The Rebel

Lies of Lesser Gods

Book Two

L.G.A. McIntyre

I0561402

Per Ardua Productions Inc.

Vancouver, Canada

For information about special discounts for bulk purchases please contact
Published by Per Ardua Productions Inc.
103-1450 Laburnum Street
Vancouver, Canada
V6J3W3
www.perarduaproductions.com

Printed in the United States of America by Kindle Direct Publishing

ISBN: 978-0-9919120-2-5

"If ye use magic in my presence again I will kill ye!"

Gralyre stepped into her space once more, stalking her. This time Catrian took a step back. "No. You are going to teach me."

Catrian's face blanked of all emotion. "I will do what I must t' protect my people. Do no' doubt me in this."

"I do not."

"Then why would ye think that I would take such a risk?"

Gralyre's glare softened, and the mockery and confrontation left him, as he acknowledged her very real concern. "Because your people are dying, and you need all the help that you can get. Because all will be lost if you do not find allies. Because sometimes the gain is worth the risk. And because…"

"Because?" Catrian's breath hitched. His assessment of the resistance's tenuous hold on life was brutally exact. Her expression became stark as her gaze dropped, searching an inner landscape of horrors that only she could perceive.

Gralyre took the final step, closing the distance between them, drawn to the sudden vulnerability he sensed within her. The scent of heather and woman drifted to his nose, and he breathed deeply. "Because I am here. And you need help. And because of this…" he murmured as he bent, and softly touched his lips to hers.

Catrian froze, still and warm beneath his kiss, then shied away from him, her face flaming. She swung hard and slapped him, rocking Gralyre's head. "No! That canno' be!"

For all the caregivers of family
suffering Alzheimer's and other Dementias.
Sometimes you have to be strong,
though it breaks your heart.

D R E A M W E A V E R S

Northern Fortress

Eastern Fortress

Verdalan

HEATHREN MOUNTAINS

SOUTHERN FORTRESS

Elevor

Fennick's Island

PROLOGUE

RAINDELL – LATE WINTER

It stalks the night-shrouded ruins of Raindell.

The fires of retribution are long burned out, and the villagers executed or scattered. The stillness is broken by a windswept whisper of snow that drifts into corners, an icy pallor that overlays the blackened, skeletal remains of burned buildings, ghostly flesh that glows coldly in the weak light of a crescent moon.

Having arisen with the darkness, It snarls Its hunger, and turns Its rapacious gaze upon Its fawning minions.

The Demon Riders wisely scatter in fear of Its cruel talons and insatiable appetites, but one is not quick enough. With a dart of claws, It snags the straggler.

The Demon Rider struggles and squeals. The others see that It has snared Its meal, and creep back from whence they hid, eager to share in the bounty now that the danger has passed.

It sneers at the ones who return, and dangles the prey just from their reach, taunting them with the wriggling, screeching prize. The minions snap, and growl, and drool. The spectacle makes It chuckle, and the sound rasps a dark counterpoint to the high-pitched screams of terror, the hungry begging, and the sighing wind. A demonic symphony.

The wind eddies and swirls, bringing a new scent to Its nostril slits. It freezes in response to the teasing aroma, and Its stomachs rumble and clench in ecstatic anticipation.

'Human!'

It releases Its prey to scamper to safety within the Demon Rider pack. It will not sate Its hunger upon the bitter flesh of 'Rider when there is the warm, succulent scent of Human in the air! Thick saliva spools in long strands from between Its razor teeth, as It swivels Its massive head to capture more of the appetizing odour, and sups deeply of the wind, pinpointing the source of the warm-blooded prey. There are but few Humans remaining in the cleansed territory surrounding Raindell, and this is a rare treat, too long denied.

When It springs, Its predator speed scatters Its underlings like mindless farm hens. It bounds across the lane, and smashes through a flimsy barrier erected across the mouth of an alley between the blackened wreckage of two buildings. The crude shelter is well camouflaged, and could have remained undiscovered in the ruins had the Humans not been betrayed by the capricious wind.

Its roar of triumph startles three Human males awake. It kills two of them quickly, and then relaxes upon Its haunches to feed while It watches the futile antics of the last man attempting an escape through the back wall of the enclosure. As the Human almost wins free, It grabs an ankle and drags him back. The scrabbling captive is a delightful entertainment while It rips through steaming flesh, and crunches marrow from bones. The wild fear reminds It of the great feasts of Dreisenheld.

Thoughts of Dreisenheld remind It of Its duty to the Hunt, and to the Master, and Its appetite wanes. It tosses the half-eaten carcass back through the gap in the wall It made to reach Its meal, placating Its begging minions with Its leavings while It hoards the second dead Human for later, for after It discharges Its obligation.

It pounces on the survivor, and settles Its bloody talons around the man's throat in a gentle caress. Its smile is a parody, a lie told by double rows of lethal, serrated teeth.

The Human soils himself.

It leans nearer, nostril slits flaring, savouring every nuance of the scents of terror. "I seek a Human male." Its guttural voice rumbles and grates like a landslide, for Its jaws and throat are ill suited to spoken language.

The man freezes like the prey he is; a rabbit caught in the jaws of a wolf. He swallows his hysterical whimpers, and his eyes scrunch to shut out the terrible sight of his captor. "Torren…and Galen…ye killed them! Ye…ye ate them!"

"Human, if thou dost aid me, I will let thee live." It can barely suppress Its glee when the man's eyes fly open with wild hope. "Thou believeth me?" It revels in the predictable gullibility of mankind; this is a game It knows well.

The Human's tongue darts out to wet his lips. "Who do ye seek?" His voice is a tremulous whisper. Sweat and tears roll in slick rivers down his face.

It flares Its shoulder plates in an aggressive display that

makes the Human recoil.

'*Delicious.*'

"A stranger to thine eyes. He arrives with death, and leaves strife and destruction in his wake! Tell me all thou knowest of the murder of thy Lords, and the attack upon thy Woman Tithe!"

The man coughs fearfully but his face animates with the desire to please. "F-Findlay? Maybe ye be speaking o' Master Findlay?"

It increases the pressure of Its blood-soaked talons, and the human gurgles, hands flailing to gain air. In the end, the man is too afraid to touch It, and his hands hover, fluttering. "He were the only stranger t' the village. 'Twas said that he were a cousin t' Wil Wilson."

"Didst kill thy Lords?"

"Aye, the Lord human collaborator for certain, I witnessed that m'self, but that were only because o' Wil's youngest son, Dajin!" The man's bitter words spit out between pants of fear. "I was there, ye see, when Dajin Wilson started the fight what killed the human Lord, and brought the purge down upon us! The stupid boy attacked his lordship o'er a woman, and then mucked it up! Findlay acted t' protect the lad. He threw a spear right through the collaborator's heart! From across the room! I 'ave never seen the like! Is it 'im that ye seek? Ye...ye will let me go now?" The Human is pathetic in his desire to please.

It leans back on Its haunches, and hisses Its discontent. This is naught but the work of Human imprudence; a Tithe disrupted, a Demon Lord murdered and a collaborator slaughtered. No matter how firm a grip Doaphin has upon the land, little embers of rebelliousness ignite, for Mankind is a fractious stock. Destroyed villages are the coin of their punishment. The anomaly that has drawn It hence is of no import, proving that this Hunt, as with all others that have gone before, is naught but a product of the Master's obsession with the prophesized return of the Man. Its claws tighten in frustration. How much longer must It brave the colds of winter afore It may return to Its warm den in Dreisenheld?

Sensing his usefulness draws to an end, the Human begins to struggle, and squawks loudly, "Findlay was the same man who attacked the Tithe Wagon! I recognized his eyes! I will ne'er forget his eyes! Black ye thought, aye, until ye saw closer that they was blue! I 'ave never seen their match!"

It rears in surprise, and chills of excitement set the spines of Its back to quivering. Could it be Him? That cold, blue gaze is seared into Its memory. Unforgettable. "Who art thou, to have seen His eyes?" Talons click and grind against each other, as It adjusts the pressure around the man's neck.

"Dolper, me name be Dolper. I am...was the Innkeeper o' the Running Wolf. After the attack on the Tithe Wagons, I kept him prisoner in me brewery until Lord Mallach collected him! And then later, after he escaped, when he returned, he was in disguise, and I did no' know him right away. I served him many drinks! Many drinks!" The Human's struggles for life-giving air finally give him the courage to pull ineffectually at Its talons.

"Silence!" It shakes the man, and Dolper's head bobbles

violently. It can make no sense of the Human's hysterical patter, but It has other, more pleasurable means to extract the answers It seeks!

It shreds the Human's will, and forces Its consciousness into the depths of the Innkeeper's tiny mind.

Dolper screeches when It possesses him but, as his resistance abates, he falls silent, his face slackens, and his head pitches forward limply with one eyelid at half-mast, and the other eye locked open in a glazed, horrified stare. The Human's pupils dilate, round and black, swallowing his eyes just as It has swallowed his soul.

It loathes Human minds, so filled with the emotions of love and loyalty, hope and joy, emotions alien and offensive to It. As It sifts through Dolper's past, what It finds useless It destroys out of petty villainy. It rips apart this memory of a pleasant summer day; obliterates that joyful memory of holding a firstborn child. But there is darkness here as well; hate, jealousy, rage, fear. This is familiar territory, emotions that do not afflict It so, however It is too impatient to linger over these succulent morsels, and soon finds what It hunts; the Innkeeper's recollections of a tall, heavily muscled Human with black hair, and darkest blue eyes.

It will absorb Dolper's memories in order to share them with the Master, though there is danger in doing so, for Human memories are created of more than the five common senses; vision, sight, sound, taste and touch. It is the sixth sense, Human emotion, that It must guard against while It makes these memories Its own, or risk being driven to madness by the incomprehensible chaos.

It braces to endure the antithesis to all that It is, to steal Dolper's memories as they were experienced, all the while besieged by a tangled web of Human emotions, impressions, sights, sounds and scents. It merges... It... he... becomes Dolper.

The women return. The Tithe Wagon attacked? How? Who would dare?

My daughter... "Ye canno' linger here! Ye will bring the 'Riders down upon us all. Get out! Leave!"

Her face so sad, so betrayed. "But Papa, where will I go? How will I live?"

"Take this." Cold coins press into a quivering hand. "Flee! Do no' return." *Watches as she disappears into the forest. Dawn's wind whispers of grief. 'Tis what must be! She did her duty. I canno' ask her t' do so again... Had t' send her away... 'Tis her only chance to live...*

It is catapulted from the memory when Human grief and love taint Its perfect darkness. It gags, and Its heart races from the bombardment of unfamiliar, unfathomable sensations. Seeking relief, It destroys the sickening, cloying memory of the loss of Dolper's daughter. Beneath Its claws, the Human's body convulses, and a single tear trickles from a clouded eye.

It riffles the memories at Its command for more pertinent

information, and moves forward in time to the arrival of the stranger who attacked the Tithe Wagon; a brutal, selfish memory... much better...

The village elders meet at the tavern. Who would do such a witless thing as attack the Tithe Wagon? Does anyone recognize the description the women gave? Gods save us! The Demon Lord will kill us all! What t' do t' stop the oncoming purge? How do we save our skins?

The ale flows, profits are good. Perhaps enough coin t' flee? Those who could are already gone...

A man, all shaggy black hair, black unkempt beard, black rags, enters the Running Wolf and demands ale.

'Tis him! The madman who has destroyed us! The women saw all, told all. He is the one! Ye saved my daughter, but no matter. Raindell is doomed unless...

Take him! Do no' let him escape!

The mob screams for blood. Blows fall heavy. The broken body lies upon the ground.

"Wait, wait! Stop! Do no' kill him! We must give him t' the 'Riders alive, as proof o' our innocence! They will be more lenient on us then! If he is dead, they may no' believe us."

"Good idea, Wil." Relief. Hope. May yet survive.

"I only hope he is no' already dead!"

The man, the prisoner, dumped on sacks in the corner of the brewery. Blood, so much blood. Chest is raising and falling. Good. He lives. No remorse, must save Raindell, must save myself. "He will no' escape from there." Laughter. Desperation. Pats the pocket where the key rests...

...The prisoner, bruised, weak, yet never pleads for succour. Just that steady glare. Those eyes, proud, scornful...patient. Stop looking at me! Let the others bring the gruel...

...The Demon Lord Mallach arrives with a platoon of Riders. Stare at the floor, bow low. The key! He wants the key! Get it! Quickly! Do no' make him wait! Fumbles with the lock.

The prisoner is given over to the Demon Lord. Will it be enough? Will the town survive?

They are t' take him t' Doaphin's Towers. Serves him right. Should have known better than t' attack a Tithe. He is so weak, they are dragging him out. Those blue eyes, accusing, I canno' meet them. 'Tis as it must be. The life o' one for the life o' many! We must survive! But those eyes, defiant, angry...no fear...Why is he no' afraid? He is mad!

The broken prisoner struggles, tripping his guards. Excitement, fear, secret pride. There is still life in our kind! No' all o' us are cowed! But it serves him naught; he goes t' the wagons with our women. Ignore it all. The Tithe wagon will be gone soon. Draw no attention!

Surprise! Savage pleasure! What is this? First Councilman Cramer, his sons, all taken t' the pyres! The collaborator is t' bear the brunt o' the town's punishment! A righteous punishment for all betrayals!

But no! Now eight innocents, who have gathered to watch the spectacle, are dragged from the tavern t' their ends on the fires.

Relief. No' me. No' me. I will live. I will survive.

The pyres flare high; the screams die away, overcome by the snap of the flames...

The scent o' roasting meat. How can I feel hunger at such as this? Gods! When will it end? How much more can we endure?

Do no' see. Do no' see...

Its interest grows keen, for Lord Mallach was later killed on the road to the city of Tarangria, his Tithe lost. But It still cannot see the prisoner clearly. The extreme bruising distorts the man's face, even without the wild beard and unkempt hair.

Here now, begins Dolper's memories of the night of the Mid-Winter's Moon. A strange male arrives with three other men. It purrs with excitement. Can it be? That face, so familiar! But the eyes will speak the truth of it...

Wil and his sons, Rewn and Dajin, come through the door, stamping their feet t' drop the snow. The stranger must be their cousin, Findlay, come t' stay with them. Curious. Something about the man...

Must warn them o' the unwanted guests before they say or do something t' incur wrath. "Brace yourselves, lads."

Faces fall at sight o' the 'Riders circulating in the crowd, at sight o' the new Lord, the human collaborator, sitting across the room. Obscene splendour. What does silk feel like?

Keep everyone calm. Maybe no one will die tonight. Wil's cousin, Findlay, tickles awareness, recognition. Familiar.

Where? When? No matter. Too busy. A new crowd o' revelers t' greet, t' warn, t' disappoint...

...Saliana Greythorn, sold for a coin by her father, delivered into the lap o' the Lord. What is the man thinking t' bring the lass t' the festival? Turn away. No one can save her now...

...A crushed tankard clanks onto the bar. Cold, blue-black eyes freeze a complaint in my throat. Keep calm, do no' draw attention. A clay cup filled and returned. A sigh o' relief when Wil's cousin, Findlay, turns away. At least he paid for the destruction o' the vessel. The coin is cold t' touch, jingles into a pocket. Pats the pocket, Pats the key... O' course!

Those eyes! Findlay is Him. The Prisoner!

How has he escaped Doaphin's Towers? Was he the one t' kill the Demon Lord Mallach? O' course! Who else! 'Tis why we are saddled with that whoreson violating the only woman here.

Why is he with Wil? Does Wil know he harbours a criminal? Is Wil a...Rebel? Ah! Valuable knowledge! Wil has much that I desire. He will give it all t' me, or I will tell his secret, and he will burn for it!

A Demon Rider's command t' Findlay to dance. What is the creature thinking? Does he no' know? Can he no' see? Oh Gods! Surely Findlay will slay them all!

Relief! Findlay consents meekly, yet makes mockery o' the order, swinging sticks acrobatically, leaping, dancing.

Laughter. Look at how confused they are! The 'Riders can do nothing...

A Sword Dance! And those eyes! It must see more. It must posses all of this memory! After all these years, could it be Him?

"Chastise him!" the Lord Collaborator yells. Demon Riders grab Findlay, and beat him for his insolence. Look away. Do no' watch. Do no' see. Do no' draw attention.

Wince! Fists hit flesh. Cringe! Surely it will be over soon?

"Music! Dance! I command you to dance!" The Lord glares at all.

Dance! Do it! Give the son o' a demon what he wants! Fiddles scratch a tune. Villagers shuffle, a mockery of merry making. Survival. Survive the night. How soon can I shut the doors? Drag feet, heart pounds, dance, dance.

What is this? Dajin Wilson stalks the Lord from behind. Gods! No! NO! STOP HIM!

The boy raises a broken table leg. Others see. Screams from the crowd alert the Lord. He turns, catches Dajin before the blow can fall. Dajin freezes. What are ye doing, boy? RUN!

The Lord draws his sword, slowly. He is relishing this, the dirty demon lover!

Do no' want t' watch what comes next... known that boy all his life...Poor Wil!

A spear smacks into the Lord's back, piercing him through. He staggers. In the hush, the clang o' the sword falling from loose fingers.

What? Who?

Tracks back the trajectory.

Wil's cousin, Findlay! His arm is just dropping. 'Twas him! O' course! Who else?

And Dajin? Ugh! Stupid Boy!

Dajin's club swings, knocks the Lord t' the ground. Rises. Falls. Rises. Falls. He has gone blood mad!

'Tis the end! Must Escape! Get out! Panic and people everywhere, tramples, stampedes. 'Riders Dead! The Lord Dead! 'Tis the end for Raindell. Flee! Get out! Escape!

Punch out the hatch under the bar. There it is, the tunnel, freedom, escape! A last look at my home. Dead Demon Riders twitch, they rise, they kill.

DEATHREN!

Grabbing, killing, eating. Death moves among the fleeing people. Doomed!

And Findlay, sword in hand, protecting the Wilsons' retreat. Who is he? Why does he stand when he should flee? Deathren heads roll, the reanimated corpses drop. Findlay yells in horror. "That is why you have to behead them?" He dashes an oil lamp to the floor. Flames.

Fire! All is gone! All is ruined! Everything! Everybody! Lost! Raindell is Lost! No help for it now. Enter the tunnel, belly down. Draw the panel back into place. Hidden... Safe...Crawl away! Escape! Survive!

When It disentangles Its consciousness from the Innkeeper's mind, It snips his neck with a click of Its talons. The warm wash of Human blood anoints It in a hot, pumping rain, as It falls to

Its knees in concert with the truncated corpse, gasping and sick. Dolper's head drops, bounces, and rolls away through the churned snow, leaving behind the melt of a steaming, red track. It comes to a rest against a charred beam, the slack face staring up at the indifferent crescent moon. Truthfully, the Human is already brain dead long before this final indignity.

It struggles to reconnect to Its own malignancy, to purge the contamination of Human emotion, smothering strand by strand of light with Its perfect blackness. This is where lesser Stalkers fail, and die or go mad.

It howls triumphantly, as It succeeds in eradicating the glowing infection of Humanity, howls until Its minions cower, and then flee in terror. At last the real Hunt begins! The Man has returned! The Master will drape It in glory!

It sends Its awareness winging into the night sky, "Master," It invokes while Its tail thumps, as furiously as that of a hatchling.

The response is quick. '*Sethreat, my Stalker! What news of the Hunt?*'

"Master, thy servant hast discovered the trailhead. The Man hast returned!"

It cries out in painful ecstasy, as the Master's malign essence merges with Its own. The memories It has just stolen from the Human are now, in turn, taken from It.

It feels the Master's excitement when the face and the voice of the Man within the memory are recognized.

'*Go to the Garrison of Brannock. Two Stalkers await you, and shall join the Hunt. There can be no mistakes this time! He cannot be allowed to slip through our grasp once more!'*

It cannot contain Its discontent. After all this time, to find the Man only to share the Hunt…but many accidents happen along a trail…

'Sethreat! Dare you defy our will?'

The Master has sensed Its deceit. Only death awaits It if It is not cunning in Its machinations. "I am thine to command! Always and forever, my Master! Always and forever!"

'Yes, Sethreat. You are.'

An unseen force bludgeons It into the blood soaked snow, as from across the many miles that separate them, the Master's power smites It for Its insolence. It mewls when the magical weight increases until Its spine creaks a warning.

'Whom do you serve, Sethreat?'

"Thy Will! Thou art all, my Master, as I am thine!" The weight punches harder, and drives the air from Its lungs. The smell of blood rises to Its nostrils, fresh human gore now mixed with the distinct, acidic tang of Stalker; Its own blood. "Thy will is my being!"

'And what is our will?'

"To Brannock, and retrieve two others to aid thine Hunt!"

'And the Man, my Stalker?'

"Thence returned unsullied to Dreisenheld!" The weight lifts, and with it, the Master's presence departs.

'Fear!'

Only the Master can give It fear! It breathes deeply of the exhilarating sensation.

ഹരു

DREISENHELD – LATE WINTER

The Master capers an impromptu jig in the middle of an opulent bedchamber, and crows triumphantly. The madness of the whoops echo among solid silver furniture set in alcoves of heavily gilded plaster moldings and marble columns. An empty bed awaits, massive and encrusted with jewels and gold leaf, draped in a thick, luxurious ermine fur that trails from the bed to the floor, discarded in the rush of awakening. The cloth-of-gold sheets, thrown back in rumpled readiness from a disturbed slumber, shimmer in the cold, prismatic lights cast by hundreds of crystal sconces throughout the enormous chamber. Within each lamp a small core of magic glimmers, slaves to the Master's will. Overhead, between the gilded and ornate mouldings, ceiling coves are painted vividly with images of barbaric slaughter. In the undulating prismatic light, the realistic battle scenes appear to move, bleeding down the walls where red and gold tapestries seem hung for the sole purpose of soaking up stray, bloody drips from above.

'He has returned! He has returned! Finally, the wait is over!' The laughter trails away, but the smile remains, and would terrify any who witnessed it.

All the long years spent scheming and planning, longing and hoping, all towards the possibility of this one miracle, three hundred long, long years…

'Old, so old now.'

The thick carpets, woven of vibrant reds, blues and golds, cushion the sound of rushing steps when the Master darts towards a full-length, gilded mirror, and peers deeply, examining pale flesh for signs of sagging, signs of dissipation.

'Nothing. Still the same. The magic sustains us.'

Blood-red lips twist in a snarl, creating lines of debauchery where before there were none, but the Master does not see, has turned away from the glass, glaring at a memory.

'Fennick, for all his interference, has lost! Curse him for the time he has stolen from us! Finally, it is time! No force will halt His coming. The fleshless will be made whole, and the world will shatter at his first steps!'

಄ಇ

NORTHERN REBEL FORTRESS – LATE WINTER

Dara Wilson awoke broken and bleeding in the lane, her body mantled by a heavy layer of new-fallen snow. For a moment, she flirted with the notion of remaining where she was. They said that death by cold was a gentle passing. She could pretend that she had never awoken, and allow the endless sleep to claim her, to release her...

'No!'

Dara found some fight for life still left within. Her body ached from new bruises and old, as her bare hands dug deep into the icy powder to support her pain filled pushup, and she surfaced from the drift that had buried her while she lay insensate. Shivering, on her knees, wet clumps of slush melted off her face and chest to plop back into the frozen depression her body had left, dislodged as she quaked from the bitter fingers of wind dancing across the dampness on her skin. In the chill of the late winter night none were abroad to witness her shame, only the crescent moon watched over her, and it was a cold and disdainful comfort, uncaring if she lived or died, and in that way, as indifferent to her plight as the people of the fortress.

Hysterical puffs of frozen air steamed from between her trembling lips, as Dara pulled her torn dress closed, fastening what few buttons remained with fingers made clumsy by more than the cold. Sobs that she dared not release convulsed her body, and she darted a glance at the sealed flap of the Stewards' tent. If they heard her they would beat her again. Or worse. She had been abandoned long enough that the new snow had blanketed her, discarded with no care, to freeze to death outside of their pavilion.

She levered herself up onto her numb feet, and only then realized that her shoes were missing. All sensation was truncated at her ankles, her feet lost to her sight and her senses within the deepening drifts. She staggered to a nearby cart, and propped herself woozily against it. It was hard to walk when you could not feel your feet, and when bone deep bruises made your body feel a thousand years old.

She was so tired. And everything hurt. And she was so very

cold, so cold. And hungry. She could not remember when last she had eaten. Food was scarce and people were starving to death, and lowlanders received the scantest of portions. Every day those who had not survived the night were carted through the fortress gates to a place in the forest, to be burned on the pyres. Would her corpse be found in the morning, and be slung, uncaring, onto a death cart?

Her teeth chattered from so much more than the bitter cold that she instinctually wrapped her arms about her torso in an effort to both conserve heat, and seek comfort. Steam puffed from between her lips with every tremulous exhalation, hazing the air in front of her eyes before frosting the lank strands of brown hair that hung down around her face.

Where was she to go? What was she to do? She had no tent of her own to return to, for the women she had been billeted with had made it abundantly clear that a whore was not welcome in their midst. They did not make the distinction that the rapes were not of Dara's choosing. Her shivers became harder, deeper, rattling her bones with overwhelming hopelessness while tears of panic prickled and froze upon her lashes.

She considered the neat rows of tents marching off along straight avenues to be lost in the haze of the blizzard, but by now the banked cook fires in front of each dwelling would be snuffed by the deep layer of snow, so there would be no heat from that quarter, and she knew better than to disturb any of the sleeping Rebels in their snug tents. Born of bitter experience she knew that no one would bestir themselves for a whore. If there were any good people here, they were too cowed to stand against the Stewards by aiding her.

A whore was what the Stewards had made of her - for the food in her belly, the clothes on her back, and a warm place to sleep. She had no choice. The things they did, the degradation of it...

She could smell them on her. The stickiness of her blood and their seed soiled her clothing, her legs. She leaned to the side, and vomited what little was within her stomach, heaving, gasping. She had to get clean...had to remove their stink from her body!

The bathhouse.

One of the few wooden, permanent structures in the Northern Rebel Fortress, the baths were reserved for the high-ranking officers. She had heard rumours that hot coals were left beneath copper tubs of water to ensure they did not freeze during the cold dark, and so they would be warm for use in the mornings. The baths would surely be deserted at this time of night and, if she could slip in unseen, she might get warm and clean. Dara would be whipped if they caught her, but her need was too great for her to care. Her thoughts were growing ever more sluggish, and the snow beckoned her as would a pillow and a soft bed, to lie down and abandon all burdens. She had to move!

The tented rows and avenues surrounding her were militarily uniform, and even after half the winter spent at the Northern Rebel Fortress, Dara was still prone to losing her way. She knew the general direction but not the exact location of the baths, only that the building was set near the creek for easy access to fresh water. The small stream bisected the fortress somewhere near the centre, though at this time of year it was frozen solid.

It would have to be near the laundry, she reasoned, a place she knew well, as she was often tasked with seeing to the Stewards' clothing.

Staggering through the deepening drifts, while the flakes continued to fall around her in a jester's frolic of feather touches and cold kisses, she became lost twice, and wasted precious moments of life to rediscover her way. She fell when her feet finally betrayed her commands, and made the rest of the journey on hands and knees, dragging her deadened limbs behind her in a rough crawl that left deep furrows in the snow behind her. By the time she located the log building that was home to the bathhouse, the cold numbness had spread up her legs, she could no longer feel her hands, and her nose, cheeks and ears were stinging with pain from the cutting, icy wind.

With a soft cry of thanks, she crawled the last distance to the door, reached up to try the latch with deadened fingers, and found that it was unlocked! She used her grip upon the handle to raise herself to her knees, and lurch within. Mindful of her trespass, she quickly shoved the panel shut behind her before collapsing to the rough plank floor, hating herself for still wanting to live even as she gave thanks for this sanctuary, gave thanks that the rumours were true. Heat!

She leaned against the door with a deep moan, as blessed warmth and steam assaulted her flesh with stings and tingles, and strained her ears for any signs that her break-in had been detected, readying herself to flee should she be discovered.

She was huddling in a tiny vestibule, most of the space of which was owned by a neat stack of split firewood. Within the gloom she spied a closed doorway in the opposite wall that hid the rest of the building from her sight, and realized the foyer acted as a heat trap to protect bathers against cold outside air. Even the log walls were expertly chinked against drafts, containing the heat within against the frigid temperatures without, but Dara was so chilled that it barely seemed to make a difference. She needed more heat than the warm air could deliver. She needed the hot baths.

Dara wiggled forward to investigate, keeping near to the log wall for concealment. She would take a quick peek through the door, and if deserted, she would try for the baths. Please, Gods, let there be no one here, and warm water in the tubs!

The door to the bathing area opened silently upon oiled hinges, and by the dim glow of banked coals, Dara saw that the room beyond the doorway ran long and narrow, a hallway of sorts, off which wooden screens were evenly placed, rising tall between each tub to sub-divide the space into five private bathing closets.

She hesitated at the threshold, listening intently, but the only sound was the dull pounding of her heart as she awaited discovery, a soft hiss of escaping steam, and an intermittent popping groan of expanding and contracting metal. It would seem that the Gods had heard her prayers for once, for steam curled from water within the baths, and the building was deserted. But her feet had passed from red to blue in colour, and her toes were a dark purple. She had to warm them! Finally trusting that the hall before her was indeed deserted, she crawled forward, dragging her deadened feet towards the promise of life.

Within each bathing closet, a large, oval, copper tub was set within a cast iron frame, and suspended over an elongated, enclosed hearth that stretched the depth of the closet. Dara could see that this would aid a sootboy in his duties, as he would have easy access from the long hallway to stoke the fires under each tub without disturbing the bathers. The backside of each tub rested against its own river-stone chimney, capturing more of the heat from the stones as the smoke escaped to the outside. It was an ingenious design that reminded Dara of the oven she had used to bake bread for her Da and brothers, back home in Raindell. Thoughts of her family made her shudder with homesickness, and she drew an ice-hardened sleeve across her face to stem the tears before they could fall.

A thin, copper tube ran from the base of each tub into a larger, cast iron pipe that exited through the outer wall of the building. Dara pondered its purpose for a moment before she realized that it was for the draining of water.

Choosing a bath at random, she yanked her ripped, soiled dress from her body, pulling off what few underclothes remained to her, and in her urgency, left the whole in a sodden heap on the plank floor instead of hanging on the provided rows of hooks attached to the wooden screen. The copper of the tub gleamed dully, reflecting little in the low light save for the faint red and yellow glow that the banked coals in the hearths cast against the log walls. To her exhausted, desperate gaze, it was burnished gold, a wealth of heat and luxury that she shook with impatience to steal, a thief courting disaster for a precious few moments more of life.

A wooden riser abutted the tub to be used to scale to the height of the bath for ease of entry, but to Dara, those six steps seemed mountainous. With the last of her desperate strength, she struggled up the stairs, sitting and using her arms for leverage to lift her rump onto the height of each tread. Forced to use her legs to help lift upwards, she had to watch her feet carefully, and work to place them flat to ensure they did not twist onto an ankle as she pushed, for they no longer recognized her dominion. Upon reaching the top, she bit her lip with anticipation, as she beheld the shimmering black surface of the water with its warm fingers of steam wafting and beckoning to her. Without further consideration, she rolled clumsily down into the warm water.

A scream of pain shocked out of her from the scalding heat. She tried to flop back out, but her violent convulsion only sent the deep water sloshing over her in waves, preventing a purchase upon the slick copper sides of the tub.

By the time she had scrabbled a grip upon the lip of the bath, the burning had receded to a tolerable level. She sobbed quietly, clinging to the side, as she slowly acclimatized to the heat. It was not that the water was too hot, only that she was so very, very chilled that had made the liquid seem to blister her skin.

She whimpered in relief when her skin stopped burning, and released the tub edge, floating back into the water, as her body greedily soaked in the life-giving heat. The tub proved to be so deep and long that she could lie suspended, sunk to her chin with her legs outstretched.

Her shivers abated, as the heat penetrated deeper, leaving her entire body aching in their aftermath though after a time her strained muscles loosened, and even her bruises eased. But her frost-burned feet still remained lost to all sensation below her ankles. She laid her head back in the warm water, letting her hair float free upon the surface, and tried to reconcile herself to what this meant.

She remembered back to her old life, when she had been much younger, and to a bad winter in Raindell when many of the wretched living in the gutters of the town had been unable to find shelter. Their blackened limbs had been horrible to see. To a one, the limbs had perished, and then so had they. Was this to be her fate? She gazed up into the darkness of the ceiling with dread. She had no more grief to spend. Perhaps it was for the best…

A sharp jab of pain suddenly pierced the sole of her left foot, as though she had stepped upon a nail, and she yelped, jerking her knee upwards with a splash but the sting stayed with her, enduring and intense. More needles stabbed her toes, her heel, her ankle, until her foot jerked and kicked from the agony, and her mouth opened in a soundless scream. Soon her right foot was also being afflicted. Around the torturous reawakening, tears of pain and joy leached from Dara's eyes. Her feet were alive!

The pricking was intense, as deadened flesh reclaimed the heat of life, each moment worse than the one before. Dara clutched at the edge of the tub when her vision blackened at the edges. Gods! What if she fainted and drowned? A low moan of pain escaped despite her best efforts to remain silent.

Then the worst happened. She heard the outer door creak open, then slam quickly amidst sharp thumps upon the wooden floor of the entryway, the sound of snow being knocked from boots.

Trapped!

A woman spoke, and Dara stuffed a fist into her mouth to muffle the soft whimpers that she could not quite contain, even as she tried to still her convulsing legs by dropping them deeper into the water. Above her improvised gag her eyes grew round and wild with terror.

"Ha! I told ye the sootboy would leave the door unlocked! 'Twas worth the ha'copper bribe t' the little leech!" The woman's voice was followed by a long span of silence. A soft glow of lantern light spilled through the doorway, and down the long hallway, setting distorted shadows to undulating upon the log walls.

Her voice came again. "No, no one will catch us. I will eunuch the little villain if he betrays us."

Dara's wide, panicked gaze spied the sodden skirts that she had discarded on the floor outside her bathing closet, made visible in the low light thrown by the lantern in the far room.

When the woman and her companion came down the hallway, she was sure to be discovered! There was no escape, and no way to flee for she could not stand! Her feet felt like Stalkers were gnawing upon them! Dara opened her mouth in a silent scream of suffering. The pain! How could it be growing worse? It was all she could do to cling to the edge of the tub, and await the devastating moment of detection.

"Because I thought it would be a nice treat for your birthday."

Again a short, silent pause. Who was the woman talking to?

"Ah, I know. Ye are most welcome. I love ye, Mayvin!"

Dara was in the second to last bathing stall at the far end of the hallway. If they came no further than the first two from the door, she might yet remain unnoticed. Then came a sound that Dara dreaded - the long, lengthy rasp of a sword leaving a scabbard. A distorted, nightmarish shadow, sword to the fore, began to slink along the log wall towards her bathing closet.

"Mayvin? What is it?"

Quiet footsteps followed the shadow, padding down the corridor towards Dara, as she whimpered and quaked, able to do naught but await her doom. The beatings, the pain of her reawakening feet, and her despair all crashed into her; a rippling, blackness that sank her beneath the warm waters.

∞⧵⧸∞

Dara awoke, sputtering and coughing. Two figures loomed over her in the low light, and she screeched in fear, punching out to escape. She barely registered that she was now lying in the hallway upon her bundled clothes, and that her feet were still cramping in their violent, painful reawakening.

"Easy girl, easy, we are no' going t' hurt ye!" one of the shapes said, trying to catch Dara's arms and restrain her. "Ye were under the water! Ye fainted!"

Dara scuttled backwards, stopped only when her shoulders met wood, and her head rapped sharply against the log wall, snapping her from her hysteria. Expecting blows to fall at any moment she curled her legs up tightly to her body to hide her nakedness, and reached for her toes, kneading them in an effort to ease the sensation of walking upon a bed of sharp nails. If she could get them functioning she might be able to run, for she was fortuitously between the strangers and the doorway, but the massage helped little to ease a pain borne deep within her flesh.

The rest of her wet body was quickly growing chilled, prompting her to abandon her feet and hug her knees, rocking. She gazed through her dripping, straggling hair at the two shapes that had, as yet, made no move to pursue, panting lightly from her fear and pain, and succumbed immediately to a coughing fit, as the last of the bath water left her lungs.

"'Tis alright. No one is going t' hurt ye. Ye are safe. We are no' going t' hurt ye," the woman chanted softly, and Dara realized she had been doing so all along.

"My name is Aneida, and this is my sister, Mayvin." She unshuttered a low-burning hurricane lamp, revealing herself and her companion by its increased glow.

Mayvin gave a short wave, but did not speak. Her dark hair was hacked short, curling in the moisture of the air to frame a face, round and pale in the lantern light, which seemed too pretty to wear so hard an expression. Her large, dark eyes were brimming with rage as they travelled over Dara's massive bruises, made visible now in the brighter light.

Aneida was her sister's opposite, and had she not named them so, Dara would never have suspected a family connection. Two long braids of brilliant, fiery red cascaded past her shoulders, almost to her waist. Her face was strong, her jaw was sharp and angular, and golden freckles peppered a deeply tanned face. The glint of lantern light shone off a silvery scar on her neck that spanned nearly from ear to ear, catching Dara's attention, as Aneida rubbed a finger absently to and fro along the seam. Just now, her mouth was set in a grim line. Both women were dressed as warriors, and wore short swords at their waists.

Dara shuddered in dread. "What do ye want with me? I was doing nothing wrong! I had t' warm myself, I was freezing t' death. Ye canno' fault me for this!" She drew a quivering breath as her defiance lost momentum. "Please." A simple plea that she knew from experience would be ignored. She curled tighter and winced, awaiting the first of the blows.

"Who hurt ye?" Aneida demanded.

Dara shrunk at the unexpected question. "What does it matter?"

"Tell us. Who did this t' ye?"

Dara's quivers increased. The Stewards had warned her time

and again of the consequences of bearing witness against them, but somehow, here in the dark, alone with these two fierce women, a kind of fierceness was born in her as well. "The Stewards."

"Which ones? North District? West District?"

"South," Dara admitted hoarsely.

"Hofar, Jorrod and," Aneida snapped her fingers to jog her memory as she glanced at her sister, Mayvin, "...what is the fat bastard's name?"

Mayvin's hands moved in a quick dance even as Dara supplied the name. "Strier." Dara's soft voice was carried on a fear-filled breath, for naming the men who raped her meant her death.

"Aye, Strier. Fat bastard. They did this to ye? Beat ye? Raped ye?" Aneida sighed and rubbed a finger along the fine scar at her neck while she evaluated Dara's posture, curled up against the corner like a beaten dog. "'Tis obvious t' see that ye are no' a whore by nature. How did ye come t' be in the trade? Ye are a lowlander?"

Dara wet her dry lips, and nodded. She could not run yet, her feet were lumps of agony, and besides, she could not reach her clothes. Fleeing naked into the teeth of the winter storm was not an option. She had no choice but to stay and tell them all, give them what they wanted, and be rid of it. "Last fall, Catrian Kinsel arrived at our farm, in the lowlands near Raindell. My Da, his name is Wil Wilson, is a spy for the Resistance. A couple of days after she arrived, Catrian and I were taken by the

Women Tithe, and my father could do nothing, though I knew that he would follow us."

"Catrian Kinsel allowed herself t' be taken by the Tithe? The Sorceress? I find that hard t' credit!" Aneida snorted.

Dara's mistrust surged to the surface, and her mouth clamped shut.

Mayvin nudged her sister, bringing Dara's reaction to her attention.

Aneida's mouth worked in disgust. "Never mind. Tell your story."

It took most of her remaining courage for Dara to resume, and her voice was hushed as she began again. "'Twas horrible! I thought we were going t' die, but we were rescued before the day was out by a man..." Dara's words drifted while a whimsical smile of regret touched her mouth. "I have never seen a man such as he. Outnumbered ten to one, he killed all the 'Riders by himself. The way he moved was like..." Words failed her. "Have ye ever seen a stag running, and how they seem t' float as they leap, the gracefulness, the power? He was like that. He stole my breath." She gave a jaded huff of amusement at her past self's girlish fantasies.

"After our rescue, my Da sent me away, for I could no' return t' Raindell, or risk being recaptured for the Tithe. Lady Catrian arranged an escort for me t' the Heathren Mountains, t' here, t' this fortress, where I would be safe..." She gave a bitter laugh, but the watery sound was without humour.

Aneida remained quiet and attentive. The sisters were naught but vague shapes in the low light of their lantern though Mayvin's mouth could be seen to hold a cynical twist, as though she had guessed the rest.

Dara coughed a little to clear her throat of the last of her near drowning. "Da, and my brothers were supposed t' arrive afore the winter snows, but they must have been delayed. I hope that when spring comes, so will they."

"And what o' the Stewards? How did ye come t' be noticed by the likes o' them?"

Dara swallowed thickly, and her shivers intensified again as horrific memories assailed her. "They said that I was no' but a lowlander whore, who would work for her food and shelter. They…they…" words failed her and a deep, heart wrenching sob shook her body, but remained unreleased.

"And tonight? What happened t' ye?"

Dara drew a shuddering breath, then another, calming herself so that her words emerged wooden and emotionless. "They raped me, beat me, used me as they would. Usually they will give me a bit of food…after. But Jarrod was so angry, because I would no' pretend to like it, and he was hitting me, hitting me, and his hands were around my throat, and I could no' breath…"

"I thought I was dying, instead I awoke in the snow, no shoes, no cloak, and nowhere t' go. My feet were freezing. I was going t' die if I did no' seek warmth. Are ye going t' beat me now?"

Mayvin made a series of sharp gestures to her sister, punctuated by naught but the rustle of clothing until she pulled a knife from her belt, and made a jab at the air, twisting the point viciously.

Dara cringed away from the brandished weapon. Did Mayvin mean to kill her? But Mayvin's hands began their dance once more, and Dara watched the intricate movements uncomprehendingly, though Aneida nodded in understanding. Could Mayvin not speak? What was wrong with her?

Aneida snorted. "Ye are right sister. Those are three men in need of gelding."

The terrible burden of Dara's hopelessness shifted slightly. "Ye will help me?"

Aneida assessed her for a long moment, her body still, and her gaze intent. "No."

Dara recoiled, as though she had been struck. She had been turned away before, but never by one who genuinely seemed to care about her circumstances.

"But we will help ye t' help yourself."

CHAPTER ONE

HEATHREN MOUNTAINS – LATE WINTER

There are events that resonate with the thunderous crash of portents. They seep into stone and bone, and incite a shift of perceptions and of ideals, an historical pivot.

All that comes after can trace its origins back to that one moment in time. It is the breeder of regrets, and laments of "if only". It is the path running off a cliff, unnoticed until the rock crumbles beneath imprudent feet, and it is too late to take it back, to leap towards safety.

Sometimes, a place will forever resound from such presages; a deafening aftermath that echoes in the thick pounding of hearts, in the slick sweat on palms, and in the flicker of movement caught by the corner of an eye. This is the maker of ghosts upon ancient battlefields.

In the end, perhaps the storm is naught but the echo of thunder from the dice of the Gods of Fortune, tumbling end over end in endless wagers over the fate of men; to see them ruined in the pursuit of destiny. Sometimes the storm starts within the beat of an eagle's wings, sometimes within an imprudent kiss.

The taste of Catrian's lips vibrated through Gralyre's body while her passion echoed back from their entangled minds, desire, rage, and dismay in equal measures, though it was her distress that prompted him to finally release his embrace. He eased back from within her thoughts, even as she released her grip upon his. It was not a truce so much as an acknowledgement that the war had taken a shift towards battlefields that neither was prepared for.

Breathless, they glared at each other with fascination and horror, as much from the violation of ultimate privacy that had ripped secrets from each other's deepest thoughts, as from the vibrancy of their unexpected desire. They were sequestered from the rest of the cavern within the quiet eye of Gralyre's magic-born cyclone. The din created by the whirlwind of packs and pans, bedding and weapons, made their space seem all the more intimate, completely obscuring the Rebel warriors awaiting their reappearance.

Light and shadow played over their faces from the fires of smashed oil lanterns that littered the cavern outside, while their hair whipped lightly from the passage of the wind, the longer strands moving to coil and tangle against each other in the tight space, black weaving to golden brown, as though bits of themselves were still unwilling to abandon the passion that had momentarily stolen their senses. The cataclysmic moment strung taunt, as the full significance of their encounter settled deeper. There was no coming back from their kiss. What they had acknowledged to each other could destroy the world.

Gralyre released his magic, allowing the wind to dissipate, and the amassed detritus to settle back to the cavern floor with crashes and clangs. Nothing had been resolved. Their discord remained. "So am I innocent, or am I guilty?" was his parting shot as Catrian turned to face her men.

"Fire!" Commander Boris Kinsel yelled, as they reappeared from the dissipating funnel.

Gralyre's warrior reflexes yanked Catrian protectively into his body, shielding her, as with a harsh note, dozens of arrows were released.

"NO!" Catrian screamed. She threw up her hands, and her blue shield snapped into existence, encompassing both her and Gralyre in its defensive radiance. It crackled with power, as crossbow bolts smacked into the surface and stuck, quivering, with sparks of electricity arcing between their deadly iron points.

Gralyre measured the seconds against Catrian's panting breaths. Outside the glowing shield, the Rebel warriors were also momentarily stilled by the ineffectualness of their attack.

By the glow of the blue light, Gralyre scanned the shock on Catrian's face, and realized that were it not for her intervention, he would now be lying in a pool of his own blood. He had yet to release his tight grip upon her shoulders from where he had tucked her protectively into his chest. With a will of their own, his fingers gently moved to brush strands of loosened hair from her cheek. "Are you harmed?" Many of those arrows would have made their way to her flesh as well.

Catrian's moss-green eyes met his, and her lips compressed with temper. "Let me go." A shutter dropped over her expression, shutting him out, as she shrugged free of his hands.

Gralyre's jaw knotted, as he stepped back, and pivoted

smoothly to face the Rebel warriors. Through the undulating shimmer of Catrian's blue shield, he examined the ranks for further threats. Some of the men had lowered their weapons, while others were in a struggling panic to reload.

"Enough!" Catrian roared. With a violent dash of her hand, the shield vanished, and the suspended arrows clattered to the floor, their iron tips melted, blackened, and smoking from the magic that had halted their deadly flight.

"Stand down!" Commander Boris yelled in concert. His face was stark, a man awakening from a nightmare to realize that he had almost murdered his own niece. The deep lines of his face boasted of a lifetime of victories for survival, but his expression whispered of a grief that would have been unendurable had Catrian come to harm by his hand.

The cavern was awash with the harsh breaths of the frightened people who cowered against the rough granite walls, gargoyles huddling within the flickering light and shadow cast by the small oil fires of smashed lamps. The tableau held until Little Wolf slunk towards Gralyre, unsure if it was safe to do so.

Gralyre drew a calming breath, and beckoned to the frightened animal. *'Little Wolf, come to me. All is well. Are you injured from the stones they threw?'*

Little Wolf bolted towards Gralyre's outstretched hand, dodging and leaping over masses of bedding and loose equipment, to lean his quivering body against Gralyre's legs, begging for reassurance. Unlike the wolfdog's usual fluency, an incomprehensible jumble of images and emotions peppered

Gralyre's mind.

'Fear! Attack? Stones hurt! Wind! Screams! Fear! Safe?'

'You are safe, Little Wolf. 'Tis over.' Gralyre gently caressed the frightened wolfdog's ears, belaying his violent gaze journeying aggressively over the cowering Rebel warriors. Thick blood from the scalp wound that Matik's axe had delivered, the unprovoked blow that had started their battle, burned into Gralyre's left eye, before flowing unchecked down his cheek to drip off his chin. Like Little Wolf, bruises pained his chest and face from the stones the warriors had hurled. He ignored it all. The next man to attack him would die.

But there would be no more assaults this day. The Rebels struggled to their feet, their horrified glances dashing between Gralyre, Catrian and Commander Boris, searching for someone to reassure them that it was safe, much as Little Wolf was demanding of Gralyre. Several of the warriors began to beat out the small flames that dotted the space, salvaging what supplies they could from the wreckage, while others sought to calm the frightened horses who whinnied and reared their terror from within their makeshift coral.

Boris swiped a trickle of blood from the corner of his mouth, sustained during the maelstrom that had dragged warriors and equipment across rough rock. Setting his jaw, he stomped through the crowded cavern towards Gralyre and Catrian, kicking debris from his path as he came. His tunic was torn off at the shoulder, revealing a rash-like scrape, and his short, iron-grey hair stood on end. His attention shifted from one to the other as he advanced, making it unclear as to which of them he was more wroth. But Boris never reached their sides, forced instead to arise to his toes for balance to avoid a collision when Dajin Wilson pushed rudely across his path.

"General! General Matik!" Dajin yelled dramatically. The Commander's disgruntled growl followed the younger man, as Dajin skidded to a stop next to a slack hand protruding out from beneath a pile of loose bedding and packs.

"Please do no' be dead! General!" Dajin moaned theatrically while he flung away debris. He rolled the warrior over, and was rewarded by a groan of pain that sifted out from behind the man's bushy brown beard. Matik lifted an arm made bloody from the multiple, small cuts that Gralyre had bestowed during their battle, as though to push Dajin away, but his hand dropped limply when unconsciousness claimed him once more.

Dajin cradled Matik's head in his lap, and glared up at Commander Boris. "Gralyre tried t' kill General Matik!" Dajin was wild-eyed, and spittle flew from his mouth, as he sought to rally the men to further attack. "He tried t' kill us all!"

"Enough, Dajin!" Rewn roared, as he pushed to his feet, and lurched forward. He was bloody and bruised from the beating he had sustained trying to come to Gralyre's aid. An ugly wound swelled the lid of his left eye, and his arms banded around his ribs to ease the pain, as he confronted his younger brother. "Ye and I both know that if Gralyre had wanted Matik dead, we would no' be seeing his chest rise. Matik attacked without provocation! A lesser man than Gralyre would have killed him for such an assault!"

"How did I just know ye were going t' take his side?" Dajin sneered.

"When did your soul grow so black, brother?" Rewn asked quietly. Disappointment colored his words when he shook his head in dismay.

Dajin blinked to stop the tears that threatened, and glanced away, running a trembling hand through his mussed brown hair, so like his brother's, while he tried to negate the blow caused by Rewn's disapproval. Even his momentary, heady control over the mob was seeping away, as many of the Rebels were now turning from him. "Gralyre must have done something, because the Commander ordered Matik t' attack!" Dajin defended petulantly, gratified to regain the immediate attention of all.

Boris charged Dajin, grabbed him by the collar, and hoisted him into the air. "Keep your tongue behind your teeth!" He shook him roughly.

Gralyre's hands fisted, as his rage spiked. Dajin was a thorn in his foot, but the lad was Rewn's brother, and Wil's son. Like it or not, he was family. When he reached for his magic it easily rose to his will, and wind stirred in the cavern once more. He did not question how it could be so for it was merely another mysterious skill found in a time of need, the whys and wherefores of its origins lost within his missing past.

Boris hastily dropped Dajin back onto his heels to confront the greater threat of Gralyre, as a gust of wind slapped his face.

Dajin stumbled away, forgotten in the heat of the moment, to slide from sight behind a group of warriors who were engrossed in the unfolding drama. In his quest to be the centre of attention, he knew that he had seriously overstepped, and in his hypocrisy, was now more than willing to let Gralyre bear the brunt of protecting him from the Commander's anger.

"Stop that!" Catrian snapped at Gralyre. "Ye know the order came no' from Boris, but from me!"

Gralyre's ire refocused upon the Sorceress. "And was it worth it? Did you find your answers?" Gralyre shivered, as he allowed his power trickle away, and the wind to still once more. The harshness of his previous question still hung like a quivering presence between them. "Am I a liar and a spy, or just unlucky enough to have no memory, and be near you?"

Little Wolf cringed behind Gralyre's legs, as his master's deep voice grew heavy with dark threat and accusation.

"Your memories are still hidden from me," Catrian muttered, her face militant.

"That is not what I asked you!" Gralyre gritted out, his hands flexing, imagining them around her throat. "I asked you if I am good or evil!"

"I canno' answer ye! All I know is that ye are no' the cause o' your affliction!" she protested hotly. "Without knowing your past I canno' make a sound judgment!" The hostility of their gazes, and the stiffness of their stances stated to their riveted audience, louder than any words, that they were at war.

"Yes, you can!" Gralyre insisted. "You see standing before you the sum of all my past deeds! My memories may be gone, but they shaped who I became."

A small smile chased across Rewn's mouth, and he nodded righteously, as he recognized the very argument that he had once presented to Gralyre. He crossed his arms, awaiting the Sorceress' verdict. Any doubts that he had once harboured about Gralyre's allegiances had long ago been laid to rest. He was certain of this man's quality, and would go to war with any who spoke differently.

"'Tis no' the same!"

"Yes it is! Everything we see and do shapes that which we become. Even when those deeds are far in the past, they still cast a shadow over our present lives!" Gralyre argued eloquently, convincingly. "So I ask you again, my Lady Catrian," he drew a steadying breath, and spread his arms wide in supplication, "I stand before you, as the sum of how my life has shaped me. Am I good or am I evil?" His deep voice resonated within the small cavern, the echoes of his words slowly dying away into the stillness that gripped the watching Rebel warriors. His gaze bored into hers, watching her struggle with the logic he presented. Her answer would be his salvation, or his doom.

'He has no right!' Outrage roared through Catrian as, out from behind the blood-matted black hair, his midnight-blue eyes challenged her. *'No matter what his logic, the danger can no' be denied. He might be Doaphin's spy!'*

She broke contact with his angry gaze, and scanned the hushed cavern, assessing the bedraggled warriors who awaited her verdict. Confusion knit her brows when she realized that, though she had certainly given him cause to do so, with all the power that he wielded Gralyre had not killed a single Rebel, although most of the men were bleeding from severe scrapes and cuts from being dragged along the rough walls by the cyclone. Even Matik, who had awakened, and was attempting to rise, was alive. At the last moment, when Gralyre could have so easily killed him, he had glanced her way, seen her grief, and spared her man.

Through all her carefully orchestrated torments he had maintained a nobility of spirit foreign to her rough existence. Everything she knew of him proclaimed his innocence – but it was still not enough to allay her concerns.

At the very least, this debacle had revealed to her that the barrier within his mind, hiding his past, was not a construct of his own magic, but a deliberate affliction created by another. Could Doaphin have carefully sliced away Gralyre's memory of their allegiance, and hidden it behind the wall protecting Gralyre's past? Could the Usurper have done so complete a job, that he was able to change the fundamental personality of the man?

Could she have done so? Did she have the power and surgical dexterity to perform such an exorcism? The logistics of such a task were staggering. Add to the mix the fact that Gralyre had powers of impressive magnitude, and a mind strong enough to have resisted even her magic, and the task grew near to impossible! Unless Gralyre had colluded with Doaphin... Her doubts remained.

"All that I know o' ye…as ye are now," Catrian qualified, "is good." She chose her words carefully so as to admit nothing that could not later be spun in an advantageous direction. "Otherwise ye would no' still live."

Unspoken remained the fact that she still did not trust him, and their audience sensed it. Catrian watched the men relax upon her pronouncement, but the way they kept Gralyre within sight when they began to collect strewn gear, stated loudly that they would take their cue from her, and remain suspicious.

'Perfect.'

She spun away in a swirl of cloak.

Gralyre reached out to catch her, incensed at the way she had dodged his question, and couched her words with insinuation, but when his hand grazed her shoulder it blossomed with fiery pain! He recoiled, shaking his burning fingers with a hiss through clenched teeth. Slowly, the pain lessened, dying away to be replaced by a dull numbness.

Catrian tossed a triumphant smirk over her shoulder, as she walked away.

Gralyre tamped down his frustration, and stomped to the opposite side of the cavern to gather his belongings back together.

Little Wolf followed, and dropped to his belly to watch quietly while items were stuffed, uncaring, back into the packs. He had never seen Gralyre quite like this before, and decided it was best to remain out of the way.

Boris moved to the centre of the cavern, and raised his hands for attention. "The storm is over, and we will be travelling tomorrow. Make ready." A slight cheer erupted at his announcement. Almost unnoticed, the magic-born blizzard had died, as Gralyre's anger had boiled off.

Gralyre paused his repacking to flex his hand, massaging it gently to relieve the persistent tingling left behind by Catrian's magical clout. His brooding gaze circled the cavern to where she was tenderly wiping the blood from Matik's face.

Reminded, Gralyre lifted his hand to his brow, probing the gash hidden within blood-matted hair, and accidently releasing a throbbing pain to stampede through his skull with dizziness as its rough rider. He backed weakly to the heated cavern wall, and sank to the warm floor, holding his head to combat his nausea. From under heavily beetled, black brows, he glared at Catrian's concerned ministration of Matik's injuries, and wished them both to the darkest pits of the underworld.

Did he believe his own arguments? Did he believe, unequivocally, that he was not an ally to evil? It had been a while since he had challenged the abyss of his missing past, but Catrian's attack now forced him to do so once more. He had, in his early days at the farm, often wondered at his nature. Was he a good man, or bad? Craven or brave? Cruel or kind?

From across the cavern, Matik's glance touched upon his, and deadly enmity arced like heat lightning between them. Matik scowled, and his hand rose to capture Catrian's where she dabbed at a seeping cut. At the proprietary gesture, Gralyre's jaw bunched, and he had to fight the need to leap across the cavern space between them, and finish what had begun.

Was he a good man, or bad? Craven or brave? Cruel or kind? He was unforgiving of grievous insults. He was that kind of man.

Gralyre's nerves were so frayed and primed for a fight that he started from his dark musings when a hand lightly touched his shoulder, but it was only Saliana Greythorn holding a damp rag, and a poultice in her hands.

"I though ye might need some help with your wound," she suggested shyly, avoiding eye contact, her tangled white-blond hair obscuring her face from view.

"Thank you," Gralyre replied gently, not wanting to scare her. He was surprisingly moved by her offer. She was so timid that a simple *'Good morn!'* could often still send her scurrying.

The night that Raindell had been destroyed, her father had sold her to the new Lord for nothing more than a copper coin, that same ill-fated night that Rewn and Dajin's father, Wil, had perished under the teeth and nails of the Deathren. She had travelled with Gralyre and the brothers ever since, and though they had never harmed her, she would still shy away if they moved towards her too quickly, or spoke to her too harshly. It made her offer even more touching and brave.

"Are you injured? Did the wind harm you?"

Saliana glanced up, and smiled sweetly at Gralyre, "I am fine." Just as quickly, her eyes flitted towards Rewn's approach. Rewn smiled encouragingly back at them both, and Gralyre's burdens lessened at the unspoken support of his friends.

Rewn grunted when he sank down the wall to sit beside Gralyre, mimicking his friend's posture with his back propped against the warm cavern stone. He glanced at Gralyre from the corner of his good eye, and shrugged. "Ne'er boring around ye," he smirked quietly with a little cough of pain.

Gralyre evaluated Rewn's wounds, injuries that had been earned championing him. "Are you going to live?"

Rewn grimaced. "Aye, I will be fine by tomorrow," he rolled over on a shoulder to address Gralyre more directly. "About Dajin…"

Gralyre lifted an exhausted hand to halt his words. "He will come around."

"Gralyre, my brother tried t' stone ye t' death." Rewn's brown eyes were crinkled with sorrow and concern.

Gralyre's lips quirked. Of all the assaults he had born this night, Dajin's was the least of them. Out of respect, Gralyre was willing to make some allowances for Rewn's brother. He owed that much to Wil's memory. So he shrugged as he turned away to look up at Saliana, who hovered above him with the dripping cloth. "He did not succeed. I will talk to him about that later."

Rewn loosed a harsh chuckle. "Only ye would take him t' task for failing t' kill ye." His levity faded. "'Tis a conversation that is long overdue, methinks!"

Saliana brushed her white-blond hair from her face, and bit her lip indecisively, as she considered the gash in Gralyre's hairline near his temple, before she leaned forward and began to dab roughly at the wound, her pale face intent and determined.

As the damp rag was applied, Gralyre winced deep within but neither by word nor deed would he show the pain she inflicted, gallantly suffering in silence the not-so-gentle ministrations of his would be healer.

But Little Wolf heard his unvoiced pain, and lifted his head from his paws, thumping his tail in commiseration. This was the master he knew and loved, returned from his dark place.

ℰᴑᏅ

BRANNOCK – LATE WINTER

The Garrison of Brannock is less than a day's march southeast of the ruined township of Raindell, yet the despised cold makes It sluggish, and Its journey takes all of one night, and part of another. It finds the garrison gates ajar and unmanned, and the snowy courtyard unmarred by footsteps. Its snout wrinkles, for the scents tell tales of murderous excesses. The Stalkers that the Master has ordered It hence to procure have been at play.

A herd of Deathren rushes out of the darkness with their mindless screams, and corpse reek. Their shredded red uniforms, and grotesque wounds reveal their own stories of massacre and mayhem.

Its Demon Rider minions draw sword with shouts and curses, and form a defensive circle to ward off creatures that were once one of their own.

With a snarl for the inconvenience, It scatters the Deathren, removing the heads of the ones too maimed to be of use, and using magic to tether the rest to Its will. Thus subdued, the Deathren quieten, and form a pack, their dead gazes rapt to Its every gesture.

"Search for survivors."

It watches to ensure compliance, as Its minions disperse throughout the deserted garrison, kicking in doors of outbuildings and sheds. Growing bored, Its attention wanders toward the citadel, where smoke curls lazily from the chimneys above the squat stone tower, and where It senses a warm pocket of heat emanating from the great hall. Time to collect the Stalkers, as tasked by the Master.

The Deathren pack shuffle mindlessly along in perfect mirror to Its movements, as It crosses the abandoned marshaling yard and, with a mighty kick, bursts open the heavy, ironclad door of the citadel keep.

It invades the great hall, and sneers at finding two Stalkers curled amid bones, fecal discharge, and rotting flesh, so fat and lazy from their indulgences that they have not even bothered to arise with the night. The stronghold has been claimed for a warm, putrid den, and aside from the Deathren staggering and moaning in confusion, the only live Demon Riders seem to be those minions It has brought with It from Raindell.

That It must ally with such as they!

Two heavy, unlighted, cast iron chandeliers that suspend upon chains from the smoke-blackened ceiling beams, hover perfectly above the denmates, while a heavy cord travels from the fixtures to an anchor upon the wall beside It, designed to allow the chandeliers to be lowered for new tapers. It suppresses the urge to sever the cord that would see the massive sconces crash down upon the worthless duo, opting instead to scent mark the wall with a spray of urine and kick furrows through the filth overlaying the stone floor, laying claim, for It owns all It surveys, and owes allegiance only to the Master.

'The Master's will is all.'

The denmates stir, and snarl threateningly at Its dominant display. "What dost thou, ancient one?"

It flares Its shoulder plates aggressively at the lack of deference, and vibrates Its throat sack in a rumbling warning. It judges the speaker's youth by the mottled grey specks of a recently grown hatchling that still pepper its tail. "Silence! Hast any survived, or hast thine debauchery consumed all?"

The denmates roar and lash their tails, so It yawns Its mouth wide to show the rows of serrated teeth that announce Its superiority, for Its size has obviously not cautioned them to prudence.

Through the open doorway of the keep, a minion steps smartly into the hall, and bows low. "We have found survivors, Lord Sethreat. They have barricaded themselves in the armoury."

At the appearance of the 'Rider, the lounging Stalkers stir at last, bursting free of their nest, jaws snapping, and howling. As though no better than mindless Deathren, they leap to consume the fresh meat. The minion yelps, and dives for the open door.

It plucks the young, speckle-tailed Stalker from mid-leap, slamming it into the floor so hard that the stones beneath splinter.

The second Stalker, possessed of an unusual green crest upon its skull, alters course to protect Its denmate. Though larger, and exhibiting a dull, cunning gleam in its eyes, its indolence has made it rotund and weak.

It meets the charge head-on with a bellow that is loud enough to dislodge cobwebs and dust from the ceiling beams, disdaining caution or tactics; these should never be wasted upon the unworthy. It answers the challenge with the brutality of Its dominance and superior strength, grabs Green Crest by the jaw, and smashes it on its back next to its denmate, Speckle Tail.

It stomps a horned foot across the throats of Its inferiors, and urinates. The hot splash rains down upon Its felled brethren, and announces Its victory with their degradation.

The denmates whimper, and lash their tails in their submission like raw hatchlings, talons open and unthreatening while they lie on their backs, and allow themselves to be debased.

It is appeased by their subjugation, and moves away, but growls when they attempt to stand, and lunges just to watch them flinch and mewl.

The two Stalkers are young and foolish, and lack self-discipline. It loathes sharing the pleasures of the Hunt with these unworthy ones, and regrets that It cannot kill them – yet. It obeys the Master.

'*The Master is terrible. The Master has spoken.*'

"Follow."

It leaves the keep, exiting into the cold darkness, and never doubts that Its will is obeyed. The Deathren pack shadows Its every move, slaves in the truest sense. It hears claws on stone, and knows the denmates trail obediently after, no less slaves to Its will now than the reeking, animated corpses.

The Demon Rider, who ran in fright like a puny Human, hovers in the courtyard, and It contemplates whether It should kill the minion for cowardice.

The Demon Rider bows low, hands open and harmless. "The last o' the survivors o' the garrison, are this way, mighty Sethreat."

The 'Rider attempts to mimic the mannerisms of a hatchling. Smart 'Riders are hard to find. Perhaps It shall allow this minion to live - for a time.

After the murders of Demon Lord Mallach, and of his temporary replacement, the Human collaborator, 'tis obvious there has been no authority curtailing the appetites of the two young Stalkers. The garrison Demon Riders, those that the denmates have not murdered out of boredom, lust, and hunger, barricade themselves in the only other stone building, an armoury.

Through the fortified door that the survivors refuse to open, neither for threats nor for bribes, they tell It of the murder of the Lord at the Midwinter's Moon festival, the human killers who escaped the destruction of Raindell, and fled northeast, taking the road to Verdalan, and the Deathren set upon their trail to run them to ground.

It considers the two Stalkers with distaste. The fact that the Deathren were sent without supervision speaks to their inexperience and laziness, a lethal combination of stupidity.

The Man must be dead.

Its talons open and close in time with the tides of frustration washing through Its cold heart at being denied the Hunt just as the first spoors of a fresh trail have been discovered. It sinks to bended knees, and invokes the Master.

The Master's presence slices like a knife into Its mind, and It squirms in pain and adulation, as Its knowledge is torn from Its black soul like a hurricane, leaving orders strewn like debris in its wake.

'Sethreat! Trust nothing! Find what is left of Him, and bring proof of His death back to Dreisenheld.'

"Thy will is all, my Master!" It grovels, but the Master's presence is gone.

It swipes a trickle of blood from Its nose slits, and licks it clean of Its talons, awaiting the abatement of the ecstatic quivering that always follows the Master's visitation.

"Come."

It leads the way out into the wilds surrounded by the Deathren Pack, the Stalker denmates, and Its own Demon Rider minions. It is eager to be done with the Hunt now that the promise of live prey has been extinguished. There is no solace in following a real trail instead of the phantoms of the Master's paranoia.

It hurries, certain that It will find the slain Man this night so that It can finally return to the dark warmth and debauchery that is Dreisenheld. But not before It takes pleasure in a kill or two. Its serrated teeth gleam in the weak light of the moon when It turns Its head to leer at the trailing denmates.

The denmates huddle together like hatchlings in the face of the implicit threat.

ﮙﮙﮙ

"Noooooooo!" Screams a long ululation of madness and loss. Fawning creatures explode, nothing remaining but pink mist drifting in the air, as the echoes bounce off the pillars and stones in the throne room.

'It cannot be! To have waited so long! To have come so near only to lose Him now! To be given hope, only to have it snatched away! No! Never! The resurrection must happen! Nothing can halt it. Not now!'

Grabs a sword and throws it at the large, gilded mirror in the corner, splintering the silver. A tantrum of magic shatters the stones of the marble floors, implodes the stained glass windows with showers of glass, and melts the gilding from the walls.

"Master...?" Five Demon Lords attending the throne room are crushed into tattered bundles of flesh and blood at the impertinent interruption.

Panting, exhausted. Grieving.

'*To have come so near…*'

ഩരൃ

It disperses the Deathren to either side of the road, and awaits the howls that will announce the presence of spilled blood. But as the night progresses towards the hated Dawn, there is still no sign of the kill site.

Day arrives all too soon, for the night was already half spent when they left Brannock. It takes refuge in a stone fissure, compels the Deathren to follow in after, and pulls fallen brush over the top of the crevice to protect all from the deathly rays of the sun.

It chuckles, as It listens to the denmates whimper and beg at being left outside to face the dawn, but eventually they leave to dig their own shallow pits for survival. The Master orders that It cannot kill them, not that It cannot leave them to die. The Deathren, It finds useful. The two young Stalkers are naught but an irritant.

The cold saps Its strength, and leaves It lethargic though the Demon Rider minions keep fires burning throughout the day to warm Its flesh where It hides from the light. It is slow to arise until the narrow-faced moon is high.

The pack travels out of the forest, and onto a boulder-strewn plain. The snow of the road is pristine, save for random tracks of wild game. The traffic that would have come from Raindell, or from the Garrison of Brannock, will never pass this way again, and this road, like so many others in the land, will fade back into the wilderness it bisects.

Just before dawn, a large hill looms ahead. Execution cages swing on the summit to warn all Humans who travel the road of the consequences of defiance.

Unexpectedly, the Deathren pack wails, and runs ahead on their corpse-stiff legs. Undaunted when confronted by the steep grade of the hill, their strides, mechanical and tireless, climb towards the summit. The Deathren sense a killing field keenly; the merest drop of blood is enough to send them into mad frenzies of hunger. This is either the place where the Man made his last stand, or the Deathren sense the frost desiccated corpses swinging in the crow cages at the summit of the Tor.

The stars are fading rapidly from the sky, as It reaches the base of the Tor, and the lazy wastrels that the Master has saddled It with grumble in self-pity and fear of the oncoming daylight. It glares at the denmates, who turn their heads submissively to avoid the challenge of eye contact.

Satisfied by their show of deference, It gestures them upwards, to follow in the wake of the Deathren. Perhaps It will dine on one of them to celebrate the end of the Hunt. It glances skyward, and judges that there is yet time to discover the Man before the light begins to burn.

Halfway up the side of the Tor, the Deathren fall upon the ground, scrabbling with their pale hands, thrusting away ice, snow and rock to reach what is buried. The Deathren, uncaring, unfeeling creatures that they are, dig until the thin layer of flesh that covers their dead fingers rips away in bloodless, pulpy strips. Soon it is white finger bones that scratch against ice and stone.

In the end, they uncover no more than the stripped carcass of a horse.

'Failure!'

It reaches over the newly dug pit, and tears the head off of a Deathren. The creature collapses to the ground, and It kicks the felled corpse with Its clawed foot, sending the body skidding away to strike a boulder with shattering impact. Shards of flesh and bone, hardened by the freezing temperatures of the winter night, fall amongst the rest of the pack in a grisly shower. The Deathren continue their baying screams, unaffected by the spectacle.

It calms Its disappointment, for if the horse is here, the bodies cannot be far. But it has grown too late to continue. The Deathren are mindless beasts that cannot seek shelter on their own, and if It wants Its slaves to track and dig, It must protect them from the sun's burn.

It exerts the will of Its magic upon the Deathren, and they fall into the hole they have just dug. It kicks mightily, and covers them over with loose dirt, rock and snow. That will suffice.

It leaves the denmates to find their own shelter, and digs into the side of the Tor. Its hind claws make short work of the ice, then the loose stone, and then the frozen ground. It crawls into the shallow cavern, pulls the tailings in behind, and settles down to wait out the day, confident that the coming night will see the fulfillment of Its quest.

Its kind requires no sleep so, though It shuts Its serpent's eyes, It does naught but pass the day in pleasant fantasy of death and blood, murder and sex. When the temperature in Its hiding place drops sharply, It knows that the hated fire of the sun has been extinguished by the smothering cloak of night, and the world is Its to dominate once more.

It roars mightily when It bursts forth from Its hole, spraying dirt, rock, and icy snow in a large radius. The 'Rider minions, who have tended the fires all day, scatter, for It often feeds upon them when first arising. However, this night it is the Hunt that it gorges upon, and It will not feed again until 'tis over.

It is the first to arise, and sets about impatiently to dig the other Stalker denmates free from their holes. It unearths young Speckle Tail first, and it keens like prey when It drags it free of its lair. Instinct rules, and It lashes out, sets Its teeth to the young Stalker's neck, and for a long instant thinks of naught but Its need to Kill, but the Master's edict still holds sway.

'The Master's will is Law. The Master must be obeyed.'

It releases the struggling Stalker, content It has proven Its superiority over the weaker minion once more.

It sets the Deathren to sniffing out blood, forces them in a zigzagging loop towards the top of the Tor. Excitement grows as time passes without finding a corpse. Anticipation rekindles. Does the Man somehow survive? Will the Hunt continue?

Just south of the flattened hilltop, and uphill from the carcass of the horse, the Deathren shatter the quiet with their insane baying, and fall upon an iced pile of stone, digging to find the contents of the grave.

"Thy Hunt is over. Thy prey is dead," hisses Green Crest.

'Insolence!'

It backhands Green Crest, and its speckle-tailed denmate roars protectively, and takes two aggressive bounds to intervene before it remembers its place and grovels, lashes its tail, its talons open in supplication.

It leaps the distance between them, and clouts Speckle Tail hard enough to slam its horned chin into the ground. "If they all perished, from whence came the diggers of yonder grave?" It bares Its teeth in promise of violence.

The pitch of the Deathren's howls change as they reach flesh, and draws Its attention from the impudent denmates. It plucks the slaves from the grave to clear a path to reach within, and rips the frozen corpse free of the icy clasp of the cairn. Wisps of grey-haired scalp cling to the desiccated skull. Its nostril slits flare, collecting and evaluating the stale scents.

Old. Human. Male. Killed by Deathren.

Not the body of the Man, and the Deathren have sensed no other deaths upon the hillside. Pleasure shivers the spines on Its back. It will remember this Hunt forever, for the prey is elusive and cunning; the Man and his companions survive save for this old infirm one! It tosses the frozen meat to the screaming mass of Deathren, who fall upon the carcass, ravenous to devour the meager remains.

It falls to Its scaly knees, and once more opens Its soul to the burn of the Master's possession. The Man yet lives. The Hunt continues to Verdalan.

„℠„

The blood is thick and sweet, still warm from the throats of the slaves. Immersed to the chin, raises a bloody arm in a sensual stretch, admires the shimmering red sleeve. The bath meant to sooth despair has become a debauched celebration.

A purr of pleasure, as the blood drips, swirls and eddies in cloying, clotting, caresses. Whispers echo from the inlayed tile, the patterned mosaics of gold and gemstones, as attendants quietly drag away the Human corpses.

'He Lives!'

CHAPTER TWO

HEATHREN MOUNTAINS – LATE WINTER

The fury of Gralyre's blizzard had left hidden dangers in its wake. Drifts of deep snow had leveled the landscape, filling small gulches and crevasses, and smoothing over entire forests of tangled, storm-felled trees. As the Rebels trekked through the treacherous winter mountains, their safety tethers stayed firmly in place, linking man to man, beast to beast, and the leaders took no step that was not first probed for surety with a long pole. Despite this slowed travel, all agreed that the bright sunlight sparking off the high peak glaciers was a sight to see after the long days spent trapped within the claustrophobic confines of the heated cavern, listening to the roar and rage of the gale attempting to entomb them in ice. The storm damage eased the further they travelled from the epicentre, and after a few days of toiling through deep snow and hidden pitfalls, they were able to gradually increase their pace.

The Rebel warriors studiously avoided speaking of the blizzard, or of the cyclone within the cavern that had tossed them about like chaff on the wind; the fearful memories were still too vivid and hard. To a man they were exquisitely polite to Gralyre lest he find need to vent his temper with magic once more.

Though Gralyre would have preferred the hand of friendship from the men, their fear-born courtesy was a welcome change to their slings and barbs. He was still ostracized from the company of warriors, but none of them were rushing to resume past antagonisms. An uneasy truce had been declared.

Most notable was the absence of Matik. Gralyre's hirsute tormentor remained at the front of the line, and Gralyre near the rear, the most space that could be placed between them as they travelled. Though Matik's attack had been precipitated by Catrian's need to discover if his amnesia was self-inflicted, Gralyre knew that Death had ridden them both that night in a fight that had little to do with Catrian's agendas. Despite all this, the uncertainty of his future, and the mystery of his hidden past, Gralyre's mood improved daily.

The Sorceress was the one blight upon his peace of mind. Despite her intrigues, he would find himself instantly distracted by a glimpse of her, or by the distant sound of her voice, and cursed himself that it was so. In the dark of night, when he was exhausted and should be sleeping, he tossed and turned with visions of the kiss they had shared, tormented by the memory in a way not unlike the brutal nightmares of his beheading, and the pulsing void. Gralyre could not fathom his fascination for her, unabated despite what she had put him through.

෨෧෬

Matik reclined on his pack in front of the campfire, sharing a meager supper with Commander Boris after their long day of travel. The fire snapped and smoked from the damp wood, yet still threw enough heat to make him drowsy. He still had not recovered his full strength after the bloodletting Gralyre had given him in the cavern, and found that he nodded off easily.

"He is here again," Boris remarked, as he sucked a tough string of meat from his teeth, and forked another bite up into his mouth from his wooden plate.

Matik roused enough to glance up, and saw Dajin Wilson lingering at the edges of the firelight, and snorted. "Yea, the pup has been fawning over me since a fortnight outside o' Verdalan," he muttered quietly.

Dajin caught the glance, and raised his hand in a friendly wave.

"Are ye going t' do something about it?"

"Like what?"

"'Twould seem t' me t' be a useful thing, t' have a spy in the enemy's camp."

Matik smiled cunningly. "I had no' thought o' that. He was useful t' me before the storm, as a flail against Gralyre." He raised a hand and beckoned.

Dajin approached General Matik and Commander Boris, smiling widely. "Good eve'n, sirs. I do no' mean t' disturb your meal, but I wanted t' wish ye well, General Matik, and ask after how ye are?"

"Thank-ye, lad. I am on my way t' full recovery." The crusted scabs from the multitudes of cuts were healing without infection with thanks to Catrian's magical intervention. Though he would be left with scars, he would soon be hale. "I heard what ye did on my behalf when that traitor, Gralyre, knocked me down." He indicated a spot at the fire where Dajin was welcome to sit.

Dajin squirmed with the pleasure of being recognized for his deeds, and quickly took his seat. "Anyone would have done the same, sir." His face darkened petulantly, and he glared down at the ground. "Except my brother. Rewn thinks I acted dishonorably."

Matik rested a commiserating hand upon Dajin's shoulder. "Well, I have been meaning t' thank-ye. 'Tis good t' know that ye can be trusted."

Dajin frowned, uncertain if he was being complemented or his brother insulted. "I am no' like my brother. I do no' wish t' associate with a spy. The man is dangerous," he hastened to distinguish himself further from Rewn.

"Dangerous, how?" Matik rumbled encouragingly.

Dajin shrugged. "Everything bad has happened t' my family since Gralyre arrived. We lost our home, our village was destroyed," Dajin had the good graces to blush at his lie in laying the blame at Gralyre's feet, "and he has somehow convinced my brother o' his innocence, so that Rewn will no longer see reason."

Matik's smile dripped with understanding. "Ye have had a hard go o' it, lad. If I accept ye into my guards, ye will train with the axe. Do ye have a problem with that?"

"No, sir! Thank-ye General! I will make ye proud!" To be accepted by the Rebels had seemed an unattainable dream. Dajin's chest puffed out. Rewn and his disapproval could piss up a rope!

Matik's flat brown eyes hardened to agates. "Good lad."

෨ඊ

Word trickled back down the line that Matik had taken Dajin under his wing, which explained why Rewn's younger brother no longer sought out their campfire at night. Dajin had, through words and deeds, firmly distanced himself from Gralyre, Rewn and Saliana to win a place within the Rebel warriors.

Though Rewn mourned his brother's defection, Gralyre suspected that Dajin would fair better by being away from his brother for a time. The lad had yet to come to terms with his guilt over his father's death, and this independence might be what Dajin needed to finally grow into the man that his father, Wil, had always hoped for.

On the twentieth day of hard travel away from the cavern, on a cloudy afternoon, the group of travellers paused at the summit of the last mountain pass, and cheers erupted from the men, as the Northern Rebel Fortress came into view. Resting upon the lap of one of the tallest mountains in the Heathren range, mist wreathed the massive wooden walls that overlooked a forested valley from high above the timberline, fostering an unimpeded line of sight in all directions. No army could approach their walls without being in constant view for almost two days. Gralyre was amazed at the size of the fortress, for it was easily larger than the lowland city of Verdalan.

Commanding the high ground, its defenses seemed nearly impenetrable. Guard towers and gates protected three visible entrances located at west, south and east points, while the high craggy cliffs of the mountain encircled the northern back of the fortress city. A steep, switchback trail led from the forested valley floor, up the side of the mountain towards each gate. Boulders stacked beside the wooden walls lay ready to roll downhill to decimate any attacking force.

Though the slopes of the mountain itself had been deforested, the trees harvested for firewood and defense, the valley had been left untouched and primordial. Densely growing pine trees thrust their boughs skyward, creating an interlocking green canopy that left the world at their roots a mystery to all but Gralyre, who sensed wolves on the hunt, leaping joyously through deep drifts after rabbits and mice, while deer held their stillness to avoid detection from the predators.

The forested, bowl-shaped valley beneath the mountain was locked on all sides by craggy peaks, an oasis hidden away from the outside world. Turning slowly to encompass all vistas, Gralyre could discern only three other possible mountain passes leading into the vale, all of which would be too high and narrow to allow a large force to traverse en masse, and was willing to bet the Gods of Fortune that all were as well guarded as the one they were currently threading their way through.

Rebel sentries challenged them from the security of craggy stone nests, waving them onwards only after Commander Boris spoke the correct passwords. It was not enough to recognize the Commander, the sentries were charged with ensuring that no enemy force made use of the resistance leaders as hostages. Only when they were certain that all was safe did these warriors use bits of reflective mirror to signal safe conduct for the road-weary party to travel onwards. Those same mirror signals would have allowed the fortress time to marshal their defenses, had the approaching men been enemies.

"Gralyre, what do ye make o' that?" Rewn nodded towards a far off column of smoke that had its origins deep within the forest below the west gate. Lofting high into the air, the prevailing winds carried the smoke over the mountains, away from the fortress and its valley.

Gralyre's mouth turned down at the corners as he studied the distant, undulating, pillar of ash. "A pyre," he pronounced grimly.

"'Tis large."

"There are no fields for crops." Gralyre glanced back at the train of laden horses that followed in their wake, carrying the last of the grain from Wil Wilson's farm, saved from destruction when they had fled Raindell all those months ago. "Everything they eat has to be imported from the lowlands. This deep into winter, they must be starving."

Welcome news interrupted their dark musings, as Matik bellowed down the line of horses, "We will make camp at the outpost tonight, and have an early start tomorrow!" Cheers from the warriors erupted that this day of travel was to be cut short.

The outpost turned out to be little more than a large clearing on the far side of the pass, hidden amidst the evergreens, and ringed by high snowbanks from where winter had been shoveled away from tents and trails. There were no walls, but the snowbank buttress made up for the lack, and would give them a fair protection against any attack.

There was more than enough room within the clearing for the tired travellers to pitch their camp, and a rough-hewn coral in which to stable the horses. The accommodations were sparse, but the welcome was warm from the men who were awaiting their shift to guard the pass.

Soon the weary travellers were supping warm stew and mulled ale, and drowsing by hot fires, secure in the relief of reaching home alive.

಼ೞ

They left the outpost at first light, and it took the rest of day to navigate the deep, forested valley, and to climb the steep, switchback road up the side of the mountain to the fortress. When finally they passed through the western gate in the palisade wall, they were met with cheers from a small crowd that had assembled to greet them, and the influx of sounds and smells, the sudden overabundance of people, was a shock to all their senses after being so long surrounded by naught but the quiet of the wilderness. The clouds parted and golden light from the setting sun added another layer of unreality to the scene.

Sensing Little Wolf's panic, Gralyre dismounted to walk beside him, and Little Wolf pasted himself tightly to Gralyre's side with a warble of distress. The surging crowd was unexpected and frightening to the animal. Gralyre dropped a hand to Little Wolf's shoulder, and sank his fingertips deep into the wolfdog's ruff. The touch worked to calm them both, as they were shuffled and jostled along with the current of excited people.

A runner from the outpost had carried news to the fortress, ahead of their arrival, of the much-needed supplies that they brought. Surrounded by hundreds of laughing men, women and children, they were paraded towards the central square, footsore heroes carrying the salvation of all upon the backs of the heavily laden packhorses.

Friends and family of the returning warriors hailed from the crowd, and one by one the men peeled off from the group to be greeted with hugs and slaps on the back, until only a few travellers remained to deliver the supplies. Rewn's face fell with each hail that was not meant for him, and Gralyre realized how greatly the man had missed his sister, Dara.

Gralyre could not help comparing the Rebel stronghold to the occupied lowland city of Verdalan that he had briefly visited. Large tents of tightly woven canvas, oiled against the elements, were staked in militarily precise lanes with cook fires spaced evenly in front of every dwelling. Gralyre noted that the tents could be swiftly dismantled, leaving nothing permanent save the high wooden walls that encompassed the fortress in security. The Rebels had designed their stronghold for a quick and efficient evacuation, should the need to flee arise.

They passed by old men sitting in a circle whittling shafts for arrows, attended by an audience of small children who listened to their boastful stories of the past with wide eyes while they gathered the prepared shafts together in bundles. Gralyre smiled as tales of heroes and battles drifted to his ears through the babble of noise from the happy, laughing crowd that escorted them. It spoke well to the health of the thriving community, that their weakest members were well cherished and cared for.

The old, the young and women had all been noticeably absent from Verdalan, yet here was an intact community, the first Gralyre had ever encountered. There were many women with children clutching at their skirts, tending cook fires, and doing other domestic chores outside their tents. So many children! It just served to accentuate the horror of what Doaphin's edicts, and the Woman Tithe, had inflicted upon the rest of the land. Now he could clearly understand Catrian's vigilance. What would he not do, to protect a place such as this?

Rewn dismounted and grabbed Gralyre's shoulder roughly in his excitement. "Gralyre! Look at all the people! All the women!" Rewn's head swiveled to take in all the sights at once.

How much stranger must this all be for Rewn, Gralyre mused, after being raised in the lowlands? It was a bounty laid before a man who had lived all his life in famine. Gralyre punched him lightly in the arm. "Careful you do not feast on what you cannot finish! A couple of these women look like they would not take kindly to it."

Rewn blushed around a wide grin.

Gralyre referred to the many women who wore light armour, and strode confidently beside the men. Most carried bow and quiver, although some had short swords sheathed by their sides. Gralyre met the gaze of a warrior maid, and all misgivings of the women's fighting ability dispersed. Her look was direct and confident, and her physique was sleek and well muscled from long hours of practice. She smiled at him, an invitation.

Gralyre glanced away first. How long would it be before rejection shone from the welcoming faces surrounding him, before they learned of his odd circumstances? A day? Two?

"Hey lowlander!" she shouted after him. "What is the matter? Canno' handle a woman who can fight back?"

Gralyre's head snapped back around in surprise at the taunt, but the undulating stream of humanity had already swept him away from where the woman had stood.

The Rebel fortress was a thriving bastion of humanity, and although the occupants were thin and lacking of belongings, they seemed stronger and healthier than their neighbours trapped in the cities and towns under Doaphin's despotic regime; their shoulders back, and their heads up, they carried themselves with pride. Perhaps their vitality stemmed from their precious freedom, something that their neighbours in the lowlands knew naught of.

The boisterous crowd spilled into a large central square at the heart of the fortress, delineated by several large, log buildings. Other than the fortress walls, they were the only permanent structures to be seen thus far, and Gralyre speculated upon their use for weapons or food stores.

The parade halted, signaling that they had finally reached journey's end, and Commander Boris and Catrian turned their horses to greet their people. They were met with roars of welcome. The Commander smiled, holding up his hands for silence. "'Tis good t' be home! We have been successful on our journey, and have brought much food."

Catrian had to await the happy buzz to subside once more before she could add, "Starting tomorrow, ye may visit your Stewards t' receive your share o' the supplies." The crowd cheered again before surging forward to help in the unloading of the packhorses.

"Gralyre! Do ye see her? I do no' see Dara!" Rewn craned his neck, trying to see above the undulating swarm of humanity.

Gralyre also scanned the throng. "I do not see her."

Rewn rubbed an urgent hand through his shaggy, brown hair, rubbing the back of his head in frustration. "How are we t' find her? She could be anywhere!"

Gralyre shrugged free of his pack, and dropped it at Rewn's feet. "I will go forward, and ask Catrian." With Little Wolf fast on his heels, he abandoned Rewn in the mob, his attention, as always, captured by Catrian, marking where she dismounted to ensure he did not lose her in the crush of people, though he need not have bothered, for though Gralyre had to wind and push his way through the throng, the people instinctively flowed around the Rebel leaders, leaving a respectful circle of privacy.

Gralyre watched as Catrian handed her reins to a soldier waiting to take her horse, and joined Boris and Matik who were already in deep conversation with a large woman who owned a face that could spoil meat. Tall and built of muscle and menace, the two long braids of muddy, grey hair hanging beside her jowly cheeks undulated wildly as she gesticulated to make her point. Her hoarse voice rattled among oddly angled teeth that flashed fangs at all, as she made her report to the Rebel leaders.

The Commander took a prudent step back from the passionately waving hands, nodding solemnly as he listened to her words and, as Catrian joined them, moved aside to include her in their conversation. Whatever was spoken of was ill news, for all three leaders wore looks of concern as they listened.

Gralyre halted at a respectful distance to await their notice, just free of the flow of people around the Rebel leaders. Catrian's voice arose over the babble of the crowd, and her anguished outburst brought Gralyre an instinctive step nearer.

"...one hundred and thirty?"

"Aye, milady. Dead from the cold and the lack o' victuals."

"Thank ye for the account, Beaurice," Catrian sighed. "Ye can start cataloguing the supplies. People will be needing them more than ever."

Beaurice's eyes, placed in narrow proximity to her large nose, were reddened and seeping from a winter ailment, and she snorted loudly to prevent a similar discharge from her flaring nostrils.

Boris shook his head sorrowfully. "The people who have died! And the hunting parties that did no' return! We are no' so many that we can suffer such losses!"

"The hunting parties may no' all be lost, uncle. They may have been delayed or been unable t' find supplies. Ye know the rules. If they canno' find the goods, they stay in the lowlands wherever they are so as t' no' add t' our burden."

"But ye have said that something has Doaphin stirred up like a hornet. Your scry showed..."

"Shh," Catrian cut him off sharply. "No' here, uncle!"

Gralyre met her accusing stare. Knowing he could not hide the fact that he had been eavesdropping, he merely nodded in her direction and stepped forward.

Matik took an aggressive stride to intercept, and halted Gralyre with a heavy hand on his chest. "Where do ye think ye are going, spy!" he snarled. Multitudes of thin red lines were all that remained of the slices Gralyre had given him during their battle in the cavern. They bisected nearly every bit of exposed flesh, but Catrian's care had seen all but the deepest of them heal smoothly, and the scarring would fade with time.

Gralyre stiffened, and glared down into Matik's face. "Get your hand off me."

Little Wolf seconded Gralyre's edict by growling, ugly and guttural, while crinkling his muzzle to show off his impressive, adult teeth.

"Gralyre! Matik! Enough!" Catrian hissed, as she joined them both, placing a restraining hand upon Matik's muscular arm to ease him away from the confrontation they both knew he would lose.

"Boris needs ye," she easily lied to extricate her General.

Matik sniffed loudly. "I will be just there if ye need me, m'lady," he rumbled protectively, holding Gralyre's glare as he backed away a few steps, and crossed his arms truculently.

Little Wolf subsided, but his gaze was locked to Matik's face, ready to act should the man become aggressive once more.

Gralyre ignored Matik, content that Little Wolf would warn him of impending attack, to focus upon the more dangerous of the duo. "Rewn was wondering how he is to locate his sister."

Catrian frowned, shaking her head at the unexpected digression of the conversation. "What?"

"Rewn and Dajin's sister? Wil's daughter, Dara…?"

Catrian rubbed her brow with impatient irritation, nodding, "Yes, o' course." She glanced over to the Quartermistress. "Beaurice, the lass I sent here last summer? Where did ye place her?"

Beaurice snarled a smile Gralyre's way, baring her randomly placed teeth. "She is billeted in South District. Check with the Stewards there." She gesticulated widely back over her shoulder towards the general direction that Gralyre should travel. "Ye will like t' find 'em dicing in the guard house, south gate. Tell them they are t' find ye and yours lodging as well."

Gralyre bowed his head courteously, and returned what he

assumed to have been her smile. "Thank-you."

Beaurice snorted her impressive nose, and stomped off, yelling at some skinny young boys to come help her. With looks of terror on their faces they complied. The Quartermistress quickly had the group organized and working to unload and catalogue the newly arrived supplies.

Gralyre nodded his thanks to Catrian before turning on his heel.

"Gralyre, hold a moment." Catrian placed a restraining hand on his arm. "My tent is just there." She indicated a larger pavilion set beside one of the wooden buildings. "Return t' me once ye are settled." There was no doubt that this was a command to an underling. She was firmly setting the tone for their future dealings.

Her order made his midnight-blue eyes flash before he was able to control his expression. Gralyre inclined his head with cold civility, plucked her hand from his sleeve, and turned away again. Walking back to where he had left Rewn and Saliana, the hair on the back of his neck rose eerily at the feel of Catrian's glare boring into his back.

ഇരു

"Rewn."

Rewn glanced around at the sound of his name to see Dajin staring at him from the milling crowd, rocking from foot to foot with nervous energy.

Dajin wet his lips. "General Matik says I should billet with ye…if that is… if ye want?"

Unnoticed by either man, Saliana edged away, placing Rewn between her and his brother.

Rewn frowned, ill at ease with this politer version of his mercurial brother. "Are ye no' afraid that we will taint ye?"

Dajin's face tightened with the familiar petulance that it had worn since their Da had died, and he spun on his heel to stalk away.

"Wait."

Dajin halted but did not turn around, his stiff back announcing his affront.

Rewn grimaced, and kicked at the icy ground, wishing back his poorly chosen words. His brother was not the only one with a reckless temper. "I am sorry. We are going t' find Dara." Dajin turned back around, and Rewn gestured with his hand, awkwardly trying to build upon the truce that Dajin had initiated. "And ye are always welcome with us, little brother."

"What about him?" Dajin nodded towards Gralyre, who was striding back through the crowd.

Rewn glanced from Dajin to Gralyre and back again, for Gralyre had spotted Dajin, and though his gait had not changed, somehow his approach had adopted an aggressive undertone. "That, Daj, ye will need t' brave all on your own."

To his credit Dajin tried to stand his ground, but as Gralyre advanced without slowing, he paled and tried to back away, but it was too late to retreat.

Gralyre drove his fist up into Dajin's chin, lifting him a foot from the ground, and dropping him on his back. He bent and gasped Dajin's shirtfront, delivering a punishing blow to his nose that snapped his head back into the snow.

Dajin yelped and put a hand to his bloodied face. "Are ye just going t' let him beat me?" he whined at his brother.

Rewn shook his head in mock sorrow, almost ashamed at the gratification he was deriving from Dajin's comeuppance. "Ye did try t' kill him," he reminded with a commiserating wince. He trusted that Gralyre would not carry the punishment too far, but the man did have a right to seek retribution, and Dajin needed to reap what he had sown.

Little Wolf dropped to his haunches with his ears perked, and his head cocked to the side to watch the one-sided fight. Rewn took heart at the wolfdog's relaxed posture for the animal was always an excellent augury of the emotional state of his master. Gralyre was in control of his rage.

But Dajin did not know that.

Gralyre's expression was icy, as he glared down at the younger man. He used the gathered fabric of Dajin's woolen coat to haul him to his feet. With little effort he hefted Dajin to his toes, and shook him roughly. "Shall I find stones for you to throw, little man?"

Dajin swallowed heavily. "No! No! I am sorry!"

Gralyre shook him once more. "I will not kill you, out of respect for Wil and Rewn, but the next time that you come at me, I will end you," he promised grimly. "Do you understand?"

Despite the cold, a bead of sweat rolled down Dajin's cheek. "Yes, I understand!"

Gralyre glared at him for a long moment, making certain that his point had been made before releasing him back to his feet. He smoothed the rumpled fabric of Dajin's coat. "Good. 'Tis done." He turned on his heel, and headed south. "Dara is this way."

Little Wolf, wearing what Rewn swore to be a canine grin, scrabbled to his feet to trot after his master.

Rewn dug into his jerkin and pulled out a clean rag, handing Dajin the cloth to wipe the blood away, as he clapped his brother on the back to get him moving south. "That went far better than I expected."

Dajin glared out from under the cloth that he was pinching to his nose, and forbore an answer.

Trailing them by several feet, Saliana used her hand to hide a small smile of enjoyment that teased about her mouth.

ଚୁଠା

Dara spied upon the south gate from where she hid behind a row of empty barrels that were stacked five high, conveniently placed where the avenue opened up into the busy courtyard in front of the large wooden doors. The Stewards were not in their customary places within the gatehouse, throwing their dice, yet still she hesitated to move, mistrusting the scene, scanning the men guarding the gate, the wall, the sea of traffic in and out of the postern...they could be anywhere. The thought made her snug her borrowed cloak tighter about her shoulders against a shiver of fear.

Since the night of the bathhouse, Mayvin and Aneida had allowed her to bunk with them, and Dara had gratefully accepted their sanctuary. Avoiding the South District Stewards completely, her bruises and pains had almost healed, while the sisters' friendship and strength had become a balm for her abused spirit. In return, Dara had taken over the household chores of cooking and cleaning. Aneida had told her it was not necessary, but Dara knew that the two women had saved her life that night, and it was little enough that she could do to repay them.

The sisters were exiled lowlanders, like Dara, but there all similarities ended. Where Dara feared every Rebel that approached, Aneida greeted them with a brash laugh, and swaggering bravado that more often than not sent the warriors fleeing. Even Mayvin was not bothered, for her cold mute glare frightened all into believing her mad though there was nothing wrong with her that Dara could detect beyond her lack of voice. It took concentration, but Dara was slowly learning simple phases of Mayvin's hand language, though Aneida was obliged to translate most of sister's thoughts. Somehow, the two women had made a life here, something for Dara to aspire to.

The sisters had promised to teach Dara how to protect herself, and had told her of a forest glade below the south gate where they could practice in secret. When Dara felt that she was ready to learn, she was to join the sisters in training, but that meant passing a test of sorts; exiting through the gate, and braving the undisputed territory of her abusers – the Stewards.

This was not the first day she had hidden like a frightened mouse, lacking the courage to expose herself in order to follow the sisters through the gates. Every day, she had lost her nerve, and slunk home at sunset with her tail set firmly between her legs. But not today! Dara was determined that this was the day she succeeded.

Dara watched the traffic passing through the gate, biting her lip, and working to find her courage. Aneida had been right, that cold, bitter night that they had met. No one could fight her battles for her! If she did not find a way to conquer her fear, forever would it hold sway over her heart. She watched a wagon stacked high with firewood rumble and slide through the dirty, churned snow, returning from the forest piled high with much needed firewood, and realized that she could use it for cover in a dash across the open space leading to the gates. This was her last chance before the setting sun made the task impossible. She could leave, but she had to move now!

"Dara!"

She whirled fearfully at the sound of a man's voice calling her name, and could not prevent the squeal of happiness that erupted from deep within.

"Rewn!"

Dara was barely able to speak around the tears that suddenly burst free at the impact of seeing her family at long last, and all thoughts of following the sisters through the gates vanished. "Ye are here! Ye are finally here! Rewn! Dajin!" Crying and laughing, she tottered towards her brothers with her arms raised in welcome and need.

Rewn did not wait for her to reach him but ran to Dara, and grabbed her in a huge hug, lifting her feet clear of the snow, as he twirled her dizzily. When he had put her down, it was Dajin's turn, and for the moment Dajin's face lost the insolent sneer he had adopted, and was instead split by a wide grin of happiness, as he embraced his twin.

Dara looked over Dajin's shoulder, and smiled at Gralyre. "You came as well? I am so glad!" She brushed happy tears from her cheeks, her gaze running greedily over her siblings. "Ye are here! Ye are finally here!" She repeated as though unable to believe it was true. She laughed joyously and hugged Rewn again, needing the familiar comfort to prove to her reeling senses that she had not gone mad. "Ye are here!" she reiterated quietly to convince herself finally of the happy truth.

Rewn laughed. "We are here!" He brushed his sister's hair back from her brow, and pressed a smacking kiss in its place.

೮ು೦ನ

From a side road that spilled into the marshaling area in front of the south gate, Steward Hofar spied his little lowland whore embracing another man, and his face curdled. So that was where she had hied herself off to! She had been peddling her wares to another!

Honestly, he had thought that Jorrod had killed the little pigeon, as he had not clapped eyes upon her twitchy skirts since the night they had tossed her limp body out into the snowstorm. He had assumed her frozen corpse had been carted off to the pyres in the morning, but it would seem that the little whore was more resourceful than he had thought. Well, she was his to do with as he pleased, and she could leave when he was done with her, not a day before.

As his strides ate the distance towards the embracing couple, and his hand caressed the hilt of his sword, he imagined Dara's devastated face when he split her swain from gullet to crotch.

"Dara!" he yelled. "I have missed ye, pigeon!"

Dara leapt away from Rewn, her face pale and scared, before her chin firmed and lifted. Her family had arrived. She need fear the Stewards no more.

Rewn frowned at the man's aggressive approach, and stepped protectively in front of his sister. "Dara?" he questioned over his shoulder, as Hofar halted a few paces off.

"Rewn, this is Hofar, one of the South District Stewards," she said coldly. "Hofar…meet my brothers."

Shock immobilized Hofar for a moment, as he finally noted that the man was not alone. Another stood at Dara's back, alike enough in appearance to name him kin, while a larger, black-bearded man, his hand stroking the ears of a black wolf, looked on with quiet intensity.

Assessing the size and breadth of the three men facing him,

an unfamiliar spit of worry skewered Hofar's cold heart, though from the mulish look on the little whore's face, she had not yet tattled her tale of woe to her family, and she would not if she knew what was good for her!

He smiled smoothly, and inside howled with glee as he watched the men relax their guards. "I am sorry t' have mistaken ye for someone beleaguering our Dara! With no family, we have been watching o'er her t' keep her safe from unwanted attentions," Hofar lied easily with an effacing shrug, and had to bite the inside of his cheek to prevent his laughter from erupting, as he watched thankfulness and guilt wash across the faces of Dara's brothers; thankfulness that their sister had been well protected, guilt at not being there to do so themselves. It was too easy.

Dara scowled, and opened her mouth to speak, but Hofar quickly cut her off. "'Tis difficult for lowlanders in the camps," he confided to Rewn with a concerned frown. "Sometimes terrible accidents happen t' those unwary o' the dangers." Dara's voice froze in her throat at the veiled threat, and her mouth snapped shut.

Rewn stepped forward with an affable grin, and his hand out in friendship. "Thank-ye for taking care o' my sister. I am Rewn Wilson."

Dara choked on a cough at the sham, and Hofar cut her a sly glance as he shook Rewn's hand. "Now that ye are here, ye can look out for her. Dara speaks o' ye often," Hofar held out his hand in greeting to the other men in turn, effortlessly allaying their suspicions.

"Dajin."

"Gralyre."

"'Tis good t' meet ye all." Hofar craned his neck to look beyond Gralyre. "And who is this pretty little one?" His gaze ran up and down Saliana's shrinking form.

Gralyre instinctively moved to block his view, and was not surprised that Rewn's shoulder met his to present a solid wall. There was something about this man's demeanour that set his back teeth to grinding. "Saliana Greythorn. She is with us."

Little Wolf, alerted by Gralyre's disquiet, lowered his nose and fixed his feral gaze upon the Steward, snuffling deeply at the air to affix the man's scent in his memory.

Hofar quickly back-stepped from his lascivious slip, and rubbed his hands together as he smiled. After all, they could not protect her forever. As soon as starvation set in, they would serve both women up for an extra scrap of meat. 'Twas well known that the lowlanders affixed little value to their women.

"Well, I know Dara is very glad t' see ye. She was billeted with several other women, but now that ye are arrived, ye will be needing a tent all your own. It has been a hard winter," he shook his head with a large show of woeful regret, "and many people have died from starvation," he met Dara's frightened gaze meaningfully as he delivered the threat, gratified to see her quail, "so there are several empty dwellings t' choose from. Once ye are settled, report t' the gatehouse. We live as a unit. If ye want food, ye have t' work. For strong men such as yourselves, that should no' be difficult." He motioned for them to follow.

"And what sort o' work did Dara do?" Rewn asked, suspicious of the odd flavour of Dara's reaction to the Steward, as he fell in beside the man.

Dara held her breath, her stare wide and anxious.

Hofar's expression was perfectly innocent, as he glanced back over his shoulder. "Dara very kindly did chores for myself and the other two Stewards, whom ye will meet shortly. Perhaps we can persuade ye t' continue to aid us," Hofar smiled wickedly at her. "After all, your brothers will likely be away much o' the time. We should no' want t' see ye pine away from loneliness."

Dara spoke through tight, bloodless lips. "I will see t' my own household from now on."

"O' course," Hofar's smile did not change yet Dara sensed the rage hidden behind it, and stumbled.

Dajin caught her with an arm around her waist and a carefree laugh. "Whoa, sister! Watch your feet!"

Rewn's stare met Gralyre's in a wordless communion of disquiet, as Hofar led them through the narrow avenues and passages between tents, directing them towards the pavilion that he had decided to allocate to their family.

Unable to bear the anxiety caused by Hofar's oblique barbs regarding her brothers' safety, Dara fell behind the group, and was soon walking in step with Saliana. She had thought that when her family arrived, that all would be made well, only now was she realizing that their arrival had made her even more vulnerable. How was she to protect her family?

Seeking a distraction, Dara ventured tentatively, "Ye are from Raindell, are ye no'?" At Saliana's nod, Dara continued, "Aye, I thought I recognized ye. Ye were in the tithe wagon."

Saliana risked a quick peek at Dara's face, evaluating her friendliness, before dropping her gaze downward again. "Yes. I should have run, like ye, when I had the chance. If it were no' for Rewn, and the others, I would be dead. I am safe now though."

"Safe," Dara reiterated, chewing on the concept, a tough mouthful to swallow. Her face assumed a sour tightness, rendering her years older. "No, ye were right t' stay. I wish I had."

Saliana glanced her way in surprise, but Dara had looked at her feet, her cheeks flushed with shame. She should not have said anything. Hofar's threat was clear. She could tell no one of what the Stewards had done, or they would kill her family.

"Here it is," Hofar announced grandly.

It was a wreck. In the last light of the setting sun they could clearly see that the canvas of the tent Hoffer had chosen for them was ragged with age and wear, but it was to be theirs, a new home for a new start, and Dara did not care so long as her family was now with her.

"Remember t' report t' the gate for assignment." Hofar smiled toothily at the men, and before Dara could escape him, he had grabbed her fingers, squeezing brutally under the guise of a genteel gesture. "Make sure that your brothers learn the lay o' the land now, pigeon. I would hate for them t' have any problems."

Dara nodded stiffly, bravely meeting the threat in his gaze. Hofar released her with a broad grin of satisfaction, and left them all to settle in their new home.

The weary family entered the tent, and dropped their heavy packs with relief, while Little Wolf circled the interior, sniffing and exploring the unfamiliar scents.

The pavilion was roughly ten feet square, and would have room for little more than just their sleeping pallets. Staining of the canvas fabric in the corners bespoke of leaks that would have to be patched, and the floor was bare, dusty earth that had been pounded flat by countless generations of feet. What little heat they would enjoy at night would come from the banked embers within the misshapen and dented brazier that was set near the centre post to allow smoke to exit through a small, blackened hole near the tent's peak. Wooden bins lined the back wall opposite the doorway, in which they could store cooking utensils, spare bedding, clothes, weapons, and perhaps some food. It was shabby, mean accommodations, but it was theirs. It was to be their new home.

"What is Hofar's talk o' problems, and fitting in, Dara?" Dajin demanded as he kicked his pack into a corner. "We are no' mewling babes!"

"Things are no' always easy for lowlanders here," she mumbled evasively. At Rewn's suspicious expression, she found herself prattling nervously to avoid expanding on her telling statement. "Where is Da? Why is he no' with ye? Did he send ye t' collect me? 'Tis safe t' come home now?" she asked eagerly.

Gralyre saw pain flare in Rewn's face when Dara asked after Wil. Tactfully, he took Saliana's hand, called Little Wolf to his side, and left the large tent.

ഇരു

Dara read her brothers' expressions well enough that no words were needed to tell her the awful truth. She barely noticed when Gralyre and Saliana left them.

"No!" She shook her head, her hands pressed tight to her mouth. "Argh, Gods! No!" She stumbled backwards, fetching up against the centre tent pole.

Rewn placed his strong hands on her shoulders, and held her still, his gaze never leaving hers as, succinctly as possible, he told her of their flight from Raindell. "There was nothing any o' us could do," he finished. "We were being chased by Deathren. Da sacrificed himself so we could live."

"Oh, Gods!" She moaned again. She was shaking so, that only Rewn's grip upon her shoulders kept her on her feet. "Ye are unharmed? Ye are both unharmed?" Her head pivoted wildly between Rewn and Dajin, as tears streamed unchecked down her cheeks.

Dajin sneered. "Aye! No thanks t' Saliana!"

"Dajin!" Rewn gritted warningly.

"Saliana fell from her horse," Dajin exploded unheedingly.

He wagged his irate finger under Rewn's nose. "If she had no', Da would still be alive, and ye know it!"

Rewn's eyes turned agate hard, as he grabbed hold of, and twisted Dajin's wagging finger, bringing him to his knees.

"Owe! Ouch! Stop it, Rewn!"

"Her fall could have happened t' any one o' us. The horses were exhausted, the ice, the loose shale o' the slope… Shall I tell Dara the part that ye played in that battle, Dajin? How your attack upon the Lord Collaborator caused the destruction of Raindell, and forced us all t' flee for our lives in the first place?" Rewn demanded scornfully.

"Gralyre was the one t' kill the Lord…"

Tears stood out in Rewn's eyes; tears for the loss of his father, and for his brother's dishonour. "Ye would be dead had Gralyre no' acted t' protect ye! And Gralyre and I would both be dead were it no' for Saliana! She rode out o' the safety o' the sunlight t' save us from the Deathren. Her! No' ye!"

"Stop it, both o' ye! Stop it! Rewn, let him go!" Dara begged. "Just let him go," her words trailed, as she collapsed to the floor, sobbing.

Rewn let go of his brother immediately, and crouched beside his sister, hugging her as tightly as he could, trying to absorb her shaking. "I am sorry, I am so sorry. Dara. Shh. Do no' cry," his voice broke at the last, and all he could do was rock her, rock them both, as they grieved.

Dajin gained his feet slowly, staring down at his siblings, excluded from the circle of their grief. His hands fisted at his sides. He could not let his tears fall.

∞∝

The walls of the tent were thin enough to hear all that transpired within. When Saliana heard Dajin's words her chin dropped, and she shrunk into herself, hunching her shoulders and hugging her waist.

Gralyre reached out to comfort her but let his hand fall to his side when she shied from his touch. "Saliana? Are you all right? No harm will come to you. Please do not trouble yourself with Dajin's witlessness!" She was silent for so long that Gralyre thought she meant not to answer him.

From within, Rewn came to Saliana's defense, and a defiant light entered her pale eyes. Colour washed back into her cheeks while she glared unseeingly at the empty firepit in front of the tent, avoiding Gralyre's concerned gaze.

"I shall gather some wood," she announced suddenly.

"Would you like me or Little Wolf to accompany you?"

Saliana shook her head, her chin firming with a rare show of defiance. "No. I can do it."

A ghost of a smile teased Gralyre's lips while he nodded proudly that she would not let Dajin's harsh opinions cow her. "I saw a wood pile back at the crossroads down that row." Saliana ducked her head and bobbed, in what Gralyre assumed was concurrence, before she flitted away.

Gralyre crouched down and snugged Little Wolf into his side, trying not to listen to the grief that now emanated from within the tent. Now would be as good a time as any to visit the Sorceress. The Wilsons needed their privacy, and Little Wolf would alert him to any trouble.

'Stay here. Keep Saliana company.' Though Gralyre could not identify the source of his disquiet, all his senses warned him to be wary of this place.

ഇൠ

Dusk came upon Gralyre, as he walked across the fortress towards the centre square, and Catrian's tent. He was deep in thought, his heart filled with sorrow for Wil's death and Dara's grief.

The first time he was struck by a passer-by he thought nothing of it, a mere trifling of two strangers bumping into each other along a crowded byway. The second time, was an irritant. By the third instance, Gralyre realized that he was being deliberately targeted.

"Filthy lowlander!" The yelled insult was accompanied by a horse's plop that sailed over the heads of passerby, and spattered against Gralyre's arm.

Gralyre whirled and pushed through the crowd to the edge of the avenue, from where the assault had originated. But whoever had done it, had melted away into the swirl of humanity to avoid retribution.

Gralyre used clean snow to brush the filth off his arm, and

thereafter paid attention as he walked, vigilant to more of the not so subtle bullying. There was no welcome in the faces he passed.

Gralyre rounded the last turn to his destination, paused to allow a man pulling an empty cart to pass, and hesitated even after the path had cleared, frowning at his first sight of the two warriors standing sentry duty outside of Catrian's pavilion. This would be the first time they had spoken at length since the cavern, and Gralyre had hoped to have his audience with Catrian go unremarked. To withdraw flashed briefly through his mind, but he suppressed the craven notion. This meeting had been delayed for far too long already. Drawing a deep, bracing breath, and straitening his shoulders to ready for battle, Gralyre started across the square towards Catrian's tent, weaving through the steady traffic of people that crisscrossed the open space.

The fully armoured guards stood to either side of the tent's entrance, poleaxes held at rigid attention, but as Gralyre approached they crossed the staves of their weapons across the flap, blocking his entry. The sentry to the left eyed Gralyre's rough clothes with a disdainful sniff. "Where do ye think ye are going, lowlander scum? State your business!"

A muscle flexed in Gralyre's jaw, as the rudeness spiked his temper, already frayed around the edges from the gauntlet of disdain he had just endured. The Sorceress *knew* that he was coming, *had invited him*, and then had deliberately set the two guardsmen here. There was no better show of power than to order him to attend her, and then deny him entrance!

But Gralyre had had more than enough of dancing to another

fiddler's tune. Something had shifted since the events within the cavern; something deep and powerful had stretched awake. There was nothing he could do to affect the Rebels' opinion of him, but he had changed how he perceived himself, and he was a man who would suffer no more insults.

Gralyre slammed his elbow into the face of the contemptuous guard, knocking him to the ground while nimbly liberating his weapon.

"Halt!" the second sentry yelled while scrabbling to bring his arms to bear, but he could not match Gralyre's speed.

Gralyre twirled the stave of his stolen poleaxe with a precision flourish, before finding his grip upon the haft at the perfect balance point, the elongated spike of the axe centred with deadly accuracy above the heart of the second sentry, rock steady and lethal.

The sentry gaped, and he froze at the threat of impaling, releasing his own poleaxe, and letting it fall to the snowy ground with a thud. "Please…no!" Into the pregnant pause that followed, the man shivered fearfully at the controlled, deadly ice in Gralyre's face.

Gralyre pivoted the stave, gaining momentum as he levered it around, and slammed the butt end into the guard's crotch. As the sentry collapsed with a heaving gasp, Gralyre reversed the spin of the weapon, and gave him a smart rap on the back of the head to accelerate his decent. He tossed the heavy weapon down onto the moaning guard he had struck first, returning the poleaxe to its original owner. The way now clear, Gralyre lifted the flap and strode through, unannounced and unrepentant.

The familiar, imperious voice of the Sorceress rolled over him. "Why are ye in here? What have ye done t' my sentries?"

Gralyre's gaze adjusted to the interior gloom well enough to clash with Catrian's. She was seated at a large battered table, a cup at her elbow, and a brassbound book opened before her. He did not bother with pleasantries any more than she had. "You invited me."

Her eyebrows rose slowly, arrogantly, as she pushed her chair backwards and stood, brushing her loosened hair back over her shoulders, and rippling the sleek brown length almost to her waist. "I did no' mean this instant. Tomorrow would have sufficed."

In the time since he had left her side, she had bathed, and changed into a clean, baggy dress. She seemed garbed for relaxation, not for an audience, which reinforced his notion that she had sought to play more games with him, but if he had taken her by surprise she masked it well. She snapped the volume shut, and sauntered casually around the table to place the tome back onto a shelf with twenty or thirty other books and scrolls.

Gralyre took a few steps further into the tent, circling to maintain the distance between them. They resembled stalking cats, neither wanting to move forward, both realizing that a step back was an invitation to attack.

The two sentries stumbled through the entrance, poleaxes at the ready, shouting and posturing in an effort to intimidate the man that they were not quite brave enough to re-engage in battle.

Gralyre remained relaxed, and kept his attention upon the only real threat in the room. The Sorceress did the same.

"I am sorry, m'lady! He pushed right past us!" The first guard that Gralyre had hit glared murderously, and swiped blood from his nose. The other sentry seemed to be having trouble standing upright, and leaned heavily upon his weapon.

"I am fine. Leave us," Catrian ordered with a dismissive wave. Her mouth compressed with displeasure as she glared at Gralyre, her expression taking on a censorious overtone. The two sentries bowed stiffly, and reassumed their posts outside the entrance.

Gralyre smiled slightly at her disgruntled expression. If she had not wanted them injured, then she should not have placed them in his way. His warrior gaze assessed her quarters quickly, missing nothing. As a leader, Catrian had the luxury of privacy, but her tastes ran towards the functional, and there were few indicators of the personality of the woman who lived here.

The interior of the tent seemed spacious when compared to what he would share with the Wilsons, though as a leader, Catrian's pavilion was certainly larger by half. A coarse, woven mat of reeds and grasses covered most of the earthen floor, tickling his nose with the warm scents of the summer past. Set to one side of the central tent pole was a long oak table, with several mismatched chairs clustered around it. Battered and gouged, it was obviously used for much more than supping. Close at hand were the bookshelves that lined the tent wall, housing scrolls, and bindings of leather embossed with worn gold lettering. The proximity of the shelves to the table aided the impression of war room rather than dinning space.

A rough green curtain, suspended from the ceiling, separated her sleeping quarters from the rest of the room, and through the gauzy fabric Gralyre could see a narrow cot that was still barren of bedding after her long absence. The remaining space was owned by a couple of comfortable chairs with padded seats and arms placed before a small, unlit brazier. They seemed her one concession to homey comfort, and Gralyre frowned, as he wondered who she would share her cozy space with. He could see her in the evening; her hair unbound as it was now, catching the light… He blinked to dispel the image.

Suspended above him, a softly glowing ball of energy hovered near the central tent peak, shedding heat and subdued radiance. His gaze travelled from her magical display back down to her face where she waited patiently for him to finish his inspection.

In the time it had taken Gralyre to examine her quarters, Catrian had regained her composure, and a light sneer now pulled her lips, as she gave him an insulting once over, from the toes of his muddied boots, to his bearded face and overgrown hair. She cocked her head to the side, and seemed to contemplate his arrival as though it was a test that she was surprised he had passed. "Ye could have taken the time t' bathe." She sniffed and wrinkled her nose.

Gralyre's jaw clenched at her barb, but he would not be distracted by petty skirmishes when there was a war to be fought. "You ordered me to attend you. You knew that I would come."

"And why did I know that? Ye have ne'er shown a willingness t' follow my orders in the past."

"Because I need you."

Her expression froze at the bald statement, and a flush touched her high cheekbones. Her grey-green eyes blinked once with an unexpected confusion.

Gralyre shot her a hard smile, and took a step forward, invading her space, keeping her off balance. "I need you to teach me magic," he clarified. Anger increased her blush, and her chin rose in challenge. He had definitely drawn first blood.

Gralyre felt Catrian's magic probe for entry into his thoughts, and for a moment he considered blocking her. Somehow, he knew that he now had the ability to do it, but he was not above using his innocence to punish her for her constant mistrust. Gralyre mockingly dropped his barriers to her invasion, inviting her to search him for the taint of evil.

She did her duty, searching his intentions, coldly and clinically, and Gralyre recognized that she gained no pleasure from the encounter. It seemed her one redeeming trait.

"So this is the way it is going to be, then?" Gralyre jeered softly.

"This is the way it has t' be, yes."

"I asked you a question before, in the cavern." Gralyre took another step nearer, using his massive bulk to try to intimidate her. "Do you believe me to be an evil man?"

"And I gave ye my answer." She remained unimpressed by his looming presence, and took her own step forward to match his. So intent were they upon their encounter that they failed to note that they were drawing dangerously nearer to one another.

Gralyre's hands fisted, though he kept his arms hanging passively, a mockery of relaxed control. "An evasion, Sorceress. You need to come to a decision."

"Do I?" She drew herself up imperiously, and stepped to the side, instinctively circling him to keep from becoming trapped against the bookshelves.

"About many things." Gralyre pivoted to face her as she moved.

"Such as?"

"If I am a spy, I already know magic, so teaching me harms you naught. If I am not a spy, teaching me magic can only aid your cause."

"If ye are a spy, awakening your magic might be what ye want!"

A small breeze ruffled through the tent, billowing the cloth walls, and puffing through Catrian's loosened hair before dissipating. "The magic is already awake." Gralyre's ruthless smile answered her scowl. He could almost hear her teeth grind, and his pulse pounded with the thrill of their conflict.

"If ye use magic in my presence again I will kill ye!"

Gralyre stepped into her space once more, stalking her. This time Catrian took a step back. "No. You are going to teach me."

Catrian's face blanked of all emotion. "I will do what I must t' protect my people. Do no' doubt me in this."

"I do not."

"Then why would ye think that I would take such a risk?"

Gralyre's glare softened, and the mockery and confrontation left him, as he acknowledged her very real concern. "Because your people are dying, and you need all the help that you can get. Because all will be lost if you do not find allies. Because sometimes the gain is worth the risk. And because…"

"Because?" Catrian's breath hitched. His assessment of the resistance's tenuous hold on life was brutally exact. Her expression became stark as her gaze dropped, searching an inner landscape of horrors that only she could perceive.

Gralyre took the final step, closing the distance between them, drawn to the sudden vulnerability he sensed within her. The scent of heather and woman drifted to his nose, and he breathed deeply. "Because I am here. And you need help. And because of this…" he murmured as he bent, and softly touched his lips to hers.

Catrian froze, still and warm beneath his kiss, then shied away from him, her face flaming. She swung hard and slapped him, rocking Gralyre's head. "No! That canno' be!"

Gralyre stepped back in confusion, shaking his head. Why had he kissed her? It had not been his intent. She had somehow slipped passed his defenses. Again. "My apologies, Sorceress. I did not mean to…I would not…"

A flash of hurt in Catrian's face halted his stumbling apology. Male instinct told him that he was damned if he apologized, and damned if he did not. Gralyre raised his hand, and rubbed his cheek in confusion. "Owe," he griped.

A woman powerful enough to destroy worlds had slapped him for stealing a kiss. A genuine smile caught him unawares, and he began to chuckle at the ridiculousness of it.

Catrian's anger could not be sustained when she met Gralyre's laughter crinkled eyes. No man had a right to be so appealing. The tension broke, and she could not hold back her answering smile, as her shoulders relaxed. "I could kill ye," she grinned ruefully.

Gralyre's smile faded, his gaze searching hers, as he dropped his hand away from his cheek and back to his side. "Like I said, sometimes the gain is worth the risk." Her blush fascinated him before she turned her back, and took a couple of steps away, creating safety with distance.

"Gralyre, I will consider your arguments, but..." her voice held little hope of changing her decision. The laughter had fled, and her shoulders held a familiar tension.

Gralyre interjected before she uttered words that could not be taken back. "Catrian, you kept me alive for a reason. Either allow me to help you or..."

"Or?"

Gralyre's jaw hardened. "Set me free."

"Set ye free?" Catrian whirled back around in surprise.

"I only wished to see the Wilsons reunited. 'Tis done. If I cannot find a home here, then you must release me, and I will seek a place to belong elsewhere."

She assessed Gralyre's stubborn ultimatum for a long moment while her gaze searched his. It was a reasonable solution, but why then did her instincts scream that he must not leave? She sighed and nodded. "Give me some time t' think on this."

Gralyre's expression darkened at what he considered further avoidance.

Catrian recognized his reaction, and rubbed a strand of hair off her face with a tired grimace. "We have only just returned, and there are a thousand things drawing my attention. Please. Give me a few days."

Gralyre was left feeling like a petulant child. He bowed low. "Forgive me, lady. I had not considered... Of course there are important things demanding your time." He had not meant to add to her burdens.

Catrian frowned. Sometimes the mannerisms that Gralyre displayed were confusingly archaic. The thought made her shudder inside at the possibilities inherent in that observation. "Give me four days t' reach a decision."

"Agreed." He reached out his hand, and after a hesitation she clasped it. His large palm swallowed hers completely, as they shook to seal the bargain.

She cleared her throat, and reclaimed her hand. "Fine. Return in four days time. And Gralyre...?"

He paused in her doorway to glance back.

"This is my home. Next time wait for the sentries t' announce ye."

Catrian remained seated long after Gralyre had left, staring blindly at the play of shadows cast from the hovering glow of her magical light. She had not lied to him; there were many pressing issues that she had to address, not the least of which was what to do with him now that they had reached the fortress.

His ultimatum burned through her thoughts. Teach him or release him. She was loath to do either, though she was reminded that the only reason she had not killed him outright was because of his potential to become a powerful ally to their cause. If she was not going to explore the possibility of using his magic, should she not release him?

Questions with disagreeable solutions shimmered through her mind at a reckless pace.

What sort of ally was she creating through her constant suspicions and trials? But how could she not be wary of the great gifts Gralyre offered, a possible spy with a hidden past, and hidden motives? By taking the chance to teach him and to increase his strength, she could be placing her people in worse jeopardy.

But to set him free in this world, without a past, without a future, and with no mastery over his magic? Gralyre would be easy prey for any Demon Lord whose path he crossed, which he had proved once already when he had been captured in Raindell. Catrian could not forget that she had already rescued him once. Had she not intervened he would, even now, be imprisoned and tortured in the dark depths of Doaphin's Towers.

Her mouth tightened at the memory of his brutally beaten face pressed against the bars of the Tithe Wagon, unrecognizable as the man who had so recently left her pavilion.

In many respects, Gralyre was like unto a child. He had memories that extended back in time for only a few short months, and life experiences to match, for not even a year had passed since he had awakened in the forest. His induction into this world had been brutal, yet he still harboured a frightening sense of nobility and integrity that would be the death of him if he were not careful. Though he could certainly act ruthlessly, he was not a ruthless man by nature.

Hers was a world that demanded brutal pragmatism in order to survive, and Gralyre was like to sacrifice himself for anyone he considered under his protection.

No, releasing him would be no favour - far better to end his life humanely than to leave him to become a Demon Lord's plaything - but allowing him to stay meant contending with the alarming attraction hovering between them. Catrian could no longer deny it, and needed to understand and control it.

Her fingers rose to touch her mouth, as she relived the kiss in the cavern. It had been her first. No man she had ever met had been daring enough to court a sorceress. She was frightened by the intensity of the passion that she had felt then, and now again, here in her tent.

Unconsciously, she smiled at the memory of his deep laughter after she had struck him for his boldness. His humour had been unexpected and contagious. Most men would have responded with rage at such a rebuff.

She sobered, her fingers sliding from her lips, and clenching into a fist that she pounded onto the tabletop in frustration. It could not be. It could never happen again. She smoothed down her dress as she stood, and lifted her chin in defiance of her own emotions.

Boris had warned her. He had seen what she would not, and now she was left feeling a fool. His words in the sewers of Verdalan drifted back to haunt her.

'We are all susceptible t' loneliness, Cat.'

She had arrogantly thought herself immune to such desires, and in her hubris, she had been unguarded and unprepared. Now she was paying the price.

To teach him, to release him, or to kill him; this was a decision that she could not make, especially as it was now clear that she was emotionally compromised where Gralyre was concerned. She would consult her uncle. Boris would make the decision, and she would abide by it, come what may.

℘℘℘

Night found the Wilsons, Gralyre and Saliana clustered around their cook fire in front of their new home, their hunger hushed but not quite silenced by their meager meal.

Saliana sat apart from the family, and Gralyre suspected that she was fretting over how the brothers had fought yet again over her part in the deadly escape from Raindell. She was curled into a small, quiet haunch at the edge of the firelight to avoid notice. Her loosened hair hid her face, another layer of camouflage so that only her eyes, glittering in the firelight, watching everything, gave her movement.

Dara's face was puffy and red, and though she put forth a brave front, her grief over her father's death was raw and painful to witness, only softened by the bittersweet joy of her reunion with her brothers.

She was unrecognizable as the lively lass Gralyre had rescued from the Tithe. At first Gralyre thought her unease was due to the news of Wil's death, but as the evening progressed, he began to suspect that there was something else at play here. Dara's gregarious nature had been supplanted by a careful seriousness during the months that she had been apart from her family.

When Rewn asked Dara to speak of her life in the camp, Dara bit her lip indecisively, and glanced anxiously over her shoulder at the encroaching darkness that was broken only by their neighbours' flickering cook fires.

"'Tis no' at all as I expected," she murmured quietly, darting another furtive peek over her shoulder at winking firelights marching away in straight lines along both sides of the avenue of tents. She leaned forward to be better heard, and dropped her voice to a soft whisper that would not carry beyond the ring of light thrown by their fire. "Da always told us that the Rebels fought Doaphin."

"They do!" Dajin interjected hotly. At his sister's frightened glare, he quickly lowered his voice to a rough whisper to match hers. "Why else do ye think they are here?" he asked snidely, rolling his eyes.

Dara leaned over, and gripped his arm. "They do fight the 'Riders," she agreed in a harsh whisper, "but only when 'tis convenient or they can ambush without being seen." She patted Dajin's arm, and released it as she leaned back, and performed yet another anxious scan of the shadows.

Gralyre's concerned gaze met Rewn's, as Dara's anxiety smote them both. Her vigilant watchfulness had them keeping careful scrutiny upon the night as well.

Seeing no movement, she shifted even nearer to the fire, and addressed the men in turn, trying to impress upon them the dangers that they would now face, while not relinquishing her deepest shame. "These are no' the brave Rebels that Da spoke o', they are naught but raiders who loot lowland farms and towns for supplies, and only fight Doaphin's forces when they are caught in their thievery!"

Rewn nodded in grim understanding. "So instead of liberators, they are as dangerous t' the lowlanders as the 'Riders are. So the people become doubly taxed." He heaved a log onto the fire, and the burst of flame revealed his disillusioned face.

Dara bit her lip. "They are no' all like this," she reassured her brothers. "Many seem intent upon breaking Doaphin's rule, and saving the lowlands, at least, 'tis what they like t' tell themselves, but it feels false." She shook her head, and then lifted a hand to impatiently brush away the strands of hair that fell loose from her braid. "Like a lie they have told themselves until they believed it t' be so," she snarled bitterly. "They despise all lowlanders as cowards. They wonder why they should risk their lives saving us from Doaphin when they could stay safely in the mountains. How can they understand, when they have ne'er lived with the terror o' the Tithe, or suffered the rule o' the Demon Lords?" She drew her legs up, and curled her arms protectively around them. She seemed very small in the flickering light as she tucked the hem of her cloak over the toes of her boots. Her fingers remained to play with the fabric, bunching and smoothing the cloth.

Rewn moved closer, and wrapped an arm around her shoulders, snugging her into his side. She smiled wanly up at his concerned face, and leaned her head on his shoulder. "They think Doaphin does no' move against them because they are strong," she whispered, "The truth they will no' hear is that Doaphin does no' move against them because he has no' gotten t' the task!"

"Hush!" Rewn frowned squeezing her shoulder.

"What are ye saying, Dara? These people are our saviours!" Dajin argued, feeling the foundations of what his father had taught him quaking and crumbling.

"Lowlanders are nothing t' them, Dajin. They believe that we," Dara's mouth quivered as she worked to loose the words, "...deserve what we get. They think us less than they, because we do no' fight. If ye are a lowlander in this fortress, they use ye as harshly as Doaphin himself!" Tears welled in her eyes, and spilled down her cheeks. With irritated disdain, she dashed them away, as though she had cried over this many times before, and knew its futility.

"How so?" Gralyre sensed a horror moldering within her spirit. His gaze shifted to Rewn's grim face, then back.

Dara clenched her eyes, and a muscle flexed in her cheek when she gritted her teeth against a nameless pain. She seemed to be fighting a battle to stop the words she wanted to utter.

"Dara?" Rewn asked fearfully, hugging her tighter.

Into the silence the fire popped, throwing sparks at the sky, and she started at the noise, shattering the intensity. "Nothing," Dara sniffed, "I am being maudlin, 'tis all. I am just so sad about Da." She hugged Rewn hard. "But I am very happy that ye are here. You must be careful though. Please do no' trust them. They are no' what they seem."

"Words to live by, 'twould seem," Gralyre agreed. "I ran afoul of this prejudice when I visited the Sorceress earlier." He relayed his encounters brusquely.

"Ye are cracked!" Dajin protested sharply. "I have been travelling with Matik and his men, and they have always treated me as one o' their own."

"Dara has been living here, Daj," Rewn reminded. "She would no' tell us t' beware without reason." He squeezed Dara's shoulders, rubbing her arm comfortingly. "What has happened t' ye, Dara?"

Dara shook her head, and her face became devoid of expression. "'Tis as I have told ye. Just…be careful. Trust no one." Her bald statement hung in the air, affecting them all with its sinister undertones until Saliana spoke up.

"I will have my things packed in the morning, and will ask the Stewards for a new placement. I thank ye all, Rewn, Gralyre, and…and Dajin," she stuttered, "for seeing me t' the safety o' the mountains, but I can no' longer… I heard ye fighting about me. I have brought enough harm t' ye, been enough trouble for ye. I will leave, tomorrow." She heaved a shuddering gasp, as much from her bravery in speaking up, as from her decision to leave.

"Good. Get out and do no' come back!" Dajin smirked.

"No," Gralyre said firmly to her, "Ye stay." He glared at Dajin across the flames. "You are no burden, you are part of our family."

Dajin sneered at Gralyre. "Who are ye t' tell me who my family is? I see only my brother, and my sister, no' a spy and a whore! Ye can leave too!"

Dara gasped. "Dajin! Shut your mouth o' things ye know naught about!"

Simultaneously, Rewn growled, "Saliana has no people here! Have ye heard nothing o' what Dara experienced on her own in the camps? She stays!"

"Ye are a fool, Rewn!" Dajin yelled and threw himself to his feet. He stomped out of the firelight, with a last shot, "I am going t' get the lay o' the land. I'll be back when the stink o' your decision is no longer choking me!"

CHAPTER THREE

A Demon with eyes that burn emerges from a boiling red mist. An executioner's sword hangs suspended for a wild moment. Sunlight sharpens the edge.

'Cannot move! Cannot Escape! I will not cry out!'

The sword drops! My terrified face is a distorted reflection in the shimmering blade. The sword bites my neck, and I am wrenched into the swirling blackness of forever... forever, but not the end...

Agony harries me into an infinite void that pulses like the chamber of a giant heart, flaying my soul in a savage rhythm. All is pain.

I am lost, I am everywhere, I am the universe... the void throbs... I am nothing, I am smaller than the smallest grain of sand...

For brief flickers between pulses I am still myself, eroding with every violent cycle, and slipping away into the grinding maw of a voracious darkness. Soon I will cease to exist.

This then, is death; this then, is my punishment for failure.

Wildly thrashing limbs produce no movement. Screams from blinding suffering go unheard. Infinity swirls and boils, terrifying, with no eyes to shut against it. Whatever power tortures me, forces me to gaze into the face of eternity...

Gralyre awoke with a moaning gasp, bolting upright from his sleeping pallet, and shivering in the cold, for as he had thrashed with the madness of the dream, he had tossed away his coverings. He glanced down in confusion for his hand was fisted around the hilt of his sword, instinctively grabbed for protection against the menace of his nightmares.

The soft sighing of breath from the others continued unabated, as Gralyre rubbed a rough palm across his face to wipe away the sweat that sheened his skin. He rolled to his feet, still gripping his sheathed blade against the lingering need, stepped into his boots, and exited the tent so that he would not disturb his friends' slumbers any further than he already had.

He stepped into dawn's first light, letting the tent flap drop quietly behind him, and stood straight and tall, breathing deeply, as he sought to lower his heart rate to normal, and negate the intense paranoia screaming at him to run, to escape what was hunting him. The morning was crisp and cold, steaming his sweat away from his body, the vapor catching the sunrise so that he seemed otherworldly, an elemental creature awakening to first steps upon a new world.

A light dusting of winter had fallen throughout the night, and shimmered in the brightness where it had accumulated in the peaks and valleys of the neighbouring tents. The acute angle of the new risen sun reflected diamonds from the avenue, where the snow added a clean layer to the previous day's churned slush.

Little Wolf followed Gralyre from the tent. Used to the morning routine, he yawned noisily, breath steaming in the cold air as he stretched, his paws forward, his rump high, his tail waving lazily in the air. He settled himself upon his haunches, blinking lazily in the bright morning sunshine, to await the advent of breakfast.

After a time of standing still, and breathing deeply of the crisp mountain air, Gralyre calmed but did not immediately begin his sword dance, instead he crouched, staring into the banked embers of the cook fire. Dara's strained behavior of the night before still occupied his thoughts, and had menaced his dreams with uneasy imaginings, even before the nightmare had consumed him. Her talk of the abuse meted out to lowlanders smacked of first-hand experience.

He dropped a handful of wood shavings into the firepit, and poked the coals to encourage a spark to awaken. As fire leapt upwards, he placed a log into the flames, and cupped his palms to the welcome heat, considering options. Dara might not wish to tell her family of what she had endured, but she was no longer defenseless. He beckoned Little Wolf to his side.

Tail circling happily, Little Wolf trotted over and leaned his full weight against Gralyre, inviting a scratch by flipping his master's hand up over his head with a practiced nuzzle of his snout.

With a small smile, Gralyre obliged him, rubbing Little Wolf's ears, and then his chest, until finding the spot that made the wolfdog's eyes drift shut in pleasure, and a hind leg begin a rapid tattoo upon the ground. *'Stay by Dara for the next few days, Little Wolf. Do not leave her for a moment, not even to follow me.'*

Little Wolf grew solemn, and cocked his head questioningly, his contented panting momentarily suspended as he listened.

'If any man frightens her, memorize their sent, for we will hunt him later.' Gralyre grinned his own dangerous wolf's smile back at his pup.

Little Wolf thumped his tail twice, and strutted proudly back to his place by the entrance to the tent. He sat watchful guard, honoured that Gralyre was including him in the protection of the pack. Having been given a serious, adult chore, when Gralyre gripped his sword's cold hilt, and flung the sheath aside as he drew his blade, Little Wolf resisted the urge to chase after the discarded leather scabbard. Besides someone was stirring within the tent.

Gralyre took his stance to begin his practice, but paused as Rewn slipped outside through the loosened flap. One side of his brown hair stood up in a comical rooster tail, and his sleep deprived eyes blinked heavily at the brightness of sunrise. They nodded their hellos. Something about the newborn day, the perfect stillness of the snow, or perhaps the ritual of the sword dance itself, proscribed the want of speech.

Rewn, the bare blade of his sword glinting in the early morning sun, took his place beside his mentor, and together they began the sword dance, as the fortress of the resistance stirred into life around them.

ଛଠଔ

Saliana accompanied Dara, each woman carrying a large reed basket braced against a hip as they walked, piled high with the dirty laundry that had arrived with the weary travellers the day before. They chatted quietly, as they sauntered towards the communal washhouse, and Dara was happily surprised at how quickly they were becoming friends. They spoke of people that they had known in Raindell, and places that they missed, their mutual nostalgia bonding them, as though they had known each other for years instead of hours.

Though Dara counted Aneida and Mayvin as friends, she was never completely relaxed in their presence for the fierce warrior women were so very different from her, and oft times, through no fault of their own, they left her feeling inadequate and weak. It was nice, then, to have found a more familiar connection with Saliana. But would that bond remain should the sordid details of her trials within the fortress come to light?

Little Wolf trotted at their heels, a silent guardian. Dara was uneasy with the large wolfdog's presence, though the threat of the animal seemed to be keeping the Rebels from harassing them as they walked. Saliana seemed to think nothing of Gralyre's pet's determination to trail after. Dara did her best to ignore him too, but could not prevent her shiver of unease each time she glanced back, and saw that Little Wolf was looking directly at her, his head cocked slightly, and his ears up, as though about to begin an earnest conversation. It was eerie.

"Do ye miss your family?" Dara asked into a comfortable lull of the conversation to distract herself from thoughts of the trailing wolfdog.

Saliana shuddered delicately, and looked away, breathing out with a harsh sigh, "No' really...is that bad?" She glanced up with distress writ clear upon her face, that her new friend would think less of her.

"No' after what they did t' ye," pronounced Dara grimly, her tone coloured by her own bitterness.

Saliana shrugged her shoulders fatalistically. "They did nothing, no' really. 'Tis just the way o' things."

"They gave ye over t' the Tithe!" Dara huffed in amazement at Saliana's equitable acceptance.

Saliana did not meet her gaze as she reminded quietly, "So did your Da. 'Tis the law after all."

Dara sputtered. "Yes, but my family followed after, looking for a moment t' rescue me."

"Gralyre rescued us."

"'Tis true, but at least my Da sent me away after."

Saliana lifted her chin as her face swept with colour. "My Da did no' have your connections. He survived as best he could, and tried no' t' grow too attached t' his sacrifice."

"Sacrifice?"

Saliana nodded. "'Tis what he called me. Saliana Sacrifice. I was always destined for the Tithe, and so I was kept separate from the family. I slept in the barn, I obeyed my Da, I cooked and cleaned, I did no' talk unless I was spoken t' first, and I did no' make any trouble." She listed the rules by rote, as though required to do so many times over the course of her life.

Dara swallowed heavily, horrified by the life Saliana described. "I had no idea. I am so sorry."

Saliana shrugged. "I knew no difference. When the 'Riders came for me, I did my duty. I climbed into the wagon without protest. But after Gralyre rescued us, I did no' know what t' do, and I thought to myself, *'Maybe life holds a future for ye, Saliana Sacrifice!'* So I defied the law!" Saliana's face animated with an unusual defiance. "I took what the Gods o' Fortune had offered, and I stayed in the woods, foraging for what little food I could find, and I was content for a time. Until the snows came, and I had t' return t' my Da's house."

Saliana smiled sadly, as her thoughts turned inward. "He beat me when I came home, but it did no' matter for by then I was safe. The Tithe had moved on."

She darted a glance at Dara, and then quickly back to her feet. Her voice became defensive as she recognized Dara's pity, and she resettled her heavy basket against her hip in her agitation. "Everything was different afterwards, like Da had been released from his prison too. He did no' call me Saliana Sacrifice anymore. He was almost… kind… t' me. For the first time in my life, he called me daughter. He mentioned that I should even marry one day."

Saliana defended her father in a way that confounded Dara, so that all she could do was listen, for there were no words to act as balm for what Saliana had survived. As bad as her experiences over the winter had been, she had always known that her father and brothers loved her dearly.

"'Tis why he brought me to the Mid-Winter's Moon festival. I was so excited. I had never been allowed t' attend before, and I had such dreams o' the dancing, and the feasting, and o' meeting a kind man who would want me as his own." Saliana sighed deeply at her heartsick longings, and her mouth turned down at the corners, tense in remembered terror. "But I was the only young lass there, ye see, and the Lord Collaborator claimed me," Saliana finished in a rush, as though hurrying to release the burdens of her story.

Both women had stopped walking by then, and Dara stared at Saliana in heartsick horror.

For the first time, Saliana's voice dropped to a whisper of anguish. "The Lord gave my Da a single copper, t' use me as he would, and my Da walked away, and never looked back."

Dara dropped her basket, spilling some of the clothing out into the muddy slush at their feet, to place her hands on Saliana's shoulders. "I am so sorry." She well knew the helpless terror of being at the mercy of a monster, with none to come to her aid.

Saliana's head came up, and determined happiness shone in her face. "I am no' sorry! If I had no' gone t' the festival, I would have been trapped in Raindell forever! I would never have known...."

Dara's confused smile was in response to Saliana's vehement joy. "Known what?"

Saliana blushed. "That there is another way t' live! That there are men who will lay down their lives t' protect ye. That they will treat ye with kindness, as though ye are important t' them."

As if confused by her unaccustomed fervor, she seemed to fold into herself, becoming the small, colorless mouse once more.

Dara was arrested by Saliana's declaration. Perhaps this was a lesson that she had forgotten over the bitter time she had spent at the fortress. Saliana's story could have been a tale of horror, but instead it was her journey to triumph. Dara was left re-evaluating how she had responded to her own trials, and was stunned to realize that this pale woman, who jumped at shadows, and worked to fade into every background, had more courage than she.

The tableau was shattered by Aneida's brash voice. "Dara! Where have ye been? Ye did no' return last night!"

"Aneida!" Dara placed a hand over her rapidly beating heart, as she watched her friend approach.

The warrior woman's strides were long, her hand rested on the hilt of her short sword, and a frown of concern marred her face. "What has happened? Did they…"

"I am so sorry! I did no' think t'… I would like t' introduce ye t' Saliana Greythorn, who arrived with my brothers yesterday!"

Aneida relaxed with a huff of relief, and smiled widely. "Your brothers have come? That is a good spot o' news for ye! I am so glad! I was worried that…"

Dara quickly interjected again to stop the flow of Aneida's words from revealing too much.

"Saliana, this is my friend, Aneida." The two women shook hands.

Dara leapt into conversation in an effort to steer Aneida away from the subject of the Stewards. Fervently she wished it had been Mayvin who had found her, for Dara could but barely interpret a few of the mute woman's hand gestures, and she was willing to bet that Saliana would understand not a one of them! Dara's face was smiling, but her eyes were wide with fright, as she urgently tried to influence Aneida to remain quiet. *'Please do no' mention it! Please!'*

"I am sorry I did no' return t' the tent last night, or send word t' assuage your worry, but my brothers brought news that my Da has been killed," her voice choked on the shame of using his death to silence her friend, "and I did no' even think t'…"

Aneida embraced Dara, hugging her tightly. "I am so sorry for your loss. From your stories he sounded like a wonderful man, and a good father."

Dara sighed brokenly, and fought to keep the tears from falling. Her grief would be just in reach for a long time. "Thank ye," she whispered.

Aneida released her and stepped back. "I take it ye will be staying with your family from now on?"

Dara nodded.

Aneida smiled. "That is good. Family will help ye t' heal. But do no' forget that we will be waiting t' train ye when ye are ready."

Dara blushed, and did a quick scan of Saliana's expression to see if there was any light of understanding, but Saliana had disengaged from the conversation, picking at one of Rewn's frayed shirts atop the pile of clothes in her basket, and did not even glance her way.

"I do no' need t' learn t' fight, Aneida. No' any more. My brothers will protect me from now on."

Aneida regarded her for a long moment while her hand arose to trace the thin scar on her neck, a gesture she was prone to when she was upset. "I hope that is no' a decision ye will come t' regret."

Dara shivered. "I think 'tis for the best," she mumbled. She sensed that she was betraying all the faith that Aneida and Mayvin had placed in her, as they had worked to repair her broken spirit, and rebuild her independence. But she was not like them. She was no warrior, only a frightened woman who was back in the bosom of her family.

Aneida smiled, a quick flash of teeth. Her hand dropped away from her scar. "I would like t' meet these brother's o' yours!" she announced boldly, one hand on her hip, the other caressing the butt of her sword.

Dara smiled wanly, and extended an invitation for the evening meal, giving Aneida directions to their bivouac. She prayed to the Gods of Fortune that the woman would keep her secret.

₮₯ℂ₱

Catrian hailed her uncle from outside his tent, and awaited his invitation to enter. She slicked her palms down the sides of her shirt to wipe away the nervous moisture as she ducked inside.

The Commander's pavilion was sparse of furniture and comforts. One of the most admirable things about Boris was his need to lead by example, for he would accept no luxuries afforded his position unless they were common items to his people. So his tent held little more than a cot and a rough table, upon which a carefully drawn map had been rolled out, and anchored with small brass weights that were worn smooth from generations of use. A small shelf resting against the tent wall beside the table contained more scrolls that Catrian knew to be precious maps showing exquisite details of the passes and mountains of the Heathren range.

The ubiquitous wooden bins opposite the entrance contained her uncle's weapons, clothes and bedding. Atop one of these, a washbowl and ewer were partially covered by a damp, crumpled cloth, while a precious scrap of mirror, attached to the tent wall above the bowl, shone reflected daylight back from the brightness that leached through the loosened tent flap, painting a bright spot against a canvas wall. More sunshine filtered down the smoke hole at the peak of the tent, illuminating the deep cracks and crags of Boris' face in curling undulations of shadow, as the hole carried away the smoke from the small brazier that held back the chill of the morning.

Boris was a hard man, entirely devoted to the cause, and Catrian was heartsick at what she feared was to be his verdict, as she presented Gralyre's case to him with as little sentiment as possible. She did not speak of her impaired emotions, for she was embarrassed that she had allowed herself to somehow become invested in a man who could be a dangerous spy. Instead she took a deep breath, and placed Gralyre's fate firmly into the hands of the man she trusted more than life itself, the man she trusted more than she could trust herself in this decision.

"Should I train him t' harness his powers, he will be a great ally, great enough perhaps t' turn the tide. But should he prove t' be Doaphin's pet, the consequences will be devastating." She shivered as she finished describing her conundrum. "Uncle, this is too large a decision for but one person. We must be o' like mind afore I will proceed."

Boris fixed her with a shrewd stare. "'Twould seem t' me, lass, that ye made that decision yourself when ye chose t' allow him t' live. Are ye having second thoughts?"

Catrian flushed a deep red. "My reasons for granting him life, then and now, remain."

"Do they? Then why seek my council?"

"His magic is strong uncle, so much stronger than I expected. He was no' even winded after he created the storm!" Catrian began to pace, a sure sign of her agitation.

"Listen, lass, I do no' know how strong that is." Boris shrugged, uncertain of her comparison. "How strong is he compared t' ye?"

Catrian rocked back on her heels, her face very serious. "Had I created a storm o' that magnitude and duration, I would have been hard pressed t' stand for days afterward and would, in fact, yet be recovering."

Boris whistled through his teeth.

Catrian nodded in concurrence. "What would ye advise, uncle?"

Boris regarded his niece for a long, assessing moment. "Doaphin's purge begins in the spring?"

Catrian nodded.

"None survive?"

Catrian shrugged despondently. "I have seen no survivors. First Doaphin's forces slaughter the lowlanders, and then they come for us. And we will fall. Unless we find some way t' prevent it, this is Humanity's last winter o' life," she confirmed through fear-tightened lips.

Boris rubbed his scalp through his short silver hair, his expression distant and grim, as he thought through all the ramifications. His hand dropped and he sighed heavily.

Catrian's breath suspended, as icy uncertainty flowed through her veins.

"Then the choice is easy. We must give our people every chance we can, even if that chance ultimately hastens our deaths. We are in a swirling river, being swept t' our doom. We canno' afford t' ignore a lifeline, lass, even if the lifeline leads t' the point o' a sword. Train him. Ye were right t' allow him t' live."

Catrian nodded, working to contain a flash of traitorous relief. "I shall begin at once. There is no' much time remaining, and there is no guarantee that he will be prepared in time."

"Just be careful, Cat. This man," Boris made a vague gesture, "is dangerous t' ye. Watch him. Do no' let your guard down."

"I will be careful, I promise."

As she turned away to leave, Boris' knowing voice followed her to the tent flap. "Would ye have killed him, if that had been my verdict?"

Catrian's hands tightened on the edge of the heavy canvas she had been about to push aside. Her shoulders stiffened, and she would not glance back for fear of what he would read in her face.

"Yes."

೮೦೧೮

Erupting from within the boiling cauldrons, hot steam rose into the cold air in billowing white plumes, mingled with the blue wood smoke from fires beneath the large cast iron pots, and created a thick haze that shrouded the laundry. Spaced throughout the smoggy mists, indistinct figures used large, wooden oars to stir cauldrons of boiling clothes, while yet more women crouched beside tubs of soapy water, scrubbing fabrics against washboards. Contented chatter murmured from all around Dara and Saliana as they worked, though they were hard pressed to perceive the hazy figures of the women to either side of their fire. High above, clouds scudded across the face of the sun, and beams of light traced through the fog, adding a pleasant mystique, as though magic were at work to transform filth to cleanliness.

A small shed oversaw the operations of the communal laundry, from whence the women could obtain the lye soap, cauldrons, tubs, and washboards that they used. Thick ice formed by the endless, rising steam, encased the small wooden building, growing massive stalactites upon every overhang, a pretty, yet dangerous, decoration that in places stretched into crystal columns, a palatial decoration for such a rude building.

Located along the shallow banks of the frozen creek that bisected the fortress, the laundry was set far back from the nearest road at the lowest point within the stronghold to aid in the safe runoff of the discarded wash water through a small grate set into the base of the palisade wall. The heavy cauldrons of boiling wash water, suspended over fires on cast iron tripods, were fitted with a simple lever for tipping the pots to empty them, accounting for the ice, multi-coloured from leeched fabric dyes, that flowed away from the laundry in layered cascades towards the small grate. The accumulation of months of discarded wash water awaited the warmth of spring to release it to complete its journey down the mountainside. With the terrain so sloped and slippery, the women were obliged to wrap their boots in rags to create the traction necessary to maintain their footing.

Saliana knelt next to the washboard, applying the harsh lye soap liberally to remove the stains of many months of travel before scrubbing clothes and bedding against the rough ridges. When the task was completed, she passed them to Dara, who used her large paddle to stir the scrubbed fabrics within the large cauldron of boiling water for several minutes. She then lifted them out, and over into the cool rinsing tub, swirling them some more, until she judged the soap gone. Pulling the fabrics out of the cold water, she wrung them, and folded them neatly back into the reed baskets. Between the two women, the chore progressed rapidly.

Saliana dropped the last shirt into the cast iron cauldron, and placed a tired hand into the centre of her back to stretch while Dara undulated the fabric through the boiling water with her large wooden oar.

"Done!" For once Saliana's pale face held a pleasant flush of exertion that kept her from fading colourlessly into the background. She dipped her hands into the cool rinse water, wincing as she washed the harsh lye soap out of the cracks in her winter-chapped skin.

Dara grinned at her through wisps of hair, that had escaped from her braid to curl wildly in the steam from the boiling water, as her arms worked. "Aneida and Mayvin have some lanolin that will help sooth those chilblains," she nodded towards Saliana's hands. "When they arrive for dinner, I will ask them if they can spare us some," Dara promised.

Saliana smiled gratefully. "That would be nice."

Dara glanced casually up at the distant road, as the movement of a wagon caught her eye through the fog, and her smile froze on her face as the mists eddied in a small swirl of breeze, revealing her worst nightmare. It took everything to keep plying the oar and not alert Saliana that there was anything amiss.

Jarrod, the man she feared most in this world, was standing on the thoroughfare glaring at her. Dara had not seen him since the night that he had strangled her, and left her for dead in the icy avenue outside the Stewards' tent. Hofar must have told him that she was alive.

Jarrod's pocked face was partially hidden by a greasy length of thin hair that hung limply out from under a filthy knit cap he wore to cover his baldpate against the cold, but even so, Dara could see that his mouth was twisted with ire. Though Dara knew that it was not possible from this distance, she swore she could smell his unwashed, filthy body, and had to fight back a gag at the sense memory. There was no doubt that he had seen her, and that there was nowhere she could hide.

Ever by Jarrod's side, looming like a chained bear, Strier grinned nastily, his eyes all but disappearing within folds of flesh. While the rest of the camp was starving, Strier seemed ever well fed. He gestured towards Dara, and she could see his mouth moving as he bent low to make a comment to Jarrod. Whatever was said, it motivated Jarrod towards her, his legs eating the distance towards the wash fires in long angry strides. Strier shambled after, rolling his shoulders, and making a show of cracking his knuckles in anticipation.

Dara's blood drained to her feet. Strier was Jarrod's weapon, and he would do anything the man wanted. She had intimate knowledge of that fact, for her flesh still bore the scars. Saliana could not be here when they arrived!

Striving for normalcy, Dara smiled at her new friend. "Here,

Saliana, there is no more for ye t' do. Take these, and start back t' the tent," Dara handed her one of the wicker baskets piled high with neatly folded, damp clothing. "I'll be along with the remainder o' the load soon. Best t' get them hung to dry over the fire, or we will have nothing t' sleep on tonight!" She joked awkwardly. Her voice sounded odd and strained to her own ears, but Saliana did not seem to notice as she accepted the basket.

"Are ye sure? I can wait for ye…"

"No! No…go on. I will be right behind ye."

"Alright then." Saliana hefted the heavy basket against her hip, "I will see ye back at the tent," she called over her shoulder as she left, picking her steps cautiously to maintain footing on the icy, sloped surface.

'Go! Go!' Dara urged, willing the woman to move faster, to get clear of the Stewards. Saliana disappeared into a swirl of fog, and Dara sighed in relief, as she turned back towards the fast approaching threats. She licked her lips nervously, and gripped the long handled paddle tighter, pulling it from the boiling water, and steadying her footing, for she had nothing else with which to defend herself. She replayed the conversation she had shared with Aneida that very morning, and the irony of the situation was not lost upon her, for where were her brothers now?

Jarrod hit the ice field surrounding the laundry, and was three strides in before his arms windmilled. He caught his balance, but was much slowed, adapting his rapid attack into an aggressive shuffle.

Behind him, made awkward by his ungainly weight, Strier

was not so lucky, as his feet shot out, and he landed upon his back, cracking his head against the frozen ground for good measure. Cursing roundly, he struggled gingerly to his feet, and minced after Jarrod with hands outstretched for balance.

Dara was too petrified with fear to flee. There was nowhere for her to go in any case, nowhere that the Stewards could not find her; they owned her food, her clothing, her shelter, and her life.

"Where have ye been hiding, lowland whore? Hofar mentioned that he had found ye at last!" Jarrod yelled when he was in range.

Dara quaked as the victim within her panicked. *'If I just go quietly, he probably will no' beat me… I will just submit and get it over with…'*

Then she looked into Jarrod's merciless glare, and remembered the truth of it, and her resolve returned in full force. Her pain and humiliation were what fuelled his pleasures. Fighting or submitting; the result would be the same, but only one course guaranteed her dignity. Dara licked her dry lips, and stood taller, determined to defy the Stewards to the end. "Safe from the likes o' ye!" she screamed back.

"What did ye say t' me?" Jarrod roared. He was nearer, and Strier was right on his heels.

"Ye stay away from me! Leave me be! I am no whore!" Dara screamed the words, a cornered animal. Her rage bubbled to the surface, leaving her almost giddy in a triumphant release. Suddenly she knew, with no doubt, that she would rather be dead than suffer Jarrod's filthy, grunting body on hers ever again.

The laundry went silent, as all the other women stopped talking to try to see what was happening through the occluding mists.

"Ye do no' say when we are through, bitch! I say when we are through!" Jarrod bellowed back as he and Strier arrived.

Strier lunged forward to grab her but lost his footing once more, and stumbled to his knees. "Lowlander slut! We own your scrawny pink arse!" His face was twisted and animalistic, his hands still reaching out, fattened fingers opening and closing in anticipation of inflicting harm.

Dara's vision reddened, and she tipped the edge of the cauldron's lever with her paddle, sending a river of scalding water towards Strier's kneeling body.

He yelped, and threw himself backwards to avoid the splash of boiling liquid. Within seconds the water had flash frozen against the ice, as it flowed downhill towards the grate. He grunted like a boar from the exertion of his narrow escape. "Bitch!" he yelled while he regained his feet, careful now of sudden moves towards her, the cowardice of a bully when faced with a defiant victim. "Ye will pay for that. I will make ye beg t' live afore I am through ploughing ye!"

Jarrod's gaze flicked from the tightly gripped paddle to Dara's contorted, maddened face, and he hesitated, shocked to realize that she meant to fight them. But there was more than one way to beat a dog! "So your brothers have arrived, and ye think ye can disrespect us now? Is that it? Say one more word, whore, and I promise ye that I will gut your precious family in front o' your eyes, and piss on the carcasses."

The breeze eddied, and this time Dara did catch a whiff of his unwashed flesh. Her stomach roiled at his threat and his reek, and it took every ounce of willpower to keep from vomiting. She gulped, tears welling, when she realized that her resistance was futile. She could do nothing but submit or endanger her brothers. She did not doubt Jarrod's ultimatum.

Jarrod saw capitulation in her face, and the filthy pockmarks peppering his cheeks stretched thin as he smiled slowly with triumph. Strier began to laugh, clutching his big belly in amusement. They had won.

"Leave her alone!"

"She told ye t' get away!"

"What kind o' men are ye! Ye need t' threaten a girl t' get her attentions?"

"Bastards! Get out o' here afore I call a real man t' come set ye straight!"

Catcalls, boos and hisses began to emanate out of the fog, and Jarrod and Strier's heads swiveled in surprise at the abuse being heaped upon them by the surrounding women.

Dara's tears overflowed, and spilled down her cheeks, as she listened to the sound of the women rallying in an instinctive outpouring of protectiveness for, not a lowlander, but a fellow woman who was threatened.

"By the gods, ye bitches shut up or I will put a sword through the lot o' ye!" Jarrod roared.

Strier drew his blade in response to Jarrod's threat, ever ready to carry out any order.

From out of the mist came a deep-throated growl of a beast that knew naught of extortion. The jeering women went quiet at the unearthly warning, and Strier recoiled, his feet dancing to keep from falling. "Jarrod! What was that?"

The silence was deafening.

The menacing sound came again, but from a new location in the mist.

Both men whirled to track the threat. "'Tis circling us, Jarrod! 'Tis circling us!" Strier cried in panic, his voice raising an octave.

"Shut up, ye stupid bastard!" Jarrod's blade left its sheath, his eyes intent and narrowed, his teeth bared. There was nothing to see in the fog, just the swirling mists, and the silence, and the sense of being stalked. His hand worked the hilt of his sword nervously.

Dara barely dared to breathe. 'Twas Gralyre's pet! Little Wolf had dogged her heels all morning, but when they had reached the laundry, the wolfdog had settled into a quiet spot, and fallen asleep. The poor beast! If they caught him, they would kill him!

Little Wolf set up an aggressive barking right behind the men, before melting away into the mists.

Strier's voice became shrill. "Where is it? Where is it?" He slashed at tendrils of fog, one swipe coming dangerously close to Jarrod's shoulder.

Jarrod parried the blow on his sword, and slapped Strier across the face. "Get control o' yourself!" he hissed. "'Tis but a dog!"

Little Wolf blasted out of the fog at full gallop, and knocked both men from off their feet before melting away into a swirl of vapour, his four paws giving him a traction that the men could not hope to equal.

Jarrod's sword flew from his hand, and skidded downhill with a metallic skirl, as he came down on top of Strier's barrel chest.

Strier screamed, high and girlish, and thrashed, hitting out at anything nearby, which include Jarrod. In his hysteria, he forgot that he still held his blade, using it as a cudgel.

Jarrod grunted in pain as the blows connected. It took some effort for him to straddle Strier's chest, where he promptly clipped him in the face as hard as he could. "Stop it, ye stupid pig!"

"Dogs hate me! 'Tis goin' t' kill us! We gotta get outa here!" Strier's phobia almost had him weeping.

As though sensing the man was close to the tipping point, Little Wolf howled a full wolf ululation. The sound echoed from the ice and the mist, seeming to emanate from everywhere at once.

Strier shrieked in response, and bucked Jarrod off his chest, as he scrabbled to his feet. Comically, he ran in place for several seconds before gaining enough traction on the ice to move. He fell several times, as he fled away from the static fogbank entombing the laundry, and towards the safety of the far, sunlit road.

In the distance, down in the valley, a wolf pack responded to Little Wolf's howl with their own songs.

Little Wolf howled again, the threat louder, and nearer than before. Jarrod paled, but held his ground long enough to utter a final threat. On hands and knees he glared at Dara from behind his greasy, lank hair. "'Tis no' over!" But without the large Strier by his side, and his sword lost, his will for a confrontation had shrunk. He fled, with only slightly more dignity than what had been shown by his fellow Steward.

Behind him, the women cheered and threw catcalls after his cowardice, but Dara collapsed to the ground with a deep sob. Would she never be free of them?

ഇൽ

"Ye sent for me, Commander?" Matik asked as he entered Boris' tent.

Boris did not return his smile. "I need your help."

Matik stood taller. "Name it."

"Gralyre."

Matik's face twisted into a sneer. "What has he done now? Can we finally kill the bastard?"

Boris indicated a chair at his table with a jerk of his chin. "Sit. Council me."

As Matik settled, the Commander sighed and leaned forward

on his elbows. "I just had an interesting conversation with Catrian."

Matik shrugged his shoulders, resettling his axe. "If he has done anything t' her…" he growled.

Boris made a chopping motion with his hand. "I do no' believe it has come t' that, no' yet, but she is no' herself. We need her focused upon the rebellion, now more than ever. We canno' afford t' have her distracted."

Matik leaned forward, mirroring Boris' posture. "Ye know for a fact she is…distracted?"

Boris nodded. "I can sense it, see it in her when she mentions his name. We need t' remove Gralyre."

Matik began to smile. "So we kill him…"

"No. If we kill him for no good reason, we risk alienating Catrian. We must find another way."

"'Twould be easier t' kill him." Matik's smile soured. "I ne'er could stand politics."

Boris laughed grimly. "Wheels within wheels, my friend."

₨₩

Saliana halted as she entered the tent and saw Dajin seated cross-legged upon a ratty fur, oiling and honing his sword. His head lifted as she hovered at the entrance, and he glared at her, his hands stilling their rhythmic movement with the whetstone. Rewn and Gralyre were just outside, within calling distance, which gave her the courage to move forward, for she was careful never to be alone with Dajin.

Saliana knew better than to address him, falling back on engrained behaviors she had learned at the hands of her family, dropping her chin to stare at the floor, and giving him a wide berth on the way to the bins at the back of the tent for the cord with which to suspend the laundry over the heat of the fire to dry. She moved quickly and silently, watching him from the corner of her eye, while shivering fearfully at the atmosphere that seemed charged with Dajin's hate.

When she opened one of the bins, and bent within to fumble for a length of cord, when she had her back to him and was vulnerable, that was when he moved. Saliana froze at the cold touch of steel at her neck, and began to quiver as the blade forced her upright. Dajin's face was an unknowable blur at the edge of her peripheral vision, for she was too frightened to look directly at him.

"Ye may have Rewn, and that traitor Gralyre believing your story, but I know what ye are. I know what ye did. 'Tis your fault Da died, and I want t' hear ye say it." Dajin's harsh whisper was quiet enough to reach only her ears.

Mutely, Saliana shook her head, *No,* as her skin prickled with sweat at her temerity.

"Say it, before I slit your lying throat!"

Saliana licked her dry lips. "I am very sorry for your Da's death. He was a fine, honourable man, who risked himself t' save me, a stranger, when my horse threw me."

"Ye shut your mouth. Ye have no right t' talk about my Da!

Ye fell! On purpose!" Dajin's sword began to tremble with the force of his emotions.

Saliana swallowed thickly. "It was no' my intention t' fall." Finally she was compelled to look at Dajin fully. "'Twas my first time on a horse," she whispered brokenly, using the truth, as another would use a shield.

Her conversation with Dara that morning had clarified what she had gained since leaving behind Raindell, and her father's house. She had lived in terror of Dajin and his ire long enough. It had to stop if this was to be her new home or Dajin would have her dwelling in that place of fear and oppression forever. She had a taste of another way of being now, and was not going to let it slip through her fingers. Ever.

A pot clanged outside, followed by Rewn's curse at burning his hand, and Dajin blinked, as though awakening from a dream. His sword dropped abruptly, and he shook his head. "Get out."

Saliana, though no longer suffering the sword at her throat, stood frozen and frightened.

Dajin raised his fist, "Get out!"

Saliana did not move but stood mutely, waiting for the blow to fall, her vision glazing over with tears. If a clout from his fist would clear this matter from the air, then so be it.

Dajin hesitated, confused when she did not cower or flee. "Did ye no' hear me!"

Saliana nodded with a quick jerk of her chin.

"Then go, afore I give ye the beating ye deserve!" Dajin blustered.

Saliana drew in a shuddering breath and shook her head, *No.*

Dajin was confused by her response; frustrated at the courage she was showing in the face of such obvious terror. And why did it make him feel no better, watching her quake and quiver. Was this not what he had wanted?

'Twas my first time on a horse…

He backed away, his fist flopping to his side when his rage died, lanced like the festering wound it was. His shame was near to overwhelming, as he reckognized the enormity of his transgression against Saliana. Doaphin's creatures had killed his Da, not this pitiful girl. "Get out," he hissed once more, his voice containing all the grief in his heart.

This time, Saliana fled, clutching her length of cord to her chest against the pounding of her heart.

80C3

Gralyre and Rewn were cooking the noon meal when Dara returned from the laundry. Unlike the neatly folded clothing she had sent home with Saliana, Dara's basket was heaped and dripping from being thrown together without a proper wringing. Her violent strides kicked the hem of her skirts high, and threw clumps of loose snow in sailing arcs from her boots with every step. Her face was reddened and contorted from suppressed tears, and her knuckles were white in their grip upon her basket.

Little Wolf loped easily along in her wake with his tongue lolling, and his ears flattened, his nose dipping to scent for threats along their trail. Spotting Gralyre, the wolfdog veered towards his master, and reported what he had witnessed.

Dara's obvious agitation had been proof enough that something untoward had occurred before Little Wolf's confirmation, still Gralyre surged to his feet, pity freezing him with an unfamiliar sense of helplessness as he watched her pass, for it was far worse than he had suspected.

Rewn stepped away from the cook fire, and tried to stop Dara as she sped past him towards the tent. "What is wrong?"

"Nothing!"

"Dara?" Rewn asked helplessly, holding her in place with a concerned grip upon her arm. "Talk t' me! What has happened?"

"I said, nothing!" In a sudden fit of rage, she ripped her arm free, dashed the wet basket of laundry to the ground, and stomped over it as she fled into the tent.

When Rewn would have chased after her, Gralyre grabbed his shoulder, and held him back, indicating with a motion of his head that he should follow.

Within the tent, Dara burst into tears, and Dajin's perturbed voice drifted out to them. "What happened t' ye?"

"Nothing! Let me be!"

"Dara?" Rewn called out, but Gralyre's grip was inexorable, as he guided his resisting friend away. He walked Rewn out of listening range of their tent, as Little Wolf took up a sentinel position lying across the threshold in front of the loosened canvas flap.

Rewn came reluctantly, his body tense with frustration while he walked backwards, allowing Gralyre to steer him where he would. If Gralyre had not been holding him back, he would have returned to demand answers.

When they halted, Rewn's aggravation burst forth in a spate of distress. "Gralyre, what am I t' do? My family is falling apart, and 'tis my responsibility t' hold everyone together, but I canno'! Dajin is consumed by bitterness and hate, and now something is afflicting Dara, and she does no' trust me enough t' tell me what it is! I am the head o' the family, and 'tis my duty t' protect them and guide them, but I feel as though I am fighting Deathren with naught in hand but a blade o' grass!"

Gralyre gripped Rewn by the shoulders, his expression grim, and his gaze compassionate. "After the way Dara acted last night, and the warning she gave about the treatment of lowlanders, I suspected that something foul had happened or was happening to her. So I had Little Wolf attend her today." As succinctly as possible, he replayed Dara's troubles at the laundry, as Little Wolf had reported it, but was careful to omit names.

Before Gralyre was through, Rewn's face contorted, and he bent at the waist, gasping air in gulps to hold back his dismay and shock. "No' my sister! By the gods, no' my wee sister!" he moaned. "Why did Da no' let me go with her when she left Raindell? I should have gone with her! She was alone and defenseless and those filthy whoremongers…" Rewn's words drifted off in a howling snarl, as he wrapped his arms around his torso in acute pain, stumbling to keep his feet.

Gralyre patted his friend's back, a wholly inadequate comfort, but he had a more satisfying solution to offer. "Little Wolf knows who they are."

Rewn uncurled abruptly to his full height. His body vibrated with eager rage, and his face devolved into a feral grimace, as he reached to pull his sword free from the scabbard at his side. "Who are they?"

Gralyre grabbed Rewn's sword hand, pressing down to keep his blade in his scabbard, then was obliged to hold there against Rewn's resistance to draw. "'Tis not that simple." He found the uncharacteristically savage expression disturbing to see upon his friend's face.

Rewn's chin quivered, and his brown eyes blackened with hate. "I asked ye a question."

"It was the South District Stewards."

"They are dead! I want them dead!" Rewn's voice arose to a near shout. He reared back, and struggled against the grip Gralyre still held on his sword hand.

As Gralyre restrained Rewn, his gaze darted side to side, but thankfully no one was nearby to note their words. He shook Rewn to focus his attention, and his face held a strong warning of caution, as he squeezed Rewn's sword hand, grinding the bones to pry his stubborn fingers from off the hilt. His voice dropped to a murmur. "They are respected members of this community. 'Tis our word against theirs, and we are new to the fortress. Outsiders. Lowlanders. If you die, what then becomes of your sister?" His dark blue gaze continued to bore into

Rewn's, urging him to heed his words, urging him to caution, as he finally allowed Rewn to shake free of his hold.

But Rewn no longer sought his blade. The sheeting destruction of rage had been tempered with reason. His face was aged by the grief that shifted and moved beneath the surface like hot magma under a mountain, while his chest flexed deeply with the agitation of his breathing.

Rewn broke eye contact with Gralyre to stare grimly at the distant tent where his sister cried. His throat worked, as he swallowed heavily. "What are we t' do then? Nothing? They canno' go unpunished! Dara must be avenged!"

Gralyre smiled coldly. "You will take your revenge, my friend," he reassured, "but calmly, and intelligently. These are the mountains, Rewn, 'tis a dangerous place. Like that coward, Hofar, said *accidents happen.*"

"Accidents!" Rewn repeated through bared teeth.

಄ഽ಄

The dark wings of dusk cast soft shadows over the fortress. To either side, twinkling fires marched into the distance, flickering defiantly against the oncoming darkness, and illuminating the people who were gathered about the flames in gentle camaraderie to cook their scant evening meals. The scent of food wafted thickly on the restless breeze, though the gruel in the pots was thin and watery. The winter had been hard, and food was tightly rationed.

There had been a time, not long ago, when Dara had stood outside the circle of light cast by these very fires, dizzy with hunger and cold, and begging for scraps. More often than naught, she had been met with cruel words, and sometimes had been driven off with blows from lengths of kindling. Now Dara stirred her own bubbling pot, and thanked the Gods that her family was here, and that she was no longer facing the long night alone, starving and terrified.

Dara's joy at being reunited with her family was tarnished by the deep sorrow at the loss of her father, and she regretted every moment that she had been apart from him before he had died, but then, contrarily, she was also fervently glad that he had not lived to learn of the true nature of his beloved Rebels, or the horrors that had befallen his daughter at their hands. Wil would have confronted the Stewards to answer for it, and died for his folly.

After the clash with Jarrod and Strier at the laundry, Dara had spent the majority of the day suffering panic and fear for her family's safety, and pulling her emotions back under a tight rein to hide her secret, though she need not have bothered, for nobody seated around the cook fire seemed to pay her any mind. A morose atmosphere gripped the family this night, and their conversations were sporadic at best.

They sat around the fire upon stumps that had yet to be split for firewood, awaiting the arrival of Aneida and Mayvin for dinner. Dajin, as surly as ever, glared at the fire while poking it with a stick, and Dara had to scold him from stoking the flames too high, and almost burning the thin stew. Rewn responded to most conversation lures with little more than grunts, and Saliana seemed very sensitive to the sullen atmosphere, sitting off to the side, her arms locked around her legs, as she made herself as small as possible. Hopefully the mood would improve with the arrival of the sisters, else it would be a cold hospitality with which to introduce her friends to her family.

'Twas obvious to Dara that both of her brothers had been deeply affected by their escape from Raindell, and their father's death, for Rewn and Dajin had been as devoted as two brothers could be before Dara had left for the mountains. That had now changed. There was tension between them that had never been present before, and Dara wondered if it was because Dajin was jealous of Rewn's friendship with Gralyre. Dara often caught Dajin watching with envy, as Gralyre and Rewn shared deep conversations, words that would cease as Dajin approached. They were keeping secrets from him.

But then, who was not? Her own secrets were like to consume her with the fires of humiliation should they ever be brought to light.

And what of Gralyre? Dara sighed as she peered through the steam and smoke of the cook fire at the mysterious man in their midst. In her mind's eye she could still see him slaughtering the Demon Riders, saving her life, and the lives of all the women who had been herded into the Tithe Wagon of Raindell. She well remembered the power and grace of him, as he had swung his sword, and destroyed the evil that held her captive. To her, he would always stand the Hero.

He was barely recognizable as the same man. His hair and beard were now neatly groomed, and his clothes were no longer the rags he had once worn. The firelight danced upon his strong features, casting light and shadow within the hollows beneath high cheeks, and along the blade of his strong, straight nose. Gralyre was handsome, not in the boyish way of Hofar, which was just a mask for the evil thing that dwelled within, but with an indefinable presence that originated from the very core of the man. It magnetized and drew. A man such as he would never be brutal with a woman, for he carried his honour like a shield, and integrity was the gilding upon it. She sighed again and shivered in reaction to her romantic thoughts.

Just now, he was oiling his sword with a cloth, his face relaxed while he concentrated upon the task, but as though he sensed her eyes upon him, he glanced up and caught her staring. His gaze was direct and inquiring.

Dara blushed that he had caught her mooning at him, and busied herself with the pot once more, stirring at the bubbling liquid with her wooden ladle. When she finally risked another peek, Gralyre had returned his attention to his sword.

From his customary resting place by Gralyre's side, Little Wolf fixated upon every move that Dara made, as she went about preparing the meal. Periodically, his tongue would slink out around his muzzle with a loud doggy slurp, prompting Dara to glance up at him. Every time she looked, his ears perked, his head cocked to the side, and his tail thumped with enthusiasm, as he blinked meaningfully from her to the pot and back.

"'Tis not done yet," she chided him, charmed by his unusual intelligence, and no longer made uneasy by his presence. He had saved her at the laundry, and she would never forget how he had acted without any prompting. Little Wolf was a fit companion for her Hero.

When Aneida and Mayvin finally strode into view along the lane leading to their tent, Dara leapt up from where she sat, and went forth to meet them. She gave them both a warm hug while her brothers, Gralyre and Saliana watched on from their places next to the cook fire.

"Please say nothing to my family about what has happened to me. I beg o' ye! The Stewards warned me that they would kill them if I told. Please, promise me." She whispered quickly.

Aneida sighed heavily, as she regarded her steadily. "Ye know that by no' telling them, ye are placing them in worse danger. How can they survive an attack that they do no' know is coming? Ye are hamstringing them."

Mayvin nodded her head in agreement.

Dara replied through the smile she had pasted on for the benefit of her family. "I canno' think o' it right now. Just give me this night. Please!" She urged.

Aneida nodded, and replied through her own toothy grin, openly aping her friend. "'Tis your life, and your decision, but ye are making a mistake."

Aneida's gaze flicked towards the cook fire. "Hello!" She hailed loudly, and her eyes widened in appreciation as Dajin,

Rewn and Gralyre stood up to greet her and Mayvin. "Dara did no' tell us what strapping men her brothers were!" Hands on hips, Aneida strutted brazenly into the firelight. The glow of the cook fire magnified within her red hair, as she locked arms with Dajin, then Rewn, as Dara introduced them. Though the men stood head and shoulders taller, she met them with the confidence and self-assurance of one warrior to another.

Where her sister was fire, Mayvin was moonlight. She did not smile as she locked arms with the brothers. Her gaze was piercing and assessing, as she studied the men she greeted, and there was a sense that she was calculating their strengths and weaknesses, and filing the information against future need.

Women were very much a novelty to the brothers' world. They looked upon Mayvin and Aneida with interest and manfully puffed chests. Dajin sported a goofy grin, and even Rewn returned from whatever dungeon his thoughts had been holding him hostage within to smile a welcome at the two women.

"And this is Gralyre. I told ye o' him rescuing me from the Tithe?"

Aneida grinned widely, and laughed boldly. "So, ye are the swordsman? We should spar sometime!" she offered, all suggestive of meaning.

Gralyre smiled urbanely and inclined his head politely. "It would be my pleasure."

Aneida's smile turned flirty. "Yes, it would."

Mayvin rolled her eyes, and gave her sister a shove to move

her away so that she could greet Gralyre.

"Aneida, ye remember Saliana from this morning. Saliana, this is Aneida's sister, Mayvin."

Saliana smiled shyly, but her arms stayed firmly locked about her legs. Mayvin nodded politely, as she and her sister seated themselves on convenient stumps that had been placed near the fire in anticipation of their arrival.

The sisters had come bearing a loaf of bread which was a rare and welcome addition to the rabbit stew that Dara had tended over the cook fire. "We received our portion o' grain today, and ground enough t' make bread. Mayvin was cooking all afternoon," Aneida explained. "I canno' bake a potato!"

Mayvin smiled and inclined her head in response to the enthusiastic praise she received.

Gralyre frowned. "We have not yet received any stores. What you see is the last of the food from our journey north."

Mayvin's mouth turned in at the corners as she frowned, and her hands flowed gracefully. Aneida translated, acting as her sister's voice. *"Ye are t' get your share o' meat and grain from the Stewards."*

Rewn's body came to stiff attention as he listened.

"They control all access t' food, and ye are only entitled t' what ye earn. Of course they also control what job ye work at so try t' get appointed as a Huntsman, that way ye will always have meat no matter what they decide t' pay ye. Otherwise, ye walk the walls, like we do, and if ye do no' walk the walls, ye collect wood, or drive the honey wagons or worse. Either way, ye do

what they tell ye, ye keep your head down, and do no' attract
their notice."

Mayvin's hands came to a rest, and Aneida added a further
afterthought. "More than a few have died from starvation and
cold at the hands o' the Stewards. They rule. Ye bend a knee.
That is the way o' survival in the fortress."

"Your sister does no' speak?" Rewn asked. "Did something
happen t' her here at the fortress? Did one o' the Stewards…?"
Dara's trials wore heavily upon his mind, and the assumption
seemed a natural one.

"No," Aneida shook her head coldly. "It happened
elsewhere."

Mayvin lost her smile, and she glared intently at Rewn while
her hand played with the hilt of her dagger.

Rewn grimaced at his loutish question. "I did no' mean t'
give insult t' ye, Mayvin. I am sorry."

Mayvin's eyes narrowed, and her hands waved briefly.

Aneida shouted a laugh. "I am no' repeating that!"

Mayvin turned her glare upon her sister. Aneida sighed and
grinned at Rewn, but the smile was a mask for a terrible
bereavement. "We do no' speak o' it. Ye did no' know. Now ye
do." It was a threat wrapped within an apology.

Rewn nodded, and for the sake of a pleasant meal, did not
pursue the matter further. The women had a right to their
privacy.

Dara dished the hot stew into wooden bowls, while Mayvin
ripped the fresh loaf into equal chunks to sop up the gravy. Quiet

reigned supreme as they all supped hungrily.

When Gralyre was finished, he dished up seconds of the stew, and placed his plate upon the ground for Little Wolf. Rewn, Dajin and Saliana thought nothing of this but Mayvin and Aneida were aghast.

"Do no' give food t' a dog!" Aneida chastised. "There are people starving in this fortress!"

Saliana responded before Gralyre could do more than open his mouth. "Little Wolf earns his share o' the food! 'Twas many a time on the road that we ate only because o' his skill in the hunt. This stew ye are enjoying is from a rabbit he brought us. Do no' ever doubt his welcome at our fire!" Saliana's words were clipped and angry.

Mayvin frowned, looked at her sister and shrugged.

Aneida grinned challengingly at Saliana. "Touched a nerve did I?"

Saliana's gaze fell, and she shrunk back into herself, her shoulders hunching protectively.

Gralyre glanced down at Little Wolf lapping noisily at the thin gravy, and caressed his ears in a protective and proprietary gesture. He could understand why outsiders would be upset at seeing a dog feeding when humans went hungry, but Little Wolf was much more than a pet, and Gralyre vowed to go hungry before his pup did.

"Tea, anyone?" Dara spoke overly loudly and brightly in an effort to smooth the troubled waters. For the sake of social convention, the combatants retreated to their corners to sip their tea in silence. Replete from the meal, they relaxed around the blaze, shivering from the contrast of heat on their fronts and cold on their backs. Periodically, one or the other would stand to put their back to the fire for warmth, before retaking their seat. The conversation remained stilted and forced.

"It was fortunate that Dara was billeted with you," Gralyre spoke into the lull, seeking information under the guise of an innocuous statement.

Aneida blew steam from the tea in her tin cup. "She was no' assigned t' lodge with us. We took her in a while ago. Her previous bivouac had become…unfriendly."

Rewn scowled at Aneida through the flickering firelight. These women knew more about what had happened to his sister than they were sharing. "Why was that?" He could not help his suspicious tone, for he was desperate for answers.

Dara threw a log on the fire, and as the flames spat up, she glared meaningfully at Aneida. "No reason. We were friends, 'tis all."

Oddly, it was Dajin who rescued the evening when he began to regale the sisters with amusing tales of growing up on the farm. At a particularly ribald story of a prize Billy goat and a neighbour's sow, Rewn broke into the yarn with an irritated and loud, "That is no' what happened!" He took up the story, and soon everyone was gasping for breath, and holding back tears of mirth.

Watching Rewn's face resume its normal, pleasant lines, as he became caught up in the familiar tales, and forgot the horrors of the world for a time, Gralyre could see that this life could be good, not just for the Wilsons, but for himself as well. He could settle here, but it all hinged upon Catrian's decision, for she held his fate in her hands.

Both Dajin and Rewn seemed awestruck whenever their guests laughed, and started to vie to outdo each other to trigger the women's glee. Aneida would throw back her head, consumed by roars of hilarity, while Mayvin, without voice, convulsed with silent shakes, her face alive and her eyes dancing with mirth.

Gralyre's laughter was all from watching the comical brothers navigate what was likely their first flirtation with women. They were sorely outmatched. Dajin wooed shamelessly with outrageous complements while Rewn, more mature than his brother, was subtler but just as obvious in his interest. Aneida preened beneath all the male attention, laughing saucily as she parried their interest with skillful precision. Mayvin looked on with a smile hovering about her mouth, her eyes crinkled with pleasure as she watched her sister's enjoyment.

Gralyre sobered, as he began to experience vague impressions of other campfires, and of laughter and merriment with other companions. The apparitions of lost memories wafted through his mind, sensed but unknowable, wrapping his heart in warmth, and overflowing him with bittersweet melancholy. Though he tried to hold onto the sensations, it was like trying to catch sunlight glittering upon the surface of a river, forever just beyond reach. He clenched his fists to control the trembling of his hands, and tried to concentrate upon the here and now instead of upon the ghosts of his past, letting the specters fade away to nothing. These little teases of memory were rare, but always left him shaken and empty, yearning for... Nothing. Everything. Something.

One other person at the fire was also only pretending her enjoyment. Saliana was still shaken by her confrontation with Dajin earlier in the day, for she had not been so frightened since leaving Raindell. Giving him the opportunity to strike her was the only way she had known to put a stop to his constant threats, and she could only hope that her spur-of-the-moment plan had been successful, and Dajin would cease to cause problems for Rewn. Time would tell, but at this moment, all she could do was count herself lucky that Dajin had not taken the opportunity to kill her.

And now, here were these women. Saliana glared mulishly at Aneida and Mayvin, unaccountably hurt whenever Rewn smiled at one of them, afflicted with twinges of jealousy for he had never looked at her, as he was looking at these warrior women.

When finally she could bear it no longer, Saliana said good night to all, and fled into the tent. She waited until she was in the darkness before she allowed her silent tears to fall, for Rewn had barely noticed when she had left, giving her naught but a vague wave to see her off.

CHAPTER FOUR

"Your presence is requested, my liege." The taunt came from a warrior who stood just off the lane, bowing mockingly at Gralyre to the great amusement of his three friends.

Gralyre sighed and set aside his bowl of pease pottage. The rumours about his name and lack of a past had finally made the rounds, and this kind of goading had become commonplace over the last few days. Thankfully, the women were visiting with Aneida and Mayvin, and so were out of harm's way.

"What do ye want?" Rewn demanded, standing slowly.

The Rebel sneered at him. "I was no' talking t' ye, lowland pig. I was talking t' his majesty." The man leaned forward with a smirk, amused by his own cleverness, as his friends egged him onwards. "We have seen enough o' ye posing with that sword o' yours, so let us see how ye handle it in a real fight, hmm?"

Gralyre sighed, and rolled his shoulders. If nothing else, he could use the exercise. He had a need to break something after finding out what had befallen Dara at the hands of these people.

His rage over the rapes was directed at the Stewards, as was right and proper, but he could not forgive the men and women who had seen all that was befalling a young, innocent lass, and had done nothing to help her because she was a lowlander. That had given birth to a deep disgust for the Rebels and their so-called resistance.

As he drew his blade, Rewn grabbed his arm. "Gralyre, no, there are four o' them!"

"Then they aught to have brought more men."

Gralyre leapt into the midst of the Rebels, and his sword became a blur of movement, his body a reed that bent and moved so that the blades of his enemies could not touch him. Less than ten seconds after the fight had started, it was over.

The Rebels, bloodied, yet alive, lay where they had fallen, moaning and crying out in pain, with horror in their faces and hearts. Their blades were lined up neatly in a snowbank where Gralyre's master swordplay had directed them, as he had disarmed the Rebels' amateur attacks with ease.

Rewn's jaw had unhinged in amazement as he had watched the fight, and he now snapped his mouth shut. He had been Gralyre's student for a while now, and thought himself used to the speed of the man, but it was still a shock to learn how much Gralyre slowed his swordplay in order to teach him.

Rewn was still trying to work out the pattern that had disarmed so many, so quickly, for it had been far too fast to see, when Gralyre placed the tip of his blade against the throat of the Rebel who had initiated the challenge. "Thank-you for the friendly sparring," he smiled coldly. "I suggest you leave before I decide to issue a challenge of my own."

He removed his sword and sheathed the blade with a snap, his gaze never leaving the challanger's face. "Do not return!" he ordered coldly, precipitating a mad scrabble of men, as the Rebels limped away, supporting each other in their rush to leave.

Gralyre scowled, as he let them go.

Rewn came to stand at his shoulder, following Gralyre's glare to watch the last of the attackers disappear at the cross street. "There go four less men that we need worry about."

"Only about ten thousand more to go." Gralyre shook his head testily, and motioned to Rewn. "We might as well get started. We can pick up Hofar's trail at the south gate."

Over the last few days, when Dajin would leave the family tent to join Matik and his men on the practice field, Gralyre and Rewn would carefully stalk the three Stewards, memorizing their routines, discovering their weaknesses, and planning their chance for Dara's justice. The more that they learned, the hotter burned the fires of their need for retribution. They witnessed many atrocities, for Dara was not the only victim of Jarrod, Hofar and Strier.

Jarrod's status as a Steward gave him power; a power that came from the fear he inflicted upon the people cowering beneath his rule. The foulness that the other two Stewards suckled upon spewed forth from the recesses of his tiny mind.

Rewn and Gralyre needed no help from Little Wolf to track Jarrod through the camp by scent alone. He was a repulsive man, unwashed and unkempt, and the thought of his beautiful sister being defiled by this repugnant animal would haunt Rewn for the rest of his life.

Ever by Jarrod's side was the giant, Strier. Judging by the hatred in the faces of their victims, Jarrod kept Strier nearby for protection against anyone fool enough to fight back. Alone,

Jarrod was not an imposing man, but with Strier as bodyguard and enforcer, his will was absolute.

Steward Strier cowed all of the trio's victims into compliance through brutality and pain. He was a large man, but his bulk was composed of heavy slabs of fat, not muscle, for working as a Steward brought enough profit that he could spend his time lazing and eating. He was cruel in the extreme, but it was the cruelty of a bully, and had he not partnered with Jarrod and Hofar, he would have had neither the initiative nor the wit to instigate the tortures that Rewn and Gralyre witnessed.

And lastly, there was Steward Hofar, who on the surface seemed Jarrod and Strier's opposite. His beard was neat, his hair clean and trimmed, his teeth were white and strong and often shown; a handsome, well-groomed young man, who at first blush seemed good-natured and kind. He did not seem the type of man to be Jarrod and Strier's willing accomplice in depravity, but his handsome face was a mask hiding unwholesome appetites.

Time and again, Rewn and Gralyre witnessed the Stewards' victims turn to Hofar for protection only to discover to their distress, and Hofar's amusement, that they had found a man just as bereft of morality as the other two, and their hopes for rescue would burn to forsaken ash. Hofar needed Jarrod's cruelty as catalyst for his depravity. In turn, his villainy egged Jarrod to new heights of corruption, while Strier reveled in whatever brutality might be asked of him by the other two. The three Stewards fed off of each other's corruption; a trifecta of symbiotic degeneracy.

The people within the South District had no recourse for complaint due to the hierarchy of the Northern Rebel Fortress. The fort was divided into four districts; north, south, east, and west. Each district reported to a different group of Stewards, and out of courtesy, one district did not interfere with the internal affairs of another.

The Stewards were responsible for protecting the fortress wall encompassing their district, manning their gate, policing, acting as judges for minor disputes, organizing hunting parties, witnessing legal contracts, and allotting the food, weapons and firewood to the people living within their jurisdiction. They answered only to Quartermistress Beaurice, reporting to her at the end of every seven day, and receiving the stipend of grain, clothing and weapons that were to be distributed to the inhabitants of their district upon their discretion.

Jarrod, Hofar and Strier, as the Stewards for South District, held undisputed, absolute authority over its inhabitants. Those who sought to stop their despotic reign, by reporting the corruption to the Quartermistress, would soon disappear, or die from privation or the elements, so that ultimately, there was no one left brave enough to bring charges of the depravities of the three men.

That was all about to end.

෫ඁ

Gralyre waited impatiently outside Catrian's tent as one of her sentries went within to announce his arrival. The other guard glared daggers while his hands twisted nervously against the haft of his halberd. He obviously remembered their previous encounter.

Gralyre smiled coldly, daring him to retaliate.

The man's expression darkened to match the sky, his knuckles tightening to white where they gripped his weapon, but he did nothing more. He looked away as his partner returned through the canvas tent flap. "She will see ye now," he muttered grudgingly.

Gralyre brushed past them both to enter the tent, trying to tamp down his eagerness. He told himself that he was impatient to discover Catrian's verdict, but knew in his heart that it was more, something deeper and wilder that eased slightly when he spied her.

Catrian stood near her bookshelf with a steaming mug in hand, watching him enter. She was dressed in her habitual leggings and jerkin, with her hair braided neatly in one fat rope down her back. Her grey-green eyes narrowed at him through the steam from her cup as she took a small sip.

Gralyre had taken pains to appear more presentable than when last they had met. He had bathed, and wore his least travel stained clothes. He had clubbed his long hair back with a strip of cloth, and trimmed his wild, black beard to tameness. Even his sword gleamed at his hip, and his boots were clean of mud. Using his best manners, he bowed to her with a formal grace.

"Good morn to you, lady." He could not tell what she was thinking, if it was good news or ill, and his drumming heart bespoke his unease. "Have you decided?"

Catrian nodded. "Ye were right. We are too desperate in our struggle against Doaphin t' ignore any potential ally."

Gralyre swallowed around a hard lump that rose suddenly to choke him. He had not realized how much he had wanted this; to be trusted by her in some small way, and to find a place of belonging. "Thank-you for your decision, Catrian."

Catrian trailed her fingers across the carefully stacked volumes on the bookshelf. "Gralyre, I will teach ye what I know o' magic, if ye will pledge t' stand by us in our fight. Until now, ye have drifted aimlessly from one place t' another, skirting death for no reason. I offer ye an opportunity t' stand and fight for something, instead o' dying for nothing" Golden streamers of light trailed from her fingertips, as she pulled them from the books, and motioned him to one of the chairs at the table.

Eyeing the fading motes of golden light, he complied with her silent request and sat. To Gralyre, her show of magic felt more like intimidation than the natural gesture she had tried to make of it. "I will not betray you. I will do everything in my power to protect you!" he vowed earnestly.

Catrian sat gracefully in the chair across from his, placed her steaming mug on the tabletop, and folded her hands precisely in front of her. From her forays into his mindscape, she knew him better than anyone could, and knew that his sincerity was real, even if his motives were still a clouded mystery. She fixed him with her penetrating gaze, and in that moment she was all Sorceress. "Do ye agree that I know more o' Magic and its properties and abilities than ye do?"

"Of course. 'Tis why I am here."

"Then I will have ye swear t' be my apprentice, t' accept without comment or argument whatever task I demand o' ye. I will have your unquestioning obedience and loyalty. In return, I swear t' teach ye all the knowledge ye need in order t' excel at the craft o' Magic. If at any time ye break with this oath, ye will no longer have my protection, and I will kill ye." She eyed him distantly, coldly, as if she were hoping he would be too proud to subjugate to her will.

Gralyre stared back fearlessly. His instincts told him that at one word of protest, or at one look of discontent, she would deny him all, and this was too important to allow his pride to jeopardize. "I swear that I will be your obedient student, that I will be a loyal guardian to all the secrets that you reveal." His vow sealed his fate to hers.

She seemed neither surprised nor relieved by his reply, but instead leaned back in her chair, watching him warily. "If at any time I sense the awakening o' evil within ye, I will kill ye," she reminded quietly. "If at any time I find ye consorting with followers o' Doaphin, interfering with the administration o' this fortress, or eavesdropping upon private councils, ye will be executed as a spy."

Gralyre's mouth curled derisively. It was not the most affable way to begin an apprenticeship, but since what she threatened him with was the aegis under which he already lived, it was a moot point. "Agreed."

Catrian took a long sip from her mug and eyed him over the rim, assessing his demeanor. "I have been considering your situation." She set her cup down and stood, walking serenely to the brazier placed in the corner of the tent upon which a small kettle burped and boiled.

She took up a rag to protect her fingers from the heat, swung the kettle from the metal hook holding it suspended over the hot coals, and poured some of the steaming liquid into a pewter tankard resting upon a small side table. "Ye would no' have reached adulthood without control o'er your powers. They did no' suddenly manifest from nothingness when ye lost your memory."

She returned and set the steaming mug in front of Gralyre, indicating he should drink, as she sat down opposite to him once more.

"That makes sense," Gralyre agreed. He blew across the surface to cool it before taking a large swig from his tankard. He paused, swirling the liquid appreciatively in his mouth, as it took a moment for his amnesia to supply a name for the taste.

'Apple cider.'

'Twas not bad, except for a bitter aftertaste left upon his tongue as he swallowed.

Catrian continued, as if he had not interrupted. "This means that I will likely be teaching ye that which ye already know. Ye once said that ye did no' know how t' fight until ye picked up your sword and swung it. Chances are, ye will remember much o' the nature o' magic as ye use it."

At Gralyre's nod of understanding, Catrian smiled, "Finish your drink and we will begin."

Gralyre paused, suspicious of her affability, with the tankard halfway to his lips. "What is in this?" a slight ringing had begun in his ears. "You have drugged me!" He slammed the mug down, sloshing liquid over the rim, and tried to surge to his feet, but his coordination would not respond to his will.

Catrian shrugged. "Be at ease. There is nothing in it that will harm ye. 'Tis a tisane t' relax your mind while still allowing ye t' maintain concentration and focus. It will help ye t' tap into your powers. Now finish it."

Gralyre hesitated grimly, suspicious of her motives, for when had Catrian ever had his best interests at heart? But he could not so soon break his oath of absolute obedience so he subsided back into his chair, and raised the tankard with clumsy fingers, spilling some of the cider upon his shirt, as he drained it as swiftly as possible. He grimaced at the aftertaste, carefully placed the cup back on the table, and blinked rapidly as his vision tunneled, and the room began to undulate.

"All that I know o' magic, I learned from these few books." Catrian indicated the shelves behind her. "But 'tis no' much."

Gralyre smiled at the whimsical way her words trailed colors into the air. He reached out a hand to catch a ribbon of green to thread through his fingers as he listened to her.

Catrian frowned as she witnessed his drugged movements,

wondering if she had dosed him with too much of the herbal mixture. She had followed a recipe found in one of her books, but he was such a large man, she had had to guess at the strength of the brew.

"There are still many mysteries hidden from me. Even now, I have an edict for all foraging parties t' bring back any books they find." She shook her head in deep sorrow. "Doaphin burned so many libraries. So much knowledge has been lost. I heard that once there were thousands o' tomes about sorcery and magic, but these few have been all that have ever been found."

She stared grimly into the distance, remembering her struggles. "And o' course, no one with the talent survives to adulthood, so no knowledge has been passed down. Until ye, I was the only human Sorcerer in the land, so I had t' teach myself. I read, and I practiced, and I learned through every encounter with the enemy, first, how to protect and hide, and second, how to attack and kill. I am very lucky t' have survived."

A strange floating sensation had overtaken Gralyre as she spoke. Catrian's face seemed blurred, but her hazel eyes were oddly focused and intense. He was not sure if her voice was coming from within his head or without. "I am glad you lived," Gralyre slurred. His suspicions of moments ago seemed churlish now, belonging to another Gralyre, a paranoid, untrusting version of his true self.

Catrian glanced up at him through her lashes, her hand tracing the grain in the wood of the table. "Thank-ye. However, we are here t' discuss your abilities, no' mine. What I have given ye is a traditional brew that has been used for eons t' test the strength o' an adept. Before I can teach ye, we must know how strong ye are. Relax and listen t' my words."

Gralyre's eyes drifted shut, and his existence folded inward until his entire universe was naught but the sound of her voice.

"Are ye ready, Gralyre?"

Gralyre was not sure if he managed a nod or not. "I am ready," he murmured. "Your voice is lovely. You are lovely." He breathed in deeply and his voice lowered to a sensual rumble. "You smell like heather."

Catrian blushed, glad that his eyes were shut so that he could not see. "Um, Thank-ye." She drew a deep breath, and tamped down the pleasure born of his drugged confession. "Do no' talk. Just listen. Magic is simply a connection between yourself and the world around ye, and your ability t' affect a change in its state o' being. The stronger your connection to the world, and the stronger your will, the stronger your magic will be.

"Reach out with your senses, and feel the world around ye. 'Tis alive. Its breath is the air ye breathe, its earth and rocks are the bones that support your flesh, its fire is the warmth o' the sun upon your face, the furnace that heats your body, and its waters slack your thirst, and pulse through your veins. The perfect balance o' it, the power o' it. Do ye feel it?"

"I can feel it," Gralyre intoned after a moment then frowned, for the vastness he sensed suddenly seemed akin to the horrible, expansiveness of the nightmare void, but without the sudden, painful, contraction to nothingness that inevitably followed. Drawing on his courage, he relaxed into the sensation, focusing entirely upon the teeming life that filled the space, utterly different from the void of his nightmares, which was like unto death; empty and cold.

"That is good. Now turn your thoughts inward. Feel the earth and stone o' your flesh and bones, heated by the furnace o' your fire. Feel the water o' life pumping through your veins. Feel the air in your lungs. Feel the balance within yourself, and how enormously powerful these forces are, and how they mimic those o' the world about you. It is through this pathway that you will exert your will."

"Yes, I see now! 'Tis so simple!" Gralyre was delighted as he followed the rivers of power running through his body, riding the crests and waterfalls of energy that circulated throughout him.

Catrian's voice continued to reverberate in his head, as she taught him, step-by-step, how to consciously connect to his magic. "Ye are special, Gralyre, ye have been given the gift t' use the balance within t' change the balance without. Within, without, 'tis linked, 'tis the same. You need only change yourself t' change the world. Can ye feel the connection Gralyre?"

"Yes, I feel it!"

Catrian's voice continued soothingly, hypnotically. "Ye have felt the power o' the wind. Call the wind t' ye now, Gralyre!"

Effortlessly, Gralyre sought and found the powerful sense of freedom and power that was his connection to the breath of the world. He felt disconnected from his body, but immersed in the powerful hum of the magic, as he summoned the wind, for it was the breath in his lungs; it was not separate from him. He was the wind. He could rage, or he could caress with a soft sigh.

"Good, very good," Catrian praised. She shivered in the blast of cold that harried a flurry of snow into the tent. The fabric of the roof and walls belled outward, as the canvas tried to contain the force of the gust. "Now, call the earth. Bend it t' your will!"

Gralyre sought the strength in his body, the stillness and patience of ancient earth that was not within him at all but was his body beneath the tent. The floor heaved and buckled as a spray of earth showered upwards.

Catrian gasped and barely had time to erect a protective shield around her precious books as earth rained down. She looked upon Gralyre's rapt face with fear. She had known he was strong, but... by the Gods!

"Water!" Catrian's demand came to Gralyre from far away.

Moisture beaded their faces as the air began to weep. Seconds later, a deluge soaked them to the skin. Gralyre smiled as the raging river of his blood pounded through the air.

"Fire!"

Heat radiated from his skin, as Gralyre mindlessly obeyed Catrian. The deluge stopped, and steam arose from his clothes. The damp coals within the brazier in the corner suddenly burst into flame.

Gralyre's opened his eyes in dreamy wonder, and through a

wreath of fire, he saw Catrian's face bent to his, her look intent, urgent. She was saying something, but he could no longer hear her for the ringing in his ears. She grabbed his face in her hands, shouting.

In a power drunk haze, Gralyre remembered her kiss, her fire that night in the ice cavern. He leaned forward and captured her mouth with his, stilling her words. *'This is fire. Is this what you want?'* Licking flames wreathed his face, her face.

Pain lashed through him, breaking his concentration, and severing his connection to his magic. Gasping, he jerked back from her, his eyes slid upwards, and he slumped unconscious in his chair.

Catrian sat back with a gulp, her heart pounding with fright. Only by knocking him unconscious had she been able to stop him from incinerating them both!

At a muffled noise, she glanced up to see her guards hammering at the barrier she had erected to protect her pavilion. With a wave of her hand, she released the spell long enough to assure the sentries that she was unharmed. She put the barrier back in place, shutting out all noise and intrusion, and returned her attention to the man slumped at the smoking table. A pool of pewter congealed on the surface of the blackened wood; all that remained of the tankard she had served him.

Her hands wandered over her lips, feeling the burn of his kiss through her scalded flesh, as she surveyed the destruction of her home. When he had called forth fire, he had burst into flame, igniting everything around him. The table still smoldered from the heat, and his clothes were ruined. It took her but a moment's concentration to extinguish all the remaining live embers.

Catrian was stunned, for Gralyre was more powerful than anyone she had ever sensed, more powerful than her, than Doaphin, and any of his Demon Lords combined. From all that she had read, no one had ever been able to master the forces so effortlessly, so quickly. A mound of dirt had almost knocked down the tent pole when the ground had ruptured to his calling. She willed it back into a smooth surface, leaving nothing but stray clumps of mud on her disheveled woven mat.

She had expected mild responses to his first attempts to consciously tap into his magic; light dew, a candle flame, a breeze, if there had been any reactions at all. According to the texts, most adepts were unable to master this lesson, even after years of study, a fact born out by her first stumbling tries, which had produced pitiful results by comparison. It had taken her years of dedicated practice to master her arts. She had neither expected the violence of Gralyre's responses, nor the depth of the powers he had tapped.

Across the table, Catrian saw Gralyre shiver, and was compelled to minister to him. She grabbed up a damp fur from her disheveled sleeping pallet, and cozied it around Gralyre's shoulders. He shuddered lightly at the pressure of her hands against his scalded shoulders, and his midnight eyes fluttered open hesitantly, unfocussed and confused from the potion that he had drunk. She could see he was exhausted. "Sleep," she murmured gently. As his body slumped, she eased him forward to rest upon the burnt surface of the table.

Catrian fell into the chair opposite to his once more, studying his face intently. What was she to do with him? Such power, harnessed, would turn the tide, and force Doaphin back to the demon-spawned hell from whence he came. Such power, turned against the Rebels, would be their certain destruction.

Unable to stop herself, she reached over to brush a lock of overlong hair from his face, and singed strands crumbled into dust against her fingers. She drew back her hand, testing the feel of the ash against her rubbing fingertips, as she stole a moment for herself, taking advantage of this rare opportunity to study him.

He had such a strong face. A strong man. Felled now from her magic, and his first efforts. The skin beneath his eyes was smudged with exhaustion, an ongoing wound from the nightmares he suffered. He was never given a moment's rest in his dreams, and even now his thick lashes flickered violently, as his brow twitched together, and then smoothed out restlessly.

His mouth was soft and full, and she felt again the burn of its touch upon hers, the mouth that had delivered her first kiss in the cavern. Men feared her, or they pursued her for their own love of power, but they never saw her for herself, nor valued her for who she was as a woman - no one until Gralyre.

She yearned to trust in him, but knew that she dared not because of the sinister mysteries that swirled around him. The risk was too great, both for her people and for her heart.

To have grasped this lesson so quickly, and been so strong,

meant that he had to have been exposed to magic before, and the implications of that knowledge caused a seed of unease to be planted, its fruit yet to ripen.

Either he had never used his magic, which could not be true for he tapped his powers too easily, or he had found a way to shield his powers from detection at a very young age. Or...

'...he is not from this world? Not from this time? The Lost Prince?'

Ridiculous! Impossible! She would not pin the survival of her people upon a hearth tale! Besides, in all the stories told, the Lost Prince had never possessed magic. All sorcery had come from King Lyre's Court Sorcerer, Fennick.

The dark shadows beneath Gralyre's eyes adopted a sinister cast. Catrian needed time to deal with her suspicions, and time to decide exactly what it was safe to teach him. Unfortunately time was a luxury in short supply, as was trust.

Gralyre needed to learn to control his powers, and it was a lesson that might be drawn out though she suspected he would master it as quickly as he had everything else. Yet, she would set him to the task, and give herself the time she needed to discover the truth.

She drew on her magic, and summoned some of her men to carry Gralyre back to his tent.

∽∾

Traffic around the south gate was brisk in anticipation of the oncoming bad weather; wagons trundled back and forth, men reported for their duty upon the walls, and teams of Huntsmen and Woodsman organized their forays. The day was cold, and overcast by gravid clouds. The scent of ozone and snow from the pending blizzard mingled with the oily smoke from the fires burning in iron pots at intervals along the wall-walk that provided meager heat to the sentries, and beacons of light in the premature twilight to anyone returning from outside the fortress walls.

Hofar loitered near the entrance to the gatehouse, his breath misting in the frigid air with every order that he gave, sending men ducking and fleeing to do his bidding. He was well insulated against the strengthening wind within a thick fur, luxurious when compared to ragged woolens worn by the rest of the warriors. His commands seemed more for his own amusement than in the interest of seeing things run smoother, but the warriors had no choice but to jump to his whims, for to gain the Steward's displeasure was to lose their allotment of food, possibly their bivouac, and ultimately their lives.

Rewn stilled his rage, seeking the calm mask he needed in order to do what must be done. Gralyre had warned him to patience, but this was an opportunity that Rewn could not pass upon. Hoffer was alone, and Rewn had devised a plan.

Gralyre was lying insensate in their tent after his visit to the Sorceress, and Rewn would wait not a moment longer for Dara's justice. Hofar had smiled to his face, and shook his hand, while all along he had spent the winter assaulting his sister. It was an insult that demanded retribution!

When Rewn started across the compound towards the Steward, he watched as a warrior dared to bulk at a command, and Hofar clouted him, sending the man sprawling into the snow. An extra kick to the ribs sent the hapless warrior rolling into the path of an oncoming wagon, and 'twas only through the quick intervention of others that he was pulled to safety in time.

Hatred knifed anticipation into Rewn's heart, but he schooled his features to show nothing but boredom. "Steward Hofar?"

Hofar whirled at the sound of his name, and smiled smoothly, though his stare was sharply assessing and suspicious. "Rewn, was it no'? Dara's brother?"

"Aye. Ye said that we should report for work assignment once we were settled?"

Hofar's smile remained in place, as he quickly evaluated Rewn's tranquil expression. "'Tis right, I did. I expected ye long before now. 'Tis been four days."

"Are the other two Stewards here? I would like t' have a chance t' introduce myself." Rewn made a show of checking the gatehouse. He already knew the answer, for he had chosen his opportunity carefully.

"No, they are busy with other matters. There were two more o' ye. Where are they?"

Rewn let his face curdle with a hint of envy. "Gralyre has reported t' the Sorceress Catrian, and Dajin is away with General Matik somewhere..." he shrugged as though he did not care, nor could be bothered to keep abreast of the movements of his family.

Hofar's eyebrows rose. "Matik? The Sorceress? Ye travel in elevated circles."

Rewn shrugged again, and scowled. "No' me. I have t' work for a living."

Hofar laughed appreciatively, and clapped Rewn on the shoulder. "I have a spot on the wall with your name upon it."

"The wall? I was hoping for something less…strenuous. T' tell the truth I have never been one t' prefer work t' leisure. In fact…" Rewn's voice lowered conspiringly, as he leaned nearer, "I have come across a fine vintage cask o' oaken dramhale that I thought that ye and I could keep good company with, and perhaps come t' an agreement?"

Hofar's face lit up, and he licked his lips. "Dramhale? Real dramhale?"

Rewn waggled his eyebrows suggestively, and leered. "In exchange for certain… leniencies?"

Hofar's smile did not reach his eyes. "If it is as ye say."

Rewn clapped his hands, and rubbed them together. "Ah, I knew I sensed a kindred spirit! I guessed a'right o' it. Ye had the look o' a man who would appreciate a fine drink!" He winked and grinned.

Hofar's peeled his lips back in a smile that was all teeth. "Where is it?"

Rewn clapped a hand on Hofar's shoulder. "Do ye think me stupid enough t' bring it into the fort? The Commander would have confiscated the lot, and I would have no' seen a drop!"

"So 'tis outside?"

"Aye, but I canno' get t' it without a reason t' be outside the walls," Rewn wheedled suggestively, "and 'tis too heavy t' cart home on me own."

The Steward nodded and smiled, made comfortable by Rewn's portrayal of avarice. "There will be no wall for ye, my friend," he promised airily, "Ye will be a Huntsman, a position o' importance, and able t' come and go by your own leave."

Rewn smiled widely, and dropped his arm away from around Hofar's shoulders. "That sounds like a fine job. Thank-ye, Steward Hofar!" He looked at the gate, and then with a show of reluctance, back at the Steward. "There is a blizzard on its way. Mayhap we should await less inclement weather?"

Hofar's smile hardened. "Nay, I will take my payment now. Come with me."

Hofar led the way to the gate, and introduced Rewn to the gatekeepers as a new Huntsman, then passed Rewn a spear and a quiver of arrows. "This is your kit. Ye will be docked wages until 'tis paid for."

Rewn frowned at the weaponry. "How much will it cost?"

Hofar glared at him, grabbed his shoulder, and pushed him roughly out of the gate ahead of him. "It will cost what I say it will!"

Rewn paused, and looked Hofar over with reluctance. "Then I will trade ye more o' the cask for the gear."

"We will see," Hofar murmured cunningly.

They set a brisk pace, as they walked the switchback road

down the mountainside. With every step, Rewn was increasingly conscious of his intentions, as though his purpose was exposed to every watcher upon the fortress wall. It was not until the forest had swallowed them from view that he relaxed fractionally.

The twilight of the oncoming storm made the forest darker, and more menacing, matching his mood. Had Hofar bothered to look back, he would have seen Rewn's face twisted with hatred. Dara had been defenseless, vulnerable, and the Stewards had shown no mercy. And so would receive none in return. Blood roared in Rewn's ears, and it took everything he had not to ram his spear through the back of the sickening creature he followed.

'An accident! It must look like an accident.'

To remove temptation, Rewn took the lead then, veering from the well-used path, and into the thickets, drawing Hofar away from any potential witnesses.

"How much further!" Hofar's manner was now all impatience and threat. His affability had been left far behind, as they had trekked deeper and deeper into the forest.

There were no tracks in the area, and they were well out of sight of the walls. It was time. "'Tis here! We have found it!" Rewn announced, and dropped to all fours to dig in the deep snow under a gnarly old fir tree. "The ground has frozen. Come help." He shuffled aside, as though to invite Hofar to join him.

But Hofar had other ideas. He held a leather sap in his hand, high above his head, and brought it down in a whistling arc towards the back of Rewn's unprotected skull.

But Rewn had come to know this man, and had been expecting just such a betrayal. He ducked out from under the swing, and rolled to his feet, the bared blade of his sword coming to a swift rest against the hollow at the base of Hofar's throat.

Hofar swallowed nervously, his apple bobbing against the point of the blade, and tried on a sickly smile as the sap slipped from his fingers, and plopped into the deep snow. "Ye canno' blame a man," he shrugged. "Have ye any notion what a cask o' dramhale can buy? If ye give it t' me I will make ye a Steward! There will be no need for ye t' work at all! How does that notion grip ye?"

And there it was. Hofar's weakness. Wealth of any sort. The man was a magpie who extorted every item of value from the people of South District. Rewn's smile did not reach his eyes. "There is no cask."

Hofar frowned in confusion. "Then what are we doing…"

The dawning of understanding, the instant screaming fear that shot through the man, sent a spear of intense righteousness straight into Rewn's heart.

"Ye canno' kill me! I am a Steward! Ye will swing for this!"

Rewn smiled coldly, and let the man rant.

Hoffer soon realized that threats would not work without the other two Stewards there to back him up, and switched to bargaining instead. "I will give ye anything!" Hofar promised as he struggled to control his fearful panting through his frosted beard. "Money? Power? Anything ye want! What do ye want?"

Rewn's smile faded, and tears of rage welled. "I want my sister's honour back, ye whoreson!" He cracked Hofar's skull with the heavy butt of his sword, and watched with satisfaction as the man folded, unconscious, into the deep snow.

Working quickly, he stripped Hofar naked, leaving his clothes scattered wherever he tossed them. Rolling the Steward to his stomach, Rewn bound him, wrists to ankles, with tight knots before gathering the loose end of the rope, and hauling Hofar's dead weight behind him through the deep drifts.

After almost an hour of hard slogging, he felt weak struggles vibrating up the rope and halted, dropping the braided cord from his shoulder with a shrug of relief. Rewn was wet with sweat under his heavy winter woolen from the exertion of dragging Hofar for nearly three miles through the tangled forest. "Good, ye are awake." He leaned against a tree, and drew out his waterskin from next to his chest where his body heat kept it from freezing. As Rewn took a long pull to slack his thirst, he assessed the Steward's condition.

Hofar did not look well. After being dragged naked through the snow, and suffering exposure to the elements, his shivers were unstoppable. Frankly, Rewn was surprised the man had awoken at all.

Hofar managed to roll to his side, but could go no further with his arms and legs bent painfully behind him. "P-p-please! D-do no' k-k-kill me! I will l-l-leave! Ye will ne'er s-see me ag-g-gain!"

Rewn bent down with his knife in his hand. "Please? Tell me

Hofar, did my sister beg ye? Did she say please?" Rewn tapped the tip of his dagger against Hofar's chest, directly over his nonexistent heart. "Did she beg ye t' stop, as ye raped her over, and over?"

Hofar winced, his shivers so violent that he almost accidently impaled himself upon Rewn's blade. "Wh-what do y-ye c-c-care! Everyone knows-s-s that l-l-l-l-owlanders s-sell their women to D-d-d-oaphin. I w-w-ill p-pay ye. J-j-just t-tell me, how m-much!"

The point of the dagger pricked Hofar's skin when Rewn twisted it, his mask slipping to reveal the extent of his rage.

Hofar realized his error and switched bargaining tactics. "Sh-she was a mistake. S-s-sorry. Sorry! Please! Do n-n-no' k-kill me! I will do anyth-thing!"

Hofar's horror filled stare never left the tip of Rewn's knife where a small bead of blood emerged sluggishly, and froze in the cold winter air before it could dribble down off his chest.

Instead of piercing the man's heart, Rewn shifted, and slit the bindings, pulling the ropes away. "I am no' going t' kill ye, Hofar."

Equal measures of hope, and malice contorted Hoffer's face. "Y-ye will regret th-this! When I g-get b-b-back t' the f-fff-fortress, ye are a d-dead m-man!" He pawed at Rewn's thick coat, and seemed confused at how easily Rewn batted his hands away. He tried to swing a punch, but his coordination was off, and the weak swipe went wide of Rewn's face. He held his hands before his face, confused by the black, frozen fingers that would not close into fists.

Rewn smiled quietly as he stood upright, wrapped the rope, and slung it over his shoulder. "Looks like we are in for a nasty blow," He mentioned conversationally as he appraised the dark sky. "Tell the truth, I will be surprised if I make it back t' the fortress afore the blizzard strikes." The wind had picked up, and the temperature on the mountainside was plummeting rapidly. Even now, the first flakes began to drift from the sky, promising a feathery death to those without shelter. Without another word, he walked away, lifting his booted feet high to clear the deep snow.

"Ye are a dead man! Do ye hear me, lowlander? A DEAD MAN!" Hoffer bellowed after him, his rage lending him momentary strength.

As he left, Rewn examined his heart. Could he really leave the man to die, to freeze to death in this oncoming storm?

For the sake of his sister, and for all the past and future crimes that this monster had and would commit, the answer was a resounding '*Yes*'.

Hofar yelled venomous threats until Rewn disappeared into the trees. Pausing for breath, he tried to stand but was unable to muster the coordination to do so. He looked down at his naked, reddened flesh, already numb and burning, and blinked in confusion, then panic, as understanding finally came to him. "Ye-ye c-c-canno' leave m-me! C-c-come b-back! Come BACK!" he screamed.

Rewn did not hesitate, as he plodded away. Soon, Hofar's

cries were lost to the howl of the wind, and the roar of the forest, as it bent to the might of the oncoming blizzard. He returned to the fortress by a circuitous route to ensure that Hofar could not follow his tracks, but the heavy snow and wind soon erased all signs of his passing. Even if Hofar had found the strength to follow him, the man would not have gotten far, exposed as he was to the elemental forces of the storm.

Despite his heavy furs, Rewn was shivering and exhausted, as he passed through the south gate, and arrived home just as the full brunt of the blizzard threw itself against the mountain.

CHAPTER FIVE

Hofar's remains were found in the forest, partially buried under the new fallen snow, after an extensive search had been initiated when he was two days overdue in returning from his hunting trip. There was not much left of him to recover for the wolves had been at his body.

All agreed that he must have become lost in the blizzard, and as happened with many who were freezing to death, euphoria had overtaken him so he had believed himself lashed by heat instead of cold, and so had stripped, hastening his death. They had found Hofar's clothing some miles away, strewn wildly about a glade, supporting the assumptions of how he had met his death.

But the fact that it had been Dara's brother who had last been seen with Hofar was enough to arouse the suspicions of the other two Stewards, prompting Strier and Jarrod to seek out Rewn for an interrogation. They found him and his brother, Dajin, hard at work splitting firewood next to their tent.

Jarrod's scent arrived upon the wind some moments before the man did, and upon catching a whiff, Rewn leaned his axe next to his cutting stump, and waited calmly as the men approached. Their visit was not unexpected.

"What is it?" Dajin asked when Rewn stopped chopping, following his brother's gaze towards the two men striding over from the lane. "Who are they?"

The murderous looks upon the approaching men's faces did not bode well. People using the avenue scattered from the Stewards' path, while neighbours ducked into their tents, leaving fires unattended and chores abandoned in their haste to vanish from sight.

"I do no' know. Keep quiet, and let me deal with this," Rewn muttered in an aside just before the Stewards arrived. There was no guilt in lying to his brother. He had not told Dajin of the attacks that Dara had suffered either, for Rewn knew from painful experience that the vainglorious Dajin could not be trusted to act with the discretion needed to seek justice nor, after his performance at the cavern, could Rewn rely upon his brother not to betray them to the Rebels for his own gain, a thought that twisted his guts late into the night.

In lieu of a greeting, Steward Jarrod shoved Rewn in the chest, making him stumble back a step to maintain his balance. "Tell me why ye did it, lowlander!"

"Hey!" Dajin yelled at the unprovoked assault, leaping towards the man attacking his brother.

Steward Strier batted Dajin back with one beefy arm, and pointed a heavy, intimidating finger in his face to hold him in place. "Ye stay out o' it!" From two feet above Dajin's head, Strier's piggy eyes spoke of pain if Dajin disobeyed.

Dajin froze, eyeing the large man with alarm.

"Did what?" Rewn growled back, as he pushed Jarrod in turn. "Who are ye?" The pretense almost stuck in his throat, but everything hinged on this encounter. The Stewards could not know of his involvement in Hofar's death.

Steward Strier, the enforcer, could not allow Jarrod to be assaulted without retribution. As Jarrod steadied his footing, taken aback by Rewn's audacity, Strier stepped in and punched Rewn's chest in blatant mimicry of Jarrod's opening volley, but unlike Jarrod's smack, this blow almost threw Rewn off his feet. "We are the Stewards! Tell us why ye killed Hofar!"

"Rewn? Rewn, what is happening?" Dajin hovered helplessly in the background, daring to do nothing to stop the assault. Everyone knew that the Stewards ran things, and that crossing them was a death sentence. And Rewn had pushed one of them! What had he been thinking? And now they were accusing him of murder!

"Hofar?" Rewn asked with innocent confusion, as he rubbed the ache left in his sternum from Strier's blow. "Hofar is dead?"

Jarrod took an aggressive step forward forcing Rewn to hold his breath to endure the man's pong. "They found him dead in the forest today. Ye were seen leaving with him before the storm! Now, tell me what ye had t' do with it!"

Rewn fought a gag as he was forced to breath in, but it gave his voice a very authentic, strained warble, as he shook his head sorrowfully. "He made me a Huntsman, and took me out t' show me good places t' track deer. We split up when we reached the timber line," Rewn confessed. "I returned early, when the snows began t' fall. Ye can check with the gatekeepers. I did no' think t' ask if Hofar had also returned." He hung his head with a saddened frown. "I did no' know that he had died."

Jarrod glanced slyly up at his bear-like companion, and gave a small nod, cueing Strier to punch Rewn in the face, knocking him to the ground.

"Lowlander pig shit! Ye had something t' do with this. I know it!" Strier grinned, enjoying the excess of force, as he watched Rewn cup his face with his hands and curl away. Strier could not resist so easy a target, and kicked Rewn in the ribs for good measure, relishing the pained yelp, as his victim rolled away from any further blows.

Rewn gasped for air, for Strier's heavy boot had connected solidly, knocking free his breath. His mind raced for a strategy. Everything depended upon convincing the Stewards that he was innocent! Rewn rubbed away the blood from his split lip, rolled to his back, and rested upon his elbows, feigning confused innocence with the skill of a stableboy caught in the loft with the farmer's daughter. "What reason would I have t' kill Hofar? He seemed a goodly man when I spoke t' him. He had just made me a Huntsman!"

As Dajin watched his brother bleed at the feet of the Stewards, his vision tunneled, making their voices distort from the ringing in his ears. The same helplessness he had experienced when his father had died under the teeth of the Deathren overwhelmed him. He wanted to run to Rewn but his feet were rooted, and his body hollow, as though he was seeing everything from inside out.

Strier snarled, revealing a gap from a missing tooth, "Because o' what…"

"Shut-up, Strier," Jarrod ordered coldly.

Strier bit off his comment with a mumble.

Rewn brushed snow off his britches as he stood. "Because why?" He tested, striving to keep his knowledge from his face and voice.

Strier was confused, as he glanced from Jarrod to Rewn. His brows lowered over his pug nose, and his chins waddled as he shook his head. "Nothing. No reason."

Jarrod glared at Rewn, but uncertainty had begun to take root. Rewn had no motive to kill Hofar if Dara had not told him of their crimes. And Dara was too well cowed to have betrayed the Stewards to her family. She knew the consequences.

Dajin tried to smooth the waters. "We are sorry t' hear o' the death o' your friend, but my brother had nothing t' do with it!" Dajin was glad to see that Rewn knew better than to retaliate for the blows. Though they had been in camp for only a few days, the neighbours had been very thorough in their warnings. The Stewards were dangerous and not to be crossed.

The two Stewards crowded Rewn, intimidating him with the fact that they could do whatever they wanted, and he could do nothing in return, save accept it.

Jarrod poked his finger against Rewn's chest, unerringly finding the welt from Strier's blow. "Best ye hope we never discover different, or I promise on my life I will see ye dead!"

Rewn looked him right in the eye. "Yes sir," he vowed, "ye will ne'er know any different." But within Rewn vowed, *'Nor see me coming.'*

Strier grabbed Rewn's shirt in two meaty fists. "Rumour has it ye have a dog."

Dajin spoke up before Rewn could. "'Tis Gralyre's dog! 'Tis his, no' ours!" He licked his dry lips, and rocked from foot to foot.

Strier shook Rewn then thrust him away. "Where is it? It attacked me the other day, and I want its head."

Rewn shot Dajin a frown, silencing him, as he would have volunteered the information. "'Tis with Gralyre, our friend, at the tent o' the Sorceress. It goes with him everywhere."

Strier slapped Rewn across the face, an insulting blow. "Ye tell him I want the beast's head." He poked his beefy finger into Rewn's chest to emphasize his words. "Ye tell him t' bring it t' me, today, or he will suffer for it!"

Rewn winced, and could not prevent his chest from caving away from the pain of the poke. Their continuous assault upon the same spot was as painful as it was irritating. He had not expected Strier's ultimatum. What was he going to tell Gralyre?

Strier grinned at Jarrod, snorting derisively, "Lying lowlander bastard. As if any o' em know the Sorceress!"

Glaring their threats, Jarrod and Strier backed away from the brothers, experience telling them to never turn their backs upon a victim. When they reached the lane they sauntered away, forcing several people from their path as they left. They never saw the murderous glower that Rewn threw at their backs, as they disappeared from sight.

ഇൻരു

The commotion outside the tent was what finally awoke Gralyre from his deep, healing sleep. He groaned when he sat up, his head pounding, and scratched at his beard, as he scanned the empty tent blurrily, noting the bright sunlight slanting through the open tent flap, and the fact that all the other pallets had been neatly stowed for the day in the cupboards. He was not sure if it was the drugged cider or the way Catrian had severed his connection to his power that had affected his headache more.

Little Wolf's tail thumped, and he gave a happy chuff, as he saw that his master's eyes were finally open. The wolfdog arose and stretched with front legs extended, an invitation to play. He had stood watch over Gralyre's sleep, but was now eager to be out.

'Awake! Awake! Cool air, run, chase, leap, snow cold against paws!'

Gralyre smiled at the wolfish poetry. Little Wolf had a way with images that painted a story of freedom and joy. *''Tis just what I need. How long was I asleep?'* Someone had thoughtfully placed an ewer of water beside him, and he gratefully downed a large drought to slack his thirst.

'Long. All winter!'

Gralyre grinned with affection. Little Wolf was notoriously unable to reckon time.

The Stewards were gone by the time Gralyre exited the tent, to find Rewn sitting upon a stump pressing a ball of snow against his split lip, while Dajin harangued him.

"Why do they think ye had something t' do with it? Ye canno' run afoul o' these men. They run everything. They can kill ye like that!" Dajin snapped his fingers.

"What has happened?"

Rewn looked up with a gleam in his eyes that belayed the innocent face he showed his little brother. "One o' the Stewards, Hofar, met with an accident. The fool got lost in a blizzard, and froze t' death."

Gralyre's brow creased in concern. "And the other two Stewards suspect you?"

Dajin answered defensively for his brother. "Rewn did nothing! They had no right t' hit him!" His cheeks flushed with anger. "'Tis your fault, I know it!" He glared at Gralyre. "Ye set your wolf on Strier, and now he want's the beast's head delivered t' him afore end o' day, or they will kill Rewn!"

"What?" Gralyre's hand dropped protectively to Little Wolf's head. There was no force in the world that could force him to murder his pup. What had Rewn been about while he had slept?

Rewn spat blood on the ground. "Let it go, Dajin. I am fine. They were just coming around t' threaten and bluster."

Dajin grumbled and kicked at snow, as he returned to splitting firewood. The heavy impact of the axe bespoke his need to expel his anxiety over his brother's life. "I should kill the beast myself!" he carped just loudly enough to be heard.

"Try," Gralyre invited in a voice of ice-wrapped steel.

Dajin cowed, swallowing nervously while repositioning

himself on the far side of the pile of firewood.

Rewn grinned up at Gralyre as, hidden from Dajin's sight, he held up three fingers and folded one away. The blood from his split lip gave his smile a bloodthirsty intensity.

Gralyre's disapproval tightened his mouth. Rewn had promised to await his help, yet the moment that Gralyre had become incapacitated Rewn had rushed to kill Hofar. If the Stewards suspected Rewn, then the rest of their plan was a tangled mess, as witnessed by the fact that they now had only until the end of day to deal with Strier before he came for Little Wolf. Gralyre silently cursed Rewn for his impulsiveness but was unable to castigate him for it, not within range of Dajin's ears.

Rewn began the story of how he had been made a Huntsman, neatly omitting the culmination of the day's activities, yet Gralyre could clearly see that his friend was bursting to share the entire tale. While Rewn spoke, the burbling pot over the fire drew both Gralyre and Little Wolf.

Gralyre retired to a stump to sup upon the thin venison stew, and as Rewn's story wound down, Gralyre searched for a more innocuous topic. "How long did I sleep?"

"Through two nights, and half o' today. 'Tis almost noon."

Gralyre scrubbed his and Little Wolf's plates clean in the snow, and set them onto his vacated stump. His serious gaze met Rewn's, and he gave a slight tilt of his chin to indicate that they should talk privately. "I must seek the gate, and smooth the waters with Steward Strier," Gralyre announced for Dajin's benefit.

Rewn nodded back in understanding. "I will go with ye. Mayhap we can convince him t' spare Little Wolf's life. Ye and he are the best hunters I have ever seen. They would be lucky t' have ye!" He glanced casually over his shoulder to see if Dajin listened. His brother was still too near for the discussion that he really wanted to engage in. "If nothing else, I can collect the measure o' grain due t' me for the work I have already done."

Dajin abandoned his axe, came around the woodpile, and dropped onto a stump next to his brother. "Are ye sure ye want t' do that? After what just happened?"

Rewn shrugged. "I am sure that they were just upset o'er the death o' their friend. 'Tis better no' t' let these things fester, but t' address them head on. We do no' want t' give the impression that we have anything t' hide," he spoke the ironic words with complete sincerity. "I am sure when the Stewards see what Little Wolf can do, they will grant clemency."

"I will come with ye," Dajin announced with a frown.

"No!" Gralyre and Rewn spoke together.

Dajin's face clouded over in sullen anger. "Fine."

Rewn gripped his brother's arm, as he would have arisen and stalked away, holding him in his seat. "If something happens t' us, who then will look after the women?"

Dajin's face relaxed fractionally, as Rewn continued to reason with him. "I do no' trust what I have seen so far o' these people, and ye are right t' fear the Stewards. I worry about the fate o' Dara and Saliana if we are no' here t' protect them. I need ye clear o' this business so that ye can watch o'er them, Dajin."

Dajin liked the protective picture that Rewn painted of him, and relaxed, signaling his compliance to Rewn's wishes. "All right, just be careful." Besides, if Rewn had already run afoul of the Stewards, Dajin had no intention of drawing similar notice. He liked it here too much to risk his place among the Rebels. Whatever his brother had stupidly gotten himself involved with, probably at the behest of the traitor in their midst, mayhap Matik could help?

Dajin glared at Gralyre and Rewn's backs as they left, for despite his self-serving reasoning, the bite of envy over his brother's preference for the company of a spy, still hurt deeply. In a fit of rage, he threw a stick of wood at the fire and knocked the stew pot over, spilling the last of their food into the coals, and sending up a thick plume of steam and ash.

ഇരു

As they walked towards the south gate with Little Wolf at their heels, Rewn bragged of the details of Hofar's last moments, his face filled with righteous glee at the memory.

This facet of his friend's personality disturbed Gralyre. He had known Rewn as a companion and champion, a fighter, a son to Wil and brother to Dajin and Dara. It was not Rewn's capacity for violence that made Gralyre uneasy, it was the pleasure he was taking in the enactment of justice. He had never suspected Rewn's bloodlust.

Though Gralyre also had a savage need to avenge Dara, and
to put an end to the Stewards' oppression, he took no pleasure in
the executions, just in the knowledge that the scales of the Gods
of Fortune were balancing. Briefly he wondered if there was a
difference between him and Rewn at all? Perhaps it was nothing
more than semantics, for in the end, the Stewards would still be
dead, their crimes avenged.

"The timing could no' have been better. I know that I
promised t' await ye, but it had t' be then."

"It was not perfect if they suspect you," Gralyre chastised
grimly. "You have placed your life, your family's life, Little
Wolf's life, in jeopardy for your revenge."

"I was careful, I tell ye!" Rewn argued, frowning at Gralyre's
lack of enthusiasm. "We will convince Steward Strier t' let ye
keep Little Wolf."

Gralyre stopped walking, and turned Rewn roughly by the
shoulders to face him. His voice dropped to a murmur, but held
the dangerous thrust of a blade. "We will convince him of
nothing! We are going to the gatehouse to kill him! Do you
understand? Little Wolf's life is at stake, and my hand is
forced!"

Rewn's mouth dropped open. "But…but we will be
caught…!"

Gralyre stalked away with a grim, "I know," snarled back
over his shoulder.

Rewn hurried to catch up to Gralyre, and they made the rest
of the trip to the gate in frosty silence. After several attempts at

apologies, Rewn gave up, finally realizing that Gralyre was right. If the execution had been perfect, his name would never have come to Jarrod and Strier's attention. He was left praying to the Gods for the ability to fix the mess he had caused before it spilled over, and took the lives of everyone he held dear.

For once, the Rebels parted before them. Gralyre's grim face froze their bigoted remarks in their throats, and had them rethinking any lewd gestures, or other subtle insults.

When they arrived at the square opposite the south gate, Gralyre turned to Rewn. "Stay here."

"Do ye have a plan, or…" Rewn was left talking to air. Little Wolf sat beside him with a loud yawn, and they watched Gralyre stride away.

While Rewn waited across the square, Gralyre performed a quick reconnoiter of the gatehouse, pausing near the open door to shake an imaginary stone from his boot, and casually glancing through to find Strier sitting alone at a table, eating a meal the equivalent to a sennight of rations for three families.

Gralyre scanned the vicinity carefully, but no one seemed to be paying any mind. This might work after all. The Steward was not flush with friends dropping by for visits, and if anything, there was less traffic nearby, as warriors had no desire to be singled out for abuse. They were all avoiding the beefy Steward.

There would never be a better chance, and Gralyre had an inspiration of how the execution could be made to appear an accident. He returned to Rewn's side, and quickly outlined his plan. Rewn had but one stipulation. "I must be the one, Gralyre.

Dara is my sister!"

Gralyre assessed his friend for a long minute, finally ceding Rewn's right as Dara's brother. His mouth twisted, as he agreed against his better judgment. "Alright, but it must be quick, and quiet!"

Rewn and Gralyre walked boldly across the compound, and stepped through the door to the gatehouse, knocking politely on the threshold.

"What do ye want, lowland scum?" Strier snarled around a bite of venison, grunting and smacking, as he tore another large mouthful of meat off the haunch he was gnawing upon. He glared at Gralyre through folds of fleshy cheek while his open mouth worked to masticate the massive chunk. Succulent juices ran off his chin, and dripped onto his jerkin. Uncaringly, Strier brushed at the drops, smearing the stains deeper into the fabric of his homespun shirt, and adding the grease from his fingers for good measure.

"Sorry to disturb your dinner, sir, but I was told to bring you my pet," Gralyre announced smoothly, as he stepped inside. Rewn loitered at the door, arms crossed, while Gralyre walked calmly across the small room towards the Steward. On cue, Little Wolf stalked stiffly into the small hut, and Rewn quietly shut the door, and drew the bolt, locking out any eyes that might bear witness.

Strier choked, and spat his half chewed meat onto the floor. He leapt to his feet, stumbled back, and overturned his chair. "What is that, then?" Strier bellowed, pointing.

With careful enunciation and condescension, Gralyre spoke as though to an idiot child. "A dog."

"I know 'tis a gods-humping-dog! What is it doing here? I told ye t' bring me its head, no' the whole beast!"

Little Wolf growled, baring his long sharp teeth, as he snapped a threat at the Steward.

Gralyre folded his arms, and lowered his chin, as though thinking about it. "No. I like his head where it is."

Strier paled, and his hand fumbled his sword free from the belt that looped his hips beneath his massive belly. "That animal attacked me at the laundry!" he pointed with the quivering weapon. "'Tis a menace!"

Gralyre smiled challengingly. "If you want my dog's head, take it yourself... if you are not too much of a coward."

"I will kill 'em, and then ye!" Strier roared mindlessly, and charged towards Little Wolf with his sword swinging impressively.

Gralyre stepped to the side, and braced his feet, sweeping Strier's neck with a stiffened arm, as the man rushed past.

Strier crashed to his back, choking and coughing from the bruising chop to his throat. Gralyre easily kicked Strier's sword away from his loosened grasp.

Strier whimpered, and cradled his stinging hand, gawking up at the looming warriors. His mouth worked though no words emerged for he had lost his breath when he had hit the floor. Finally he managed a hoarse whisper. "Ye know what we did! I can tell ye know! What are ye going t' do t' me?" Like all bullies, when threatened by a superior force, he immediately revealed his true cowardice. Enormous tears began to leach from his eyes, lingering in folds of flesh. "Let me go! I will no' tell the others. I promise! It will be our little secret, all right?"

Rewn drew his sword, and set it to Strier's neck. All he could see in his mind's eye was this massive lout raping Dara. Outrage blurred his vision, and his arm quivered with the need to sheath his blade in the man's throat.

"Rewn," Gralyre reminded quietly. "Find your control. Not like this."

Rewn shook his head, as he fought his own instincts. "Tie his feet and hands then, and be done with it."

Sacks of grain were neatly stacked in the corner, hoarded food that was supposed to have been distributed to the starving people of South District. Pulling his knife, Gralyre slit the cord that bound the neck of one of the sacks, and tugged it free.

While Rewn kept Strier cowed with the threat of his sword at his throat, Gralyre roped Strier's feet securely, then his hands, pulling them taut above the Steward's head, and knotting the cord off against the heavy leg of the table. Throughout the operation he was grimly amused by the knowledge that the twine had come from Wil's farm, for the grain stacked in the corner was some of what had been used to buy their way into the resistance, saved from the fires, as they had fled the purge of Raindell.

When Gralyre had immobilized the Steward, Rewn tossed his sword aside, and knelt his full weight onto Strier's chest, pressing his heavy palms over the man's nose and mouth. As Strier reared and squirmed to gain air, the table started to bump and knock, so Gralyre stood on the Steward's hands, pinning him more securely for Rewn's attack.

"Ye will no get away with what ye did t' my sister!" Rewn hissed in the man's ear, as Strier's struggles grew weaker. He let up, just long enough for Strier to gasp a lungful of air, before resuming the pressure of his hands to suffocate him.

"Rewn this is taking too long. Finish him," Gralyre growled a reminder, disturbed that Rewn was torturing Strier instead of killing him cleanly. His eyes darted to the door, but so far the Gods of Fortune smiled upon them, and they remained undiscovered.

Rewn grimaced up at Gralyre, his face feverish with hate and pleasure. "Hand me a goodly chunk o' that meat," he ordered hoarsely.

Gralyre reached back to the table, retrieved a large portion of greasy venison from Strier's abandoned plate, and tossed it down to Rewn.

Still holding Strier's nose sealed, Rewn waited until the man's mouth gasped open for air. Before he could cry out, Rewn stuffed it full with a handful of meat. Strier began to struggle and chew, unable to draw breath between Rewn's suffocating knee on his chest, and the hand that blocked his nose. It was over within a few minutes.

Rewn stood and spat on Strier's blue-faced corpse, smiling at the poetic justice of using the man's excesses to smother him.

Food overflowed Strier's mouth, mixed with bloody spume, and his eyes bulged with horror in a flaccid face slick with cooling sweat.

Gralyre quickly unbound Strier's hands and feet, and replaced the purloined cords around the sacks of grain. Glancing around the room, he retrieved Strier's sword and sheathed it at the side of the cooling corpse, then handed Rewn back his own discarded blade. The death had to appear to have been an accident. They could leave no trace of their presence behind.

Rewn was quivering and panting heavily in reaction when he knelt back down, and placed Strier's enormous pudgy hands to his neck, as though the Steward had been choking upon his mouthful when he had died. Rewn looked up at Gralyre. "Did we miss anything?"

Gralyre shook his head and walked to the door. "We still have to get out of here without being seen. Damn the Gods, this was ill advised, Rewn. Get ready to fight."

Rewn shrugged, excitement animating his face, and making him look more like Dajin than Gralyre had ever seen, as he joined Gralyre at the door. "I care no'. Only one is left. What can he possibly do t' us afore we finish him?"

Gralyre gripped Rewn's arms, concerned by his flippancy. "They are not the only Stewards, nor the only Rebels. If they discover we have killed two of their own, they will seek our heads. Get ahold of yourself! Think man!"

Rewn shut his eyes, breathing deeply, and slowly, until his agitation eased. Finally he nodded to Gralyre. "I am good."

"Alright. 'Tis time to establish our alibi. Act normal." Gralyre grabbed a spear from a bundle stacked in the corner, motioning to Rewn to precede him from the gatehouse, while Little Wolf exited on his heels, unruffled by the drama of death he had witnessed.

"Thank-ye Strier," Gralyre called jovially back over his shoulder, as he was shutting the door. "I will no' let ye down!"

To the bored guards at the gate, Gralyre introduced himself as a new Huntsman. Rewn at his side, already known to the gatekeepers, corroborated Gralyre's claim.

One of the gatemen noted Gralyre's hands, empty but for the spear. "Strier did no' give ye your kit?"

Gralyre grinned. "He was too busy eating half a deer, and told me to get the rest from you."

The guardsman rolled his eyes at his mate, and they shared a look of disgust. "Fat, lazy turd," the man griped with a shake of his head. "Come on then."

Gralyre was soon the proud owner of a new spear, bow, rope, net and quiver of arrows. As they walked away from the gate, he handed the gear to Rewn. "Take this back to the tent, and stay there with Little Wolf. Do nothing until we know we are clear of this mess."

"What are ye going t' do?"

"The Sorceress will be expecting me. We keep our normal routines, and pray to the Gods that no one suspects us."

80G3

Matik left the gatehouse, and was met by the surviving South District Steward, Jarrod, who dogged his steps towards the waiting death cart. "Thank-ye for taking a look, General Matik, sir. 'Tis too suspicious, do ye no' think, what with Strier kicking it so soon after Hofar? It was just as I suspected, 'twas murder, was it no'?"

Matik halted and placed a commiserating hand upon Jarrod's shoulder, bearing to touch the man in the interest of consoling him over the loss of a comrade. "Be at ease, Jarrod. I see no murder here. Strier choked upon his meal. He was trying t' reach help but collapsed afore he made it t' the door."

Jarrod peered around Matik, through the open gatehouse doorway at the large body lying on the dirt floor with a rug tossed over him. "Choked?" Jarrod had discovered the body himself. Interrogation of the gatemen had been of no use, as the guards had not noted who had been seen with Strier last, nor when they had last seen the Steward alive.

Matik stepped back, seeking fresher air. "His mouth and throat were packed with meat. Judging from the size o' the meal, and o' the man, he liked t' eat. Ye had seen him take larger than normal bites o' food?" Matik frowned as he mentally compared the bulk of the dead Steward to the starved, hollow-cheeked faces of the men and women of the South District. 'Twould seem past time to have the Quartermistress audit the districts for abuses of power. It was understood that there were certain leniencies granted to those with responsibility, but not to the point of flaunting their excesses. That was a fast way to sow dissent in the ranks.

Jarrod shrugged and nodded. Strier had been a glutton. There was no denying the fact. "But do ye no' think 'tis suspicious, General Matik?"

"Eh?"

Jarrod's mouth worked. "First Hofar, now Strier. It canno' be coincidence."

"Why do ye think that? What else could it be? Is there a reason that someone would be seeking their deaths? Did Hofar or Strier have enemies?"

Jarrod could say nothing or implicate himself in the villainy that the Stewards had all shared in. "No more than is normal when ye are a Steward," he replied cagily.

Matik shrugged. "There it is, then." He nodded to the men that were standing by, and watched solemnly, as they entered the gatehouse, and carried Strier's body out. Grunting mightily under the weight, it took five strong men to heave Strier onto the cart for his final journey to the pyres in the forest.

Jarrod watched as well, and icy ropes of dread drew taut about his black soul. It looked like an accident, but he sensed danger circling like wolves around a wounded stag.

Hofar and Strier had been murdered! He was certain of it! 'Twas impossible to choose a culprit from among the many inhabitants of South District who had legitimate grievances against the Stewards. All Jarrod knew for certain was they would be coming for him next.

"Gralyre, m'lady," the sentry announced, as he stuck his head around the lifted tent flap.

Catrian waved a hand, "Thank-ye, Eavan, that will be all."

The sentry nodded, and his head disappeared.

Catrian stood from the table, smoothed the folds of her shirt, and tucked a loose strand of hair behind her ear. Clasping her hands in front of her, she strove for serenity, and then wondered why she had even bothered to try.

Gralyre entered the tent, and filled it to overflowing with his presence; his height, his strength, his grace as he moved, and an indefinable something, a raw animal power that reached out and wrapped around her, whispering an insidious lure. Midday sunlight haloed him, sparking blue highlights from his black hair, until he stepped forward out of the brightness, and she could clearly see his face; strong, intelligent and smiling.

"Good morning, Sorceress." His deep voice caressed the title like an endearment.

Catrian's heart stuttered, then started to beat again at a much faster pace, and she was immediately wroth with herself, as a blush heated her cheeks. Guilt pierced her, and she fought the urge to return his smile, for she had no right to feel pleasure at the sight of him. "Sit," she ordered briskly, and stepped back to keep a distance between them as he took a place at the table.

She strove for detachment, as she walked to her books. One day she might have to kill this man, and she swore by the lives of all the people she protected that she would not hesitate to strike. Catrian drew a heavy tome from her shelf, and thumped it onto the tabletop in front of Gralyre, raising dusty motes to dance in the sunbeam shining down through the smoke hole at the peak of the tent.

"What is this?" Gralyre reached out, and caressed the faded gold embossing on the leather cover, his face entranced. The heavy tome was easily a foot in length, and half that in breadth, with at least a thousand leaves between the boards.

Catrian flipped the cover open, and revealed a tight, handwritten scrawl on the first page. "Can ye read it?"

Gralyre recited dutifully, "Aegon's History of Magics in the Kingdom of Lyre." He smiled with pride, for there had been a time when he had been unable to recall how to read. It had not been until Wil had read the note Gralyre had awoken with in the forest, the letter from a long dead king to his son, that the spell had been broken and the ability released.

"Good. 'Tis a rare gift!" Catrian praised. Once again she was left pondering the mystery of his past, wondering where he had learned the skill. Would she ever unravel the mystery of him?

"This is a primer o' Sorcery that Boris found for me many years ago. Before that, I had power, like ye, but I had no control. This book taught me what magic actually was, and how t' wield it with precision and finesse."

"Finesse?"

She rounded the table, and took the chair opposite Gralyre's. "Yes. There is always more than one path t' reach your goal, but some will expend more effort than others. Consider the strength it would take t' shatter a tree, but even a child can eventually cut the tree down by swinging an axe."

Gralyre nodded. "I think I understand."

"Learning t' wield Magic, is all about learning t' conserve your strength, and t' discern the easy path from the hard. Finesse."

"Why do we need to conserve our strength? Would not a hard blow be faster and easier?"

Catrian pressed her palms against her chest, and patted as she explained, "Magic is energy that comes from within in order t' effect the world without." She made fists, extending her arms across the table for Gralyre to observe the deep, red glow that began to leak from within her clenched fingers. "This energy is present within every creature, for it is the Godsmagic, the energy gifted to every life. It beats our hearts, fills our lungs, and fires our flesh. Ye do no' need t' tell your heart t' beat, for the Godsmagic compels it t' do so, all on its own."

Gralyre nodded his understanding of the concept.

Catrian's face animated, as she taught Gralyre this fundamental lesson in the nature of magic, her grey-green eyes lively, as she forgot that she was to keep separate from him, and instead became enmeshed within her enthusiasm to share her knowledge. The glow from her fists increased intensity, until she appeared to be holding stars trapped within her hands. "Ye are one o' a special, blessed few, who have more Godsmagic than other folk, more than what is needed to keep your flesh alive, and so are able t' use your energies to affect the world around ye." She opened her fists, and twin, dancing flames hovered above her palms. "But therein lies a danger, for if ye were t' spend all o' your Godsmagic at once," the flames roared high, dancing and undulating above the table, and Gralyre leaned away in instinctive reaction, "ye would be left with no way t' keep your heart beating, and your lungs filling, and ye would die." She clenched her fists, and the flames snuffed.

Gralyre blinked his eyes to clear the aftermath of the dark spots left from the bright flare of light. "That is why Sorcerers use Wizard Stones, is it not?"

Catrian nodded. "But that is a lesson for another time. I will no' teach ye anything more until ye have read this book, and have a basis for understanding."

Gralyre grimaced, and his enthusiasm to learn waned, as he leafed through the tome, skimming the small, tightly packed scrawl that adorned page after page.

Catrian could not help the smile that curved her lips this time when she recognized his reaction to the dry text. "Ye may come every morning, as ye wish, t' study the book, but for now I do no' wish ye t' use your magic beyond connecting t' the minds o' animals, which ye are already quite good at. No' until ye fully understand the consequences o' what ye affect, and how the magic can affect ye. 'Tis too dangerous for ye at this stage."

He smiled faintly, his gaze direct and intimate with remembrance. "I always wondered...I have never been able to connect to the minds of people, as I have animals. Except for you."

Catrian's face heated, and she tried to speak neutrally of it, to negate the impact that the shared memory of their passion in the cavern had upon her heart rate. "'Tis more complicated t' enter the minds o' people because, as humans, we have natural barriers, a stubbornness born o' sentience, if ye will. Ye can overcome it with enough power, and force your way in, or ye can use a whisper, and the defenses will never know ye are there, but there is always resistance if the subject is no' willing."

Gralyre frowned, for he had experienced the power of a forced entry from the Demon Lord Mallach when held captive in the Raindell Tithe Wagon on his way to Doaphin's Towers. For a moment the memory caught at him.

'I know who you are!'

Those five words were burned into his memory, words the Demon Lord had spoken while Gralyre had retched and quivered from the brutal assault upon his psyche. It took an effort to release the dark memory, and return to the present, to see his hands resting upon a book, and not clenched around the bars of a cage.

Seeking a lightness he did not feel, he sighed dramatically, and his cheeks creased ruefully, as he met Catrian's smile. "How long did it take you to read this?"

Catrian laughed saucily, and pushed away from the table. "Two years, but in my defense, first I had t' learn how t' read!" She was still chuckling, as she abandoned him in her tent.

ഏറര

Within hours of Strier's passing, Jarrod knew that his reign was over. He stood with arms folded, and his back to his tent, surveying his crumbling tin kingdom, frantically scanning the passersby for someone he could subdue and subjugate - a perfect victim. An example had to be made to bring South District back under his control.

He left his tent behind to walk the avenues, noting that the whole district had a leashed air of festivity, as the foundation of oppression crumbled away. People wore smiles and greeted each other cheerily, where before they had turned their eyes to the ground, and kept their conversations furtively short for fear that their neighbours would betray them for an extra crust of bread.

Jarrod was the only one mourning the deaths of Hofar and Strier, not because they had been friends, for Jarrod called no man friend, but because with their passing his power had begun to evaporate like mist in sunlight. Where before there had been tears and pleas, he was now ignored or greeted with jeers. He no longer had the capacity to injure these people, they knew it, and he knew it, and as one person defied his will, thirty more saw, and threw down their shackles.

He had to show them all that he was still to be feared. He needed a victim, and what he would do to them would cause grown men nightmares for the rest of their lives. When he was done, he would see how many were brave enough to defy him!

As though the Gods of Fortune had answered his prayers,

there she was.

She strode jauntily across the compound with another woman, and he tracked her progress, as the two paused outside the medical tent. As her companion entered, she remained outside, her face tilted upwards with a light smile to catch the sunlight, and her eyes closed in contentment. She acted as though she had not a care in the world.

A slow smile flattened out his lips, and pulled taut the filthy pockmarks of his face.

ಬಂಡ

Dara walked beside Saliana, showing her where the medical tents for South District were located. It was a place she knew well, often visited to receive treatment for the bruises and cuts she had suffered. At least today, no injury brought her to this doorstep.

Saliana smiled at her, a quick, shy grin, before she ducked her chin, and addressed the icy glitter of sunlight reflecting from the snowy ground. "Thank-ye for showing me the way, Dara. I have always wanted t' learn t' be a healer. Mayhap they will accept me as an apprentice?"

Dara gave Saliana a quick hug. "Ye will never know until ye ask them! Go on! They would be fools t' turn ye away!"

Saliana blushed at Dara's encouragement, and yet her hand trembled when she drew back the canvas flap, and she hesitated at the threshold. "Ye will no' come with me?" she asked with a thick quaver in her voice, peering ahead with uncertainty at the darker interior in front of her.

Dara grimaced behind Saliana's back. "No, this is something ye should do on your own. I will await ye, right here! Go on now!" She urged. Truthfully, she could not stand the thought of visiting the hospital again. They had seen her too many times, and patiently listened to her clumsy lies of accidents with pitying looks. Her pride could not bear it. Dara would never voluntarily step into that tent again.

So Dara watched, as her timid friend walked bravely into the unknown, then turned her face upwards to accept the bright sunlight, shut her eyes, and sought a place of peace that would supplant the memories of pain and injury that were thundering through her mind. A pleasing thought was easily found; two were dead, and would never touch her again. Her shoulders relaxed, and she sent a thank-you winging towards the Gods that had seen fit, for once, to punish the wicked instead of the innocent.

Dara did not hear his soft-footed approach.

"Hello, whore!" Jarrod hissed in her ear, as he seized her by the hair. The filthy paw he slapped over her mouth smothered her cry of alarm. Easily lifting her slender weight against his chest, he dragged her struggling form across the square, back down the lane, and into the dark, stale recesses of his tent. He met every eye that saw them, and gloried in his resurgence of power, as the people all turned away in shamed fear.

Inside his tent, she continued to struggle, and he cursed as she bit at his hand. Anger flared to uncontrollable heights within his fetid soul, for she would never have dared to fight so if Hofar and Strier had been present. To punish her defiance, he swung her around, and punched her in the face.

With a soft cry, Dara fell to the dirt floor, and feebly shook her head, trying to maintain consciousness, as she began to crawl on her belly towards the exit. "Help! Help me!" she screamed.

Jarrod pulled his knife, and knelt, straddling her hips, dragging her against his chest by her single fat braid, and forcing her spine into a painful arch. He brought the tip of his blade to a point just under her right eye, and grinned as Dara froze, her terrified gaze fixed upon the knifepoint, taking shallow pants of air, and trying not to move lest he cut her.

Her fear made his body swell with pleasure. The blow he had dealt had split the skin at her temple, causing a bead of blood to roll down her cheek. It was just the start of the indulgences to come. Loosing a carnal moan, Jarrod leaned forward, and licked his tongue up her face, relishing the taste of her blood and terror. As he took a moment to savour his absolute victory, he shifted so he could whisper in her ear. "Did ye miss me, Dara?"

He sniggered at her helpless shudder of revulsion, and could not stop his lower body from grinding convulsively against her buttocks.

෧෬

Saliana entered the darkened interior of the hospital, walking forward with apprehension dragging at her footsteps before pausing to let her eyes adjust to the dimmer interior. The medical pavilion was three times the size of the tent she shared with the Wilsons and Gralyre, to accommodate the rows of cots marching six to a wall. A heavy curtain, behind which a pleasant voice hummed a song to the accompaniment of clanging pots, isolated the rear of the tent.

Small, wooden cupboards separated each cot, holding a small basin, an unlit lamp, and rolled bandages. The cots were made up with clean linens, ready for patients, though they were all currently unoccupied.

Saliana's insecurity reasserted itself, and she swallowed heavily, seeking some small kernel of bravery. "H-hello?" she stuttered in a whisper, and her disquiet increased until she began to quiver. Yet some vestigial stubbornness kept her rooted, and she managed to call out with more volume. "Hello?"

With a heavy rustle, an older woman with a kindly face stepped through the curtain. Her gown was neat and tidy, and a crisp white apron covered her from shoulders to feet, upon which she was currently drying suds from off her hands. "Hello dearie," she sang out with a smile. "What seems t' be amiss?" Her grey hair was tied neatly into a bun, and her sharp black eyes were running over Saliana's quaking form, searching for clues to her distress.

Saliana froze, as the words she wanted vanished from her vocabulary. She licked her dry lips, and wavered in her intentions. This was a laughable idea! The healer would have no use for her! "Nothing! I am sorry!" she blurted and fled back outside.

Strangely, Dara was not waiting for her as she had promised, though Saliana was glad she was not present to witness her mortifying defeat. Still, Saliana had only spent a moment within the tent, but perhaps Dara had thought it would take longer, and had returned home?

Saliana started walking slowly towards the family tent, her head hanging despondently, as she berated herself for cowardice. What would she tell Dara? Humiliation seeped through her at the way she had failed.

Dara was not outside the family tent when she arrived, so Saliana drew a breath for courage, and slipped within. But only Rewn was present, rifling through the stores in the back of the tent for food with which to start the evening meal.

"Where is Dara?" Saliana blurted.

Rewn looked around in surprise. "Hello Saliana. She was with ye, was she no'?"

Saliana shook her head slowly, as the first fingers of unease supplanted her shame. "We stopped at the healer's tent, so that I could ask them about becoming an apprentice, and Dara said that she would await me in the lane outside, but when I returned she was no' there. I thought that she had come home."

Rewn dropped the lid of the wooden bin with a bang, as apprehension began to stutter to life. "She is no' here. Where else could she be? The laundry?"

Saliana was shaking her head. "No' today. 'Tis done. Dara

promised t' wait for me. She would no' have left!" Her hands came to hover over her mouth, as she whispered, "Do ye think something has happened t' her?"

Rewn paled, plucked his sword from the corner where he had left the weaponry upon his return from the gatehouse, and quickly strapped it around his lean hips. "Stay here," he ordered as he left.

Rewn debated collecting Gralyre from the Sorceress' pavilion, mindful of his promise to stay near the tent for the rest of the day, but feared the Rebel leader discovering their secret if she read his thoughts. And as usual, Dajin was nowhere to be found, having stormed away when Rewn had told him that Gralyre was to be a Huntsman.

Such a sense of urgency nipped his heels that Rewn decided to proceed immediately to the medical tent. The healer assured him that she had not seen Dara, after which Rewn spent frantic moments in the lane outside searching for a witness to what had become of his sister.

No one would speak to him, and no one would meet his eyes, so that Rewn's fear increased with every encounter. Their avoidance was as obvious as their pity. Even the usual insults flung at him for being a lowlander were absent.

"Please, have ye seen my sister? Anyone? Please help me!" he roared his frustration at the passersby. "Just tell me what ye saw! Talk t' me!" he begged as Rebel after Rebel ignored him, ducked down side streets, or walked a wide path around where he stood in the lane.

At last, a woman approached carrying a basket loaded with kindling. Three small children hid within the folds of her skirts, and peered shyly out at Rewn while they scuttled along to keep pace with their mother. As she passed she hissed quietly from the corner of her mouth, "He took her."

Rewn's blood drained to his feet, and he staggered from the horror of the terrible truth.

'He took her! Jarrod took her!'

His worst nightmare realized, Rewn sprinted for the avenue that would take him to Jarrod's tent, praying that the woman was mistaken, praying that he was not too late if she had told him true.

As Rewn raced towards Jarrod's tent, people lingering in the avenue scattered at his approach, until an eerie pocket of silence surrounded him. There would be no help from that quarter, but the whimpers emerging from the tent when he arrived shattered any thoughts of caution he might have entertained. The scene before him when he thrust aside the canvas flap ripped a howl of pain from Rewn's throat, and he launched across the small space.

Jarrod was crouched over Dara, his knife to her throat, taunting her with it, drawing small beads of blood as he pricked her skin over and over. She hardly seemed conscious of his threats or actions, with her eyes swollen almost shut, and her face battered beyond recognition. So engrossed was he in fulfilling his twisted pleasures, Jarrod was unaware of Rewn's presence, until the hard grip in his hair twisted him to his feet.

Jarrod's sweaty hand lost its grip on the knife, even as his loosened britches dropped to his ankles, tripping him up, so that he was utterly unprepared to block the hard fist that pounded into his chin. The first blow made him sag, unable to stop the following strikes that came in rapid succession.

Dara lay where she was, too injured to move, while tears of fear and shame flowed unchecked down her battered face. Weakly, her hands trembling, she did her best to hold her torn dress together while the men fought. She only caught flashes of the fight through flutters of her bruised and swollen eyelids, but even so, the murderous rage that twisted Rewn's features, as he hammered his fists into Jarrod, made him seem a stranger. She had never seen her gentle brother wear such an expression, and mourned that she was the cause of it.

Dara felt no triumph as she watched Jarrod collapse at Rewn's feet, only a shot of protective fear as Rewn leapt upon the downed man, and his fists continued to drive home. If he killed Jarrod, his own life would be forfeit. The Rebels would never suffer such an act from a lowlander! Terror for Rewn gave her a surge of strength. "Rewn! Stop!" she screamed over and over, trying to break through the animal rage to the reason beneath.

It seemed Rewn would ignore her, before gradually the madness faded from his eyes. Confused, he squinted at Dara, blinking sweat and tears out of his eyes, as his chest heaved with his panting breaths. His blows slowed, and finally stopped with a fist hovering mid-air, quivering with the need to find its target once more.

Dara sobbed thankfully, "Ye must stop! If ye kill him, they will kill ye!"

Rewn grimaced as prudence overtook rage. From his knees, straddled over Jarrod's chest, he doubled his fists into the Steward's filthy tunic, and lifted the man's shoulders until they were face-to-face. The rotting, dirty fabric began to tear away, as he brought the shorter man up to eye level. He leaned in to the barely conscious Jarrod, and whispered three words of promise in his ear. "Ye are next!" Rewn heaved the slighter man to the floor, and stumbled up to his feet.

Breathing heavily from his exertions, Rewn scooped up his trembling sister, and carried her from the fetid tent. "I promise ye, he will never touch ye again," he vowed softly as they stepped into the brightness of the sun.

೫ೢಐ

Thankful for the cool darkness that hid the worst of her injuries, Dara lay upon her pallet within the family tent, humiliation pooling like oil in her soul. Rewn knew what the Stewards had done. How was she to bear it? Deep racking sobs shook her body, and tears burned into the cuts and abrasions within the bruises that swelled her face.

Saliana made soothing sounds while she wrapped snow in a soft cloth, and set it to the swelling on Dara's face. Dara winced through her tears, but allowed the coolness to assuage the pain.

Rewn sat at Dara's other side, holding her hand, gently rubbing it, though he still trembled with a violence that had yet to abate. "Everything will be all right now, Dara. They canno' hurt ye ever again." He smoothed back her hair, and tried on a weak smile of encouragement.

Dara believed him, yet shame set her to searching for any sign of disgust within her brother's face. Seeing nothing but love and compassion, she still needed to defend what had happened, for she could not bear him to view her with revulsion. Having held the horror of her secret for too long, her confession tumbled forth in disjointed, rapid-fire sentences between gasping sobs. "They... *uh... uh...* would no' give me an allotment o' food! They said I was a useless lowlander... and did no' deserve their sanctuary! They made me..." Tears spilled unchecked down her cheeks, unnoticed to her now as she stared at the inner horror of memory. "...they made me... *work...* for food!"

Saliana gasped. "Oh, no! Oh Dara, I am so sorry!"

"'Tis all right Dara, I know. I know what they did t' ye. Ye are safe now." Rewn reassured gently, though his voice quivered with his suppressed rage, and his face contorted with a flash of intense pain before he regained control, and smoothed it back into caring lines for Dara's benefit.

"I had t', ye see?" she cried beseechingly to her brother. "I had no one t' protect me," she wailed forlornly, "and I was so very hungry, and it was so cold."

Rewn's quiet promise reached her, and calmed her sobs. "Shh, be at ease, Dara. They will no' touch ye again. No' ever!"

And Dara's breath caught as she realized the truth about the nature of the accidents that had befallen the Stewards. "Oh no, Rewn, ye did no'! If ye are suspected...! If they catch ye...!"

Rewn leaned forward and brushed a gentle kiss across her brow, though even that light touch of compassion wrung a small whimper of pain from Dara's throat. "Hush now. Do no' worry about this. Rest. All will be well."

When Dara's eyes fluttered shut, Rewn touched Saliana's shoulder, thankful beyond reason that she had warned him in time to save his sister, and drew her with him towards the exit. "Saliana! Thank-ye!" He embraced her with warm gratitude, talking quietly in her ear so as to not disturb Dara. "Take care o' her," he beseeched as he released her. "I need t' find Gralyre. We need t' end this."

Saliana nodded in response, reeling from the unaccustomed touch when Rewn left her. Her deep blush was hidden in the dimness of the tent, as her heart filled with pride and adoration for the man who placed the life of his sister above that of his own.

৪৩ও৪

"General Matik, sir?" Dajin hovered at the entrance to Matik's tent, awaiting permission to enter. The light was fading from the sky to make way for the early dark of deep winter. After pacing the camp for hours debating what he should do, Dajin had finally decided that he had an obligation to his brother, and to the resistance, to approach Matik about his concerns, especially after the incident that morning involving the Stewards.

"Can this wait for the morrow on the practice field?" Matik sat in a hard-backed chair set before his brazier, honing his axe with careful sweeps of a whetstone within the last of the light from the smoke hole in the tent's peak.

The one room of the tent was sparse of comforts. The chair that Matik sat in had a companion, and a narrow cot occupied the other side of the space. Together with the storage bins and the bare dirt floor, Matik's quarters bespoke a man unconcerned with appearances or luxuries.

Dajin's hand tightened against the canvas of the tent flap. "'Tis somewhat urgent…"

Matik grunted. "All right, come in, boy. State your piece, I was just about t' seek my supper."

Dajin strode forward, and stood clasping and unclasping his hands. "Ye said that I should let ye know if Gralyre does anything? Well I think that he is leading my brother into danger. The South District Stewards visited us this morn, and accused Rewn o' killing Steward Hofar. Then they demanded that Gralyre bring his dog t' Steward Strier, to be destroyed, only when Gralyre and Rewn returned, Gralyre still had his pet, and Steward Strier had made him a Huntsman."

Matik abruptly stopped the rhythmic scraping of his blade and glanced up, paying full attention to Dajin now. "He visited Strier today, and was made a Huntsman?"

Dajin nodded.

Matik patted down his beard, his eyes sharp and suspicious, as he considered this knowledge in light of the concerns that Steward Jarrod had voiced regarding the coincidental natures of the deaths of his fellow two Stewards. "Steward Strier was found dead. He apparently choked upon his dinner."

Dajin puffed up his chest, content with the knowledge that he had done the right thing in coming to Matik. "'Twas him. Gralyre. I just know it!"

"Ye have proof?"

Dajin frowned slightly, as his enthusiasm deflated. "No," he admitted testily. "But I feel it t' my bones t' be true."

Matik patted his beard again. "Thank-ye for bringing this matter t' my attention. Good lad!" he praised.

Dajin preened at the approval.

Matik gave him a nod. "Best ye get back afore they miss ye. Keep your ears and eyes open for aught else."

Matik watched as Dajin Wilson left his tent, before thoughtfully setting his axe down beside his chair, and tucking away his whetstone. He was well aware of Dajin's prejudice towards Gralyre, but the lad's suspicions were not unfounded. Had Gralyre killed the Stewards? But no, their deaths had most certainly been accidents...had they not? No matter. Gralyre should never have been made a Huntsman. What was the spy up to? Why was he maneuvering to escape the confines of the fortress?

ഇറ

"What is it, what has happened?" Gralyre demanded as Rewn met him on the road returning from his afternoon of study in Catrian's tent. In the light of the setting sun, Rewn's agitation was plain to read upon his face.

"Dara…" Rewn choked out, as he grabbed Gralyre's arms, using his friend's strength to steady him.

"Wait!" Gralyre cautioned, and drew Rewn aside from the teeming avenue into a deserted side alley lined with stacks of firewood.

"Dara…!"

"Shh, quietly now."

Rewn's voice dropped to a harsh whisper, and he hung his head, unable to meet Gralyre's eyes. "Jarrod took her…tortured her. Thank the Gods, I arrived just in time t' save her!"

"Gods!" Gralyre burst out. Before he could ask after Dara's condition Rewn continued his ragged confession.

"Gralyre, I made a terrible mistake. I beat the man senseless. I could no' help myself. He knows now. He knows everything. He knows I killed the others!"

Gralyre stiffened, as fear for Rewn and his family slammed into him. "Rewn…!"

"I know, do ye think I do no' know? I forgot everything. He cut her! He beat her! She is hurt so bad, Gralyre, he almost killed her! I have left her with Saliana, but what are we going t' do?"

Gralyre stilled, and his midnight-blue eyes iced over, ancient glaciers of destructive patience. "We finish this, tonight, before he can speak to anyone." He shook Rewn roughly. "Where is the Steward now?"

Rewn grimaced. "I left him unconscious in his tent."

Gralyre's eyes lost focus for a moment, as he connected to the thoughts of a raven, and sent it winging to the Steward's tent. It perched upon the peak of the pavilion, and looked down the smoke hole at the unmoving man.

"He is still unconscious. We have some time yet to plan. We need to fetch our weapons."

ഇൗ⚮

Jarrod awoke, cold and aching, upon the floor of his tent with no knowledge of how long he had been insensate. He choked and wheezed, as he shakily crawled to his pallet, and collapsed against the filthy bedding, where, overcome with self-pity, he blubbered uncontrollably into the sour mattress. How could he have been so stupid as to forget that Dara's large warrior brothers had arrived at the fortress? Without the protection of his two cronies, he was defenseless!

Rewn's words reverberated through his mind once more. *'Ye are next!'*

Jarrod moaned, as understanding ripped vicious teeth into his softened courage. Hofar and Strier had already paid the price for their attacks upon Dara. Now it was his turn. There would be no stay of execution!

But then rage slowly drew his lips back from his yellowed teeth, and Jarrod sat up, rubbing the snot from under his nose with the back of his hand.

He was still a Steward of South District! Rewn would rue the day he had attacked him, and killed the others! Jarrod had his pick of replacements for Hofar and Strier, men who would kill for the chance to be the next Stewards, and would if they wanted the job. Rewn's days were numbered! Jarrod had nothing to fear from the lowlander! He would handle this himself!

Jarrod knew that he could not go to the Commander with accusations of murder without implicating himself in his crimes. Besides, the sun was setting, and he was sore from the beating he had taken. He would await first light, collect some men he could buy with promises of becoming the next Stewards, and teach Dara's brother what it meant to cross him. He would skin the man in front of Dara's whore face, and rape her upon his cooling corpse!

Jarrod lost himself in the fantasy, as he crawled over his dirty bedding to the bins, and rooted around for a weapon. He returned to his pallet, and made himself comfortable facing the closed flap of his tent before loading his crossbow, readying to shoot any who dared enter uninvited.

He had only to survive the night.

੭੦੦੪

"Beaurice!" Matik hailed across the compound as he puffed

to catch up with the fast moving Quartermistress.

The homely woman turned, and snarled her smile at the General. "Sir?" Without looking she cuffed the two youngsters who were toting bundles for her, sending them scurrying onwards when they would have dawdled beside her.

Matik halted a prudent distance away, having run afoul before of her swinging hands and arms that punctuated her conversations. "Ye have been informed o' the deaths o' the South District Stewards?"

Beaurice bobbed her head, sending her braids to swinging, as her hands began their heavy gestures. "Two dead! It beggars the imagination!"

Matik nodded. "Strier choked on a meal that would have served ten rations to ten families, an accident surely, yet 'tis come t' my attention that there may be murder afoot. How closely do ye oversee the goings on o' the Stewards?"

Beaurice shrugged. "They report t' me upon the sennight for orders and rations for their districts, but I do no' interfere with their workings unless there is need."

Matik frowned. "I want ye t' audit them all. Could be nothing, or could be that they are taking too much advantage o' their positions, and the South District Stewards paid the price o' their neglect. As t' that, I want ye t' have a hand in choosing the new Stewards for South District. Se t' it."

Beaurice snarled her smile again. "Aye, sir." As she turned to go, Matik touched her arm to halt her, ducking and bobbing to avoid the swing of her arms as she pivoted back around.

"There is one more thing, o' a more delicate nature," he murmured quietly, mindful of the ears of the people passing by.

Beaurice sniffed through her large nose, and her eyes narrowed shrewdly, as she leaned forward to hear him.

"There is a man, a lowlander named Gralyre in South District, working as a Huntsman. I want him removed from duty immediately. His appointment should ne'er have happened. He is no' t' be allowed out o' the fortress. I need ye t' pass the word t' every gate, and t' every Steward."

"Is he a danger? Do ye think he murdered the Stewards?" She momentarily stilled. "Do ye want him killed?"

Matik rubbed thoughtful fingers through his beard. He was sorely tempted but Boris had other uses for the man, and had warned Matik against killing Gralyre. "No. Just keep him penned within the walls."

"Aye, sir! I will se t' it tonight!"

℠℣

Dajin stomped into the family tent with a less than gracious greeting. "Why is there no meal over the fire? And speaking o' the fire, who let it go out…" He stopped as he took in Rewn's ravaged face from where he huddled over the pallet containing a heavily wrapped figure. Standing throughout the tent were the other subdued gatherers, Gralyre, Saliana, Little Wolf…the only one missing was…

"Dara!"

He moved so quickly to reach his sister that he skidded on his knees when he dropped down by her side. "Uugh!" he yelped when he beheld Dara's beaten face. "Rewn! What happened t' her? Who would do such a thing?"

"Your precious Rebels." Rewn pressed yet another handful of snow into a rag, and gently laid it against Dara's puffy cheekbone. Even though unconscious she moaned from the pain of the light touch, and both brothers flinched.

"Rewn," Gralyre warned softly. "We have not much time."

Rewn glanced up at Gralyre, then over to Dajin. "Ye see what they are, what they do?" he accused.

Dajin's hands clenched into fists. "Who was it? I will kill them!" he vowed.

Rewn snorted derisively, and as he stood his sword scabbard swung within a breath of striking Dajin's face. "Ye will do nothing! Ye will stay here and protect the women. Gralyre and I will deal with this. If we do no' come back…"

"Rewn! Where are ye going? Who…?"

"If we do no' come back, try t' be the man Da always hoped ye would be!"

"Rewn…!"

But Rewn, Gralyre and Little Wolf had faded from the tent, leaving Dajin alone with Dara and Saliana. With no one else conscious to inform him of what had befallen Dara, he looked to the mousy woman who was not making eye contact.

"Tell me!" he ordered.

Saliana's lips were trembling, as she drew a ragged breath.

Being alone with Dajin was difficult at the best of times, never mind when he was as angry as he was now. "When Dara came to the fortress she was forced to…be…a…she had to…"

Dajin made a slashing motion with his arm, telling her to stop. Telling her he understood. "And who…" but he answered his own question before he finished it. "The Stewards!"

Saliana nodded her confirmation.

Dajin snarled, and flung himself up from where he had crouched at Dara's side. Once again, Rewn had cut Dajin out of the fight to hoard the glory for himself!

'Why do they not just come out with it, and call me Coward?'

Babysitting the women! The humiliation of it made his face flush red with rage.

And he could do nothing! If he went to Matik with this news, Rewn would be executed. It was all Gralyre's fault!

"D…Dajin?" Saliana stuttered. "Are ye alright?"

Dajin's lip curled into a sneer. As if she cared! Well, if he was to be the caregiver of this useless twitch, he might as well make the most of it. "Make me dinner, right now!"

Saliana's eyes widened with shock, but she was more than happy to escape the small tent for Dajin looked as though he was ready to start swinging his sword.

$$\wr\!\circlearrowright\!\wr$$

Jarrod jolted awake, and did not wait to discover who it was when the canvas tent flap rustled from someone's grip. Over the last hour, his imagination had run rampant, oscillating between his desire for revenge, and his dread of attack, until his injuries had overcome him. Startled awake Jarrod triggered his crossbow, and sent the bolt flying just as Beaurice, the Quartermistress, stepped inside.

"I said, are ye home…?" Beaurice took the shot in her chest, grunting and keening, as she staggered further into the tent, and collapsed to her knees.

Jarrod gulped. What had he done? There was no way out of this! Any number of a dozen people must have seen her enter his tent. When they found he had murdered the Quartermistress…!

Beaurice looked up, blood seeping from her mouth. "Ye bloody… bastard!" She coughed and a fine mist of red sprayed from her mouth.

"What are ye doing here? Why did ye have t' be the one!" Jarrod yelled, and launched himself onto the injured woman.

Despite being mortally wounded, Beaurice managed to grab Jarrod's arm before he could use his knife, warding it off. Her eyes were wide in panic, as she struggled to keep the last of her life.

Jarrod leaned his weight into the grip of the blade, slowly advancing it toward Beaurice's chest. Yet still she held him at bay. Who would have thought the old girl had so much fight in her? Jarrod released a hand, and grabbed the crossbow bolt imbedded in her chest, twisting it.

Even as Beaurice contorted with a pained scream, his knife in her throat choked the sound abruptly, and blood pumped out in a thick jet. He left his knife embedded, and lurched to his feet, watching, as she slowly collapsed and ceased to move.

He scrubbed a hand across his face to slough away the gore that had spattered on him, oddly calm for the first time that night. With this murder, his path was suddenly very clear. If he wanted to survive, he had to flee the fortress! Tonight!

Jarrod began to pack, throwing his few belongings, including all of his coin, most of it stolen from lowlander refuges, into a few sacks. The one satisfying thought in this debacle was that he no longer had to share the money with Strier and Hofar. It was all his; a treasure he could use to start a new life in the lowlands. With the wealth he had accumulated, he could live out his life like a Demon Lord, and hire guards for protection from his enemies!

He reloaded his crossbow, and sat a lonely vigil, fearful of every noise outside of his pavilion, and waited out the evening until the hour was late. Throughout the night, Beaurice's clouded eyes stared accusingly at him, a dark omen of justice to come.

In the quiet of midnight, long after his neighbors had retired, and the traffic upon the avenue had ceased, Jarrod shouldered his heavy sacks, and slunk from his tent. He paused at the threshold, listening, waiting, but nothing moved, his neighbours were asleep, and there was no one to witness his coward's retreat.

His pulse thundered in his ears, as he strained to see movement in the shadows, of a skulking presence or of a pending attack, but the darkness was absolute save for the sporadic glow from banked embers within firepits in front of row upon row of sleeping tents that he passed by in a stooping shuffle from the weight of his packs, and his injuries. Tonight there was no moonlight to aid his enemies, for heavy clouds hid the night sky.

Creeping from shadow to shadow, he made his way across South District to the horse paddocks, which were located in the stockyards to the east of the south gate. There he paused from a place of concealment, carefully watching for the telltale movements of would-be assassins.

If Jarrod were going to ambush a man, this would be where he would do it, far from sleeping Rebels who might startle awake, and respond to a cry for help. But nothing stirred, not even the horses that were dark shapes within their paddock, breathing softly as they rested.

Jarrod finally steeled himself to move, clicking softly to a horse to get its attention, as he approached the paddock. It nickered gently when it walked over to greet him, but shied as he grabbed its bridle. Jarrod jerked its head down, and placed a hand over its nostrils, keeping it as quiet as possible, as he walked it out of the paddock. He took a saddle from the shed, and it was but a moment's work to load up his sacks and mount.

A shadow detached itself from the darkness, and stepped forward to block his path, and Jarrod's heart stopped beating, as terror momentarily stole his wits.

"Who goes there?" A hurricane lantern was unshuttered, casting an unwelcome glow over the furtive scene.

In the time it took to regain control of his shaking limbs

Jarrod realized it was but the stableman. Still, his voice squeaked as he started to talk, and Jarrod was obliged to clear his throat and begin anew. "I am on important Steward's business! Get out o' my way, or I will run ye down!"

Not giving the man any choice, Jarrod spurred the horse forward, and the stableman had to dive from his path. For long tense moments, Jarrod feared the man would raise an alarm, but when naught was heard, he began to relax. After all, he still had power enough to bluff his way out of the fortress.

Keeping the horse to a trot was the hardest thing that he had ever done, but if he were to gallop madly through South District at this late hour of the night, he would do naught but call undue attention to his flight. Briefly he thought of leaving through the west gate or east gate to further obscure his trail, but knew that he had a better chance of remaining unchallenged within his own district, where he was still feared and could bully his way free. Upon the wallwalk, the dark shapes of men paced back and forth between cauldrons of fire, watching out into the darkness of the valley, and paying no attention to a lone horseman approaching the gates from within the fortress.

Jarrod reined in at the gate, as the two sentries stepped forward to bar his way. Hurricane lanterns were unshuttered, leaving the guardsmen in darkness while highlighting Jarrod with his many sacks, sitting upon the restless horse. "Halt! Who goes? Speak friend or die enemy!"

Jarrod lifted a hand to shield his night-darkened vision from the bright light. "Bugger ye! Open the gates for me, maggots. I have urgent Steward's business."

"At this time o' night?" One of the guards snorted incredulously. "Sod off!"

Jarrod's mouth tightened with frustrated rage, for this morning the guardsmen would never have dared speak to him thus but without Strier to enforce his will, he was the next thing to powerless.

"Hey Jarrod, looks like someone finally decided t' pretty up that ugly mug o' yours!" Chuckling and nudging each other, the two guards turned their backs to return to their posts.

If he could not cow them into compliance, Jarrod would have to bribe his way free.

The sound of jingling stopped the gatemen in their tracks. The tinkle of the coins hitting the hard packed snow, one after the other, turned them back. "Like he says," one guard said to the other, with a grin and a shrug. "Steward's business."

While one collected the fallen coins, the other guardsman lifted the heavy crossbar from place, and cracked one side of the gate open. He bowed mockingly, and indicated the open portal with a suave sweep of his arm.

With no further words spoken between them, Jarrod trotted his horse forward. The tension in his spine relaxed slightly with the sound of the gate slamming shut behind him, and the crossbar dropping with a heavy thud.

'I made it!'

Jubilation lifted his spirits, as he congratulated himself on his sly escape.

Though the night was moonless and dark, the snow was faintly luminescent. The blurry light was bright enough to follow the switchback trail cut into the slope of the mountainside. Jarrod fought the urge to kick the horse into a gallop, to place as much distance as possible between himself and the murder he had committed but he would get nowhere fast should the horse step in a rut and break a leg. Taking firm control of his flight, Jarrod allowed the horse's pace to settle to a quick walk that seemed torturously slow, as he wound his way down towards the tree line.

He could not help glancing behind at every turn of the switchback, to see if anyone had followed after him through the gates of the looming walls. The brothers of that little trollop, Dara, were the least of his worries now for they were safely back in the fortress. Should Beurice's body be discovered in his tent, riders would be sent to bring him back to face the noose.

The dead Quartermistress might remain undiscovered for a day or so, but Jarrod doubted that the Gods would grant him such a boon. He had to reach the far south pass before news of his crime could be flashed to the outpost using the mirror signals.

Breath steamed out in a thankful sigh when Jarrod entered the forest, and could no longer be seen by the men upon the fortress walls. Jarrod would reach the southern pass by mid-day if he did not stop to rest, and once through the outer checkpoint, it was into the wild, where no one would ever find him.

Triumph stiffened his spine as, mindful of the bruises that

pulled his torso, he straightened in his saddle, no longer adopting an instinctive cower in anticipation of an arrow in his back. No longer fearful of facing a noose, his thoughts turned to revenge, and the author of all his woes.

Dara's brother may have killed the others, but not him! One day, he would return and take his revenge, for he would never forget the beating he had suffered, nor the position of power he was being forced to abandon, all because of some lowland strumpet!

An owl's hoot echoed through the cathedral of trees and some small animal squealed a death cry. Jarrod, liking the omen, chortled quietly. The horse shifted and snorted at the noise, but continued to obediently plod along the trail. Over the next few hours, he spackled over all lingering cracks in his mettle with the plotting of revenge.

Aching from his beating, and exhausted by the night of fear driven flight, Jarrod shivered, and settled his thick fur nearer around his body, allowing the soft swoosh of the horse's steps in the deep snow to lull him. As the night elapsed towards dawn, his head sagged forward, and bobbed in time to the horse's gate.

ಬಿಂಞ

The horse bulked, stopping so suddenly that the dozing Jarrod almost went over its ears.

"What ill has gripped ye, nag? Get your arse moving!" He spurred the animal but not one more step forward would it take as it loosed a loud, long nicker.

Dread jolted him, as he noted an eerie silence gripping the forest, broken by naught but the constant low drone of the wind, as it creaked the trees, and clattered barren branches. Sinister vibrations prickled the root of every sparse hair on his head, as he peered into the darkened woods to either side, seeking whatever had spooked the horse. Was it wolves?

Jarrod heard a whimper, and realized with dismay that it had come from his own throat. Apprehension oozed from every pore, and he kicked the horse harder, beating it about the head with the reins.

The horse whinnied and danced from the pain he caused, but refused to take one step forward. Jarrod stilled with a gasp as three shadows detached themselves from the trees. He pulled his sword in challenge. "Who goes there? Name yourselves!"

They drew nearer, making no sound beyond the soft crunch of boots on ice, and Jarrod's uncertain courage shattered into icy shards when the dim luminescence of the night revealed the set features of Rewn and Gralyre.

"How! What…!" Jarrod sputtered. "Ye are no' here! I left ye behind! Ye canno' be here!" How had they guessed his route well enough to set an ambush?

Jarrod fumbled his sword, and cursed as it slipped from his fingers, vanishing into the deep snow beside his horse. It was too late to run but he tried anyway, sliding from the saddle, and floundering hysterically in the deep snow, as he left the beaten path to escape into the tangle of the woods.

The black wolf pounced in front of him, glinting teeth bared in an ugly snarl. Jarrod turned tail to flee back the way he had come, only to find his escape blocked by Rewn's glinting sword. He stumbled to a halt, cringing, as his eyes travelling between the wolf guarding his back, and the swordsman his front.

Gralyre spoke soothingly to the horse, examining the bloody marks left by Jarrod's cruel whipping. This was Rewn's battle to fight, as was his right as Dara's brother. Gralyre would not interfere beyond what he had already done, by tracking the Steward and halting the horse. He released the owl he had used from his service, allowing it to return to its nightly feeding.

"I will give ye more o' a chance than ye deserve," Rewn's words quivered with anguish. "More than what ye gave my sister!" He took a step back to make room, and kicked Jarrod's sword up out of the hole in the snow that it had made, sailing it towards him. "Ye may defend yourself!"

Jarrod's fear-chapped lips pulled back from his teeth in a snarl, as he snagged his blade from the air, adjusting his sweaty grip upon the hilt when the coldness of the winter night caused his wet palm to stick to the frosted metal. Blood rushed through his ears, and he knew he was drawing his last breaths of life, but here at least was a chance. If he killed Rewn and Gralyre both, he could still escape! Screaming his hatred, Jarrod attacked.

Rewn ducked his wild swing, and slashed Jarrod across the abdomen, his sword biting deeply into Jarrod's flesh before drawing away in a wicked spray of blood.

Jarrod's sword dropped away from his limp hand, and he

faltered, swaying for a moment before he sank to his knees in disbelief, clutching the cut on his stomach, as blood and steam welled between his fingers. He blinked heavily and gasped for air, as he watched the dark stain of his blood spread down across his thighs, and soak into the pristine snow, melting deep furrows of red. It was not as painful as he expected.

He glanced up in anticipation of the killing blow, only to see Rewn clean his sword with a rag before sheathing it. "What are ye doing?" Jarrod gasped, and then wailed, as the agony of his injury finally wore through his shock. "Ye canno' leave me like this! Finish it!" he panted when he could form words again.

Rewn's answer was a cold, hard smile of hatred. "If ye be lucky, ye will bleed t' death afore the wolves come!"

Images of being fed upon whilst he still lived, filled Jarrod with a horror he could not contain. "No!" he sobbed, holding up his bloodied hands in supplication. "Pity! Pity! Kill me! Kill me now!"

A predator to the core, Little Wolf padded towards the felled man, and paused to teeth red snow off the ground, glaring deeply into Jarrod's eyes while he licked his chops.

Jarrod screamed, and found that once he had started he could not stop. High pitched and hysterical, the cries echoed through the trees, but the only ones to hear did not care. He had become the mouse to their owl, he thought wildly.

In the near distance a wolf pack answered his wild screams with their eerie ululations, and Jarrod immediately choked off his cries, suppressing them to heavy panting moans of pain and fear.

Gralyre called Little Wolf to his side, as he gathered up the horse's reins, and walked it back up the trail towards the lights of the distant fortress. The wolfdog brushed past Jarrod, rocking his body, before melting into the darkness like a ghost.

"Please," Jarrod whispered one last time, as the men left him to die. Rewn glanced back once, as though to memorize the scene, and nodded at Jarrod with grim righteousness before turning away, and being swallowed by the trees.

As the silence and loneliness of the forest returned, Jarrod gasped and sobbed, trying to hold the slippery parts of his body from falling out into the snow. Throughout the remainder of the night, he had plenty of time to think on his crimes, but still, right to the last, as his blood loss and the icy air slowly put him to sleep, he regretted not a single atrocity he had committed. The wolf pack found him soon after.

∞≪

Rewn, Gralyre and Little Wolf entered through the south gate with a large stag slung over the rump of Jarrod's horse, ensuring that were no questions asked of their overnight absence, just cheers for a successful hunt.

After distributing the meat, Gralyre and Rewn parted ways, Rewn to return to Dara's sickbed, and Gralyre to continue his studies in Magic. They had stashed Jarrod's ill-gotten sacks of gold in the rocks at the base of the mountain. Being seen with the Steward's wealth would have been a sure sign of their guilt in his death. It was important to strive for as much normalcy as possible over the coming days, lest they be suspected in Jarrod's disappearance.

When Gralyre arrived at Catrian's tent, the sentries waved him through without ceremony for Catrian had alerted the guards to expect his arrival when she had left for the day.

Even empty the tent held the essence of her, a scent or perhaps a vibration of power that made him shiver, as he crossed the room. It was odd to be in the space without her there, and Gralyre was conscious of being an interloper, as he drew the book from the shelf, being careful to touch nothing else.

He settled himself at the table but hesitated to open the cover, his gaze blurring the title, as he became caught up in his inner thoughts.

He did not regret the death of the Steward. For what the man had done to Dara alone, he deserved his sentence, and Gralyre knew that his crimes had been much worse than this.

It was Rewn's loss of innocence that Gralyre regretted. His friend had killed Demon Riders and Deathren, but killing a man was different, and there were consequence to such an act. He only hoped that Rewn was able to find his way back from the bloodthirsty edge he had been teetering upon, for if he fell into the abyss of hate and rage, the essence of the good man he had grown to love as a brother would be lost forever.

Sighing, Gralyre flipped open the book and found his place in the text. Concentration came hard because of his exhaustion from the night's goings on, but he doggedly continued to read.

After about an hour, the tent flap rustled, and Gralyre straightened in anticipation of seeing Catrian. He suddenly needed her presence like a desert needed rain, and a smile broke over his face.

His enthusiasm caved when Commander Boris stepped inside instead, his face glowering and dark with anger.

"What do ye think ye are doing?" Boris dispensed with all pleasantries to demand.

Gralyre's eyes flicked down to the large, obvious tome, then up again to meet Boris' suspicious glare. One eyebrow rose disdainfully, but before he could reply, Boris clarified.

"Matik just reported t' me that ye had yourself appointed a Huntsman?"

Gralyre shrugged, relaxing as he realized the purpose of the visit did not center upon the ill luck of the Stewards. "What is the problem?" Gralyre laid a leather strap in the page to mark his place, and shut the heavy book with a deep thud that threw dust motes up into the air.

"It should ne'er have been allowed. Now that we have discovered your scheme it ends today!"

"I was not scheming," Gralyre interjected hotly.

"The South District Stewards were lax in their duties and reports. Had we known what ye were about, ye would have been dealt with swiftly! Ye are crazed t' believe ye would be allowed t' come and go at will, so allow me t' disabuse ye o' the notion. It will never happen again!" Boris snarled. "Ye are t' keep at your studies, and learn magic. For some reason Catrian thinks that ye may be able t' help us, and for the moment, I am willing t' permit it."

Boris thumped his fists upon the table when he leaned forward, looming over Gralyre, and blocking the sunbeam that drifted down through the smoke hole at the tent peak. The harsh light angled into the wrinkles and furrows of his face, eclipsed his eyes with shadows, and for a startling moment, transformed his face into a deathly skull. "Do no' think my generosity extends further! What are ye thinking, man? Ye know that if ye regain your mind, ye could turn on us all!"

Gralyre ran a hand over his bearded chin, leaned back in his chair, and grudgingly ceded the point – as he had done each time it had been thrown at him. He lived daily under the cursed handicap of his amnesia, and well knew the danger represented by his missing past. But until it happened, he wondered when he would be allowed to live a simple life, without suffering suspicions over his every motive?

"I assure you that my only intent is to contribute. I am the best Huntsman you have." It was not a boast. With Little Wolf to track for him, and his ability to hear the thoughts of animals, Gralyre would never return from a hunt without meat for the many hungry mouths within South District.

Boris grunted, and rubbed a rough hand over his short grey hair, scrubbing for a moment before letting it drop. "Just do as ye are told, and stay away from that which does no' concern ye!"

Gralyre's eyes flashed molten, as Boris' edict hit home.

Damn the Gods, both he and Little Wolf needed the space, needed to roam the wild! How were they to survive being penned into the fortress walls like chattel? A ripple of claustrophobia shivered through his tight held shoulders.

Boris noted his reaction, and nodded self-righteously, as he delivered his final blow. "That includes Catrian!"

Outrage pounded the blood in Gralyre's ears, the drums of war. "What?" His voice emerged reasonably, but there was no mistaking the edge that sharpened the one syllable.

"Ye heard me. Ye are her apprentice, nothing more. That is all ye will ever be. Do no' seek t' reach above your station. She is no' for the likes o' ye!"

"What does Catrian think of your decree?"

The Commander's smile widened, slowly, in control and knowing it. "She will do whatever is necessary for the Resistance. She will obey me!"

Gralyre forced his clenched fists to relax, seeking the calm and control of the sword dance.

Boris watched Gralyre's face blank of all emotion, and had to fight a cold shiver at the unnatural response. A normal man would lash out in anger at such an insult, perhaps even throw a punch.

His smile lost ground, as he reconsidered the rash of deaths in South District, culminating in Beaurice's murder the night before. It was assumed that Steward Jarrod had fled in the night because he had murdered the Quartermistress. It was possible that he had fallen out with his fellow Stewards, and murdered them too - not accidents, as they had first seemed.

A company of men had been sent in pursuit to bring Jarrod back to face his crime, however, no trace of him could be found. A message sent to the far outposts had returned negative results. Jarrod had not fled through any of the passes. The man had vanished into the forest.

Then there were the rumours that had reached the Commander, that 'twas Gralyre who had murdered the South District Stewards. Had he killed Jarrod before he could escape? Gralyre and Rewn Wilson had been outside the walls last night, having left at dusk… an odd time that, to set out on a hunt… and Rewn had been the last man seen with Hofar before the Steward had been caught in the storm that froze him to death. There was a lot of smoke swirling around, for there to be no fire.

'Twas difficult to get to the truth, for when tragedy struck, fingers always pointed at the lowlanders and strangers first. There was no clear evidence that Jarrod had met a similar fate as his fellow Stewards, nor that the deaths were anything but accidents, but the coincidences were uncanny.

"Did ye kill them? Did ye kill the Stewards?" If Boris thought his bald question would startle a confession he was greatly disappointed.

Gralyre's brows snapped together in anger, but he met the accusation armed with the absolute truth. "I did not end their lives." He may have helped, but Rewn had been the executioner. If Boris had been able to find one ounce of evidence to support his charge, he would have killed Gralyre already. Still his accusation hit too close for Gralyre's peace of mind.

"If I were to murder anyone, I can name others who would top my list," Gralyre growled meaningfully, perhaps rashly.

Boris reared back and placed his hand on his sword in response to the veiled threat. "Heed me, man. Ye live under my sufferance. That will surely come t' an end one day."

Gralyre watched Boris stomp from the tent. "And you mine," he muttered darkly before reluctantly returning to the thick book, and thumbing it open to the marked page.

CHAPTER SIX

The sword is falling, catching the light, my face is a terrified distortion in the flashing blade. My arms held, I can do nothing but await death. The Demon is triumphant.

The sword slips through the neck of my first captor, and blood sprays, blinding me. The henchman's head topples, and the grip on my arm loosens, as the body sags.

Struggle free... Too late!

The blade bites into my neck, a small pain eclipsed by true, torturous agony, as I explode.

Everywhere! I am the universe!

The void pulses, and I contract.

Nowhere! Nothing! Smaller than the smallest grain of sand...

Gralyre surged up off his pallet, and dove through the tent's entrance. He tumbled deftly up to his feet, as he hit the icy ground, and sprinted several strides before he got ahold of himself, halting his panicked flight.

'The demon is coming. It will find me! Run! Get out! Get free!'

His head rotated urgently, as he scanned the surrounding moonlight and shadows for an escape route, and for an attack. He quivered from freezing in place against the insanity of his paranoia, and it took long moments before he realized that the repetitive moans of fear he heard were being expelled from between his lips with every panting breath.

And even longer before he realized that he had an audience.

A stick snapped, and his fear-tightened muscles recoiled his body around to face the threat but it was just a neighbour, an old widow, shortening kindling with which to stoke her fire.

"Ye suffer night terrors. I hear ye in the darkness, mewling like a babe. Ye are too loud. Ye waken me!" she groused.

Gralyre blotted his face with his sleeve, embarrassed for the tears that mingled with the terror sweat. Every night, he died. Every night he suffered the consequence of his failure. What terrible deeds lay in his darkened past that he must suffer such penance?

She fed more shards of wood to the hungry coals, and the flames began to rise. "My son had the nightmares," the old woman continued. "He could no' stand the agony, and he faded away, became a stranger t' his ole mam. One day, he travelled t' the lowlands and ne'er returned. 'Riders got him, I suppose."

Gralyre was still trying to calm his stridulous breathing. "Sorry," he managed.

Her head popped up, glaring at him through the fire and smoke, as the kindling caught. "Sorry? Sorry! Ye, and your lot. Lowlanders!" Her wrinkled face distorted, her eyes reflecting twin flames. "Every man, woman and child in this fortress has lost their dearest blood in the fight against Doaphin. And why? T' save the likes o' ye, and your kind? Ye who will no' fight for yourselves?" She reached down and grabbed up a hefty stick, and threw it at him. "The lot o' ye can burn for all I care!"

Gralyre blocked the stick with his arm, a slight pain for she had not much strength.

"Go back t' the lowlands where ye belong! Ye do no' deserve t' be here. Ye have no' earned the right! Eating our food, taking work from us, while good Rebels go without!"

Gralyre's anger surged to the fore. The constant bigotry and discrimination, the fact that he could not escape the fortress, the starvation, and the lack of sleep all cumulated into an explosion. "Earned the right? The lowlanders ye so despise live every day under threat of death from Demon Riders, Deathren, Demon Lords, and collaborators. What do you know of fear, or what is deserved? They eke out an existence, as best they can, and count themselves blessed by the Gods to see each sunrise!" Gralyre roared. "And those few who do fight back, who do choose to put everything they know, everyone they know, at risk, see their towns destroyed, and their peoples scattered and murdered." For the first time in a long while he thought upon all the abandoned and destroyed villages, towns and cities that peppered the lowlands; proof of the annihilation of humanity.

"Then the few who escape and make it here to join you, that they may someday save their neighbours and friends, these people you treat like offal beneath your boots?" Gralyre sneered as he gave her the once over. "You are not fit to mend their cloaks! Where do you imagine the food in your pots, and the clothes on your backs come from? I see no fields of grain on this mountain!"

"My son died!" she cried, "I have lost everything!"

Gralyre sighed as his ire drained away. What was he doing fighting with a frail old woman at midnight? "We have all lost, lady. Every cursed one of us. And it will never end until Doaphin is dead."

Gralyre turned on his heal and stalked up the lane, Little Wolf ranging ahead, gleeful at the impromptu midnight walk.

෨൬

Dajin clanged the lid of the pot with angry vigor before he pivoted away from the cook fire, slopping his pease pottage from his wooden bowl when he threw himself down onto his tree stump. His dramatics were not unnoticed, as he began to feed himself with mechanical scoops, managing to maintain his sullen scowl even as he chewed and swallowed, infecting the very air around him with his displeasure. His disgruntlement had been stewing for several long days, though he had yet to give it voice.

Saliana faded back into the tent to escape the tense atmosphere around the cook fire, her hands filled with two carved bowls of hastily ladled pottage. Dara was too injured to be up and about, so Saliana had voluntarily taken over her care. Dara's brothers were too busy blaming themselves for what had happened to their sister to see how their fighting was upsetting her recovery.

Responding to Dajin's unspoken aggression, Rewn finally tossed his empty vessel to the ground, and slapped his knees sharply, a clap of thunder in the quiet of daybreak. "What?"

Dajin glowered at him, his lip curled in a sneer as he blurted out around a large mouthful of food, "Dara! Ye bloody knew what they had done t' Dara, and ye did no' trust me enough t' help ye t' avenge her!" Sprays of food flew from his lips, and he brushed a sleeve across his mouth impatiently, and swallowed thickly. "Ye trusted Gralyre t' help ye, but no' me!"

Rewn's emotions had been balancing on a thin edge since Dara's attack, so it took very little to push him into temper. "Trust ye? No' two moons past, ye were trying t' stone Gralyre t' death, and letting me take a beating without raising a voice. Ye made it very clear, little brother, that your family would no' get in the way o' your ambition!"

Dajin flushed red at the truth of the reminder, but he was not willing to cede the point. "I knew that ye were keeping secrets from me, I *knew* it! I canno' believe that ye would think that I would no' avenge Dara. *She is my twin!"* He leapt to his feet, and his fists clenched tightly, as he quivered with outrage. His bowl flipped to the ground in a wet spatter that Little Wolf was only too happy to pounce upon and lap up.

Rewn sprang up to meet him. "For all I know, ye will yet betray us t' advance yourself! What position o' power would ye be awarded for your treachery?" he demanded snidely.

Dajin's face reddened further when Rewn's taunt scored another hit upon his ego, for he would have likely told Matik all. But only because Matik would have believed him, and punished the Stewards, Dajin justified. Rewn could not see reason because

Gralyre hated Matik, and had poisoned Rewn against him!

Jealousy and guilt made for a toxic brew. "Demon Lover!" Dajin shouted, as he charged his brother.

"Enough!" Gralyre barked out, surging from his seat before the first fist could fly. He grabbed Dajin's scruff with one hand, and Rewn's with the other, lifting both men to their toes with a mighty flex of muscle. "Dajin, we did not tell you because if we had been caught and hanged, we needed someone we could trust to look after the women. And Rewn, if I can forgive Dajin for the stoning, I expect you to do the same. This is neither about you," he shook Rewn roughly, "nor you, Dajin," he growled as he meted out a similar punishment.

Gralyre dragged the brothers close enough that all three shared the same breath for an instant. His voice lowered, deadly and cold. "Your pride has naught to do with this, 'tis about your sweet sister, and what is best for her. Ye are her brothers. Start acting like it!" Gralyre released both men with a shove, and turned away to reclaim his seat. "Think on that with as much effort as you are spending nursing your bruised manhoods," he muttered darkly.

Rewn and Dajin eyed each other stiffly, as they reclaimed their seats but Gralyre's words had lanced the boil of their contention. They were mute, uncomfortably embarrassed to have been so soundly, and rightly, chastised. Breakfast continued in tense silence save for the burping of the pot's lid, as steam escaped in small bursts from the simmering contents.

Coals in the banked fire glowed with every gust of wind that threaded sporadically through the rows of tents, swirling first heat then freezing cold into their faces with every eddy. The sun had yet to climb, but the sky was without cloud, and bore a promise of crystalline blue to break the monotony of white and dirty grey that imprisoned them in what felt like endless winter.

Throughout the neighbourhood of tents, people were cooking and breakfasting with quiet murmurs punctuated with outbursts of laughter. Life was definitely more pleasant in South District since Jarrod's "departure".

The gatekeepers had let it be known that Jarrod had fled in the dead of night, never to be seen again, and the sentries walking the wall had not only born witness to the gatekeepers' testimony, but had watched Jarrod's solo descent into the tree line. Upon the discovery of the Quartermistress, murdered and left in Jarrod's tent, it was widely assumed that the man had fled to escape his crime. As far as most were concerned, that was the end of the matter - good riddance to bad company.

The three new Stewards for South District, recent appointees of General Matik's, appeared to be decent men. Already the corruption of nepotistic appointments and favouritism that had underscored Jarrod, Strier and Hofar's tenure was being undone.

Unfortunately, this meant that not only was Gralyre's short stint as Huntsman over, by order of the high command, but Rewn's appointment was also under review by the new Stewards. It was doubtful that he would receive approval to continue as a Huntsman, as Rewn was both a lowlander, and guilty of association with Gralyre.

So it had been days since Rewn had had anything to occupy his time besides his own testiness. He was doubly cursed for being forced to watch Dajin leave every morning to train with Matik, an honor that had not been extended to him, while Gralyre also left to attend his studies in magic.

Finished with his breakfast, Gralyre stood and strapped on his sword, thankful that he had those studies to escape to, or he might be going as mad as his friend.

Little Wolf pranced towards Gralyre with excitement, spinning and chuffing softly at the thought of leaving the fortress, and getting away from the tension that infected the tent these days.

'No. Stay. Protect the den, Little Wolf.'

Little Wolf stopped spinning, his body quivering with yearning. *'Run? Snow, trees, Hunt? Sun warm on fur, air cold in lungs!'*

Gralyre tried to soften the wolfdog's disappointment, for Little Wolf was also feeling the affects of being caged. *'Protect the Den. That is a very important job. Keep the women safe.'*

Little Wolf yawned a loud protest, and then heaved a sigh of acquiescence. He turned around three times and settled himself in the hollow he had carved out of the snow bank at the edge of the tent entrance, where he could monitor all the comings and goings. His unhappy gaze followed after his master, as Gralyre left without a word of goodbye to the Wilsons.

Gralyre wanted to hit something, but there was nowhere for him to spend his aggression, leaving him troubled that he had almost lost control with Rewn and Dajin. His confinement made being around the combative brothers difficult to endure.

As had become her custom, Catrian had already left before he arrived. Despite all attempts not to, he still found himself looking forward to seeing her everyday, only to experience a disquieting disappointment at her absence. He strongly suspected that the Sorceress was avoiding him, no doubt upon orders from Boris, which added degrees of aggravation to his irritability.

As he settled himself at Catrian's table and thumped the book of magic upon the table, he acknowledge that he was heartily sick of sitting in her darkened tent immersed in theorems and observations on the practices of magic, as laid down by a verbose, self important Sorcerer from five-hundred years in the past, who had used eighteen words to get to the point of one, and in the process clouded his teachings in mind numbing obfuscations. Should the volume ever be abridged, it would surely shrink to a tenth of the size. After a fortnight of heavy study, Gralyre was less than a quarter of the way through the ponderous text.

The day wore onwards, and Gralyre finally lost the light that had shone down through the smoke hole at the peak of the tent. He could fire a lamp, but his back was aching from bending over the text all day, and his body was demanding movement. Deep within, he admitted that he had been lingering in the hopes of seeing Catrian, but he knew from experience that she would not return while he remained.

After the confrontation with the Wilson brothers that morn, Gralyre's concentration had been marred by temper, and he had barely proceeded ten pages further into the text due to having to reread paragraphs. For all the effort he had expended this day, he had learned naught but that energy could not be created or destroyed, it could only be converted from one form into another. The old Sorcerer had gone on in great length with a list of all the different types of energies, their properties, and the most efficient ways to bend them to one's will.

He marked the current page with his strip of leather, and snapped the tome shut with a satisfactory bang. Gralyre stretched, lifting his arms high above his head, and yawning mightily, as his spine cracked and realigned, then rubbed his strained eyes, feeling the grit and grain of too much study. He needed to clear his thoughts and absorb what he had learned, and so would leave Sorcerer Aegon's *History of Magics in the Kingdom of Lyre* for another day.

He was impatient to begin to put into practice some of what he was memorizing, for knowledge without application was useless, but he was bound by his vow to the Sorceress. It was like reading about how to use a sword, but never once picking up a blade and swinging it.

Upon exiting Catrian's pavilion, Gralyre noted that there was an unusual buzz of activity in the square. The rhythm of life within the Northern Rebel Fortress had been disturbed by the arrival of road weary travellers. A small crowd of excited faces had gathered to watch the procession, and to speculate about the contents of a heavily laden mule train that accompanied the group of strangers.

Gralyre sidled up to the back of the crowd, his height an advantage to see over their heads, and watched as two men separated themselves from their travelling companions to be personally greeted by Boris, Matik and Catrian.

Catrian stood within the gentle light of the low setting sun, stern and beautiful, and Gralyre realized with a jolt how hungry he had been for a glimpse of her. Boris' warning was still fresh within his mind, but he felt defiance out of all proportion to the threat. It was Catrian's decision to speak to him or no, and Gralyre was suddenly burning with the need to put her interest to the test. He had to know if it was Boris or Catrian's will that had kept her away for the past fortnight.

Gralyre began to push through the crowd but froze when one of the strangers, a robust man in the prime of his life, embraced Catrian, and lifted her from the ground. The stranger's blond hair glinted golden in the setting sun, as he bussed her cheek with a smacking kiss, and swung her in a wide arc. Gralyre was unaware that he had clenched his fists, glaring heavily until the man deposited the laughing Sorceress back on her feet, and turned to greet Boris with the exuberant embrace of an old friend.

The man's companion greeted Catrian with more decorum, a brief press of her hand, before he hung back from the proceedings. His dark hair was clubbed neatly at the back of his neck, and his eyes squinted narrowly, as he carefully conducted an evaluation of the company, the crowd and the fortress.

Gralyre nudged the man next to him, and indicated the travellers with his chin. "Who are they?"

The man turned with a smile that quickly fled when he beheld the scowl that overtook Gralyre's face, as the blond stranger once again wrapped an arm around Catrian's waist with the ease of familiarity. "That is General Chartrin o' the Western Rebels," he stated nervously.

"The Western Rebels? Who are they, again?" Gralyre feigned confusion to encourage the man to continue speaking, smoothing his face of all emotion to put the man at ease.

The Rebel relaxed, and thumped Gralyre's chest companionably with the back of his hand. "Ye know how secret everything is kept, but I had it from a friend o' mine," the man tapped his nose with a lean finger and winked, "'tis rumoured that Chartrin's territories lie on islands in the waters off the mainland, near t' Dreisenheld itself, and that his people live on ships that travel the oceans! They have blockaded Dreisenheld for generations. He must have travelled a pretty length o' time t' get from there to here!"

"See those pack animals?" a woman chortled enthusiastically, spontaneously joining the conversation. "'Tis a good bet, by the Gods o' Fortune, that they are filled with fine things pirated from Doaphin's ships." A matronly woman of middle years, she patted her hair into place, and smiled, as she took in Gralyre's massive chest and arms.

"Gold and pretties!" another woman squealed with a clap.

A ripple of laughter passed through the crowd, but Gralyre remained untouched by it. There was only one reason that he could imagine that would impel a General to journey so far from his stronghold in the depths of winter. The Rebels were planning for war.

ഋᏵ

The days stretched ahead of them all. Life was made further dismal by the early decent of the sun, though every day it shone a little brighter, and remained in the sky for a little longer, as the days lengthened their reach towards the salvation of spring.

However, the ice that encased the brothers' forgiveness for each other, like the long winter, had yet to thaw.

As predicted, Rewn was denied a position as Huntsman. He was relegated to a Honey Wagon team; cleaning midden pits by chipping through frozen waste to remove it before the spring thaw, and then carting it past the north face of the mountain to be disposed of down a deep gulch. As a lowland refugee, it was the only job available to him.

Dajin's high status, as one of General Matik's chosen few, made him even more unbearable to live with, if that was possible. He was certain to twist the knife in Rewn daily, by pointing out that he was performing the lowest job in the fortress.

When the harsh words were over, and apologies had yet to be uttered, the silence was heavy with the emotional exhaustion of the little group, who no longer had the energy to do more than endure each other's company.

Once their scanty evening meals were consumed, and the coals of the firepit banked for the evening, there was little else to do besides retire for the night. Dara's attack had taken its toll upon them all, and there was little appeal to remain at the cook fire to share stories, and laugh, as they had done of old.

As with most evenings, they prepared their tent for sleep in silence, their routine a poor substitution for their past camaraderie. From within the bins at the back of the tent, Saliana pulled furs and wool blankets, which she silently doled out to the men, leaving them to spread out the bedrolls on the hard ground. Dara possessed the lone cot that Rewn had bartered for, so that she would be able to rest more comfortably while she healed. It was set nearest to the glowing heat of the small brazier that kept the beast of winter from sinking its teeth into them all while they slept. Already abed, Dara was an unmoving mass under a pile of heavy furs.

Saliana slept upon the dirt floor beside the cot, to be at hand to assist should Dara awaken in the night. Both of their beds lay at the back of the tent, nearest to the storage bins, and furthest from the freezing breeze that penetrated the tent's entrance. It was also the safest place. After what had befallen Dara, any threat that should appear had to go through the three men to reach the women.

Rewn's bedroll was spread to the right of the central tent pole, and Dajin's to the left, the maximum distance that could be placed between the brothers, though it did little to help the waves of animosity that arced between the two.

Gralyre claimed the space next to the drafty tent flap so that, should he experience one of his nightmares, which was on most nights, he could leave without disturbing the others unduly. Little Wolf curled tightly against Gralyre's side, sharing his heat and comfort.

Settled in their bedrolls, the oil lamp doused, sleep was slow to lay claim to their bodies and minds, and there was much tossing and turning. Perhaps it was the darkness that made it easier to speak, to be a disembodied voice, or maybe it was boredom that prompted Dajin to share the news he had been hoarding.

"The General from the south arrived with his warriors today. His name is Ryes. I have never seen men so pale in all my days. 'Twas like looking at ghosts."

Gralyre raised a brow at the news, and resettled himself onto his back with an arm propped under his head. Little Wolf grumbled in exhaustion, as he was forced to shift his body to match Gralyre's new position. There were no stars to be seen through the smoke hole at the peak of the tent tonight, which was fine, so long as the clouds did not snow down upon them. Gralyre had spent more than one morning shaking icy flakes from his bedding. "From the south? How many Generals do the Rebels have?"

A flash of suspicion swept Dajin, but to his credit he swallowed his venom, too tired to indulge in mistrust, and chose instead to ignore the question, as he provided the common knowledge that he had gleaned. "The southern Rebels are soft looking, sickly even, not like General Baldric's men who look like they piss fire. A man I spoke t' mentioned that the south has been swept clean o' people for generations." His words were arrogant and rote, as though memorized from the lips of another. Dajin was finding life at the fortress suited him far better than being a farmer ever had.

"Nearly all o' the leaders o' the resistance have gathered now. People say 'tis the first time in a generation that all the Generals will be sitting at the same table." His words drifted out of the dark around the sound of a massive yawn.

Laying opposite Dajin, Rewn hummed in thought, then listed off on his fingers in answer to Gralyre's question, "That would mark the arrival o' General Chartrin o' the west, Ryes o' the southeast, spy Master Baldric arrived a fortnight ago, we hold the northeast, so we are just awaiting two more Generals; General Laurazon o' the lowland north, and the midmountain Eastern Rebels under General Kierdenan."

Dajin rolled over, and glared in the general direction of his brother's voice. "How do ye know all this?"

Rewn's grin was heard more than seen. "Da was a spy, little brother. What do ye think we did during all the trips t' Verdalan over the years? We met with General Baldric many times." Rewn frowned in thought. "I believe General Kierderan's stronghold is just a short distance away t' the south, no more than a fortnight's journey, surely. I wonder why he has yet t' arrive?"

"Must be something important happening t' get them all here at the same time and place," Dajin mused with banked excitement, forgetting for the moment that he had not yet forgiven Rewn.

Gralyre's fears had long been confirmed. "Commander Boris has called a war council."

"War! O' course, that makes sense!" Dajin bolted upright, a darker outline within the shadows of the tent.

"Do no' sound so excited, brother. War is nothing t' seek." Rewn mumbled sleepily.

"Says the coward." Dajin sneered, and flopped back down again. "Do ye no' see that we will finally have a chance t' avenge Da and our family? We get t' kill 'Riders!"

Rewn yawned. "Just go t' sleep Dajin."

Dara's voice mumbled with sleepy exasperation from out of the darkness. "Will ye both be quiet?"

"Sorry Dara, goodnight," Rewn whispered.

"'Night," Dajin added.

∞∞

Perhaps it had been the talk of war, or the ongoing stress of not being able to leave the fortress to roam the quiet wilderness, too many sedentary hours spent reading Catrian's book of magic, the constant discrimination of being an outsider, or just the compounded pressures from the lack of privacy, food, and sleep totaled to all of these, but Gralyre's nightmares were especially vivid. They always came, in some form, though the intensity of late had been growing to the point that he dreaded sleep, and the horrors that it brought.

His body twitched and quivered, as he reacted physically to the chaotic and ghastly images playing out in his night terror. It always started with war...

...Swords and spears thrust and rend. Endless killing. Deafening roars and clashes. Men fight, and die with screams of rage, pain, and fear. Unceasing attacks by a sea of enemies, wave after wave breaking in bloody ruin on the tip of my sword.

No rest! Keep fighting!

Blasts of lightning fall, and strike warrior after warrior, hardening them into black stone. A bolt hits a man to the side, living only moments ago, now his spear and sword are forever raised in challenge. Surrounded by a menagerie of grotesque black effigies, despair crushes breath.

Dead! My men, dead! Must keep fighting...

...black smoke pours from a cottage in flames. The roof collapses. My pups are dying.

'SOOT! NO!'

Henchmen hold fast, arms pinned, force me to watch my pups die. I feel the passing of each, their voices in my head silenced forever. Demon Riders caper in the flames of my home, over the bodies of the innocent.

'Bastards! I will kill you all! KILL YOU ALL!'

Black smoke engulfs, chokes, assumes a red glow. The mists part. The Demon appears, carrying his massive sword. Death approaches. The captor on my left; fetid breath puffing, excited.

The blade's edge glints in sunlight, coiled for the strike.

'I will not cower before you!'

The whistling of the sword cutting through air. The touch of cold steel against his neck...

...Bound. Arms and legs chained to stone. The Demon Lord Mallach shimmers like a mirage in a hot forge. "You will never escape Doaphin's Towers!" Mad laughter. Bullwhips grow from the Demon's fingertips; five snakes of horror, caressing, coiling.

Thunderous cracks snap the air. Pain rips into flesh. "I know who you are! I know who you are!"

Lord Mallach undulates and morphs into a woman, becoming a sneering caricature of Catrian. 'Ye are nothing! I would kill ye, but for your powers!'

Flinches. Avert my gaze to the side. Wil hangs there by his wrists, chained to the stone of Doaphin's Towers, disemboweled, his eyes closed in death. Two Deathren feast upon his entrails, fingers bloody as they shove ropy flesh into their screaming maws.

'Wil! No!'

Wil's eyes snap open, fogged and maggoty. 'Ye be a spy or a tomb robber!' The words reverberate endlessly. Wil smiles and gore erupts from his mouth, arms reaching, fingers clawing...

... Must Escape!

...The images rend, and there is nothing but endless black

emptiness that pulses like the chamber of a giant heart.

'This is my punishment for failure.'

No senses, disembodied. Flayed in time to the rhythmic throb of the darkness. Large as the universe; spread so thin, too much, too far... Now smaller than a grain of sand; nothing left, almost gone... Now large again, now small again... Again... Again...

Gralyre awoke from the intense nightmare with a soft shout, smothering it as best he could so as to not disturb the others. As he lay in the dark, panting from the exertion of the dream, it was difficult to reconnect to his surroundings.

Little Wolf bellied up from where he had lain curled at Gralyre's knees, and rested his chin upon Gralyre's chest, watching his master with devoted care. *'All is well,'* the pup promised.

Little Wolf had once entered Gralyre's dreams to try to fight what it was that attacked his master night after night, but Gralyre had made him promise never to do so again, for the nightmares were a trap for the unwary, and Little Wolf's soul had almost been lost to him in the terrible, pulsing void. So now, all Little Wolf could do was offer comfort in the night, a reassuring presence that the danger had not followed Gralyre into the real world.

Gralyre dug his hands into Little Wolf's ruff, anchoring himself to reality with the heat and solidity of his pup. This was real; the rest was only the reliving of painful memories, fearful imaginings, and outright fantasies. Yet his heart still galloped, his breath rasped thinly in his throat, and ripples of paranoia bore reality away until crippling waves of terror overwhelmed him.

He was being hunted, a dark power was seeking him, and it was coming for him! Danger! He had to escape...

'Flee...RUN! He is coming!'

Gralyre struggled violently to win free of his twisted bedding, and Little Wolf scrabbled to his feet to watch.

"Gralyre, are ye alright?" Rewn's soft voice whispered from out of the darkness.

Gralyre finally disentangled his legs, and crawled to his feet, breathless with the force of his panic. "I need to get some air! I need to get outside!" he gasped quietly, stomped his feet into his boots, grabbed his cloak, and barreled out of the tent into the coldness of the night.

As the icy air flash froze the sweat on Gralyre's face, he gazed with torment up into the night sky, and sought mastery over his dread. He watched his icy breath dissipate into the air, and wondered if the nightmares would ever cease. He could not go on like this, without sleep, without peace.

'You are safe. None can attack you while you sleep,' Little Wolf assured, having padded quietly out into the night in the wake of Gralyre's skittish exit. *'I stand guard.'*

Gralyre strained to remain rooted against the overwhelming urge to flee, to keep his feet planted solidly against the ground instead of pounding in rough terror towards the gates of the fortress and freedom.

'There is no one hunting me. There is no one hunting me. There is no one hunting me…There is no one…' A gentle hand upon his shoulder made him jump, as Rewn interrupted the mantra Gralyre was repeating to in an effort to find control.

"The dreams are worsening o' late, I can tell. Ye awaken most every night now. 'Tis been a long time since the nightmares haunted ye so. No' since the early days at our farm."

Gralyre nodded, and shoved his hands through his black hair, holding his head in a vice grip, as he groaned loudly, his gaze turning sightlessly upwards at the clouded night sky. "I have not had a decent sleep in far too long, not since I was prohibited from leaving the fortress! Rewn, I cannot stay here! The fortress, the Rebels, their cause…they will not allow me to be a part of it, yet I am not allowed to go on my way. I must leave…get out! He is coming for me!"

Rewn cautiously squeezed Gralyre's shoulder. "Who? Who is coming for ye? Gralyre, what do ye know?"

Gralyre shook his head, gasping at air, as he dropped his arms to his side. "Nothing. Nothing but madness." His gaze searched Rewn's. "The dreams are just nightmares. A phantom demon wielding a sword kills me there every night, and sometimes when I awaken, I feel him still, in the darkness, coming for me." Gralyre hung his head, fighting the madness. "It must stop! I have to make it stop! I must leave."

"Gralyre, no, ye belong here with us."

Gralyre shook his head, denying Rewn's assertion. "There is nothing left for me here!"

"What o' your apprenticeship t' the Sorceress? How go your lessons in Magic?"

"What magic? She has set me to studying a book, and now avoids me. I have not seen her face in a moon. I am not being taught, I am being placated, manipulated and controlled. If I regain my memories, I could kill you all, kill her..."

His gaze turned inward, and his words quickened with anguish. "She can never forget that, I cannot forget it, must never forget it. My presence here places her in so much danger..." he stumbled over the betrayal of feelings that his unguarded words revealed. "There is nothing left for me here," he repeated.

Rewn frowned and dropped his hand from Gralyre's shoulder. "Us. We are here for ye. Ye are my friend, the best one that I have ever known. We would all be dead seven times o'er were it no' for ye. We would have perished in Raindell, and ne'er have won free o' the Deathren in the tavern if ye had no' led us t' the escape tunnel. We would ne'er have survived the attack at Hangman's Tor, when the Deathren ran us t' ground."

"Wil died."

Rewn drew a deep breath. "Yes he did, and ye will show respect enough t' no' lay claim t' my Da's sacrifice as your own!" he urged softly. "Ye led us here, and gave us all a chance at a future that we would ne'er have known had we stayed in the lowlands. And when Dara was attacked, ye did no' hesitate. Ye were there for her and for me."

Gralyre's shoulders slumped, and Little Wolf was quick to

nose one of his palms up onto his head, inviting a caress. Gralyre drew a shuddering breath, then another, as Rewn waited patiently for him to compose himself.

"Ye need only give it more time. They will come t' know ye, as I do." Rewn's mouth tightened over his friend's pain, but there was little he could do to alleviate it. Gralyre was so strong, so in control, that sometimes it was hard to remember that he was still just a man, with all the same vulnerabilities.

"Thank-you. I…sometimes after I awaken from the nightmare, I am not myself," Gralyre confessed haltingly. "I am sorry that I awoke you. You should return to bed." He rubbed the sleeve of his forearm across his face, carrying away the frozen sweat and tears before he shivered, and wrapped his arms around his middle, not just for warmth but also for comfort.

Giving Gralyre a measure of space, Rewn moved away to crouch down, and poke at the sleeping coals in the fire pit, tossing in a log to help build the resultant flames. The red glow edged his face, and turned his brown hair vermillion. "I canno' sleep either. I have no' been able t' since Jarrod." He shrugged, looking up at Gralyre from where he squatted. Irritably, he tossed aside the stick he had used to stoke the flames.

Gralyre collapsed onto one of the stumps that were placed around the firepit, and sighed in relief, welcoming the distraction of conversation. The warmth of the flames, the quiet of the night, and Rewn's steadfast presence were all working to banish the clinging residues of his irrational paranoia.

Little Wolf yawned noisily, and settled at Gralyre's side,

leaning heavily against his master's leg. His eyes grew sleepy, as Gralyre began to rhythmically caress his soft ears while gentle heat from the fire worked its way outward to where they sat.

"I have killed Deathren, and 'Riders aplenty, but the Stewards are the only men I have ever… Yet, 'tis no' the killings." Rewn's forehead wrinkled, and he peered deeply into the glow of the fire, seeking the words to describe his affliction. "I liked it, Gralyre. I liked it so much that I would kill them again, and again," he declared savagely. "'Tis no' how I want t' be, but I canno' pluck it from my mind's eye. Every night, as I fall asleep, I dream o' killing them, over and over, in different ways." Stark, fierce pleasure twisted Rewn's face, and within the flickers of firelight he became a stranger, but when next he looked at Gralyre, the foreign expression had faded away, and he had returned once more to being the warm, caring brother who had only wanted to protect his sister from harm. "What is wrong with me? They are dead, I did it, I felt it, I know it, so why do I continue t' kill them every night in my dreams?"

It was Gralyre's turn to return the comfort so recently granted, thankful for Rewn's problem to take his mind off his own. "Just because you took your revenge, does not mean that your anger has abated. You may never be able to reconcile what happened to Dara. Something so horrible…perhaps 'tis meant to haunt us. But the fact that it bothers you? An evil man would not be troubled by it."

Rewn nodded dolefully, as he considered Gralyre's words. "Aye, maybe so."

An arrow hissed out of the darkness, and hit the metal pot that Saliana had packed with snow, and left over the banked coals to afford them warm water with which to wash in the morning.

Shhhhhhhhh-CLANG!

The meltwater upended into the firepit, sending forth a plume of sparks, smoke, and steam that instantly engulfed Rewn and Gralyre in a choking cloud.

"Gralyre!" Rewn shouted a warning, as he rolled backwards off his stump, and fell into the stacked firewood that separated their tent from their neighbour's. The split wood tumbled over him, and he was momentarily entangled. Another arrow hissed out of the darkness and hit the stump where Gralyre had moments ago been seated.

There were five men standing at the outer glow of the firelight, just off the lane. One held a spent crossbow that he was struggling to reload. The others carried staves and hunting knives, and Gralyre was charging unarmed straight into their midst.

As Rewn struggled to stand, kicking wood away from his feet, Gralyre tackled the bowman, the impact carrying them both back onto the road, where they fell, struggling, to the snowy ground.

Two men leapt upon Gralyre's back, trying to pull him from their companion, staves drumming against his shoulders and skull.

Gralyre smashed an elbow back into the face of one, who

listed away with a curse, clutching a bloodied nose. A fourth man thrust his remaining comrade aside so that he could set the steel of his blade to Gralyre's throat, forcing him to still his attack.

"Uh-uh, lowlander piece o' shit. Ye let Geordie go now, easy, or I will slit ye from crotch t' craw!"

"Gralyre!" Rewn roared, as he finally stumbled free of the woodpile, having armed himself with a stout piece of kindling. He lurched forward to come to Gralyre's aid, but an older man blocked his path with a wicked, swinging slice of a large hunting knife, threatening Rewn's midsection, and forcing him to jump back or be disemboweled.

"Do no' move, lowlander! Drop the wood. Do it now!"

The kindling hit the ground with a heavy *thunk*, and Rewn's fists clenched in frustration, for he was now as unarmed as Gralyre was. Neither man had thought to strap on their swords before leaving the tent. The urgency of Gralyre's nightmare had precluded such foresight. "What do ye want?"

The older man pointed his knife at Little Wolf. "Ye have food, and now 'tis ours."

Gralyre slowly arose to his feet while the knife set to his throat followed him up from the ground, its pressure sure and unrelenting.

"No sudden moves, ye bastard," the knifeman warned.

Gralyre held his hands out to the sides, palms open in a show of compliance. "We have no more food than is our allotted due." Shivers began to wrack his body. *'They have come for you!'*

whispered Gralyre's deepest paranoid terror. He knew the madness of the thought, but all reason had fled with the attack coming on the heels of his nightmare.

The older man grinned, showing a gap in his teeth, and making the silver stubble covering his chin glitter in the firelight. Grey hair sprang out from under a knit cap, a halo that joined with the nimbus of breath-frosted air when he huffed with soft laughter. "Why, I see meat-on-the-run staring right at me." This statement prompted a round of dirty chuckles from the rest of the gang.

"Little Wolf is not food," Gralyre growled, and only the knife at his throat kept him from launching himself at the man. A house of rage began to build, framed by his intense fear, windowed by the irrational terror of his nightmare, and roofed over by his parental anxiety for Little Wolf's safety.

Little Wolf snapped and barked out a threat in counterpart to Gralyre's assertion, though he remained on guard by the tent in response to his master's silent command to do so.

The older man, who appeared to be in charge of the small band of thieves, scratched at the whitened whiskers on his starvation-hollowed face with the blunt spine of his knife. "Well, me and my lads have no' eaten in days, and I see ye here, a demon-loving lowlander, supping on fine stew, and feeding it t' your dog while we go without a scrap. Ye be hoarding food, boyo, while good Rebels go wanting. The beast is mine, and we may let ye live, but either way we are eating this night. The question is whether ye will be seeing the dawn."

He flicked a sneering grimace at the bowman Gralyre had first felled, who was painfully rising up off the ground. "Geordie, pick up that crossbow, and put a bolt in this animal like I told ye. Mayhap, ye can aim it proper this time?" he grouched.

"Aye, sorry," Geordie mumbled, as he put a foot in the cocking stirrup, and leveraged the bowstring back up to its release hook. His fingers fumbled a bolt into the flight groove.

Rewn paled, as he watched Gralyre's face alter; his eyes went cold and sharp, and his body relaxed and shifted, as though transfiguring from a mere man into something far more dangerous. "Mister, ye do no' want t' do this," Rewn rasped thickly.

The older man moved forward, and pricked Rewn in the hollow of his throat with the shiny tip of his knife. "Ye afraid o' me, ye lowland coward?"

Rewn shook his head. "No." He tipped his chin towards Gralyre. "But ye should fear him."

The night exploded.

Ripples of energy blasted out from the epicentre that was Gralyre, and bodies flew though the night. The magic hit Rewn and the ringleader simultaneously, catapulting both men into the family tent. The center pole snapped, and the pavilion collapsed onto the sleeping Dajin, Saliana and Dara.

The women screamed, as they awoke in the smothering folds of canvas with clawing, fighting men crushing them.

The shockwave travelled in a circle of destruction ten tents deep, tumbling woodpiles and sweeping belongings away, snapping tent poles like sticks, and collapsing pavilions onto sleeping neighbours.

೫ೂಟ್ಟ

Catrian bolted upright in bed, clutching her head with a soft cry of pain. Gralyre! What was he doing? Such an outlay of magic, when she had specifically forbade it? He was defying her orders!

She gasped, and her heart pounded with dread. Had his memories returned? Was he showing his true colours at last?

She must contain him before he killed them all!

Catrian sent her consciousness winging across the fortress, and attempted to sever Gralyre's connection to his magic, as she had once before. He was not difficult to locate but he blocked her, deflecting her attack.

'Too strong! Too powerful!'

It was Catrian's worst nightmare come to pass. She leapt from her bed, pulled on boots and a cloak, and sprinted from her tent. Her brief contact with him had revealed a deep and terrible rage, which fueled her fear that he had turned.

She intercepted a sentry in the square, who had just arrived for his shift in front of her tent. "Give me that horse!" she commanded, stealing the reins of the beast from the man's slackened grip, and leaping smoothly to its back. Catrian kicked it into a gallop, all the while readying herself for the fight ahead, bracing herself to kill Gralyre.

හිරැ

Gralyre wove ropes of air, and whipped them outwards to snag about the legs of the fleeing gang of would-be thieves. Satisfaction coursed through his veins, as he collected them, one-by-one. If what had happened to Dara had taught him anything about the nature of these Rebels, 'twas that they would keep coming after Little Wolf if even one was left alive. If an example was not made, others would try the same. He had to send a definitive message that the Wilsons and Little Wolf were not to be trifled with. They were protected.

Rewn lashed out with both feet, and sent the ringleader flying back out of the folds of the family tent, to land on his back in the firepit.

The older man keened, a high-pitched screech, as he hit the live coals, and rolled away into the packed snow to smother the flames that licked into his clothing. As he scrabbled up on all fours to escape, Gralyre's magic wrapped an invisible tether around his shins, and hoisted him into the air to dangle ineffectually upside-down next to his men.

"Get it off me! Get it off!" the ringleader yelled, bending upward to grasp at the unseen restraint.

Now that the threat was neutralized, Rewn rolled off the collapsed tent, and began to paw through the fabric, searching for the entrance. "Dajin! Dara! Saliana! Are ye alright?"

Screams and curses erupted from out of the tangle. "Rewn! What is happening! Get me out o' here!" Dajin bellowed.

"I will have ye freed in a moment!" Rewn promised, as he lifted heavy rolls of canvas.

Sudden, intense pain blurred Gralyre's sight, and staggered him to a knee. He grabbed his temples, and shouted his frustration. Catrian was trying to stop him.

The thieves suddenly found themselves freed, tumbling to the ground, as Gralyre became distracted with the need to block Catrian's attack.

"Dajin! Can ye reach the weapons? Grab the swords!" Rewn shouted, noting the thieves' escape. "We are under attack!"

Geordie, the bowman, took flight with the stave-man Gralyre had elbowed in the face, the two men sprinting away up the lane, slipping and sliding in the snow from their haste.

Gralyre's head swiveled back to Little Wolf when he heard his pup loose a howling snap, to see that he had cornered the second stave-man against the wreckage of a neighbouring tent.

Unbeknownst to the wolfdog, the knifeman who had held the blade to Gralyre's throat now threatened Little Wolf's unprotected back, still intent on gaining his meal, as he stalked the pup on quiet feet.

An animal roar burst from Gralyre's throat, and he threw his right arm out, snapping whips of air around the knifeman just as he surged forward to stab Little Wolf. Gralyre dragged the knifeman to the ground hard enough to throw up a spray of snow from the impact.

With rage came strength, and Catrian's interference became a buzzing annoyance beyond the ache in his temples. Blood seeped from his nose and ears from the intensity of her efforts, unnoticed in his battle madness. His nightmare terrors ruled him entirely now, and he was acting purely on instinct.

Gralyre sent his magic winging after the two fleeing attackers, so that they did not escape to return on another night. Thinking themselves safely out of range, they were felled with cries and shrieks, and dragged back into the firelight again to face Gralyre's justice.

While Gralyre was thus occupied, the ringleader, who still had some fight in him, had scrabbled across the snow, and reached the abandoned crossbow.

Late to realize the danger, Gralyre could do nothing. Overwhelmed with the different strands of energy he was weaving, he could not divide his attention further. He did not know how much longer he could block Catrian, and maintain his grip upon so many men.

"Rewn!" Gralyre yelled hoarsely.

Rewn left helping Dajin out of the collapsed tent to dive towards the older Rebel, just as the thief rolled to his back, and fired the bolt at Gralyre. At such close range there was no way that he could miss.

Rewn crashed into the older man, and wrenched the crossbow away. He slammed the heavy machine into the man's skull, knocking him out, before pushing away with a gulp to see if Gralyre yet lived.

Acting purely on instinct, Gralyre had released the theives he had captured in order to protect himself. The air in front of him had become a solid wall, and the crossbow bolt had struck the invisible barrier a feather distance away from Gralyre's breastbone.

Gralyre shared Rewn's look of incredulous relief, before he dashed the bolt to the ground, and shifted his focus back to the fight. He remembered Catrian's comments about conserving his strength, and realized that he need not divide his attention, but could corral all the theives at once.

Instead of individual ropes of magic, he created a single prison of air with which to pen the groggy ringleader. Forcing the cage to move, he dragged the older man through the snow towards the insensate knifeman, before adding to his collection the second stave-man who Little Wolf was still holding trapped against the neighbour's tent.

Little Wolf snapped at the man he had guarded when Gralyre's magic slid the Rebel away through the snow, eliciting a gratifying scream of fear. Relieved of guard duty, he sat on his haunches with his head lowered in challenge to watch as Gralyre's magic caged the last two men, Geordie and the bloody-nosed stave-man, who had both attempted to flee again.

Having penned them all, Gralyre coldly began to contract the cage. Immersed in the nightmare that so plagued him, he would not stop until the threat was annihilated.

The thieves stumbled and flailed, as they were herded closer and closer together. The Rebels threw themselves against the invisible barrier of air, their faces twisted with terror, as the walls collapsed inward until they were mashed together in a tangle of arms and legs. They had sought an easy meal, and had instead taken a bite that had choked them. Their prison compressed further, wringing screams of pain from the group, as they began to be crushed.

From out of the surrounding tents, disheveled people buckled with bits of clothing, and with weapons drawn, searched for the point of attack upon which to defend themselves. Neighbour looked to neighbour, gathering and multiplying into a small army. Torches were lit, and soon the area was flickering with light.

Pounding hooves sounded in the night, as Catrian's horse galloped up the lane towards them. Rewn stood next to Gralyre, and placed a supportive hand upon his shoulder, as Catrian halted in a spray of snow, and slid from her horse.

Dajin finally won free of the canvas, and crawled from the collapsed tent, sword in hand, to stand behind his brother. His wide eyes took in the swath of destruction, and the imprisoned, screaming Rebels, just as Catrian's did the same.

"Gralyre! What have ye done?" she cried, blue fire wreathing her hands, as she started towards him. "Ye knew the consequences o' defying my edict!"

Gralyre blinked the sweat from his eyes, returning to his senses, and spared her a glare, stiffly proud. Unbowed by her threat, he continued to compress the thieves in their prison. "They came for Little Wolf, a sneak attack that caught Rewn and

I without our weapons! They were going to kill us all, and I had nothing else with which to defend our lives!"

Dajin made a harsh sound. "A dog? Ye almost got my brother killed over your pet?"

Rewn glanced back over his shoulder, staggered that Dajin would care. Had things really fallen so far askew between them that he was surprised by a show of brotherly loyalty? "Dajin, ye know Little Wolf is like a child t' him."

Catrian's heartbreaking dread eased; Gralyre had a legitimate reason for his actions, he had not regained his memories, nor succumbed to an evil intent. The glow of magic in her hands flickered and vanished, as she realized that she could allow him to live.

"Release them," she ordered loudly for the benefit of the watchers.

"They will only come again. Let them be an example to the next Rebel that seeks to attack me and mine!"

Catrian's eyes narrowed at his defiance, and she stepped forward aggressively, until they stood near enough to touch. She deliberately placed herself between Gralyre and his cage, focusing his attention upon her instead of the dying thieves. "Ye must give me this," she gritted quietly, her eyes darting to the side at the gathering of people. "Ye must show them that I control ye, and that ye are no' a danger t' them. Show me deference!"

Gralyre blinked heavily, as he finally noted the drawn weapons, and the violent posturing of the small army of neighbours.

"Gralyre, think o' the Wilsons if ye will no' think o' yourself," Catrian advised softly, sure now of his compliance. "Trust me."

Catrian shuddered, as Gralyre's powerful magic released its influence upon the air. Just like that, the gang of would-be thieves teetered and fell, as the invisible wall released them from their tight packed prison.

Gralyre dropped gracefully to a knee in front of her, bowed his head, and plucked up her hand to press the back of her fingers against his brow. His posture was utter subservience, though Catrian was not duped into believing that there was an ounce of humility within him.

Rewn sighed in relief, and aped Gralyre by taking a knee. From the watching Rebels, there was a significant lessening of tension, as Dajin also genuflected, and laid his sword onto the ground.

Catrian rested the back of her hand against Gralyre's brow for a moment, gazing down at his bent head. The black strands of his hair tickled against her fingers. A frown knit her brow as she watched him shiver. Something was amiss, something more than fighting off an attack would account for.

"Let me in," she ordered softly, and as Gralyre relaxed his will, she folded her consciousness into his. A quick surface scan of his immediate memory laid to rest any lingering doubts over his innocence. "Ye had a nightmare tonight?" she realized.

Gralyre released her hand, and turned his face up to hers,

meeting her insight with torment. "I have this nightmare every night. You truly believed that I attacked without provocation?"

She snatched back her hand, and glared a warning at him, as she turned away. She could not show him concern. Not now. She had to appear impartial.

Leaving Gralyre, Rewn and Dajin upon their knees, Catrian faced the thieves. "Present yourselves," she ordered, her voice powerful and commanding.

Awakened from Rewn's blow, the older man stepped forward, trembling and fearful. But some of his men tried to flee. The crowd of onlookers forced them back to face the Sorceress, prodding them with swords and spears until they were gathered before her, penned now by the angry righteousness of the mob, instead of Gralyre's magic.

Catrian addressed the ringleader with the regal coolness of a queen. "My apprentice claims ye are thieves."

The man swallowed thickly, and bowed his head respectfully. "'Tis no' our fault! We are starving, m'lady! We only sought food! We have no' had a decent allotment since the old Stewards died. We did no' know that he was your apprentice, m'lady." Blood washed thickly down the side of his face from the cut on his temple, caused by the strike Rewn had dealt him with the crossbow. The Rebel winced, as he touched his temple.

Catrian recalled that, due to a rash of accidents, they had recently lost two South District Stewards, followed by the flight of the third upon the murder of the Quartermistress. If the new Stewards that the Matik had appointed were not fulfilling their duties, then they would be immediately replaced. She pinpointed a man in the crowd. "Fetch me the new South District Stewards," she ordered.

Gralyre, Rewn and Dajin remained upon their knees, and the crowd of onlookers milled restlessly, as they awaited the arrival of the newly appointed Stewards.

Any calm Gralyre had found while talking quietly to Rewn in the firelight had been utterly shattered. In the battle's aftermath, his paranoia now returned with shocking intensity. Shudders wracked him. *'He is coming! He is coming for me!'* His breath rasped with his harsh panting. His irrational instincts screamed that he must fight free at any cost!

Gralyre bent his head, ignoring all in his quest for sanity, striving to discern reality from fantasy, trying to focus upon the cold wetness of the snow against his knees, instead of the need to run wild and far, and to keep going until he collapsed!

The draped fabric of the tent undulated, as Saliana managed to find the entrance and crawl free, disheveled, but unharmed. "Rewn!" she cried as she saw him on his knees before the Sorceress. She took a couple of uncertain steps forward, and then gestured back at the collapsed structure. "Dara is still trapped! She is too weak t' get out, and the tent is too heavy for me t' shift off o' her!"

With a quick glance to the Sorceress to gain permission, Rewn and Dajin rushed back to their collapsed tent, straining and struggling with the yards of heavy canvas to free their sister.

Gralyre did not offer to help, too consumed with his battle for control. If he moved, he feared he would lose his wits.

Catrian frowned in concern, as she watched Gralyre's seeming indifference to the plight of his friends. "Ye men, there," Catrian was obliged to order some of the loitering watchers. "Come help lift this tent, and ye others, fetch some new tent poles from the stores. See to the other pavilions as well. Be quick about it!" She soon had men scurrying in the dead of night to do her bidding. After that, much of the crowd dissipated back to their homes, to right the damage done by Gralyre's explosion of magic, and to avoid being pressed into work by the Sorceress.

By the time the Stewards arrived, the Wilson's tent had been re-erected, and Dara had been released from the suffocating weight. Saliana was now within, comforting her, while Dajin stood sentinel at the entrance, watching as Rewn retook a knee beside Gralyre, and the impromptu trial commenced.

The Stewards presented themselves to Catrian, their clothing disheveled from awakening and dressing in haste to respond to her summons.

Catrian dispensed with any niceties, coming directly to the point of the would-be thieves' defense. "These men here," she indicated the thieves, "have attacked others because they are starving. They say that they have no' received a fair portion o' food."

The Stewards looked at each other, until one licked his lips nervously, and stepped forward as the spokesman for them all. "They have no' been denied food, m'lady, just forced t' eat the same rations as everyone else. The old Stewards favoured these men, and they were given larger shares than was their due because o' it. T' tell the truth o' it, the dead Stewards were no' the most honest o' men, m'lady, and oft showed such favouritism. We have found stores o' food allotted for the district that have been hoarded back from the people. We put a stop t' such dishonesty when we were appointed."

Catrian made a chopping motion with her hand to cut off the flow of words, and turned back to the thieves. "Ye received your rations?"

The thieves shuffled amongst themselves, until one finally blurted "Aye, but 'tis no' enough for a child let alone a grown man! There would be plenty t' go around if these demon-loving lowlanders were no' taking the food from our mouths!"

Catrian sighed in exasperation, as their arguments reached the real crux of the issue, revealing the bigotry at the heart of their attack. That they were hungry, she could not doubt. They were all feeling the pinch of the shortened rations, but every winter there was more than one lowlander family found dead, their goods stolen in the dead of night. Unfortunately, this was not an isolated incident, and though she could do nothing about their prejudices, she could address their attempted murder and thievery. She looked to the remaining crowd of onlookers, and summoned a random man with a wave of her hand.

"Yes, m'lady?"

Catrian took him by the arm, and led him some paces off for privacy. Her voice dropped to a murmur. "Tell me o' your food allotment. What do ye receive?"

The man nodded. "'Tis no' much, m'lady, but with careful rationing, we make due. I get a cup o' oats, and a half cup o' coarse-milled flour, some root vegetables; a potato, a carrot, and a turnip," he listed, "an onion, and a portion o' meat equal t' the size o' a hare. With this, I feed myself and my family for a fortnight."

Catrian suppressed her pity before it could show upon her face. She had known it was bad, that starvation was a constant companion at this time of year, still she had to swallow thickly around her guilt over the large bowl of thick venison stew and crusty bread that she had enjoyed for her dinner.

"Thank-ye, ye may go," she released him from his testimony.

She returned to quietly consult Gralyre and Rewn. "Tell me o' your food allotment. Best ye know I will judge it against the rations o' the man t' whom I just spoke."

Rewn answered for Gralyre, who was still incapacitated, his voice a low murmur. "Each one o' us receives an adult portion on the fortnight; a measure o' meat, a potato, a carrot, an onion, a turnip, a bit o' oats, some barley flour. 'Tis all."

Catrian frowned in concern at Gralyre who he had yet to lift his head from the bow he had assumed. Even for the benefit of the watching Rebels, this passivity was completely out of character. "Rewn?" she asked uneasily.

"He awakened with one o' his nightmares. 'Twas why we were no' caught abed."

Gralyre lifted his head then, and his torment shone from his face, as he gazed up at the Sorceress.

Catrian's mouth tightened with compassion, well aware of what Gralyre suffered when the nightmares came, for she had walked within his mind, and experienced the terror for herself. The man was far from well, but there were larger affairs to be dealt with at this time.

Leaving Gralyre and Rewn for the moment, she returned to the thieves.

"Tell me what food ye receive. I will know if ye lie."

The thieves each confirmed their allotment to be what the stranger and Rewn had given testimony of. "But 'tis no' fair! They are lowlanders! They do no' deserve t' get as much as us!" one of the thieves whined.

The older man added in their defense, "We saw that one," he pointed at Gralyre, "feeding a portion t' yonder dog! He has no right t' waste food on a beast when we are all starving!"

"Gralyre, ye gave rations t' your pet?" Catrian asked, appalled.

Gralyre lifted his head at last, and met her stare with defiance. "'Twas my allotment that I shared, mine to do with as I pleased."

She had not seen Gralyre for a moon or more, having taken advantage of setting him to study the book of magic to avoid him, and gain some much needed perspective on her erstwhile feelings. Catrian really took in Gralyre's appearance then, and realized how much weight his large frame had lost since last she had seen him. The rations were barely enough to support a grown man, never add sharing them with a large beast. She would not have it!

Catrian steepled her hands next to her mouth, seeking the words she needed, as she passed judgment. "Ye men have been caught in the crime o' thievery. I will no' hear excuses or prejudices that the people ye targeted were lowlanders. We are humans, no' Demon Riders. We do no' feed off o' each other, we protect one another. Human lives, all human lives are precious, more so now than ever before! These lowlanders are here because they can contribute t' our survival, and t' the cause o' defeating Doaphin. The grain ye have so lately enjoyed was given t' us by these men for the benefit o' all. If ye kill them, ye will be all the weaker when the real threats arrive! I will no' have this divisiveness within my fortress! I sentence ye t' ten lashes apiece, and a fortnight in the pillory on prisoner's crusts. Perhaps then ye will have an appreciation for the food that ye are given, and no' covet your neighbour's!"

A rustle of approval swept through the crowd. Some of the thieves struggled upon receiving Catrian's pronouncement, but they were quickly subdued and bound by Rebel warriors who voluntarily stood guard. Catrian watched on with no pity. They were lucky she had arrived afore Gralyre had killed them.

"Rewn Wilson, ye but defended your hearth and home, and I find no fault with your actions."

Rewn sagged slightly in relief, a harsh sigh escaping between his lips, as he shot a quick grin of encouragement at Gralyre.

But Catrian was not done with her sentencing. Though her

heart ached with what she must do, she had to make a show of strength for the crowd, to keep Gralyre safe. "Gralyre, ye are hereby ordered ten lashes, for defying my will by using magic when it was expressly forbidden t' ye. In addition, ye may no longer give your rations t' your pet. I suggest ye put it out o' its misery afore it starves t' death, and share its meat with your neighbours."

Gralyre looked up at her from his knees, his face taunt with warning, as he muttered for her ears only, "Do not harm Little Wolf. I beg of you Catrian, please. You know what it is you ask, and that I will not comply. Do not set this between us." He swayed, and blinked before he was able to steady his stance once more.

Catrian's mouth tightened, and her voice dropped low, a match to his, so that the crowd could not hear her words. "Gralyre, ye are starving yourself t' death! Ye must eat."

Rewn turned his head, and scanned his friend, really seeing for the first time how his clothing hung loose upon his large frame. His mind travelled back to Dara's attack, finally noting Gralyre taking no more than a couple of bites from his plate before giving his portion to Little Wolf, or leaving the fire to take an extra serving to Dara, as she lay abed, to aid her healing. "Ye have been giving your food t' Dara as well, have ye no'?"

Gralyre nodded, his face unapologetic. "She needs it right now, far more than I."

"And the wolf?" Catrian murmured angrily. "Ye are feeding him?"

Gralyre's jaw clenched. "If ye would but let me leave the fortress to hunt!"

Rewn looked between the two and sought a resolution, speaking loudly to ensure his voice carried to the onlookers. "The dog earns his keep, at least he used t' afore we were pulled from the hunting detail by the new Stewards. With him at our side t' track, we were always successful. Let us be Huntsmen again, and this dog will ensure meat in the pot of every last person in South District for the rest o' the winter!" Rewn boasted.

Catrian's lips twitched at his argument, impressed anew by Rewn's diplomacy, and relieved that he had presented her a valid alternative to injuring Gralyre further. "Rewn Wilson," she pronounced in a loud voice, "because I recently travelled with ye in my company, and witnessed firsthand the effectiveness o' yonder beast at hunting, the dog's life is spared. Ye will report t' the Stewards in the morning, with the beast, where ye will resume your duties as Huntsman, t' bring meat t' our tables. The dog will receive its own ration from what it is able to capture and kill, and for only so long as it continues t' be o' use t' ye in the hunt."

Rewn bowed his head in compliance. "What o' Gralyre?" he asked quietly.

Gralyre glanced at him, and shook his head slightly, recognizing that they had pushed Catrian for as many concessions as they dared. Besides, he knew that he would never be allowed such freedom. Boris had made that very clear. He was content, now that he knew Little Wolf was to be spared further hardship.

Catrian words confirmed Gralyre's evaluation. "Ye have gotten enough o' your way tonight, Rewn Wilson," she pronounced coldly.

Rewn's rose to his feet to bow low. "Thank-ye, m'lady."

He clapped a hand to Gralyre's shoulder in commiseration. "I will have Saliana prepare for your injuries," he promised despondently, and left Gralyre kneeling at Catrian's feet.

"Stewards," Catrian called. "Let us away t' the whipping post, that we may put an end t' this terrible night's business."

She walked back to her horse while Gralyre was hauled to his feet, and bound by rope in line with the thieves. He did not seek to fight the charge, nor complain of his sentence, for he had broken his vow to Catrian by using magic, despite the necessity. He was fortunate the sentence had not been harsher; she had promised him death when she had taken his oath.

As the rope pulled taut, and the prisoners shuffled forward, Gralyre wondered anew why he stayed in the fortress with the Rebels. If he truly wished to leave, there was not a man among them to challenge his decision. He did not belong here. At best, he would be discriminated against for the rest of his life, and at worst, he would reclaim a past that would destroy them all. Both paths were insufferable, but if there was a third option he could not yet see it. All he knew was that he was quickly reaching the end of his tolerance.

The prisoners were quick marched across the fortress to the

centre square where, one-by-one, they were led forward, and secured to the whipping post to receive their stripes.

The punishment came in the form of a common bullwhip, not a cat-o'-nine-tails, and Gralyre breathed out a harsh chuckle, disturbed by just how much knowledge of whips that he suddenly found himself in possession of; insights that seeped up from the black pit he had in place of a past. Though the single-tail bullwhip being plied by the executioner would split his skin, these wounds would likely not penetrate into muscle. The real pain would come from the impacts, and the resultant bruising that would linger for days. This whip had neither sharp barbs, nor a cruel tip braided with iron beads, both of which would flay away flesh, so there would be no serious wounding this night.

As was usually the case with his amnesia, the knowledge appeared when need demanded it, not through voluntary searching, and provided only the facts, not the life experiences that had shaped the knowledge.

The buzzing speed of the bullwhip parting the air, followed by the sharp crack of leather on skin, as it wrapped around trembling torsos, was easily heard throughout the square, though in the predawn, few people were awake to gather to watch the sentences being executed. An expert handler plied the lash quickly and economically, delivering ten strokes per man. All of the thieves screamed, and two fainted from the pain, before they were dragged away to begin the remainder of their sentence in the pillory.

Gralyre was the last to endure the whip. He removed his shirt and folded it neatly before he walked with his guard to stand calmly at the pillar to be bound. His face was fierce, as he controlled his urge to fight free rather than submit to the flogging. But having the ability to escape should he choose did not make it the right course. He had almost lost Little Wolf this night, and placed his closest friend in jeopardy, all because he had failed to note the men stalking them from the road. That inattention spoke volumes to his exhaustion and weakness from the starvation and nightmares. At full strength, he would have easily dealt with the five thieves, as poorly armed as they had been. Instead, he had broken his oath to Catrian and used his magic, and would now pay the penalty.

As he stood in the false dawn, awaiting the first bite of the lash, his stare met Catrian's. She was pale, but composed. He kept his gaze locked to hers, as she nodded to the executioner, and the whip flew. Gralyre watched her flinch when the first crack sounded, and the first of the pain ripped into the flesh of his back.

His breath caught on a gasp, as into his mind's eye, a ghostly memory shimmered like heat from a fire...

...He passes judgment from an ornate chair. Wine sloshes from a jeweled goblet as he gestures. The puddle soaks into the red of the deeply piled carpet...

''Tis the lash for ye! Five times five, boy! If you will not obey me, I must beat the insolence from your hide!'

...A thick leather strap, rises, snaps, burns, five times five.

Pain. Helpless…

The fragment of memory boiled over with fear and despair, and for a moment after that first brutal impact of the whip, Gralyre's ears rang, and his vision tunneled with the need to struggle free. The remembered pain of a long ago strapping became snarled up with the pain in his back, and befuddled his mind with a confusion of raw emotions. The brutal impact of the second strike brought him back to his reality, and the unremembered past faded away.

After that, he shut his eyes, and sought the coldness of the sword dance, allowing the pulse of his own heart to block the whistle and snap of the bullwhip, and mute the fire that lanced through his flesh, a now familiar pain that his body remembered how to endure.

The onlookers, watching Gralyre stand tall and hard, taking the lash without a whimper or cower, nodded their approval and admiration at the tough bravery the man displayed. When the final blow fell, two men rushed to unbind his wrists, and to place supportive shoulders under his draped arms to help him keep his feet. Gralyre gritted his teeth against the pain, swaying unsteadily, and blinking to keep the sweat out of his eyes.

"Bring him," Catrian ordered, leading the way into her tent. She paused at the entrance to talk to her sentries. "Send for Rewn Wilson, South District, t' the left o' the crossroads."

"Right away, my lady."

The men dragged Gralyre, now only semi-conscious, past the

filmy curtain, and placed him facedown upon her cot, as she indicated. "Leave us," she ordered.

As the men saluted, Catrian was already wrapping soft, clean cloths around packs of snow, and pressing their icy coolness gently to Gralyre's angry red lacerations. Her hand was dwarfed against the powerfully packed muscles of his back, beautifully defined within the golden glow of the lantern light, but marred now by the bloody bruising of the whip. This near to him, his starvation was even more evident, for there was not an ounce of spare flesh beneath his taut skin.

"I am sorry," she murmured, the words torn from her unexpectedly. He was so large, his shoulders were so wide, that his arms dangled over the sides of her cot, and his feet hung off the end of her bed. She had never bothered to appreciate the beauty of a man's back before, the large muscles that bunched and moved as he shifted, and she had to concentrate to keep applying the cold compress instead of giving in to the urge to trace her hand across his shoulder. She shivered and flushed, confused by the unaccustomed notions flooding her thoughts.

"What are you sorry for?" Gralyre slurred, turning his head to regard her with glittering, feverish eyes that in the low lantern light seemed completely black, the blue lost to the shadows.

She bit her lip, as he flinched under her gentlest touch when she applied another cold cloth. "Everything, nothing, I do no' know. Ye have no' had an easy time o' it, being here, have ye?" she asked softly, finally giving in to the urge to brush his overlong black hair away from his nape. Along the side of his neck her fingers traced the thin scar, healed, but yet ruddy, having not yet faded away to white.

'From where the sword bit into his neck…'

She snatched her hand back in confusion, disconcerted by her wayward thought. It was only a coincidence.

"No," Gralyre rumbled as he reached out, and captured her fingers in his, bringing them to his lips.

Catrian's heart stuttered, as he pressed her hand to his mouth. She was flustered, wondering if he was agreeing with her, or protesting the loss of her touch. "What are ye doing? What was that for?" her flush intensified, her eyes riveted to his, unable to glance away.

In the glow of the lantern light, his gaze was earnest, and filled with boundless pain that came from more than the injuries to his flesh. "This cannot continue, Catrian. We both know that I cannot be trusted, that one day I may turn on you." Gralyre's mouth turned down at the corners, and his brows came together over the high bridge of his nose. "I could not bear that," he whispered harshly. "The look on your face when you rode up on your horse…I never want to be the cause of such distress again. I need you to do something for me."

"What?" Catrian was mystified, and captivated by the feel of his lips brushing her fingers as he talked, the hot burn of his breath warming her hand from the cold of the snow she had packed onto his wounds. The thought that he would once again demand to be allowed to leave shot a bolt of pure panic through her. "Ye know that I canno' let ye go. Ye must stay and learn magic. Ye are needed. 'Tis what we agreed!"

He shook his head faintly. "You do not understand. I do not sleep. I cannot eat. Every night the nightmares torture me. They are driving me mad. That and the thought that I could one day cause your death. I cannot bear it any longer. I want you to take from me my memories. Everything that is left. Maybe if there is no hope of recovering my past, you will be free to trust me. Perhaps then, I can make a real home here."

Catrian was aghast. "No! I will no' do it. Gralyre, ye would be utterly lost! Only see how ye suffer with only a piece o' your past lost. Ye would be utterly defenseless! Ye would no' recognize your friends," she sputtered. "Ye would no' be able to feed or dress yourself! Ye would be as a newborn babe!"

Gralyre pressed her hand tighter to his lips then rolled, wincing, onto his side to clasp her palm against his heart. His eyes were feverish with pain as they met hers. "I beg of you!" His free arm snaked out, embracing her about the hips, and pulling her closer so that he could nestle his head against her abdomen. "I cannot bear it any longer. Every night I feel the bite of that sword upon my neck! Every night I die!" His words were muffled, but their anguish reached her all the same.

Catrian gasped, shocked at the depth of his pain, while her hands fluttered above his dark head where it pressed so tightly into her. She shivered at his need until, compelled beyond bearing, she gave in to the urge to hug him nearer, unable to deny him comfort. But she would not destroy his mind; in this she would not be swayed.

"I am sorry, but I will no' do it. Ye have come t' enough harm at my hand. I will no' do this thing, I will no' rob all that is left o' ye. Someone has already stolen your past, and I will no' be the one t' steal your future!"

She brushed his hair away from his face, a great tenderness welling within that made her catch her breath at its intensity. She bit her lip to stay words she had no right to say.

Gralyre turned his tormented face up to her. "Please. Help me."

A simple plea, made more shocking because of the strength of the man who asked. Catrian nodded, barely aware that her traitorous hand yet stroked his hair. "I will help ye t' sleep. That I can do. Ye will no dream," she vowed, her words whisper soft.

Gralyre sighed heavily, allowing Catrian's touch to soothe him while her magic worked its gentle will upon him. "Thank-you," he whispered gratefully, and went limp in her arms.

She held him against her for a moment, her heart twisting over in her chest, as she examined his now peaceful face. She reached out to cup his cheek tenderly, feeling the soft brush of his beard against her fingers, and the measured puffs of exhalation from his deep slumber.

Gently, she eased him back down onto the cot, and bent forward to brush his brow with her lips, staying to inhale the scent of his hair. "I wish…" she began to whisper into his ear, but could not allow the words to be uttered, even if he were not awake to hear them, for words held power, and intent, and what she wished could never come to pass.

She straitened just as her sentries announced the arrival of Rewn and Dajin Wilson. As the two men entered carrying a stretcher, she stepped away from the bed, placing herself a decorous distance away from Gralyre's side.

Rewn hissed air through his teeth when he lifted the icy clothes off of Gralyre's wounds to reveal the extent of the damage. "Is he alright?" Rewn asked grimly as he looked down upon Gralyre's bloody and bruised back.

"It will hurt like the devil for the next couple o' days, but he will be fine," Catrian promised. "I have induced a deep sleep so that he will no' feel the pain as ye take him home. He will no' awaken until tomorrow."

Rewn nodded to Dajin to take up Gralyre's feet, and together they hefted him from the bed, placing him upon the stretcher. "'Tis good that he canno' feel this," Dajin muttered.

"Thank-ye for caring for him, Rewn, Dajin. He needs ye, more than ye know." Catrian could not help saying as they left.

"Of course, m'lady," Rewn seemed surprised at her sentiments, but no more so than Catrian was.

As she watched the Wilson brothers carry Gralyre away, her hand smoothed a crease from the blanket, lingering to catch the last of the warmth from Gralyre body, and into her mind's eye she traced the muscles of his beautiful back, finally allowing the indulgence of fantasy. "Ah, Gods!" Catrian moaned as she stared down at her empty bed, and realized that she had stupidly stepped into a trap that she had intended to step over.

CHAPTER SEVEN

"Gralyre."

At the familiar gravelly voice, Gralyre glanced up with hostility from the repair he was making to a leather satchel, towards Matik who was standing off the lane, his hands petting his beard, as he studied Gralyre with his agate hard eyes, his ever present axe strapped to his back.

It had been a long sennight since the whipping, and Gralyre's back had mostly healed. The long scabs pulled stiffly across his back, but the bruises had faded, and there would be minimal scaring, as the whip had only sliced his thick hide in a few places.

He was terribly embarrassed by the fever that had made him beg Catrian to destroy his mind to give him peace, and had yet to return to her tent to resume his studies. The thought crossed his mind that Matik was there to remind him of his promise to learn magic, but then, why had Catrian not come herself?

Silent animosity snapped thickly between the two men until Gralyre slowly set aside the awl he was using to punch a hole in the leather, and indicated with a tilt of his head that Matik should take a seat on one of the stumps at the fire. Whatever it was that Matik wanted, he was clearly there under duress, which piqued Gralyre's curiosity enough to suffer his enemy's presence.

Little Wolf growled as Matik approached, well remembered

animosity ruffling his fur.

Matik eyed the wolfdog, as he slowly sat. "Is it safe?"

Gralyre shrugged. "For now. What do you want?"

Matik sighed and smoothed his beard again, while his face screwed up in resistance of the words that tore reluctantly from within his barrel chest. "I have been directed by both Commander Boris, and the Lady Catrian, t' seek your aid." He turned his head, and spat his disgust into the fire, raising a hiss and a spark from one of the glowing coals.

Gralyre stifled a derisive laugh, but could not hide the cold amusement that twisted his lips. "Help? Me? With what? I am a dangerous man, Matik, not to be trusted. You know that."

Matik glared and gritted his teeth, obviously resentful to be the one presenting the request. "Ye are the best man with a sword that we have ever seen." He growled out the reluctant complement. "In a fortnight, we are hosting a tournament in honour o' the visiting Generals, and we need a champion t' represent us, and give us a good showing; make us look strong."

This time Gralyre could not contain his incredulous laugh as, up from the depths of his missing past, the knowledge of what a tournament was floated to the surface, and the nature of Matik's demand became clearer. "You cannot be serious. I would as soon fall upon my sword, as use it in aid of my enemies!"

"We are no' enemies!"

"Are we not?" Gralyre growled, his amused mask vanishing to revealing the depth of contempt that lurked beneath.

Matik leaned forward, and clasped his hands around a knee,

his face intent. "'Tis no' my idea!" The man could not have sounded more disgruntled. "This egg is from Boris and Catrian's hatchery! I have already handpicked my combatants, but they feel that because o' the character o' the times, a decisive victory is required. We must win."

"Why should that matter? The purpose of a tournament is to promote civilized competition and unity."

"Boris is getting old." The reluctant admittance made Matik's voice even more of a growl. His hands stilled in his beard, clenching within the long hairs, as his eyes gazed into the distant past. "Time was he commanded the resistance through the might o' his arm, and the Generals listened t' him because they respected and feared his strength. No' longer. If the Generals should think him weak, and decide to go their own way..." His fingers combed urgently at his beard again, and Gralyre could see that Matik was weighing exactly what he could reveal.

"If you want my help, you must tell me all," Gralyre demanded proudly. It was the very least he deserved after what the Rebels had put him through.

Matik's hands stilled, and dropped into his lap. "We are facing a most terrible war, a war t' decide the fate o' humanity, do ye understand now? Catrian says it will begin in the spring. And Doaphin will likely kill every last one o' us!"

Gralyre reared back, never doubting that Matik had given him the truth. He had known that humanity's grasp upon existence was tenuous, but he had had no idea it was so very dire.

Puzzle pieces reorganized in his mind; the deserted and

destroyed villages of the lowlands, the lack of children, the Woman Tithe. Gralyre frowned in confusion, for war made little sense. Doaphin need only await a few generations more for humanity's extinction through attrition, so what had prompted his sudden desire for immediate extermination?

"We canno' allow any fractures t' form in the resistance. No' now! No' when our need is so urgent!" Matik leaned forward, trying to make Gralyre understand what was at stake. "The confidence o' the Generals in Commander Boris' ability t' lead, must be maintained at all costs. He needs t' appear strong. Our forces need t' appear strong. We need ye t' see t' it." It was as near to a plea as Matik could make.

"And you think that a tournament victory will accomplish all of this?" Gralyre snorted.

Matik shrugged. "It will no' hurt."

It made an unfortunate sense that Boris' control hinged upon appearing robust in the eyes of his Generals, and that to that end he had sought out a ringer to ensure a victory. Yet, why should he bestir himself to help, a small part of Gralyre whispered bitterly. Especially at the behest of one who had actively contributed to his torment. These Rebels had done nothing to earn his loyalty. Gralyre shifted on the stump, feeling the painful pull of his knitting wounds, and found that he was not feeling particularly altruistic this day. "What will you do for me?"

Matik roared to his feet, and Gralyre matched him. "Ye bloody demon-loving lowlander! How dare ye ask that!"

Gralyre smiled in cold challenge, thoroughly enjoying his

moment of power. "If you are going to treat me as an enemy with one hand, and an ally with the other, then I am obviously nothing better than a mercenary in your eyes. I will guarantee your victory in the tournament, and that Boris is made to appear powerful in the eyes of his Generals… if you meet my demands. You came to me. I did not seek this. So, Matik, what are you willing to offer for the use of my sword?"

Matik spat into the fire again, clenching and releasing his fists, as he shook his head slowly, glaring threateningly, his chest heaving with outrage. "What do ye want?" His voice dripped contempt.

Gralyre returned to his seat, and nodded to Matik to indicate that he should do the same, as he set out to negotiate. What did he want?

'Freedom.'

Yes, that, but also to spit in the eye of the people who had meted out so much pain and suffering. If Boris wanted Gralyre to use his prowess to make him look powerful, than the Commander must be made to release some of the power he held over him. A slow smile spread Gralyre's mouth until his strong, white teeth gleamed. It was aptly poetic.

"I want to be restored as a Huntsman, to be allowed outside the walls." It was a freedom that Boris had made a personal point of denying, and it was this one thing that Gralyre knew would humble the Commander most. Another piece of his personality was revealed. He could be vindictive. He was that kind of man.

Matik's glare went flat and cold, as his chin rose in challenge, and his beard bobbed with the violence of his response. "Never. Going. T' happen."

"I would accept a caveat that Rewn Wilson or another of your choosing would accompany me at all times, to ensure that I was not conducting myself nefariously," Gralyre bargained with an exquisitely reasonable tone of voice.

Matik shook his head, "No!"

Gralyre shrugged. It had been worth a try. "Then we are at an impasse. Good luck with the tournament." He stood and walked into the tent, rudely abandoning his guest to leave or stay as he chose, but the conversation was over as far as Gralyre was concerned.

Dara glanced up from where she reclined against her pillows on her cot. Her brow knit with unease. "Who was that, Gralyre? Who is out there?"

"No one important," he smiled, as he crouched down, and gently picked up her hand, sandwiching it warmly between his, and chafing lightly to bring heat to her fingers. "How are you feeling today? Do you want me to help you to sit by the cook fire for a spell?" It was time for her to be up and about, but the beating she had suffered, the humiliation she had felt when her plight became known to her family, had made her almost phobic about going outside.

The swelling in Dara's face had receded but the flesh was still mottled with the yellows, blues and purples of healing bruises. She nodded bravely. "I think I would like that. Will ye stay with me…" she broke off with a little gasp, as the tent flap was rudely thrust aside, and Matik stuck his bearded head through the opening.

Gralyre turned, instinctively shielding Dara from his sight. "I thought we were done," he growled pointedly.

Matik looked from the beaten woman to Gralyre, taking in the tender clasp he held on her hand, and the protective posture of his body. "What happened t' her?"

Gralyre stood, and used his bulk to force Matik back outside the tent. "She was a lowlander in a Rebel fortress," Gralyre snarled.

Matik, for all his faults, was not an abuser of women. "I am sorry, it looks bad."

"It is."

Matik sighed and rolled his shoulders, resettling the weight of his axe. "I know that there is no friendship between us, and ye have no cause t' aid us. I only ask that ye reconsider."

Gralyre's brows rose along with his amazement at Matik's unusual civility, and so chose to respond in kind. "I will consider your request, if you will bring mine to Boris and Catrian."

Matik stared coldly up into Gralyre's face for a long moment before finally nodding. "Done. I will let ye know what they decide."

Gralyre nodded. Done.

&⊃⊂&

In the early hours of the morning, there was little traffic in and out of the south gate, wrapping a sense of peace around Gralyre, as he packed supplies onto his horse. For the first time since he had become trapped in the Rebel fortress his tension eased, as he readied his mount for the hunting foray. He could hardly wait to leave behind the noise and odors, not to mention the suspicious glares, and discrimination, for the clean silence of the forest. He had missed the quiet spaces.

He had won. Boris and Catrian had acceded to his terms upon his promise of help. His one leash was that he was to be accompanied at all times by three others. He had no problem agreeing with the provision, and Rewn had immediately volunteered. The difficulty had been in finding two more warriors who would consent to hunt with him - the dangerous Sorcerer's apprentice, lowlander, and possible spy.

Dajin had flatly refused with a gleam in his eyes that bespoke glee at Gralyre's predicament. It had been Dara who had suggested that the sisters, Mayvin and Aneida, might be willing to oversee his parole, and they had.

He gave a friendly salute to them now, as the sisters rode up and dismounted to await him by the gate. Rewn had returned to the tent to fetch extra arrows, and would rejoin them soon. Then they would be off.

Gralyre's hands stilled in their task, and he breathed deeply of the air, his face alight with anticipation. If freedom had a scent it was this; the tang of a swift wind combing through ancient evergreen forests. The winter day had teeth that were cold and biting, and the sky was overcast and heavy with the promise of snow, but it mattered naught. Freedom was at hand - for a time.

He settled his thick fur closer around his shoulders, turned to pick up another pack, and felt his mood curdle when he spotted Catrian approaching. From the attitude of her challenging stride, and the stiffness of her shoulders, he knew that this confrontation would not be pleasant, and he steeled himself to endure whatever it was that she wished to bedevil him with.

Catrian crossed the snowy lane, her gait predatory, her thick fur leggings and boots lending more than a passing impression of the soft paws of a stalking mountain lion. People, wagons, all the traffic, flowed around her as though she were an immovable boulder in the midst of a stream. She paid them no heed. There was only one prey in her sights.

"So, ye have moved up in the world. Maneuvering for a position o' power?" She called out coolly as she neared, for the intimacy of the night of the whipping was a distant and embarrassing memory that gave her mood a darker turn than normal. Certainly, Gralyre had not allowed it to influence him, as he had bargained for his freedom.

It galled her that there had been no other way to compel him to act as their champion. If he sought to meet with the enemy, he would have no better opportunity than this, running unfettered in the wild. Deep within, Catrian admitted that they had brought this upon themselves by the way they had maltreated him, but still a small piece of her heart ached that Gralyre had chosen a mercenary route rather than to simply comply with their request. He did himself no favours by striking this bargain.

The old adage that a beaten dog will eventually bite the hand the feeds it slipped through her thoughts, and her mouth tightened at the residue of regret that lingered, wishing it could all be different somehow.

Gralyre clenched his teeth to contain his retort to her opening shot, collecting himself for the inevitable confrontation while his horse stomped impatiently to be away. He ran a palm down its gleaming neck, soothing the beast without, as he tried to soothe the beast within. He chose not to respond to the familiar insult, and instead finished hefting the pack up onto the horse's back, and settling it into place. His jaw was clenched tight against words that would be useless to utter, and his neck prickled from the waves of danger brought on by turning his back upon this powerful woman.

Her response was swift and definitive, as her mind pressured his, questing for entry.

Unable to maintain the illusion of calm, Gralyre spun with a glare. "I have done nothing to gain your suspicions."

The wind plucked at a lock of hair loosened from her tight braid, and ruffled the fur of the heavy cloak she wore against the cold, as Catrian raised her chin, power and control etched into her every movement. "Trust is earned. Do ye have something t' hide?" Her eyes glowed with her disillusionment, awaiting one word of dissent from him to renege upon their accord, more wroth with herself than with him, that she had expected more from this man.

Any headway towards an uneasy, cautious friendship between them had been shattered by their bargain, and Gralyre smothered his regret for the loss of something that he had never held in the first place. He turned to the horse, giving her his back. "No, I have nothing to hide."

Gritting his teeth at the unwelcome sensation of submitting to another's will, Gralyre dropped his guard, and allowed Catrian entry into his deepest thoughts, emotions and memories. It was worse than it had been before, for the cool, clinical nature of the connection was at odds with the heat and intimacy of their last touch. He did not try to engage her in more. It was better this way; he would submit, and she would finish all the quicker, and be done with it.

For the first time since they had arrived at the fortress, and the atmosphere between them had eased, Catrian delved deeper into Gralyre's mind than she would normally, and immediately gleaned what had happened to Dara, and how Gralyre and Rewn had dealt with her rapists. Surprise made her grab Gralyre's shoulder, and roughly drag his resisting body around to face her. Her stricken eyes searched his face. "Poor Dara! Why did ye no' come t' me with this?"

"Trust is earned," he drawled the words back at her.

She blinked as his harsh words hit her, and their gazes clashed for long stubborn moments before he broke the tableau, bent, and grabbed up the last pack to settle onto the back of the impatient horse.

"'Twas no' your place t' mete out justice!" she finally countered hotly, as his tacit dismissal added insult to injury. Had she ever met a more stubborn, frustrating man? On the one hand, he had no right to be judge, jury and executioner, but on the other there was a fierce gallantry to his actions. Yet that chivalry had been nowhere to be found, as he had blackmailed her and Boris for his freedom. The man was an enigma.

"You know the attitude of your Rebels towards us lowlanders. Our word against theirs?" He snorted derisively, "Who would they have believed? Who would you have believed?" He secured the sack with a hard knot that he knew he would regret later. As usual, the distraction of her presence had set him off balance. With a grimace of frustration, he pivoted away from the horse to face her directly, giving up the pretense of ignoring her.

"They would have believed me!" Catrian shouted. "I would have seen the truth!"

"Why would I trust you?"

Catrian set her feet, and crossed her arms defensively. Recognizing an argument that she could not win, she smoothly changed tactics. "Ye are a fool t' have requested t' become a Huntsman. Ye canno' be trusted t' be outside o' the gates on your own. Yet 'tis done, and now I am here t' ensure ye comply with our caveat t' take along companions!"

Gralyre nodded to Aneida and Mayvin who were conversing quietly near the gate, studiously attempting to appear disinterested in the confrontation between Gralyre and Catrian.

From the opposite direction, Rewn approached with his own saddled mount. "See? Companions," Gralyre pointed out acerbically.

"Report directly t' me upon your return. I will need t' check t' ensure ye have no' betrayed us!" Catrian ordered, just to watch the rage spike in his face with a flare of heat across his cheekbones. She would make him hate her, for 'twas the best way out of the trap she had blindly stepped into.

There had been moments when they had been almost civil to each other, and feelings had arisen to consume Catrian's imaginings. To combat it, she had distanced herself, and avoided her tent while he poured for hours over that ridiculous book she had distracted him with. Trusting him, liking him, was a dangerous pathway that could lead, not only to her destruction, but also to the ruination of humanity. Everything would be easier for her if he would just hate her, so she need only fight herself for control over this insane temptation.

Catrian's words spilled out, pointed and poisonous, and her heart bled, as Gralyre's face froze, shutting her out. "The only reason we suffer ye at all is for your magic. When ye are no' hunting, ye are t' continue with your studies! It has no' gone unnoticed that ye have no' returned t' your reading since the whipping! Should ye decide t' no' pursue mastery o' your powers, ye are o' no use t' us, and ye will be dealt with accordingly."

Gralyre clenched his fists, breathing deeply to control his need to attack, as he sought to reason with her. "You have to lengthen the leash, Sorceress. I need to get outside the gates for Little Wolf's sake, and yes, for my own. I am turning into a tinderbox awaiting a spark, and I do not want another outburst as with the storm in the mountains." The militant jut of her chin prompted him to go for her softest underbelly. "Besides, if I sought corruption, I would look no further than here," he gritted softly.

Catrian gasped, outraged. "How dare ye!" In that moment, it was not so difficult to hate. Her hand flew of its own accord, aiming for his cheek.

Gralyre grabbed her wrist before she could strike him, holding it gently but firmly, not allowing her to take it back without a struggle, as he forced her hand downwards. "Look to your own house, Sorceress, before you comment upon the dirt in mine!"

His fingers released their clasp, and she took back her hand, absently rubbing her wrist where he had grasped it, though he had not hurt her. Catrian's gaze fell away, and she seemed about to say more, but remained silent when she noticed the audience that their loud argument was drawing. Without another word, she spun on her heel and stomped away.

The people who had loitered in their tasks, scattered from her path, but their watchful eyes returned to the lone warrior who was glaring hotly after the Sorceress' trim form.

Gralyre wondered what she had left unspoken, but it was to remain a mystery to him, though considering how the conversation had devolved, that was probably for the best. He would not enter her mind to steal her thoughts and emotions as she did his. An uninvited link was tantamount to rape. However angry he was, he would never subject her to such a demeaning invasion.

"Gralyre, come on!" Rewn shouted, waving to Gralyre from where he stood waiting with Aneida and Mayvin.

Gralyre gathered the reins of his horse, his shoulders sagging against the pang in his chest, as he walked towards Rewn and the sisters. Perhaps it was better that Catrian should hate and mistrust him, for if he regained his memories and became treacherous, he wanted her as far from danger as possible.

Little Wolf ran ahead of them all, and dug urgently at the wooden gate with both paws, whining a wolfish symphony of impatience to the gatekeepers.

"Hold on, fella," one of the men grumbled good-naturedly, for the wolfdog was well known to them from Rewn's forays into the wild with Little Wolf at his side, as per the bargain he had struck with Catrian for the life of Gralyre's pet.

As the gateman hefted the heavy wooden crossbar, Little Wolf's weight burst the portal open. With an undulating gait of pure lupine joy, he ran free, circling madly in the icy, empty rocks beyond the wall, as he awaited Gralyre and company to catch up to him. *'Run, run! Horizons beckon! Leave the den! Rabbits beware!'*

"What did the lady want?" Rewn asked as Gralyre finally joined them.

Gralyre shrugged dismissively. "The usual threats," he

growled disdainfully, and stalked through the gates, as eager to leave the confining walls far behind as Little Wolf was.

Rewn, his face set in lines of concern for his friend, clicked to his horse to get it moving. "G'yup there."

Aneida grinned at her sister. "Looks t' me like Catrian has an itch in need o' scratching!" she whispered cheekily.

Mayvin hit her in the arm, and gestured. *Can you be cruder? 'Tis obvious there is feeling between them.*

Aneida rolled her eyes, as she interpreted Mayvin's hand language. "Ye are too much o' a romantic, Mayvin."

Aneida leaned back against a fallen log and sighed deeply. "Agh Gods! I had forgotten what it was t' be full!"

Mayvin's hands moved in swift counterpart.

Aneida laughed. "She says, '*One more bite and I will pop!*'"

Gralyre, Rewn and the sisters sat replete around the snapping campfire. The snowfall had never materialized, and the night was a mild one for winter. For the first time since they had reached the fortress, and become subject to the winter rationing, the four were stuffed full with the meat of the deer they had taken earlier in the day. 'Twas one of the benefits of being a Huntsman, that you were able to eat your fill of your catch.

From where he was already curled asleep next to Gralyre's pallet, Little Wolf let out a soft woof, his legs twitching from his dream. The wolfdog was utterly exhausted from his excitement of being able to run free at Gralyre's side, as with times of old.

Gralyre smiled. "He is still chasing rabbits."

Rewn stretched and yawned. "Well, I guess we should all turn in."

"I will take first watch," Aneida claimed. "I need time t' digest!"

"I will take the second," Gralyre volunteered.

Rewn's mouth turned down at the corners, and he scratched at his heavy, winter beard self-consciously. "Well, actually… ah… we were told t' watch ye, Gralyre." His face reddened with embarrassment at the insult he gave, but it had been one of the conditions applied to Gralyre's parole.

Aneida and Mayvin watched from across the flames, stilled and ready should there be a need to act.

Gralyre did his best to smooth the disgust from his face, and nodded his compliance. It was neither Rewn's fault, nor the sisters'. "I see," he said quietly.

"Gralyre I am sorry. If it were left up t' me…"

Gralyre shrugged. "Rewn, do not trouble yourself. 'Tis as it is."

"Gralyre…"

But Gralyre rolled himself into his bedroll, giving the company his back. It was a sour note with which to end an enjoyable day.

Aneida touched Rewn's arm. When he glanced at her, she shook her head. "Leave him be," she suggested softly.

Rewn nodded and, soon after, sought his own bed.

છાૢ

After a restless night sparring with his nightmares, Gralyre awoke to see Rewn crouching by the fire, cupping his hands to the warmth. The sisters were now abed, having taken the first two watches of the night.

Gralyre rolled from his pallet and stretched mightily, before drawing his sword to welcome the day as was his custom.

Little Wolf cocked his head at a sound in the surrounding bush, and went bounding off into the forest to investigate.

"Will you join me, Rewn, or is it not allowed?" Gralyre asked, flourishing his sword in a complex spin, and throwing it high into the air, a flashing blur, that he caught deftly as it fell back into reach.

Rewn grinned at him over his shoulder. "I did no' ask."

As the two men began their practice, Rewn shadowing Gralyre through the sword forms, Aneida awoke, rolling over to watch, her eyes bright and inquisitive. "What is that? What are ye doing?"

Gralyre paused to look at her, then grinned at Rewn, and attacked without warning.

Rewn gave a shout of surprise, and just got his sword up in time to block Gralyre's slash, then was hard pressed, as Gralyre hammered at his defenses.

The clang of swordplay awoke Mayvin, and she rolled to her feet with panic in her eyes, and her sword in her hand.

Aneida touched her arm, and indicated the men. "'Tis alright.

They but spar."

Mayvin sheathed her sword, leaving her hands free to flow into speech. *He is very good.*

Aneida silently nodded her agreement.

Rewn's face was wet with sweat, and his breath was steaming from his mouth with his heavy pants by the time Gralyre neatly disarmed him. "Argh! That is a new one! Show me what ye just did?" he demanded.

Gralyre beckoned to the women. "Perhaps ye would like to join us?" He had not yet broken a sweat.

Mayvin and Aneida exchanged an uncertain glance.

"You must allow me to repay you for agreeing to oversee my parole. 'Tis my only wealth," Gralyre explained with quiet dignity.

Aneida smiled boldly, and put her hands on her hips. "Why no'?" she shrugged.

After that, each morning Gralyre took an hour or two out of the day, before they started the hunt, to train Rewn, Mayvin and Aneida. He worked to enhance their abilities, to provide them an edge of survival in any swordfight.

Gralyre was impressed with the skill level that the women already owned. It far surpassed that of most Rebels he had sparred with. Even Rewn and Dajin had not been as able when Gralyre had first taken them as pupils.

"The world is a terrible, dangerous place for a woman who canno' defend herself," Aneida had explained. "Our Da insisted that we learn the sword from him, as he had learned from his Da, and on back through the ages since the time before Doaphin. He had no sons, so he passed the knowledge t' us."

For a lowlander, to own a sword under Doaphin's rule carried with it a sentence of death. It spoke volumes about Aneida and Mayvin's father, that not only had he defied the edict but that he had also entrusted his legacy to his daughters.

Gralyre gave them no special consideration, for a woman who chose to live by the sword could die by it as easily as any man, and any allowances made for their gender would be a cruelty. Aneida and Mayvin were quick studies, driven and focused to improve their proficiency, and they were soon able to hold their own against Rewn, who had a half-year training with Gralyre head start upon them.

ૐ૓

VERDALAN – LATE WINTER

Ah, Verdalan!

Sethreat breathes deeply of the seething cauldron of humanity, a thick stew of despair steeped in terror. The humans think the tall stone walls ringing the city protect them, but they are naught but the cage that will keep them penned for Its delectation. The cold winter has made It yearn for heat and death, and although Verdalan is not Dreisenheld, a poor country cousin at best, it will suffice to satiate Its need to rend and tear, murder and befoul.

Anticipation drives impatience, and the denmates clamour to enter the city. They even dare to step out of their place to precede It through the gates. It roughly backhands them both, sending them skidding through snow to fetch up against trees and rocks.

The inferior ones do not deserve to revel in blood, unless it is their own! This bounty is Its alone to enjoy, and It will not suffer the presence of another Stalker upon Its hunting grounds.

"Thou shalt stay outside in the cold. Circle the city, find the trailhead." Sethreat glories in power, as the denmates whimper and beg at Its edict. They want nothing more than to gorge themselves upon manflesh and murder, but they will not dare to test Its authority. It has schooled them well of their proper place during the cold nights of travel from Brannock.

Most of Its Deathren have been lost to the harshness of winter along the road to Verdalan. Some vanish in the fiery dawns, and leave nothing but ash drifting on the wind, and others are buried, immobilized until spring warmth thaws their flesh and sinew.

The loss of the Deathren herd is not unexpected, for the creatures have short second lives ruled by insatiable violence. Summer brings its own challenges, for flesh rots quickly, and the creatures, though animated by evil, still require muscle to move bone.

It grants Its surviving Demon Riders, and the remaining Deathren entry into the city, further insulting the denmates that Its minions can go where they cannot. The minions are necessary to Its winter travel. But the denmates are just needless competition.

It enters through the gates, unchallenged by the 'Riders that guard them. Their fear is delicious, an appetizer to the frenzy of death to come. The streets are deserted this late at night, for the Humans live under a restrictive curfew, enforced by roving packs of Deathren. They think themselves safe within their hovels. They are wrong.

It kicks in the first door It sees. Then begin the screams, and death, and wet, wet warmth of blood. It nests amid the carnage to await the next nightfall, gorging Itself, and recovering strength from the long, cold journey.

News travels fast, and by nightfall next, the Humans know that It is in the city. Now they huddle within their hovels with Demon's Bane nailed to their doors in pathetic attempts to ward off the evil that stalks them in the night. The weed does nothing to protect them.

It owns the darkness!

The abundance of filthy Human scents makes it impossible to track a single quarry after so much time has passed, but though the path has grown muddied, there are still those who remember the passage of strangers, and it is these witnesses that It seeks.

Treading icy, cobblestone streets, pausing at random doors to seek forth with magic, It steals the memories of those within, and leaves behind an epidemic of madness and death. If any Human holds memories of a tall black-haired man with blue-black eyes, It has yet to find them, but the city is large, and only so many humans can be sampled each night.

§∞∞

HEATHREN MOUNTAINS – LATE WINTER

It was a fine, warm winter's day. Rewn had deemed it a perfect time to teach Dara to defend herself, and had appropriated a corral for a training ring that was far enough from the beaten path to draw little notice.

Rewn had removed his shirt to better illustrate to Dara the vulnerable points on a man's body, and did not notice how his display of lean muscles affected Saliana, who sat a short distance away upon the split rail fence.

Dara ignored Rewn's lecture, opting instead to appraise his lean frame. "Ye have lost weight," she frowned, "ye are no eating enough. I know food is scarce but ye need t' take your share, Rewn," she scolded.

Rewn snorted. "Stop trying t' change the subject. I am going t' attack ye now," he warned. "Stop looking at my hands. Look at my shoulders. 'Tis the tell o' how the blow will fall."

He made a slow jab at her breastbone, which Dara sidestepped. Remembering his instructions as best she could, she followed through with an awkward slash at his midsection that Rewn nimbly avoided.

Rewn took Dara's hand, and patiently repositioned the short stick she was using in place of a knife, and smiled at her encouragingly. "Ye will always have the advantage o' surprise. They will no' be expecting a woman t' be able t' defend herself.

Cry, weep, whatever it takes t' lull them into thinking ye are down, then spring your attack."

Again they went through the drill, this time Dara managed to stab Rewn in the side with the stick. Rewn grabbed Dara in a bear hug, pinning her arms. Dara struggled for a moment, and then went limp. "Tell me what ye did wrong," Rewn ordered sternly.

"I got too close."

"And....?"

"I do no' know!" Dara exploded. "I am no good at this, Rewn!"

"Ye did no' incapacitate me. That little poke in the side would no' have stopped a kitten. Ye go for the vulnerable spots which are...?"

Dara rolled her eyes, sighed, and stepped back. "Eyes, groin, throat."

"And when ye have struck, do ye stand around t' see what damage ye have done?"

"No. I run."

"Correct!" Rewn praised her. "Now try it again."

Saliana spoke from the sidelines. "What if 'tis no' a man ye fight?"

"What?" Rewn called back, uncertain of what she had mumbled from far away. He was startled to see her. She was so quiet and still he had forgotten her presence.

Saliana hopped down from the split rail fence, and walked towards them, though her body language screamed that she was poised to bolt. "I asked what we should do if 'tis no' a man we fight? What if 'tis Deathren or a 'Rider? What do we do then?'"

Dara nodded her agreement. "Yes, what if 'tis a Stalker?"

A hard chuckle sounded from behind the little group. "Ye stand and fight. If ye run they will only kill ye the faster!" Aneida, hands on hips, strutted to Rewn and patted him on the cheek. "Teaching them t' fight?"

Saliana frowned at the woman's familiarity. Her chin went up. "Aye, he is!" she asserted uncharacteristically.

Aneida turned on her so fast, her red braids whipped around her head like ropes of fire. She smacked Saliana in the centre of her chest, and sent her sprawling. Before Dara could move, Aneida hooked her leg and threw her down beside Saliana.

"What are ye doing?" Rewn yelled.

Aneida spun back, and kicked him in the groin. Rewn coughed a moan, and dropped to his knees. She gave his forehead a push with a heavy finger, and smirked as he fell over into the slushy snow. "Why?" he choked, as he curled into a ball, and began to retch.

Aneida ignored Rewn for the moment to crouch by the felled women, who shrank back, staring at her in stunned awe, and not a little fear. The smile was still large upon her face and in her eyes. "Never let a man teach ye how t' fight a man," she chided amiably. "They do no' know what it is t' be at a disadvantage o' strength. Ye want t' learn how t' defend yourselves?" At Dara and Saliana's cautious nods, Aneida advised, "Come with me!"

"G'bye Rewn," Dara mumbled to her contorted brother, as

she trailed after Aneida.

"Sorry Rewn," Saliana paused. "Pack some snow on your...well...'twill take down the swelling," she blushed. She hurried to catch up with the other two.

෧෬

Aneida led them from fortress through the south gate, and down the mountain into the edge of the timberline, where she stopped in a clearing where the snow was packed firm underfoot. "Mayvin and I often come here t' practice," Aneida explained. "'Tis easier t' concentrate without prying eyes upon ye."

"'Tis the spot ye and Mayvin described t' me," Dara recognized. She smiled a little, for she had finally made the trek she had been unable to take while the Stewards had been alive.

"First things first," Aneida announced, flinging two bundles to the ground in front of Dara and Saliana. "No more skirts. Ye can no' run in them, and ye can no' fight in them. They tangle, and slow ye, and make ye vulnerable. So change."

Somewhat shyly, Dara and Saliana changed into the men's garb Aneida had provided. The warmth of the sun kept them from feeling the cold of the air, as they donned the unfamiliar garments.

Aneida frowned at them both. "Braid your hair, unless ye wish it shorn."

"Why? 'Tis just as easy t' catch hold o' in a braid, as left unbound," Dara reasoned.

Aneida stepped forward, grabbed a thick length of Dara's hair, and flung it over her face, blinding her. While she struggled for sight, Aneida cuffed her hard enough to send her sprawling. "Vanity or death. Your choice."

Saliana stepped protectively in front of Dara. "Ye did no' need t' hit her! She has only just recovered!"

Dara glared up at Aneida from where she lay in the snow, but without further protest, sat up and began to braid her hair.

Aneida's mocking laughter swelled up from her chest, and washed over them both. "Ye think me cruel, Saliana? Have ye ever been struck?"

Saliana nodded.

"When? What were the circumstances?"

Saliana's gaze slunk to her boots, as her transient courage left her as suddenly as it had appeared. "My Da, my brother, my uncles." She picked at a frayed cuff with nervous fingers. "Whenever I deserved it, they would clout me."

Aneida's face hardened, as she stared at Saliana's bowed head. "And when was that, how often?"

Saliana shrugged, and her voice sunk to a meek whisper. "Once or twice a day. When I did no' do the chores fast enough or good enough. When I spoke without leave." Her voice trailed off, and she looked away, stilling and shrinking into herself.

Dara listened to her with mounting horror, and as she rose to her feet, she embraced Saliana comfortingly. "I was never hit by Da, or Rewn, or Dajin."

"Rewn would never strike ye," Saliana sighed, resting her

chin on Dara's shoulder.

Aneida snorted. "Which is what made him a bad teacher for the two o' ye." The women parted to listen to her words. "He would ne'er strike ye, and he would be a fool for the kindness. It would be no favour t' either o' ye. Ye can no' learn t' protect yourself from a tepid attack. There is no such thing." Her voice rang with experience. "'Tis always brutal and fast. T' survive ye must be more brutal and faster." Aneida gave Dara a hard look. "Ye know what I say is true."

Dara's chin quivered, for the injuries that Jarrod had inflicted were only just healed, and her face was still puffy and bruised. The scars she bore from his knife would linger forever.

Saliana returned the favour so recently given, and hugged Dara in turn, as tears spring to her own eyes at the pain her friend had endured.

"Enough!" Aneida's voice was amused, and without sympathy.

Dara and Saliana sniffed back their tears, as they turned towards their new teacher.

"So ye have both experienced pain. So has almost every woman who has ever lived. Do ye want t' make sure it ne'er happens again?"

Dara and Saliana both nodded.

"The first thing we will work upon is your attitudes, your posture, how ye walk." To illustrate her point she strutted back and forth, shoulders back, arms swinging, chin up, and eyes searching. "Move as if ye have a destination, a purpose. Get your heads out o' the clouds, and be aware o' everything around ye at all times. Ye must always be on your guard." Aneida halted, and made eye contact with Saliana. "Ye especially."

Saliana's eyes dropped, but Aneida grabbed her chin and forced it ruthlessly upwards. "This alone will stop most o' the animals from coming after ye. They will always sniff out the weakest, the most vulnerable. Keep from looking so, and they will pass ye by for weaker fare." Aneida exerted pressure to keep Saliana's chin from falling again. Defensively, Saliana shifted her gaze over Aneida's shoulder, the only avenue of avoidance left to her.

Aneida released her chin, and squeezed her shoulder kindly. "Eye contact challenges, ye know this. Ye learned t' keep your eyes down so the animals in your household would no' notice ye. But they noticed ye anyway, did they no'?"

Saliana nodded, and then licked her lips nervously, bravely returning her gaze to meet Aneida's. "Animals?"

"A man would no' treat a beast so, let alone a woman. So animal, yes. Ye need t' make the distinction, else all men will come t' be animals in your mind." Aneida laughed. "And men, real men," she chortled, "they are too fine a distraction in these terrible days t' avoid!"

She grew serious again, and cocked her head to the side. "When ye are dealing with an animal, ye keep your eyes on theirs. Every thought they have will be writ there, and can be used against them. If you do no' watch them, how can ye know when they will attack? Understand?"

Saliana nodded.

"Good." Aneida stepped away and drew her sword to slash it through the air. "Ye have both felt the power in an animal's fists. Ye know that if the animal lands a blow, ye are done, for ye will always be smaller and weaker, so when ye strike, ye strike t' kill, and ye strike first and fast." She impaled her sword into the snow and leaned on it. "Breathe deeply and hold your air."

Dara and Saliana complied, drawing in a gust and holding it, as Aneida paced around them, lecturing. "A fight should last no longer than the longest ye can hold your breath. If it does, break and run away, if ye can, for their endurance will always outlast yours."

A few moments later Dara and Saliana released their held breath in loud whooshes. "'Tis no' a long time," Saliana fretted.

Aneida smiled. "'Tis long enough t' reach their eyes, throat or manhood, and as your endurance grows, ye will be able t' hold your breath longer." She reached into her pack and brought forth two stunted, shaped pieces of wood. "These will be your practice daggers. I will no' teach ye the sword, unless ye be set upon becoming warriors. Daggers can be hidden within your clothes, and are light and easy t' wield. Some animals see a sword upon a woman as a challenge, and I think that neither o' ye want that sort o' attention," she advised grimly.

At their nods, Aneida proceeded with the lessons. She worked at showing them how they could turn an advantage against the fiercest attacks. By grabbing only two fingers of her opponent and twisting in a certain way, Aneida could drop an attacker to the ground, leaving them vulnerable to her knife. She demonstrated over and over until Saliana and Dara could accomplish the feat themselves. That something as vulnerable as a hand could disable a large man was a skill that both women were happy to learn.

"Have either o' ye ever watched a cat fight a dog?" Aneida asked.

Saliana smiled. "There was an old mother cat that used t' share the barn with me when I was a little girl. I saw her put the run on a sow once that had come looking for her kittens."

Aneida returned the smile with a nostalgic gleam in her eyes. "Mayvin and I grew up watching how our cats fought. They were so small, yet they never backed down, and they seldom lost, no matter the size of their foe. So we taught ourselves t' fight in the same way." Aneida proceeded to show how they could use their feet in kicks and their arms in strikes, as well as their elbows for blows when there was no room for anything else. Neither Dara nor Saliana could have conceived before the lessons began that such fighting as this could exist. A chokehold from the front or the rear was no longer something to be feared, but a position to be turned to their advantage. Teeth and nails became natural weapons.

By the time the afternoon had spawned long shadows, Dara and Saliana were covered in painful welts, and wet through to the skin from their many falls into the melting snow. As promised, Aneida pulled no punches. She came at them with all her might, never taking into account their inexperience or vulnerabilities as women. She frightened them, she hurt them, but both women knew she was being cruel to be kind.

Aneida praised them at the end of the lesson. "A definite improvement."

"In what way?" groaned Saliana painfully, as she rubbed her bruised arm.

Aneida laughed. "Ye are no' cowering anymore! Tomorrow, I will teach ye how t' fall so as t' no' injure yourselves."

"When will ye teach us how t' stab?" Dara's eyes were riveted to the wooden dagger in her hand, as she slashed it through the air in wide arcs. Her shoulders were back, and her cheeks were flushed with exertion.

"When your reflexes are better, and ye are more confident in your body's strength and balance." Aneida promised.

ഇൻരു

Dara and Saliana supported each other, as they limped back to the fortress alone. Aneida had headed into the brush to hunt soon after the lesson had ended, promising that their next session would take place when she returned.

"That was amazing, truly amazing! I finally feel as if I am learning something!" Dara gushed with some of her old enthusiasm for life. "Rewn only frustrated me. I knew I could ne'er be as good as he, but Aneida is a woman, the same as us. If she can do this, so can we!"

Saliana grimaced wanly, and struggled to maintain eye

contact with Dara, for Aneida's insistence upon that had literally been hit home to her again and again throughout day. Whenever Saliana had taken her gaze from Aneida's eyes, the woman had sprung like a lioness. "I do no' think 'tis for me." She said hesitantly, quietly. "I like the thought o' ne'er being hurt again, but I do no' want t' be a warrior." She blushed and dropped her eyes, unable to continue to meet Dara's gaze. Habit was yet stronger than will. "I still want t' be a healer," she confessed shyly.

Dara stopped short, and gave Saliana an encouraging hug. "I told ye before that ye would make a marvelous healer! Look what ye did for me. Why, I would still be in my sick bed were it no' for your help!" Saliana's blush turned fiery red from the praise. "But I still think ye should attend Aneida's lessons with me. Just 'till ye learn enough t' defend yourself."

Saliana nodded her assent, and her face lit up with a rare, radiant smile.

"Then 'tis settled! We will visit the healer when we return, and we will no' leave until she agrees t' take ye as an apprentice! This time, I will go with ye t' make sure."

By the time night had taken hold of the camp, Saliana found herself swearing her apprenticeship to the South District Healer. For once, her back was straight, her eyes were direct, and she smiled proudly as she pledged herself.

There was only a sennight remaining before the tournament, after which Gralyre had little doubt that Commander Boris would rescind his consent to allow him to be a Huntsman, so Gralyre vowed to spend as much of his remaining time away from the confines of the Rebel fortress as possible, glorying in his freedom while he could.

This suited his companions, for when Gralyre's appointment as Huntsman ended, the sisters would be relegated back to their guard duty on the wall walks, and Rewn would be left hunting alone again, with no companion save Little Wolf.

The three stags caught that day were suspended high in the treetops, swinging on ropes to protect the hard won food from other predators. The company had travelled far afield to track the game, and had decided to make camp rather than trek for half of the night hauling their heavy burdens back to the fortress. It was not unusual that they did not return to the fortress, but made camp for the night in a small, protected hollow. They would return with their prizes on the morrow, but tonight was theirs, to enjoy the fresh meat, and good company, and eat until their bellies burst at the seams.

With the abundance of food that was now available to them, Gralyre's form had begun to fill back out, and his outlook on life had improved drastically. Some of his uplifted spirits were due to the new friends he had gained, in the form of Aneida and Mayvin, but mostly it was from the abatement of the Rebels' slights and prejudices.

Being able to hear the thoughts of animals gave him an

advantage over all the other Huntsmen, for where they swore there was no game, Gralyre and Little Wolf always found prey. With each successful hunt they were gaining a reputation that was overshadowing the bigotry for it was difficult to maintain hatred for someone who was saving you and your family from starvation.

Yet despite his improved circumstances, Gralyre was still unable to sleep. The nightmares were in fact worsening, and he viewed slumber with a dread reserved only for the vilest of chores, rather than as a pleasurable ending to a tiring day.

Sated and tired from their hunt, they settled into companionable conversation around the warmth of the fire. The light cast their shadows as giants against the surrounding trees, undulating and flicking in time with the snapping bursts of flames.

Gralyre and Rewn had been learning Mayvin's hand language, picking up short phrases and words, though they were still far from literate with their translations. Tonight, Mayvin was teaching them the signs for some common objects.

"Water!" Rewn blurted as she wriggled her fingers upright.

Mayvin shook her head. *No*.

"Fire," Gralyre stated definitively. He had seen that sign before.

Mayvin nodded and smiled. She pointed at Rewn and undulated her hand side-to-side.

"Water?" Rewn repeated, uncertain this time, his brows knit in concentration.

Mayvin's mouth opened in a soundless laugh, as she again shook her head. She leaned over and flapped her hand in his face.

Rewn gave a bark of laughter. "Air, wind!"

Mayvin clapped in celebration, then taking pity upon him, showed him the sign for water.

Aneida chortled, watching on with amusement as her sister taught the men. It was great entertainment to watch them navigating the complex gestures. Mayvin's language was always evolving, a secret code that previously only the two women had shared. It was a joy to Aneida that Mayvin was taking the leap of faith to teach others to understand her. It had been a constant worry to Aneida that were anything to happen to her, Mayvin's words would be forever silenced.

Mayvin's world was expanding, and it was due entirely to Gralyre. He made them believe that they could be more than what they were, more than what circumstances had made of them. They may have afforded him freedom by agreeing to accompany him out into the forest, but he had given them much more in return.

"Mayvin?" Rewn blurted. "Will ye no' tell us how ye lost your voice?"

Mayvin's face lost all color, and her hands stilled, dropping to her lap. Her lack of movement was a sentence all upon its own.

Aneida bristled, baring her teeth. "What is it t' ye!" she asked aggressively, conditioned to lash out when challenged. Her relaxed contentment of a moment before was utterly shattered.

Rewn shrugged and flushed, his eyes dropping. "I am sorry, I should no' have asked," he said regretfully, "I am just...I am curious. We have spent so much time together, and I know next t' nothing about either o' ye, 'tis all." He shrugged again, and gave Aneida and Mayvin a rueful smile, "Forget I asked."

Aneida looked at Mayvin, her index finger rubbing against the old, thin scar that split the skin of her neck, as was her wont when she was upset or uncertain.

Mayvin nodded at her sister, as her hands moved. *'Tis all right. Tell them. They should know.*

Aneida shook her head. "No, Mayvin, I do no' want t' talk o' this tonight."

Mayvin was adamant, her hands flowing quickly, *They are our friends. We can trust them. Tell them all. Tell them everything, and be done with it!*

"NO!" Aneida shouted, standing abruptly, departing the firelight, and rushing into the surrounding trees. The sounds of her passage faded to nothing.

The silence held awkwardly for a long time, as the three warriors stared deeply into the fire, each seeing their own demons dancing within the flicker of flames.

When Aneida came back into the clearing, she paced to and fro several times like a caged lion, as though arguing with her pain to stay or to go. "I will take first watch," Aneida volunteered suddenly, sternly thrusting her pain back where she kept it, tightly and safely chained within her heart, to be drawn upon for strength when needed.

With a sigh of relief that Aneida had spent her rage, Mayvin held up two fingers. She would take the second watch.

Rewn claimed the third, and last, shift of the night.

Well used to the routine, Gralyre merely rolled himself into his furs while Little Wolf nestled into the lee of his knees with a contended sigh. While Aneida leaned up against a fallen tree and scowled out at the night, Gralyre listened to Rewn and Mayvin settle into their bedrolls, and tried not to begrudge their peaceful slumbers.

Except for the night of his flogging, when Catrian had used her magic upon him, Gralyre had not slept through to dawn since joining the Rebels. The stresses of life in the fortress had increased the severity and persistence of the dreams to the point that sleep had become an act of courage, for he knew that at some point, the Demon would come with his sword, and take his head. He never grew used to the shock of the event. Every time was as the first time, yet worse for the anticipation, so that though he was afforded nights that were uninterrupted by shifts on watch, he grew increasingly exhausted.

Had he hoped that being outside of the walls, coupled with an easing of his friction with the Rebels, would grant a sounder rest, Gralyre would have been mistaken, for the horrors of his dreams followed him out into the wilderness, too deeply rooted to be so easily escaped.

Gralyre stared with reddened eyes into the flickering firelight, as he feigned slumber, and listened jealously to the deep breathing of Rewn and Mayvin. After a time, Rewn began to snore lightly, and Gralyre was consumed with envy at his peace. All the while, his fatigued body demanded what his mind was loath to give it. He was fighting a loosing battle.

Aneida kept the fire in high flame to spread a blanket of heat over the sleepers, and to ward off predators. The snap and crack of the burning wood, the hypnotic flames, and the soothing heat upon his face, all worked to lull him so that despite his dread, Gralyre's resistance was overcome, and he slipped under the dark waters of exhaustion.

His nightmare seeped into his mind like black oil wicking upwards in a lamp, and ignited an inferno. He cried out for nameless comrades lost to fierce battle, and his face grew wet with tears for men turned to black stone.

"Gralyre…Gralyre…"

A gentle hand shook his shoulder, and he jerked awake, sitting upright with a shout. It took a moment for him to blink away the lingering residue of madness in order to focus upon Aneida's concerned face. His chest heaved, as he gasped brokenly, trying to still the pounding of his heart. "Ah Gods!" he moaned and wiped the tears from his face with the back of his hands. He became aware of a peculiar silence, and realized that Aneida was staring at him. "Sorry? What?" he asked in confusion.

"I asked ye if ye always suffer night terrors?" Aneida spoke in a quiet murmur to avoid awakening the other two, who were furry humps in the snow on the opposite side of the snapping fire. "I guess that we all do in these times," she answered her own question with a grimace.

"Aye," Gralyre huffed out on a shaky breath. He sagged down to lean upon an elbow, his eyes still haunted by visions of death, his body quivering with the paranoid need to run, as he surreptitiously scanned the edges of the firelight for a Demon swinging a sword with which to lop off his head.

Little Wolf opened one eye, and grumbled quietly while he resettled himself against Gralyre's legs, before sliding back into his dreams.

Aneida tossed her red braid over her shoulder, and sat back against the trunk of a nearby, fallen tree, her face curious as she asked, "Rewn mentioned ye do no' have a past. Ye remember nothing o' your life before?"

"No, nothing. Just the nightmares," Gralyre made a helpless gesture. "Insane things that cannot be."

Aneida smiled sadly, and just like that her mask slipped to reveal a glimpse of the real woman within. "Perhaps 'tis a blessing. There are stains in my past that I would beg the Gods t' scrub clean from my memory if only I could."

Gralyre's regarded her with understanding. "I have oft thought that myself. If my nightmares are so bad, what of the truth of my past?" He settled onto his back, his hand reaching down to touch Little Wolf in a habit of reassurance. "I am sorry that I disturbed you," he mumbled, shamed by his affliction.

Aneida flashed the bold-faced grin that she used to ward off the world, as she shrugged, and stood to walk around the fire.

"'Tis Mayvin's turn for watch in any case."

Gralyre was determined to slumber no more but his sleepless nights, and the fresh air worked to counter his intentions. His eyes grew heavier, fluttered, and finally shut out the world.

In the deepest reaches of his nightmares he heard Little Wolf howling at him. *'Waken! Waken! Danger!'*

"Gralyre! Gralyre, wake *UP!*"

Rewn's roar reached out to him, and Gralyre was driven from the last vestiges of sleep by excruciating pain. He jumped from his pallet with a shout, his clothing aflame, burning his flesh. All around their small glade, trees were roaring, twisting infernos. He dove back to the ground, and rolled himself in the snow, smothering the fire, and soothing his burns at the same time with the icy wetness.

Little Wolf bounced and jumped around him, whining for Gralyre's pain, but unable to get near while Gralyre rolled to extinguish his flaming clothes.

Rewn and the sisters yelped and spun, pounding and patting at wisps of fire that licked each other's clothing.

Catrian's magic pounded for entry into Gralyre's mind, a piercing throb of agony that made him cry out, and hug his head with his arms. He had the sense that she was readying her magic for a more deadly assault, as he relaxed his will to allow her entry.

'What is happening? What are ye doing?' Catrian demanded without preamble. *'Ye have used your magic again! Must ye suffer another ten lashes?'*

'I called upon my magic from within my dreams! 'Twas unintentional!' Gralyre got a sense that Catrian was disconcerted by his explanation. *'Catrian! What is happening to me?'*

'Sleep no more, this night! Come t' me as soon as ye are able!'

Gralyre promised to present himself by late afternoon, and Catrian's presence vanished, frustrating him with her abrupt departure and lack of explanation.

Aneida leapt over the smoldering campfire, her sword gleaming, as she threatened it at Gralyre's throat where he lay gasping on the ground. "Do no' move!" she howled. "Do no' even breath!"

Rewn tackled her away. "Aneida! Stop it!"

Mayvin stuck her sword point against Rewn's lower back, and he froze. Mayvin had reacted with such stealth that he had not sensed her coming until she had already positioned herself for the kill. As the pressure of the blade increased, he raised his arms, releasing Aneida.

Gralyre propped himself up on his elbows to keep Little Wolf from crawling onto his seared chest. "I am truly sorry. This has never happened before! I had no idea that I could... I cannot control the dreams, they come as they will." Responding to the immediate danger, he drew his power, and created a tornado of snow that cycled through the trees to douse the forest fires before they could spread.

"Canno' or will no'!" Aneida swung her blade, parting the air with a frustrated whistle. "What sort o' dream can call wind and fire? If ye were no' seeking t' attack us then what was that? Start talking! Now! And it had better be the truth or I shall thrash ye both!" Aneida snarled as she glared from Rewn to Gralyre.

"Mayvin, would ye mind?" Rewn asked mildly, growing nervous of the constant pressure in the small of his back that had yet to ease.

The sword vanished, and Rewn turned cautiously to face her, but Mayvin was already several paces away, her body angled to keep both Gralyre and Rewn under full observation.

Gralyre averted his face, unaccountably ashamed, as he studied his ruined bedding. Where he had been sleeping, a perfect outline of his body was melted through the snow, and scorched onto the frozen earth. Gralyre frowned, and rubbed his hands deep into his hair, dislodging bits of ash to sift away upon the wind. He had been dreaming about the long past fire that had taken his pups from him.

What new torment was this? Was this the evil that the Rebels accused him of, appearing at last? When would his past cease to bedevil him! His hand left his hair to gently explore the patchy remains of his beard. He glanced up at Rewn with a silent plea.

Mayvin sat down, one hand still gripped to her sword's hilt, as she made a gesture with her free hand that was easy to interpret. *Begin.*

Rewn looked at the ground, and rubbed the back of his neck. "Well, ye knew that Gralyre has no memory o' his past, and that he is afflicted by terrible nightmares. What ye did no' know is that the nightmares are all about the…" He looked to Gralyre for guidance, raising his brows in a silent question of how much he should reveal.

"The Lost Prince," Gralyre finished Rewn's hanging sentence. His voice was tightly checked, suppressed of all emotion, awaiting the burst of incredulousness from the women that always accompanied the revelation. "The nightmares are of The Lost Prince, and his final defeat at the hands of Doaphin. The battle of Centaur Pass."

Mayvin's mouth popped open, and she touched her temple with her fingers while crossing her eyes. *Touched in the head!*

"Ye have the right o' it, Mayvin," Aneida nodded, as she slowly sank to her knees in the snow, her bared blade balanced across her thighs, her horrified gaze locked to Gralyre's. "Ye are mad! Even your name, Gralyre! I thought 'twas just your kin named ye such in an act o' defiance."

Gralyre eyes were steady upon hers, his voice a monotone, as retold a story he had become hardily sick of. "I awoke without memories, last spring, covered in gore. All that I had in my head was the nightmare; a dream of a terrible battle, my men being turned into black statues, and then," he drew a shuddering breath, "I am beheaded. Every night, I suffer through my own execution."

"I would ne'er have thought...I mean that ye are...Ye just seem a sane man t' me!" Aneida stuttered.

"He is sane!" Rewn defended hotly. "'Tis just a nightmare. It means nothing! Tell her, Gralyre! Tell them both about the letter, and the Maolar chainmail, the coins, the crest you took from off your shirt! The Royal Seal o' Lyre! Tell them!"

But Gralyre was through talking; he had told the tale too many times, and Rewn was doing an admirable job of it on his own. He allowed the familiar arguments to wash around him, retreating into his thoughts while he gently crumbled singed fur from Little Wolf's side from where the wolfdog had been pressed to him for warmth during the cold winter night.

The disaster had been so narrowly averted! He must gain such control that, even in his sleep, even in the grip of his most violent and fearful nightmares, he would keep his magic leashed. Either that, or live apart from people until the end of his days.

Gralyre spent the remainder of the night afraid to doze lest his magic consume him again, fearful that were he not careful, next he would burry them all in a deluge of ice. He paced around the camp, eager for morning and their return to the fortress. The irony was not lost upon him.

Rewn watched Gralyre more than he did the surrounding forest, though he was in no mood to converse. The two men shared an uneasy silence, staring into the campfire, and awaiting the first blush of dawn to herald their return home. Now and again, one of the women would toss fitfully, alerting the men to the fact that they were also awake.

CHAPTER EIGHT

VERDALAN – LATE WINTER

Sethreat has been in Verdalan for several assaults of the hated sun, and there is still no trailhead, no sign that the Man trod these streets. Dawn nears, and It is alone in a darkened, deserted, neighborhood of Verdalan. It has sent the baying Deathren away to their daylight holes, preferring silence to contemplate a new strategy, for soon It must report to the Master, and face the consequences of Its lack of progress. Unaccustomed fear twists Its guts. The Master does not suffer failure.

A tickle dances over its rough, scaly skin, sending the spines on Its back skyward with quivering excitement.

'Magic!'

It pivots Its head until It pinpoints the source. Its snout lifts, scenting towards the distant mountains. Many miles away, to the northeast, someone releases a spell of destructive strength!

It seeks contact with the denmates. Speckle Tail is easily found, lurking outside the city's western gates, chewing upon the remains of a 'Rider, a cow with its cud. It has felt the magic but pays it no mind.

Sethreat breaks contact with the youngling in disgust of its sluggish wit, amazed to be of the same species as one so stupid. It seeks the mind of Green Crest, but a yawning void answers the summons.

'Dead?'

Sethreat probes against the emptiness.

'No, not dead. Hiding. Green Crest shrouds its location.'

Sethreat's teeth glint in the weak moonlight, sneering at the lower Stalker's puny efforts to veil its intentions. *'What hast thou to hide?'* It glories in the minion's pain, as Its superior magic and strength rips aside the denmate's puny shielding.

Pure rage makes Sethreat bellow a challenge into the night!

Not only has Green Crest the scent of the Man, but it also follows the trail for these many nights. While Sethreat wastes time searching Verdalan, Its rival has stolen the march, and is far ahead, upon the north road towards the Heathren Mountains!

Sethreat's claws rip up icy paving stones, as Its bulk gathers traction for speed. The rival seeks to find the Man first, to curry favour with the Master! It roars again, as It accelerates through the streets, hearing screams of terror come from within the hovels It passes.

'Brainless chattel!'

Not bothering with the city gate, Sethreat gathers Its powerful hindquarters, and launches over the thirty-foot walls, impacting hard enough on the far side to crater the earth with an explosion of snowy spray. It bellows a summons for Its minions to follow after, and hastens upon the north road. It can claim but a few miles before sunrise to begin shortening the gap.

Foregoing the strength and concentration required to keep its shielding in place now that it has been discovered, Green Crest dares to taunt, *'The Man is no longer thine!'*

Sethreat gnashes Its teeth in rage at the betrayal. *'No matter! Thou shalt suffer a horrible death long before thou hast opportunity to flaunt thine success to the Master!'*

Green Crest's reply is swift. *'Thy speed is as slow as thy wit, old one. Save thy strength for thy punishment, for soon thou wilt face the Master with empty talons.'*

୨୦୯୧

NORTHERN REBEL FORTRESS – LATE WINTER

'Twas a subdued hunting party that returned to the Rebel fortress late that afternoon. Suspending the three stags on poles between the four of them, it had been a hard trek home that had taken most of the day, but their efforts were made worth while when they were given a hero's welcome at the south gate. Many hands eagerly unburdened them of the venison, for 'twas enough meat to fill many a pot in South District.

After overseeing the distribution of the food, and bidding farewell to Rewn, Mayvin and Aneida, Gralyre sought out Catrian.

Dread and anticipation warred at the knowledge that he was to see her, and Gralyre tried to suppress both emotions for they held no place upon a battlefield. Control gave the mind a chance to function, but where Catrian was concerned, Gralyre knew his discipline lay only loosely within his grasp. They had not parted well, and he could only guess at her state of mind after his unauthorized use of magic for a second time.

His strides lengthened, quickly eating the distance to her pavilion where, upon arrival, he waited impatiently for the sentry to announce him, before rudely pushing past into the tent. Gralyre's anxious gaze went straight to Catrian, and at first sight of her his worries eased, as though her presence were a balm against all the ills in his world. He shivered as the warmth of the air within the tent began to warm the winter wilderness from his flesh.

Catrian was dressed as she often was, in loose buckskins and a homespun shirt, with her brown hair woven into one fat braid that dropped to the middle of her back. She leaned a hip against her shelves, as though she had been returning a book when the sentry had announced his arrival. Her brow knit slightly, as he entered. "Good, ye have arrived. We have much t' discuss."

Gralyre's eyes, hollow with his exhaustion and worry, searched into Catrian's, trying to gauge her mood, as he lowered his mental defenses, a silent invitation for her to scan his mind.

Catrian took full advantage of Gralyre's compliance to skim quickly and clinically through his latest memories. "I see," she murmured as she disengaged.

Confused by her calm, Gralyre thrust his hands through his hair, rubbing the back of his neck against the disturbing remembrance of the previous night. "You see what? That I am a menace to everyone around me? In the midst of my nightmares, I summoned fire. I nearly burned down the forest! I do not think that a beating will aid me this time," his hands dropped to his sides, and his eyes were unguarded in their suffering. "'Tis my every nightmare come to pass! Is it happening? Am I changing? Becoming evil?"

She sighed heavily, and sank into a chair at her table, thwarted in her intentions to avoid being alone with the man in the face of his crisis. "Sit," she ordered when she realized that Gralyre was hovering with uncertainty. Still, she would keep their contact as brief and as dispassionate as possible. She had no choice.

The chair creaked from his weight when Gralyre settled across from her.

"I had no' expected that ye would reach this point so quickly," she contemplated, "nor that it would manifest so powerfully. 'Tis common, as ye learn magic, t' begin calling upon it as ye sleep, like twitching your legs, as you dream of running. I should have suspected that your nightmares would cause ye t' react with much more violence than is normal. That coupled with your strength…I suppose this was inevitable." She sighed. "I should have realized that ye were nearing this point after your instinctive use o' your magic on the night that the thieves attacked ye, and warned ye that it might occur."

"So, what happened last night is normal?" Gralyre's anxiety abated with the realization that he was not turning into a monster. At least, not yet. "So what is to be done, Sorceress?"

Catrian smiled faintly. "Now, I shall teach ye that which ye have been reading o'. But there are dangers in learning, Gralyre, especially with the amount o' power ye draw upon. Perhaps 'tis fortuitous that ye blackmailed us into letting ye become a Huntsman," she mused. "The isolation o' the forest will keep the rest o' us safe while ye learn control."

Gralyre nodded his compliance, relieved that he was to continue on as a Huntsman, despite the circumstances that had brought it about. He tried not to think on the destruction he could have wrought if his uncontrolled magic had manifested within the closely packed tent neighbourhoods of the fortress.

"Ye will practice only outside the confines o' the fortress, during your hunts, so that any accidents will no' cause the deaths o' your neighbours," Catrian ordered, unknowingly echoing his deepest concern. "Ye will inform me o' when ye begin and end your practice, that I might know the purpose o' your use of magic, and can monitor ye from afar."

"You will not be accompanying me?"

Catrian scowled. She could not allow herself to spend any more time in Gralyre's company than she had to. "Do no' question me so. Ye are no' my only burden!"

Gralyre's brows drew together, and he reared away from her. A burden? Was that all he was to her? Suddenly the warmth of the tent held a chill that had not been present before.

Catrian stood to fetch a candle, disturbed by the flash of pain she had seen in his face. 'Twas to the good. There could be no future here - a lesson that her treasonous heart needed to learn.

She returned to her seat, sparked the wick of the candle with a flash of magic, and thumped it on the tabletop between them.

She continued her lecture, as though the harsh words had not been spoken, keeping their relationship firmly in the arena of Master and Apprentice.

"Judging by your instinctive use o' wind t' create the blizzard, and t' defend your home when attacked by the thieves, ye have a strong affinity for that connection, so we will begin there. I want ye t' use wind t' make the fire flicker without snuffing the flame." She indicated the candle

Gralyre raised a brow, still offended by her words of moments before.

Catrian glared at him. "Are ye questioning me?"

Gralyre shook his head, and a hard smile curved his lips, as he realized that she had just very clearly defined their relationship. He should thank her for releasing him from the chains of his fascination. "'Tis just a strange request. I ignited a tree last night. Surely a candle is of little challenge?"

Catrian's gaze snapped cold fire in the face of his provocation. "Is it? Ye have no idea o' the power ye wield. Last night, it was as if Doaphin and all o' Dreisenheld were massing an assault at my doorstep! I would be surprised if they could no' sense ye all the way t' Verdalan!" she lambasted. "Everything ye do is like an avalanche, when most times all that is needed is a small nudge o' a stone. If ye are no' careful ye will sap all your Godsmagic trying t' cudgel a Demon Rider, and stop your own heart in the process! So ye will practice this, and only this, until ye can manage the smallest nudge o' power. No more!"

"I can nudge!" Gralyre defended, insulted, as she praised his strength with one hand, and castigated him for his lack of control with the other. He was a master of the sword dance. Every nuance of wielding a blade was his to command. How much effort could it be to produce a trickle of magic instead of a roaring flood?

"Prove it."

His first attempt blew the candle off the table, out between the loosened flaps of the tent, and onwards into the square beyond. Catrian's braid blew back as the canvas of the tent billowed. Beyond the walls, a shout and a crash followed not far behind. A horse gave a loud, startled whinny of distress, and took off at a loud gallop over the heated curses of a man.

Gralyre shot a wry grimace at Catrian, as he finally recognized that the task before him would not be so easily mastered.

Her face set in patient lines that hinted loudly of smugness, Catrian stretched out an arm, and summoned a second candle to fly from the shelf into her hand, mocking him with her control. She balanced it on the tabletop, and set the wick aflame with a snap of her fingers. "Again!"

Many hours of practice later, and Gralyre could finally nudge - after a fashion. The flame flickered and sputtered, but did not douse, and though the candle teetered in place, it did not topple, nor light the rug afire, nor punch a hole through the fabric of the tent.

"Good, well done," Catrian complimented. "That is enough for today. How do ye feel? Tired?"

Gralyre shook his head with a small smile of pride at his success. "No, not at all. I feel better than I did when I arrived. More rested."

Catrian frowned.

"Why? What is it?"

Catrian's face smoothed out, and she smiled reassuringly. "Nothing."

Gralyre was coming to know her quite well, and by now could easily recognize the lie. "Tell me, Sorceress!"

It was his imperious tone that made her answer with far more sharpness than had been her intent. "Ye are no' tired."

Gralyre shrugged in confusion. "I fail to see that as a problem. That is good, is it not? It means that I am strong."

Catrian leaned forward, and glared at him. "Do ye remember our first lesson, and the nature o' the energy within ye that is used t' work magic?"

Gralyre leaned back, and crossed his arms. "The Godsmagic. Use too much, and ye can no longer sustain your own life," he paraphrased the lesson succinctly.

Catrian rewarded his flippancy with a stern glare. "Every time a Sorcerer uses magic, he uses his stores o' Godsmagic, and that saps his strength. With the amount o' energy ye used today, ye should be as exhausted as if ye have been running for hours. In need o' rest."

She blew out the candle with a small puff from her lips, and a thin snake of smoke wafted into the air. The harsh scent of burnt tallow assaulted their noses for a moment before the odor was drawn up through the smoke hole at the apex of the tent.

Gralyre shrugged. "But I do not feel tired."

Catrian pointed a finger at him. "Exactly!"

Gralyre rubbed a hand over his chin, feeling the bald patches of burned away hair from the fire of the night before, then slapped the table, causing the traitorous candle to topple. Ignoring it, he leaned forward contentiously. "I cannot feel other than I do! So what does it mean? You must tell me, Sorceress, as I am not like to guess what is in your mind!" His hands tightened into fists.

"What do ye know o' Wizard Stones?"

"An object that a Sorcerer uses to store energy against future need to prevent over-exhaustion of internal stores while working magic."

Catrian raised her brows at his perfect answer.

Gralyre shrugged, and a tight smile lifted his mouth. "Read it in the book." From her query, Gralyre extrapolated the nature of her concern, "You think me connected to a Wizard Stone, using its stores, and that is why I do not tire from using my magic?"

The Sorceress nodded. "It would make sense. Your ease in learning what I teach suggests that ye underwent training in your lost past. 'Tis a good bet that ye connected yourself t' a Wizard Stone as well. In fact, I have long suspected that ye have created such a link with the element o' air."

"Air? But I thought that a Wizard Stone needed to be indestructible, a physical object like, well… a stone?"

A crinkle appeared in Catrian's brow. "So much knowledge

has been lost, and what I know, little enough though it is," she indicated over her shoulder at her shelves, "is contained within these few books, and from what I have observed and learned through experience over the years. But I can divine no other explanation, Gralyre."

Forgetting herself for a moment, Catrian stretched her arms across the table, and covered his clenched hands with her palms. They rested like small, pale glaciers atop the large mountains made of his fists. "'Tis easy enough t' discover the truth o' it. Search within your mind. Seek the place o' your Godsmagic. It is a place beyond thought, beyond memory, a physical foundation for all the life force in your body. It may appear to be a silver lake, and your connection to your wizard stone a tether, or glowing rope, that travels outward away from ye, towards another place."

Gralyre breathed deeply, willfully ignoring the sweet sensation of her touch, as he steadied his concentration, and sought within for the glowing tether of which she spoke. After a few minutes of fruitless searching, he shook his head and shrugged. "There is nothing there. Could it be hidden from me, behind the dark wall that guards my past?"

Catrian frowned. "Will ye give me permission t' seek it?"

Gralyre was so startled by her request that his automatic "Aye," slipped out. Since when did she ask permission to invade his thoughts?

He closed his eyes, relaxed his will, and tried to control his body's visceral reaction to her presence inside his consciousness.

When she inadvertently unearthed his chaotic emotions surrounding her, he gently forced her away from those thoughts with a rumbled warning, "I do not think it there, Sorceress." These longings were his, they were private, and she had made it clear that she did not want this of him.

He felt her chagrin, mixed with acute, sensual curiosity, and had to leash his instincts to pursue her presence for a taste of more, as she moved on, moved deeper than she ever had, seeking the place of his power; his Godsmagic.

He experienced the landscape of his mind from her perspective, filled with more colorful, rich memories than ever it had, not empty, as it had been when he had first awakened in the forest the previous spring. The memories were like the leaves upon the branches of a massive tree, all rustling and moving and living, and at the roots, lay a vast lake of shimmering silver, his Godsmagic.

He finally understood why she had asked his permission, as a sign of trust to allow her this deep into his soul. From where she was, standing at the fount of his power, inside all of his defenses, she could easily destroy him.

She did not linger but soon returned to her own body, and Gralyre fought an urge to keep her deep in the heart of him, where there were no boundaries to their being together forever. He was bereft when she left.

"Ye are right. There is nothing there. But that makes no sense, unless…" she looked at him, and horror began to dawn in her face, as her hands tightened convulsively where they still rested upon his fists.

She had never looked at him like that before, and it concerned him worse than any rage or cutting remark could. Gralyre's hands turned under hers, and captured her fingers before she could draw them away. "Catrian, what is it? What is wrong? Surely 'tis but lost somewhere behind the black wall that keeps my past from me?"

Catrian shook her head and swallowed. "No, that canno' be, because your Godsmagic is there, glowing, I can see it, and that is where the connection would be, but there is no tether t' a Wizard Stone. That means that ye would have t' be..." she swallowed thickly.

"Tell me!"

"...possessed of more Godsmagic than any Sorcerer who has ever lived."

Gralyre grinned, and his chest puffed slightly. "That is good, is it not? The stronger I am, the more I can aid in the fight against Doaphin!"

Catrian was shaking her head, and her hands tightened, her fingers tangling with his. "Gralyre, I could no' see it! The great stores o' magic that ye must surely have at your disposal, do no' exist within ye. So where is your power coming from, if no' from a Wizard Stone?"

When she did not return his smile, Gralyre's faltered, and his brows lowered in a frown over his midnight-blue eyes. "No great stores? I saw a boundless lake of Godsmagic within me..."

She shook her head. "'Tis normal. 'Tis no different than what

I possess."

Catrian had always believed that if the worst happened, and Gralyre turned evil, that she would be powerful enough to kill him, and protect her people. She had thought that the one barrier to this would be the emotional attachment she was unwillingly forming to the man. But having just discovered that, in comparison to his, her strength was that of a breeze before an oncoming storm, a fearful shudder racked her body. She had felt many things with Gralyre, most of them beguiling and unexpected, but she had never been terrified of him until this moment. An unusual sensation of weakness, that she was no longer the strongest in the room, made her blink in confusion.

Her one advantage, should it come to battle, was her superior skills, and by training him, she was quickly losing that edge. The abnormal speed by which he had mastered this lesson spoke loudly of previous expertise, something that she had long suspected. Coupled with his abnormal and unseen stores of power, a whirlpool of terrible doubt began to boil upwards from her subconscious.

...A trained Sorcerer, grown to manhood, when all others perish at the hands of Doaphin...

...Hints of the tale of the Lost Prince in his missing memories...

Gralyre was the perfect spy, and the perfect hero, rolled into one being.

And she wanted him.

So badly that nightly, as she lay in her lonely bed, she would often stare into the darkness while her heart pounded and yearned with desires that could not be acknowledged by the light of day. He had become a weakness, and should she succumb, he would steal away her ability to protect her people.

The terrible suspicion cleared the murk of her subconscious, and the light of understanding finally shone upon an unspeakable realization, made even more so by her undeniable longing to be his.

Catrian snatched her hands free of Gralyre's, and she stood abruptly, forcing a smile. "No, ye are right. 'Tis no' so bad. Ye will have t' train harder t' gain control, 'tis all. In the forests, where ye will cause less damage," she babbled, working with all her might to keep her fear from her face, and out of her voice.

Gralyre's grin returned, as he prompted, "I need to learn how to nudge."

She fought his charm and charisma with everything she had, and nodded. "'Tis all for today. Practice what I have taught ye, day and night, until ye can do it in your sleep," she ordered in a strained voice. She wanted to scream and cry and throw things and destroy him and save him, yet all she could do was hide this chaos behind a benign mask, and it was killing her. He had to leave. Now!

Gralyre snorted at her unintentional pun, and pushed his chair back to stand. "In my sleep, aye, that I will." He hesitated for a moment, and Catrian feared that he would ask her more, and she needed him gone! But in the end he turned away, as confused as she by the sudden undercurrents, and headed for the tent's exit.

"Good night, Sorceress."

As the flap rustled shut behind him, and the crunch of his footsteps in the snow receded into the night, Catrian collapsed back into her chair with a sob that stabbed through her like a knife to her soul.

'Gods! What have I done?'

No adept reached adulthood without being found and destroyed by Doaphin, and as powerful as Gralyre was, there was no way he could have remained hidden. She had survived only through the continuous vigilance of her uncle and the resistance, until she was old enough and strong enough to defend herself.

An adept was bound so tightly to the Godsmagic of the world, that any strong spells they wrought created a disturbance that could be sensed by other Sorcerers, like the beating wings of a fly tickling the strand of a web, and alerting a spider to its presence. The greater the magic, the further the sensation could travel.

Catrian had sensed Doaphin and his Demon Lords all her life, their dark magic like a bitter acid at the back of her throat, and she had even sensed several Dream Weaver sorcerers in the mysterious far west, whose magic was deep and rich, but she had never sensed Gralyre until recently.

But these were facts that she had considered before, and dismissed for the need of Gralyre's magic to add to hers in the coming war.

What scared her, what she had only just realized, was that she had not sensed his sorcery creating the blizzard that had trapped them in the ice cave on their journey home. She had guessed he was responsible for the storm, after days of observation, but she had never felt his outlay of magic, save for when he had talked to his pet. She had even posited that he had made the wind his Wizard Stone, without once noting that he had not created a disturbance in the world's Godsmagic to create the storm.

It was not possible! Why had she not realized this before? Had she deliberately hidden from the truth? What could this mean?

'I must consult Boris!'

She stood, and moved towards the tent flap, shock making her stagger slightly before she changed her mind, veering to sit on one of her cozy chairs near the glowing brazier. She covered her mouth with her hands, her eyes wide and full of horror, as she stared into the heart of the smoking coals.

'No! I canno' share this with Matik and Boris! They will kill him, and I have no proof that this is a danger t' us. Nothing has changed.'

Gralyre could be innocent, or he could be guilty, but regardless they needed his magic.

'No! Everything has changed!'

Gralyre had to be a pupil of the mad butcher who had ruled this land for three hundred years! How else had he survived? As powerful as he was, he could not have remained hidden to adulthood. He must have been allowed to live! Someone had shielded and trained him! And there was nowhere he could have received such knowledge of the magical arts, except at the knee of the Usurper, in Dreisenheld.

For a moment she shivered in purest terror. *'What if he is Doaphin?'*

No! She was mad! Of course he was not! He looked nothing like Doaphin, whose image she had gleaned from sifting the minds of captured 'Riders. In fact, Doaphin featured greatly in Gralyre's nightmare. 'Twas he who wielded the executioner's sword while Gralyre was restrained by two Demon Riders. But of course that was one of Gralyre's false memories, the nightmare beheading at the hands of Doaphin. The beheading that had befallen the Lost Prince.

Doaphin was an effeminate, blond man, slight of build and stature, with a withered hand. Gralyre's polar opposite. But that did not mean that Gralyre was not a willing pawn in Doaphin's regime, a collaborator, for how else did Doaphin's countenance feature in his nightmares? Doaphin had not left Dreisenheld since being cursed by Fennick after the battle in Centaur Pass three hundred years ago, when the Prince and his sword had vanished. Dreisenheld was the only place that Gralyre could have seen Doaphin's face

As far as Catrian was aware, she was the only human sorcerer in the land, save for the Dream Weavers in the east, and what she knew of the nature of magic was pitiful when compared to Doaphin's three-hundred-year lifespan. What knowledge was he privy to? What sorcery did he command?

Gralyre had to be lying to them all! If he could create such a storm without disturbing the world's Godsmagic, what more was he capable of?

'No!' she vacillated once more, *'Gralyre is innocent! There is no evil within him!'* Unless it was all locked away behind the powerful barrier that bisected his past from his present...

But none of this explained where Gralyre's vast stores of magic were coming from. Something had to be feeding his power, but if not a Wizard Stone, then what? 'Twas not the first time she cursed the dearth of knowledge in her tiny library.

She prayed for another explanation for the enigma of Gralyre's existence, as tears rolled down her cheeks, and her heart shattered. Did she have the right to roll dice against the Gods of Fortune for the lives of her people? Did she have the right to afford Gralyre the benefit of the doubt?

৪০৫২

Soon Gralyre could create a puff of breeze so light that it could barely be felt to caress his cheek, or a thundering gale that could uproot trees. He could cause a single dewdrop to form upon the tip of a branch, or deluge the forest with sleet and hail. He could tear open the earth, like giant fingers ripping into soft bread. He could even lift a single pebble from the ground or dislodge boulders from the mountainside. Earth, Wind and Water bowed to his every command.

"Gralyre, if ye would no' mind?" Aneida swept an arm to indicate the stacked firewood awaiting a spark.

But he could not make fire.

"Alright, Rewn, Mayvin, ye better stand back," Gralyre cautioned.

Mayvin rolled her eyes, and Rewn grinned.

"Aye, as if it will work any better this time than the last thirty tries," Aneida heckled under her breath. But all three took several cautionary steps back from the firepit, and sat upon a felled tree to watch. Their hunt was finished for the day, and as usual, Gralyre practiced his sorcery in the evenings, honing his skills as much as possible with the lesson that Catrian had set him.

Find control and learn how to nudge.

Focusing his will, and using as little effort as possible, Gralyre strove to create only a small spark within the wood that Aneida had gathered.

Nothing happened; not a puff of smoke, not an ember. Frowning, he tried again and again. The effort caused sweat to shine across his forehead, yet the wood remained stubbornly cold. Absently, he called up a light breeze to cool his brow.

Of all the energies he could now manipulate, fire and heat still remained stubbornly difficult for him to conjure. Gralyre instinctively knew how wind came into being, its mood, its strengths, and how it interacted with eddies created by the landscape as it roared over mountain peaks. But he could not capture the essence of illusive fire.

In theory, as remembered from the ponderous explanation in the thick book, in order to work any magic he needed to find the right combination of matching energies within both himself and the object. By reaching out and bonding with the similar Godsmagic in the wood, then exerting his will to change himself, he would cause the kindling to catch fire.

From his studies, he knew that the wood stored three kinds of Godsmagic. First, Gralyre could pick it up and swing it like a club. He sent a large branch sailing into the forest where it knocked loudly against a couple of trees before it fell into the snow. It was a small snit of a tantrum that made him feel slightly better. This seemed the most common, and easy of energies for him to identify with, the simple Godsmagic of movement. This was why the winds were so easy for him to conquer.

Aneida cleared her throat. "No' going so well, eh? Are ye going t' light this anytime soon? 'Tis getting dark, and 'tis Rewn's turn t' cook. Ye know how long he takes."

Mayvin shoved her. *Quit distracting him.*

Gralyre shot Aneida a frown before returning his attention to the firepit.

Secondly, the wood had absorbed the heat of the sun, as it had grown from seedling to tree. This was the warmth and light that Gralyre sought to release back into the world. But he could only do that by inducing the third energy, the Godsmagic that would ignite the stored sunlight. And therein lay the problem.

Aegon's theories had been overlong and obtuse, and Gralyre was not entirely certain of what he was seeking. Try as he might, he could not seem to voluntarily connect to the Godsmagic that would cause the combustion. In theory, he should be able to induce even rock to burn by creating movement within its essence such that it would heat, as with two sticks rubbed quickly together will create an ember. But to move the essence but not the object itself… it was a frustrating concept!

Though he had made fire instinctually in his sleep, he had yet to reproduce its effects in a deliberate manner, not since that long ago day in Catrian's tent when she had fed him the concoction that had allowed him to see the Godsmagic of the world as clearly as he could now see the stacked pile of wood awaiting a spark. Control and subtly. Frustration roared through him at his continual failure. How could he nudge fire?

Perhaps he was going about this the wrong way. Perhaps the answer lay within the Godsmagic that controlled the heat in his flesh. If he could tap into that, would it make it easier to identify the same Godsmagic in the wood?

He knew the part of himself that was drawn to wind; his need for unfettered freedom, and to smash, and break like a child in a temper. But what was the nature of his inner fire?

Gralyre delved deeply into his stores of Godsmagic, mentally swimming in the silver lake, diving deeply, as he searched for a clue to his own nature, following the lines of energy that controlled the furnace of his flesh.

As clearly as though someone had opened his eyes to a bright day, he suddenly understood. He was holding too tightly to control. Fire was the epitome of chaos. Fire was heat, and destruction, and rage, and battle, but the Sword Dance controlled the battle rage, suppressed the fire with cold ice.

But fire burned, and consumed. Control had no place in the world of fire, and there was only one constant in his life over which he held no restraint - passion. His body flamed to life, and the heat of lust rose in his blood, as he relived the taste of Catrian's lips. Overwhelming chaos.

Holding tight to the energies that now seethed within, he returned from the silver lake and opened his eyes. Looking deeply within the fuel he had been laboring over, he recognized the chaotic energy that matched his own, and drew it forth. Billions of motes vibrating against one another; chaos, sex and passion. Fire.

The wood detonated in a fireball that blew everyone off their feet. Several trees surrounding the clearing burst into flame with roars. Gralyre slapped at the fire licking at the cuffs of his shirt while Rewn, Aneida and Mayvin dived for cover with shouts of surprise.

For a moment, stunned by the sudden success, all Gralyre could do was stare at the flaming pine trees and hoot in victory. "I have made fire!" he yelled.

"Gralyre! The trees!" Rewn shouted back.

Summoning wind, Gralyre smothered the flames in a cyclone of snow. His grin remained, unfettered and delighted, as Rewn and the sisters popped their heads up out of the snow they had dived into. Slush and ice clung to their singed hair and sooty faces, and Gralyre began to laugh. He pointed at the merry crackle of flames surrounding the wreckage of the firepit. "I made fire," he smirked at Aneida.

Aneida stood up and rearranged her disheveled cloak with a smart snap. "Humph!"

Gralyre laughed deeply, crossed his arms, and surveyed the clouds of smoke that were still billowing from the smoldering trees. He had toppled a barrier, but like a young lad wielding a sword for the first time, Gralyre needed to build the muscle to lift the blade before he could start to swing it. Now that he had created fire, he needed to discover how to restrain it.

ഇൽ

During the time remaining before the tournament, Gralyre's control grew, and with it, his successes. The nature of magic was quickly making itself known to him, and he gloried in his newfound abilities. The world was so much larger than he had ever suspected, filled with power and possibility. A stone was not merely a stone, nor a tree just a tree, but a limitless fount of energy and transformation. Truly, *'Godsmagic'* was an appropriate description of the power that was beginning to obey his commands.

So much good could be wrought with magic, yet the land and its peoples had experienced nothing but the evils of power run amuck. As with all great forces, Godsmagic was impartial, 'twas the intent of the sorcerer that coloured its nature good versus evil.

Spring was starting to shake off the cold weight of winter and the melting snow had turned the avenues of the fortress into thick mires that pulled and sucked at Gralyre's boots, as he strode towards the centre square and Catrian's tent. His steps were steady and sure, but pleasurable anticipation lifted his spirits. He was not certain when her opinion had come to mean so much to him, but after a sennight of practicing in the forest, Gralyre presented himself with pride before the Sorceress, eager for her verdict upon his progress.

Catrian glanced up from papers spread across her table when the sentries announced him, and as Gralyre entered the tent, she stacked them together neatly, and turned the pile over. She stood and approached him, her feet quiet upon the reed mat that covered her floor.

Gralyre's grin spoke of his enthusiasm. "Catrian, I finally made fire! At first, I had half the forest in flames but…" his words stumbled to a halt at her stern expression.

Something had changed. She did not speak, only quickly scanned his mind, as though she were indifferent to his progress. They had been many things to each other in the past, but indifferent had never been one of them. Confusion made him frown.

"That is fine. Continue t' practice using the barest amounts o' energy t' accomplish your feats, as I have instructed ye. When ye can draw forth naught but an ember ye may return t' me." She walked back to her table and sat, flipped the stack of papers over, and began to shuffle them, scanning them, as though they were of upmost importance. "That is all, ye may leave." She dismissed with a distracted wave.

"I…ah," Gralyre sputtered at the abrupt rejection.

"What?"

"I wanted to talk to you about doing more."

"No."

Gralyre reared back in surprise. "You have not heard me out!"

"I will no' change my mind."

Gralyre ran a rough hand through the hair he had combed so carefully in preparation of seeing her, ruffling the overlong black strands back from his temples. "I have enough control that I will not kill anyone accidentally, but I want to learn more. A blade in a sheath is no danger to anyone!"

Catrian's face remained cold and intractable, and Gralyre had a suddenly perception that she was curtailing his lessons. "What is this?" he growled.

Catrian laced her fingers together primly, resting them atop the stacked pages. "I do no' know t' what ye are referring, but I have told ye t' leave." She nodded pointedly towards the exit.

Being directly insubordinate, Gralyre took a step forward, and leaned heavily onto the tabletop with both fists, looming above her. "I have mastered the lessons you have given me, and I wish more." He saw her face darken at his demand, and experienced a moment's qualm. She had enough power to squash him, but his grievance was real, and he would have her explanation. If he was going to learn to wield his magic, Catrian had to honour their contract of student and teacher.

"You have been curtailing my progress," he quietly accused.

"Why?"

To his surprise, something that looked almost like grief contorted her features, a flash of intense pain that was quickly shut away, yet her mouth trembled with sudden vulnerability, and as she spoke the words rang of truth. "Gralyre..." she cleared her throat, looked down at her hands, and began again. "Gralyre, there are too many unanswered questions about your past. I thought that I could look beyond them, for the sake o' adding your powers t' our arsenal against Doaphin, but..." She seemed to sag in her seat.

Gralyre dropped into the chair across the table, and traced a pattern upon the wooden surface with a fingertip, to keep his hands from reaching for hers. He sighed heavily, and his mouth twisted with cynicism. "'Tis to be the old argument, then? You think that I do not understand, Catrian, but I do. I dare not trust myself either. I do not know what that dark place of my mind hides. But I do know that I would never seek to harm you," he promised, his midnight-blue gaze caressing her face. His voice deepened, a soft baritone. "I do not want to ever be your enemy. Never that."

Catrian's eyes grew shiny with unspent tears that would not spill. More than anyone else in his life, she was intimately aware of how the constant mistrust hurt him. Gralyre was a man of great integrity, and the suspicions did grave injury to the very fabric of his being. Yet she could not allow it to be other than what it was, for who he was now could be naught but a mask for who he had been then.

"Ye learn so fast, lessons that should take ye years. I am no' teaching ye, ye are just remembering that which ye already knew. I fear where that knowledge came from, Gralyre. Who taught ye?"

Gralyre searched her eyes. "You know I cannot answer that."

Catrian nodded stiffly. "Please. Just give me time. So much is happening so quickly…" she drew a deep breath. "Please."

She had never asked him for anything. Told him, ordered him, threatened him, aye, all that. But never once had she pleaded with him. He did not like it.

He reached out for her clasped hands, and she jerked them back. "No! Do no' touch me!"

"Catrian…?" A little piece of Gralyre's heart chipped away at the rejection. Was she afraid of him?

"Leave me!" she snapped. "Go! Do as I tell ye!" As quickly as that their accord evaporated.

Gralyre stood so abruptly that his chair toppled. Looking her in the eyes with a hard gleam in his, he righted the chair with a small burst of magic. "This is not over, Sorceress," he warned quietly, watching her with deep concern. "Sooner or later you will share with me what has changed between us."

On the way out of Catrian's tent, Gralyre passed Commander Boris, Matik, and several road-weary, roughly dressed men he did not recognize. They stared at him coldly, as he passed by but Gralyre ignored their presence, except for Matik, whom he took the time to glare at. Was this the reason for Catrian's odd behavior? What new weeds of deception had Matik and Boris been cultivating?

Gralyre walked onwards into the square before turning, his interest piqued, as he recognized the Generals of the Resistance approaching from the right. He watched, as they also vanished within Catrian's tent, and realized that the men that he had passed with Matik and Boris must have been the latecomers, General Kierdenan and his entourage. The leadership of the Resistance was now all assembled.

After allowing servers carrying platters of food to enter, the men guarding the entrance to Catrian's tent jerked their pikes together to bar all other entry. Something important was happening. The heightened security outside the tent bespoke that.

Briefly, he thought to contact the mind of a rodent, and send it to the tent to listen, but quickly subdued the idea. He was no spy, despite their suspicions that had him doubting himself.

ഓരു

"General Kierdenan. I bid ye and your men welcome," Catrian smiled courteously, smoothing away all agitation from her encounter with Gralyre, as she rose from her place at the table, nodding pleasantly when Boris and Matik led the way into the tent.

"I do no' appreciate a summons in the dead o' winter, Sorceress. This had better be worth my time," General Kierdenan complained, his expression pulling at an old scar that travelled from his left temple down the side of his face to curve around to disappear under his chin. Other scars lined his cheeks, and bisected the flattened, crooked nose of a pugilist, distorting his unpleasant expression further. From beneath heavy, thick brows that just narrowly avoided growing together, he glared at her with flat cold eyes, and rudely appraised her form with a lascivious intensity. He was built like a bull, heavy of muscle, and massive in size and intimidation.

"We appreciate your attendance, General Kierdenan. We would no' have issued the summons save for the most dire o' needs," Catrian intoned diplomatically.

The other Generals entered the tent, followed closely by a team of servers carrying platters of meat and drink.

"Finally!" General Chartrin grouched, as he took in the new arrivals. "Ye would think ye had t' travel as far as I did! What took ye so long, Kierdenan? We have been cooling our heels here for half the winter!" He tossed back his golden hair, exposing the jewel earing piercing his lobe. Though he had been a long time away from his pirate ships, there was still something of the scent of the ocean clinging to him.

Kierdenan sneered, seeming his usual expression, caused by the scars pulling at the lines of his face. "I am but a day or two late, am I no'?"

One of the Generals moved forward with the grace of a cat. He was tall and lean, almost slight of build next to the bull-like Kierdenan, but his intense blue gaze was sharp and clever, calculating. "We have no' met. I am Laurazon." He held out a hand in greeting.

Kierdenan ignored it, turning away rudely to address Boris. "So we are all here. What senile madness is this? Even your pet Sorceress could no' protect us should the Demon Lords get wind o' this summit!"

Matik stepped forward with a rumble of warning rattling out from beneath his thick beard, but Boris stopped him with a hand upon his shoulder. "In good time, Kierdenan," he smiled coldly. "Tonight is for feasting. Now that we are all here, we will arrive at our business in two days time."

"General Kierdenan, we have arranged billeting for your men." Catrian indicated one of the servers with a graceful sweep of her hand. "Hagen will see them settled."

Hagen saluted and herded Kierdenan's men from the tent, leaving Commander Boris, Matik and Catrian alone with the assembled Generals.

Please," Catrian indicated the table, "will ye no' all seat yourselves."

With ill will, Kierdenan threw himself into a chair, grabbed a leg of chicken, and took a savage bite from the roasted flesh.

ഇരു

Catrian touched her uncle's arm, holding him in place, as he would have left with the other men. Boris was tense with suppressed rage, having endured the barely veiled barbs and slings from General Kierdenan all evening. The man's deliberate tardiness, when he had the least amount of distance to travel for the summit, had been only the first of the insults.

When the last General had exited, and walked a fair distance from the tent, Boris barked, "What is it?"

Catrian's eyes widened, startled at the brisk tone.

Boris sighed and patted her shoulder awkwardly. "Sorry, Cat." He sighed. "What do ye need?"

Catrian indicated the comfortable chairs set before her kindled brazier. "Sit with me awhile, uncle." The blast of heat was welcome, for the temperature without had dropped several degrees as night had fallen. In the dim light of the tent, the soft, golden glow of the coals burnished their faces, and soothed away the stress of the evening.

After a few minutes Boris broke the comfortable silence. "Something is bothering ye, lass. Out with it," he ordered as he settled deeper into the soft padding.

Catrian's mouth quirked in amusement. "Am I so easily read, uncle?"

Boris grunted, and his returned smile lightened his careworn face. "Just by one who knows ye well, my lass. Ye have been fidgety all night, and I suspect 'tis more than the presence o' the Generals that has made ye so."

Catrian nodded, and her eyes shifted to stare into the embers in the brazier. "I think that ye should reconsider using Gralyre as our champion tomorrow."

Boris stirred, and leaned forward to rest his forearms along his thighs. "Where is this coming from? Ye thought it a fine idea when we proposed it."

Catrian shrugged. "Nothing really, just a feeling…"

The Commander's gaze sharpened, steely and hard, as he stared up at her profile. "Has Gralyre revealed himself? Is it time t' kill him?" He straitened aggressively in the chair.

"No! No nothing like that…just…I do no' think it wise t' put so much faith in him. He is unstable, unpredictable. He could betray our trust out o' revenge for past slights. We have no' been kind t' the man, uncle."

Boris grunted. "Cat, ye witnessed Kierdenan's demeanor tonight. The man thinks me weak. He would see himself replace me as Commander. I canno' permit that. A show o' strength is needed!" Boris' jaw jutted mulishly. "Gralyre canno' be trusted, but he is the best swordsman I have ever seen. We need a victory, a decisive announcement that we are no' t' be trifled with!" Boris punched a fist into his palm with a hearty smack.

Catrian nodded. "Yes, I know, uncle." General Kierdenan had taken every opportunity to insult Boris' age and wit, but at least the other leaders had still paid their Commander the proper respect. How long would that continue if Boris did not retaliate in some way for the insults? Diplomacy was all well and good, but outright sedition had to be addressed. The Resistance could not go to war suffering divided leadership.

Yet she instinctually wanted to keep Gralyre from the eyes of the Generals, and was confused by her sudden protective urge.

Boris' eyes narrowed suspiciously. "Why the sudden concern? Did he say something that led ye t' believe he will no' fulfill his pact?"

Catrian's brow knit. "No, o' course no'. He is trust…" her words trailed when she realized how she was contradicting her own statement of just moments before.

Boris snorted. "Trustworthy? 'Twas what ye were going t' say?" He grimaced heavily. "The man is as trustworthy as a carrion crow on a battlefield. So what is he? A moment ago ye said we should no' trust him, now ye tell me we should!"

Catrian frowned. "He will fulfill his bargain, uncle. I just do no' deem it wise t' expose him t' the Generals. He will draw a great deal o' attention when they see him fight, and they will want t' know where we found him. They will no' understand why we have allowed him t' live. I should have thought this through more thoroughly!"

Boris sagged back heavily in the chair, his gaze steady on her face. "Ah, finally. There is the crux o' it. Ye fear for his life," he stated. He rubbed a hand over his short-cropped hair. "I warned ye, lass. I warned ye t' guard your affections."

Catrian stilled, and even her breath held suspended for a moment. Her eyes burned, as she stared fixedly at Boris.

"Ye were right, uncle." She breathed out a harsh sigh, relieved to say the words aloud. "Ye were right. I did no' see it, until it was too late."

Her voice lowered into a monotone; a chant, a vow. "I did no' choose it, but still I will kill him should it come t' that. Is that what ye want t' hear?" she demanded. "I will kill him! I have even chosen how I will do it. Fast. With fire. He is no' good with flames, and would no' have the skill t' stop me…"

Boris gripped her arm, giving her a rough shake. "Calm yourself, girl. I did no' question that ye would do your duty, only the suffering that ye will now endure because o' your foolishness."

Catrian nodded morosely, and her gaze rose to meet the Commander's. "Ah Gods!" she breathed out in a near sob. "Do no' use him tomorrow. Do no' make me have t'…" her words trailed into silence, as she shook her head, staring down into her lap at her tensely twined fingers. "If they find out about him, they will demand his death. How could they no'?"

The Commander's face was harsh and unyielding. "I am sorry, girl. 'Tis done."

CHAPTER NINE

Located outside the west gate was a flattened field, the only part of the mountain plateau not to be contained within the walls of the fortress. The field was usually used by the Rebels to train in arms, but otherwise for mustering troops in times of war, and just now, it drew merry crowds that surged and laughed with a festive abandonment in anticipation of the tournament. The winter had been bitter and long, and many people had been lost to hunger, cold and disease. The Rebels were more than ready for a bit of entertainment, and the pageantry of the tournament fit the bill perfectly. The morning sun slanted warmly down upon the field with a teasing hint of spring, prompting many to throw off their heavy woolens and furs to parade defiantly in the face of the winter snows that blanketed the mountainside.

Along the perimeter of the field near to the steep drop that overlooked the valley, cooks had set large cauldrons of thick venison stew over hot coals, ladling servings into crusty trenchers as, in celebration of the gathering, all rationing was suspended for the day. Frothy tankards of ale were clasped in many a hand, and distributed alongside dried strips of venison and rabbit, salted and full of flavour. The air was redolent with the scent of small, savoury pies of spiced meat that were eagerly snatched up by swarms of hungry Rebels.

Many confections had been created over a fortnight of

preparations. Tree sap had been rendered into syrup, and poured over fried dough, a sticky sweet that people smiled and sighed over, as they ate their fill for the first time in months. Rendered further, the sap became so thick that when drizzled over a trough of snow it hardened into a gooey toffee that the children laughed and fought over, popping it into their mouths as quickly as the cooks prepared it. The practice field was filled with happy chaos.

A large awning had been erected at one end of the marshaling field, under which Catrian and Commander Boris were seated centre amidst the full pantheon of Rebel Generals enjoying refreshments. Catrian's gaze met Gralyre's, as he walked onto the field, but she pointedly ignored the hand he raised in greeting, leaning over to say something into Boris' ear instead, and making Gralyre's hackles bristle at her snub.

Gralyre's attention settled upon the assembled Generals, studying their ranks to match face to name. General Chartrin, the pirate, he readily recognized seated between two other Generals to the right of Boris. The bronzed and blond seaman slouched in his chair with a tankard in one hand, and a haunch of venison in the other, smiling and gesturing, as he talked to the General seated between him and Boris. General Laurazon of the lowland north, Gralyre guessed.

Rewn had been vague about the man, but Gralyre needed no further observations than his own to sense the dangerous intelligence that rolled in waves from the man. Laurazon nodded politely, taking contained sips from his tankard, his eyes watchful and moving, as he scanned the field of assembling warriors. Dark of hair and eye, his clothing outlined a fit and lean body that seemed coiled for action, even amidst his allies.

To Chartrin's right, seated in a comfortable chair at the end of the row, Gralyre recognized General Baldric, for he was just as Rewn had described; long black hair that hung straight to the middle of his back with thin braids at his temples to keep the strands back from his strong face. A long moustache, thin and silky, hung to his chest, but otherwise he was cleanly shaven. Chartrin laughed and elbowed the man roughly to share the joke, but Baldric's face remained cold, his eyes burning fervently, as he glared his displeasure.

Rewn had described Baldric, as a man utterly devoted to the destruction of Doaphin. Baldric oversaw the extensive spy network that ferretted information from deep within Doaphin's occupied territories, and sent it onwards to the resistance leadership, which was how Rewn had come to know him, during trips to Verdalan with his father. He was not conversing with his fellow Generals, nor did he partake of the food and drink that was placed upon the long table behind which the assembly sat in comfort. Gralyre had a sense that Baldric trusted nothing and no one, not even his fellow Generals.

Catrian was seated to Boris' left, and Gralyre recognized the man seated to her other side as the one he had passed at the entrance to her tent after their last disastrous meeting, General Kierdenan.

Just now Kierdenan's thin lips were twisted into a sneer

beneath his flattened nose, as though he judged everything he saw, and found it lacking. Gralyre did not like the way the General's small brown eyes, peering out from beneath thick, furry brows, roved over the sorceress whenever she turned away. Gralyre knew that Catrian could take care of the insulting behaviour on her own, but that did not supplant his urge to add to the scars on Kierdenan's face with a hard beating to school him in manners.

From his position of prominence seated next to Catrian and Commander Boris, Gralyre suspected that this was the General that most threatened Boris' leadership, and the reason why Gralyre had been contracted as champion.

To Kierdenan's left sat the last General, who by process of elimination, Gralyre knew to be General Ryes of the south, even if his extreme paleness had not revealed his identity. He seemed well into his cups, even this early in the day. His thin blond hair receded to a fringe around his pate, a halo for his moon shaped face with its drunken smirk that made him seem a soft dullard in comparison to his predatory companions.

"Gralyre! Over here!"

Gralyre turned at Rewn's hale, dismissing the Generals from his mind, as he sought the blue pennant that marked his team's location on the field of battle, the small group of handpicked warriors who were to represent Commander Boris in the tournament.

Though he did not know most of the men that he would fight beside, Gralyre had insisted to Matik on the inclusion of Rewn and Dajin. Having trained them, Gralyre was confident that their abilities far outstripped the skills of any other within the fortress. After a quick practice bout with Rewn, Matik had ceded. He had already included Dajin, as he had been training with him since they had arrived at the fortress, and was well aware of the superior knowledge that Gralyre had bestowed upon the younger Wilson brother.

As Gralyre arrived, Matik had just finished untucking his beard from the neck of his leather practice armour. "Gralyre! Ye are late!" Matik castigated. For once the axe was missing from his back, for the first of the contests was to be the sword.

Gralyre raised an eyebrow at the man's surly greeting, for to his knowledge he was early. "Why are you not at table with yonder Generals?" he asked pointedly, as he received from Rewn the lightweight, boiled leather that would serve to armour his body against blows.

Matik sneered at the slight, and as he walked past, struck Gralyre's shoulder with his. "I would be, but I am here t' make sure ye remember your bargain, spy!"

Gralyre froze in place at the aggressive posturing, and drew a deep, steadying breath to contain the instinctive need to grab Matik, and beat him to the ground. That was not the fight that he was commissioned to win this day, he reminded himself sternly, as he drew the armour's flattened shoulder boards over his head. Boris had granted him the freedom of the forests, now Gralyre would grant him the glory of the win. He took a moment to examine the neck-guards; wing-like protuberances that rose from the shoulder boards to offer minor protection, yet still provide mobility. They would not stop an overhand blow, but would protect the neck from any side sweeps of a blade.

With economy of motion, Gralyre settled the moulded breast and back plates into place that would protect his torso, and fastened the leather buckles at his sides, designed to keep the armour tight to his body. A simple cap of boiled leather went onto his head to complete the protective gear, held in place by a strap fastened under his chin.

They were to be pitted against General Baldric's forces for the first bout, and Gralyre took a moment on the sidelines to offer last minute advice to the brothers.

"Dajin, remember to keep your stance solid. If you lose your balance you lose the fight."

"I know!" Dajin flared with exasperation, as he rolled his shoulders under the boiled leather armour. He shook out his hands and kicked his feet, much like a horse stomping and snorting, eager to run.

"Hold still. You have missed a buckle." Gralyre cautioned, and strapped the armour tighter to Dajin's body. "How does that feel?"

Dajin huffed out a breath, and jerked himself away. "Fine!"

Gralyre nodded, and turned to Rewn, who rolled his eyes. Gralyre smiled, and pounded his fists down on his friend's shoulder plates, testing the armour to make sure it was tight. He nodded his approval. "You are ready."

Rewn grinned and nodded. A horn sounded, and he turned his

head to see that the combatants were being called to the field. "Wish us luck!"

"Luck!" Gralyre called back. He was suddenly caught up in the excitement of the competition, and filled with an unfamiliar sense of belonging. He met the eyes of a stranger, one of his teammates, and they shared a grin of anticipation.

Together, the warriors representing Commander Boris, and those representing General Baldric walked out onto the field, and were handed their blunted swords. One by one, the warriors drew runes from a sack to pair off, and took their places on the field opposite their opponent. The men that remained undefeated in battle after the initial one-to-one duels would then face a free-for-all melee that would determine the ultimate champion of the blade.

Gralyre ran a professional eye over the terrain, noting that the hard packed snow of the practice field had started to melt in the heat of the sun, creating soft spots of slush that would trip up the unwary, especially as many feet churned it up. As the day progressed, the footing would grow more treacherous. Everything was a weapon to be used.

"Begin!" Boris shouted, and the horn blared.

With a roar, the warriors attacked, and the sound echoed by the cheers of the watching crowd. The clanging of the swords had the spectators lining the field yelling encouragement at the fighters, and many coins exchanged hands as bets were made.

Gralyre's opponent was a nervous looking man who twitched his sword timidly at Gralyre's chest. Gralyre cuffed it aside with his bare hand, and smacked the slighter man in the chest with the blunted end of his sword. As the Rebel stumbled back, Gralyre hooked a leg behind his, sprawled him to the ground, and set his sword to his neck. "Yield," he commanded softly while the crowd roared approval of the first win of the day.

The man's mouth gaped in surprise, as he stared up at Gralyre, before his head swiveled so that he could look at his General.

Under the awning, General Chartrin roared with laughter, and nudged General Baldric hard enough to rock him. "Is that no' your second, Iptus, lying on the ground with his twat in the air, Spymaster?"

Baldric's face remained without expression, as he stared stonily at Chartrin until his grin faded. "Iptus' talents lie elsewhere. Blunt instruments are o' no use t' me. But then, what would a pirate know o' subtlety?"

Chartrin's eyes narrowed, and he carefully set his hand upon the hilt of his sword. He lifted his tankard for a long deep swallow, his gaze challenging and unrepentant. Stillness surrounded the two Generals, a calm before the breaking storm.

Baldric gave a cold, barking laugh, shattering the threat of violence, and turned back to the field. He gave his man a negligent wave of consent.

Iptus, the warrior beneath Gralyre's blade, licked nervously at his lips, and then nodded his surrender.

Gralyre glanced towards Boris and Catrian. Boris gave him a slight incline of his head, approval for the quickness of the win, though Catrian's face was averted, watching elsewhere. Gralyre saluted the Commander with his sword, and then offered a hand to his felled opponent.

"Iptus," the man gave his name, as he accepted Gralyre's help up.

"Gralyre." He walked with the smaller man to the sidelines to watch the remainder of the bouts.

"As in *'Lost Prince'*?" Iptus asked, his eyes darting so, that his words seemed to be addressing an empty tankard that had been left sitting upon a stump.

Gralyre shrugged. "Just Gralyre." He was not about to go into the obscure circumstances surrounding his past, not with a stranger.

A man met them at the sidelines, armed with a piece of chalk, and marked a small slash on the armor of Gralyre's back, and an X upon the back of the loser, baring Iptus from further swordplay, though he could still participate later at other competitions such as archery, knives, axes or riding. However, a warrior who received three X's, in three events, over the course of the day, would be eliminated from further participation in the tournament.

Gralyre sighed in disgust, as he watched Dajin yell wildly, and attack with an ostentatious and wasteful flurry of blows. He had not trained his former pupil to such excesses, and wondered what nonsense Matik had been teaching him.

Dajin's opponent was a man of about the same age, who was diligently blocking Dajin's darting sword. The warrior wore an intense frown of concentration, but was no match for Dajin, who had received private tutelage from a master swordsman.

With a swift thrust, Dajin managed to slip his sword past the man's defense, and whack him hard across the temple with the flat of his blade. The blunted edge, and the leather helmet protected the warrior from serious injury but it was enough to cause him to wobble. Dajin moved in for the kill, striking hard and fast about the man's head and chest.

The warrior held up his hands in a sign of yielding, but Dajin ignored him. He was not satisfied until his opponent was sprawled at his feet, spitting blood from blows to his face.

Proudly, Dajin paraded to and fro for the benefit of the crowd, enjoying their celebratory cheers of victory.

Gralyre shook his head at the ignoble way his former pupil had dealt with his opponent, followed by his vain preening before the audience.

"That one," spat Iptus in disgust, "he needs someone t' kick the piss and vinegar out o' him." He left Gralyre's side to assist his bloodied teammate from the field.

One by one, the bouts concluded, with Commander Boris' forces winning the majority of the duels, leaving Rewn and his partner the last upon the field. The two men were evenly matched in size and age, but as with Dajin, Rewn had the advantage of education. Gralyre smiled and nodded with appreciation, as he watched Rewn catch the man's blade on his, and send it soaring. Rewn lowered his guard, and stepped back, having won the bout.

The Rebel stared disbelievingly at his numb fingers, before he closed them in a fist, and threw a punch at Rewn's head. "Demon-loving lowlander!" he bellowed.

Rewn ducked the wild swing, and as the man fell off balance, kicked him hard in the stomach. The man dropped to all fours, gasping for air. Rewn's face darkened and twisted with rage, making Gralyre stiffen as he recognized the expression. Though Baldric's man was already down and beaten, Rewn stepped in, and kicked him again in the ribs, sending him sprawling away in a spray of slush. The horn sounded, and he hesitated a moment before he spun on his heel, and stalked from the field, leaving his dishonoured opponent to the tender jeers and boo's of the crowd.

From across the field, Catrian frowned, as she watched Gralyre leave off leaning against a stump to meet and calm Rewn's wild-eyed rage. Catrian leaned over to comment to Boris, while she watched Rewn gesticulate angrily, "I remember him as the reasonable brother."

Boris chuckled, unable to contain his smile. His forces had won the majority of the opening battles, and he gloried in the success. "Ah, refreshment!" he chortled enthusiastically, as he accepted a mug of ale from the woman who was serving them from a barrel set in the deep snow beyond the pavilion. The frothy brew was chilled and welcome for the sun grew warmer the further it rose into the pristine blue of the sky.

"Here, Laurazon," Boris nudged him with a shoulder, "give this a try," he enthused, indicating to the serving woman that she should top the General's cup as well. "Beats any o' the piss they serve in the lowlands."

"'Tis our piss. We sent ye this barrel last summer," Laurazon quipped dryly.

Boris laughed loudly, his mood high at the good showing of his warriors. The horn sounded, and the next group of men trotted onto the field, and paired off; General Kierdenan's men against General Ryes' warriors. The contest was quick and decisive, as Kierdenan's men routed General Ryes' on all fronts, permanently eliminating the southern General's forces.

Kierdenan laughed cruelly at Ryes, who slouched in the chair beside his, "By the gods, Ryes, did ye bring warriors or women?"

Ryes' blurry eyes met Kierdenan's. "Why?" he mumbled drunkenly. "Are they done already?" He slid sideways, amber liquid sloshing from his tankard, as he caught himself from falling.

Kierdenan sneered, and beckoned to the serving wench. "Ryes' cup is empty."

Far across the field, as each General's team faced off against the other, Gralyre studied the men who won, searching out their weaknesses and strengths, and pointing them out to his team, preparing them for the melee.

Insightful comments such as, "He looks fast, but he uses the same three moves…" or "His chin tics upward when he goes on the offensive…" soon had the team paying close attention to his every word, as they studied the bouts together.

Matik frowned, as the dynamics of leadership shifted towards Gralyre, but held his tongue. After all, Gralyre was only fulfilling his bargain. And he was not wrong. He might despise the man, but in battle he had no equal.

General Laurazon and General Chartrin's forces were the last to take the field. They were very closely matched, and each experienced an equal number of wins and losses.

There was a short interval before the melee began in order to allow Chartrin and Laurazon's forces time to recover their breath. Matik took the opportunity to rally his team.

"All right, lads, there are thirteen o' us t' take the field, which would be very good odds, save that General Kierdenan still has his full compliment o' twenty due t' the south's poor showing. Laurazon and Chartrin each have ten, and then there is Baldric's seven. For the benefit o' our lowlanders," he sneered the insult towards Gralyre, Rewn and Dajin, "I will remind ye o' the rules o' the melee. No attacks from behind, 'tis considered bad form. No interfering with someone else's battle, even if they are losing. No ganging up onto one warrior, one-on-one fights only. When ye finish a man, move on t' the next. There is no need t' be greedy, there are plenty o' fights t' go around. Keep fighting until the horn blows, which will no' be until only one team remains undefeated upon the field."

"With honour!" Matik yelled.

"With Honour!" they all responded.

Echoes of the same chant came from the other teams, as the horn blew, the crowd cheered, and the thirteen walked onto the field to pit their metal against the other warriors who had won their opening fights. Each team gathered at one of the four winds, and immediately began to taunt and jeer, inciting the men in the groups across from them, and picking their first fights.

The horn blasted three times, the sound echoing off the rocks of the mountain, and rolling out over the valley below.

"Begin" shouted Boris.

The crowd roared their excitement.

The warriors surged forward, and the melee began.

The coldness of the sword dance descended upon Gralyre, and his heartbeat slowed, steady and even, even as his reflexes increased. He was unstoppable. No man faced him for more than three or four passes before he was felled.

For the first time in memory, Gralyre was surrounded by the clang of swords, and the din of a large battle; men screamed in rage and pain as they fought.

Upwards from the black depths of his soul, the nightmare leached into his thoughts, and Gralyre faltered, as flashes of another war overtook his mind's eye.

Standing alone against a wave of thousands. Blood sprays in wide arcs with every swing of my blade. So many enemies, every stroke kills two or more. Lightening blasts from the sky. The warrior at my side hardens, blackens, frozen for all time with spear and shield raised...

"Mercy!" screamed a fighter, and Gralyre blinked heavily, as he returned to the present, and realized that his opponent was on the ground, arms raised in supplication. Gralyre was poised to remove his head.

He mumbled an apology, and stumbled back, wiping a quivering hand across his eyes to clear them of imagined gore that was really only the sweat of exertion.

Gralyre's wide, panicked gaze met Catrian's, and her face crossed with a look of concern, as though she knew what he was feeling. Oddly, just seeing her calmed him, her presence grounding him in a way he could not describe. He reclaimed the coldness and rhythm of the sword dance, and was immediately engaged by another warrior, from whose camp he was unsure. All he knew was battle, and he cut a wide swath through the ranks of his challengers.

Now that he had regained his wits, Gralyre clung grimly to the reality of the present, and did his best to ignore hints of the familiar nightmare that continued to beset his concentration. It was fortunate that there was no warrior on the field who could match his skill. Even distracted, he finished his bouts with finesse and ease, but Gralyre's pleasure in the day had waned.

He consoled himself with a master's pride, as Rewn and Dajin defeat warrior after warrior. They had learned their lessons well, and their greater skills were obvious.

As the field of men grew smaller and smaller, the crowd began to pick out individuals to cheer or boo, and as Gralyre's wins mounted, the crowd was quick to roar its approval at the falling of each warrior.

"Tell me, Catrian, who is yonder champion that ye canno' seem t' stop watching?" General Kierdenan asked with a wide leer.

"'Tis just one o' our men," she replied offhandedly, her body tensing, as a warrior attacked Gralyre from the side, just as he felled his current opponent.

The crowd booed with shouts of *"Bad form!"* Though technically, Gralyre had vanquished his first foe before the second had attacked from his flank. Two passes later, the man was down, and the crowd was roaring approval again.

"He is good."

"He is."

"I am surprised that ye are no' fighting, Boris?" Kierdenan shifted his focus when he could not get the engagement he sought from the Sorceress with his thinly veiled innuendos.

Boris swallowed carefully from his tankard, and pasted on a benign smile. "No more than any o' us are, Kierdenan. We agreed t' let our men have the fun."

Dajin ran afoul of the softened terrain, stumbling and sliding in slush at the wrong moment, and giving the warrior he fought the opening he needed. His face was red with rage when he quit the field, kicking at humps of snow; an undisguised poor loser.

"Bad luck, that," Kierdenan taunted Boris. "That leaves ye with only five men left t' my eight."

Boris' smile soured but before he could reply, a groan of defeat came from Chartrin.

"Demon take ye, Boris, who is that warrior? He just went

through the last o' my men. I am out!" Chartrin threw up his hands with another grimace. Seconds later he leaned over to Laurazon, "And there goes the last o' yours! Who is he?"

Laurazon met Boris' eyes with an appraising, clever tilt to his mouth. "Who indeed?"

"His name is Gralyre." Baldric also joined the conversation, as Gralyre defeated the last of his forces. It was no surprise to any of the Generals that the spymaster already knew the mysterious warrior's name.

"Gralyre?" Chartrin frowned. "'Tis a forbidden name."

Catrian braced, but kept her attention fixed upon the field to avoid the conversation that swirled around her. 'Twas precisely the circumstance that she had feared; Gralyre had drawn the attention of the Generals.

Laurazon gave Boris a lazy once over. "There is more t' this man than there seems."

Boris wore a ghost of a smile, and winked slyly at Laurazon before allowing his attention to slide back to the fight, and to the man that he had bribed to be his champion; a man that he would soon be well rid of.

"There is enough t' him t' suit me," Chartrin grouched as Gralyre fought through the last of Kierdenan's men, and the crowd screamed approval. Chartrin leaned out around Boris to bait Kierdenan. "Did ye no' start the melee with a full twenty?"

Kierdenan threw his tankard onto the field with a shout, his face enflamed and mottled white around his scars.

Boris signaled the end, and the horn blew. He covered over

his small smile of triumph with a sip of ale. Gralyre had caught the attention of the war council; the hook was baited. And with victory came a Gods sent bonus, for Kierdenan had been embarrassingly routed.

Kierdenan glared at the field, where the last three men standing were all men who owed allegiance to Commander Boris. "Wench, fetch me another tankard!" he bellowed.

The server was quick to comply.

Victorious on the field, and one of the three remaining warriors, Matik slapped Rewn on the back, and even managed to spare a smile for Gralyre. "Well fought. I may hate ye for the demon-loving lowlander that ye are, but 'tis a pleasure t' watch ye fight. Ye are peerless." He held out his hand.

Gralyre considered it with surprise before reaching out to take it. As far as complements went, it was a sorry one indeed, but he would accept it.

Matik jerked Gralyre nearer, using the hand he grasped as leverage. "I will still see ye dead if ye betray us!"

Gralyre narrowed his eyes, and squeezed Matik's hand, wringing a wince of pain before he released him. "You will try," he corrected with lazy menace.

Matik smirked his confidence, and stalked away.

Flushed with triumph, Rewn laughed and slung an arm across Gralyre's shoulders. "Forget him! We won!" Together, they lifted their swords in a salute to, first the Commander, and then the cheering crowds.

General Kierdenan glared at Catrian. "It must be satisfying t'

be able t' vanquish all your foes with but a wave o' your hand."
His face was tight with spiteful anger. He was looking for a
fight, and his tongue was barely leashed.

Commander Boris' face lost all trace of convivial hospitality
at the implication that his men had cheated.

"I did no' aid our men, General. There was no need," Catrian
responded with a serene smile. She placed a calming hand over
one of the Commander's clenched fists.

Kierdenan smiled craftily, and ignored Catrian's attempt to
smooth the waters. "He is very skilled, this Gralyre. I have seen
no better fighter, except for ye, Boris - in your prime," he added
snidely. "I wonder if we are seeing the new Commander, waiting
for the old t' make way?"

Boris' face darkened, as the well-placed barb pricked his
vanity. "What are ye saying? Speak plainly."

"Only that it would seem that ye are no longer the supreme
force that ye once were. In fact, without the Sorceress by your
side, ye are naught but an old, tired horse whose race has run!"

The conversations amongst the other Generals suspended,
and they waited tensely to see how this confrontation between
the Commander and General Kierdenan would play out.

Catrian's restraining hand atop Boris' tightened warningly.
"Were I no' here, still would ye be bending a knee to
Commander Boris." Her words were cold and proud, the regal
tones of a queen.

"Would I? Would any o' us?" Kierdenan's smile was full of
spite, as he looked beyond Catrian and Boris towards Baldric,

Chartrin and Laurazon.

Boris pounded a fist on the arm of his chair. "How dare ye infer that I hide behind the skirts o' my niece!"

"Prove it!" Kierdenan verbally lunged for the kill. "Pit your sword against that o' your champion. Prove that ye are still fit t' lead. And if ye lose…"

"I will no'!"

"If ye do, I believe that a forfeit must be paid."

Boris shook off Catrian's cautioning hand. "Name it."

"Your niece is mine. She comes home with me."

Catrian gasped in outrage. "Uncle, no! I am no' coin t' be gambled away!"

Kierdenan sneered and leaned back in his chair. "If ye do no' need her t' rule, then ye do no' need her by your side, and should share her with the rest o' us. Or was I correct? The sorceress is making all the decisions?"

"Done!" Boris rasped, and leapt to his feet, spilling the dregs of his tankard in the process.

Catrian met Kierdenan's smug smirk, resisting the urge to reduce him to ash. That would come later, should Boris lose. Her eyes narrowed angrily for she would never consent to be his, no matter what Boris promised.

"Ye!" Commander Boris yelled at Gralyre, as he strode out onto the field, and pointed challengingly. "There was no one here t' match your skill. Come here! Ye and I will fight!"

The crowd went wild with excitement, and bets began to exchange hands. It was common knowledge that Boris was the best swordsman in the fortress, but how would he fare against this new champion? Word spread back through the masses, drawing more people at a run to watch the bout.

Matik approached Boris under the guise of bringing him armour and a blunted sword, and muttered softly, "What are ye doing?"

Boris met Matik's concern with leashed rage, as he snatched the sword. "Do no' make me appear weak! Kierdenan challenged me, and I canno' renege!" He left Matik standing helplessly, still holding the armour.

Gralyre eyed Boris' lack of armour, and motioned to Rewn to help him strip his own. Why had Boris challenged him? This was not part of the bargain that had been struck.

It was a relief to remove the sweaty helmet, and welcome the caress of the cool breeze. He lifted his face momentarily to enjoy the sensation.

Rewn slapped Gralyre on the back. "Do no' hurt him," he advised, as he quit the field.

The horn basted loudly; a demand to the fight. Gralyre eyed Boris up and down, taking in the professional way the sword was held, the no nonsense stance. His face lit up in anticipation, as he wondered what it was like to sword dance with someone who knew what he was doing.

The two men circled one another, and the crowd fell so silent that a simple cough reached out from the mass of people with the clarity of a shout. As if it was a signal, Boris attacked, and Gralyre brought up his sword and blocked.

CLANG! CLANG! CLANG!

The reverberations of metal on metal echoed throughout the field, as they parted and circled each other warily.

"What is this about, Boris," Gralyre asked quietly while he effortlessly returned the compliment of blows.

CLANG! CLANG! CLANG!

"You contracted me to win. Would ye have me throw this fight?"

CLANG! CLANG! CLANG! CLANG!

Gralyre easily blocked the blows, disappointed to recognize that his skills far outstripped the Commander's.

The men parted again.

"No! Ye must fight me! If I lose, the demon-humping black heart Kierdenan wins Catrian."

CLA - CLANG! CLANG!

"Ye bet your own flesh on the outcome of our bout?" Gralyre snarled, aghast. He had no chance to analyze why the thought of another staking claim to the Sorceress bedeviled him. He was always confused where Catrian was concerned.

CLA - CLANG! CLANG!

It did not escape Boris' notice that Gralyre returned the exact same blows, in the exact same sequence, only faster and harder.

"If I lose, I lose the right t' lead! But if I win with too much ease, after your performance thus far, they will know it t' be a lie, and I will lose all respect, and I will lose the right t' lead! There is no way out o' this!"

Their blunted swords skidded off each other in a skirl of

metallic shrieks.

"Ye have surely cocked this up!" Gralyre bit out coldly. "You worry about power when you should be worried about Catrian! I will not allow her to be treated as a pawn in your power struggle!"

"I canno' allow another t' lead in my place. No' now. No' yet!"

Gralyre saw the change roll over Boris' face, and braced himself for the older man's attack. It was time for this sparring to end, and the real battle to commence. The attack came, fast and furious. Boris was good, far better than the men Gralyre had fought so far this day, but was still nowhere near his level.

The rhythm of the battle pounded through Gralyre's blood, and his concentration narrowed to the smallest of points, as his blade became a silver blur, blocking blows and returning them. As the glory of his sword craft washed over him he began to formulate a plan.

Boris was frustrated, as all his best moves were countered, and he was forced back again, and again. In all his years he had never found a man who could outmatch him at swordplay, and fear began to churn in the pit of his stomach. He had made a serious tactical error in engaging Gralyre in battle. How had he lost such control, as to allow Kierdenan to provoke him into this fight?

'I have been out-maneuvered by a thug,' Boris thought with disgust.

What were Gralyre's intentions? Would he throw the fight?

Sweat rolled down the Commander's cheeks, and he knew, as only a veteran knows, that if he did not finish with Gralyre soon, his strength would succumb to the youth and superior skills of his opponent, but try as he might, Boris was unable to find a single hole in Gralyre's defense. Not an error was made. If anything, Boris sensed Gralyre withheld his full prowess. That thought sent a cold shiver down his spine, as Gralyre continued to spar with relentless power.

Silence penetrated Gralyre's concentration. As they fought, the crowd had grown quiet with suspense. The reason exploded in his mind when he blocked a brutal overhand blow. Boris was the resident champion; the crowd's reaction beside the point, Gralyre had sensed it himself, as he had taken up the challenge. The Commander's power stemmed from his strength of arms, and his people depended on that strength in their leader. If Boris lost on this field, he would lose face, and likely be deposed.

Gralyre had seen younger men than Boris whittling wooden shafts for arrows, and telling stories to the young. The Commander could not afford to be seen as anything but completely, ruthlessly strong. To show weakness was defeat.

Not that he truly cared what Boris suffered, but from what Gralyre had observed, the Rebels were barely leashed, and if the resistance were to lose any of its leadership, it could devolve into an undisciplined den of thieves and bandits, even further than it already had.

And Catrian could not be made to suffer for Boris' lapse in judgment! If Gralyre won, she was lost. If Boris won, the outcome would always be suspect. As the smell of ale wafted from the Commander's panting breaths, Gralyre wondered how much the drink had to play in the mire they now found themselves in.

Gralyre breathed out with a controlled hiss, and swung his sword viciously at Boris' midsection, forcing the Commander to leap back. There had to be a way for Boris to save face, and to rescue Catrian from being given over to General Kierdenan to settle the bad bet.

And then it came to him. Neither a win nor a loss. Gralyre was willing to bet that no one had ever witnessed an engineered draw.

Leaving his left side unprotected for a moment, Gralyre waited until Boris' sword darted for the breach in his defenses. The timing was perfect, as Gralyre brought his own sword up, catching Boris' blunt edge with his. A quick step to the side, and a hard thrust, and they ended with their swords at each other's throats.

The crowd went wild. Their champion of the day had not been defeated, but neither had their Commander. They were equally matched. The battle was already being recounted to the people in the back who had not had a clear view of the fight.

Boris' chest heaved with exertion while he blinked in confusion at where his sword now rested, against the steady pulse in Gralyre's neck. That was not where he had been aiming, and he grew cold as he recognized the skill it had taken for Gralyre to direct both of their blades. The man was inhumanly good. Boris knew the younger man could have taken him at any moment; he had never been in control of this fight.

Boris' eyes clashed with Gralyre's over their crossed swords. Though the clever outcome was the only way to confound the bet, if he saw one ounce of condescension in Gralyre's face he would continue the fight! But Gralyre's expression was enigmatically bland.

Boris grudgingly lowered his blade, his chest still heaving with exertion. "A draw then," he growled, trying to regain his wind, annoyed that Gralyre was but barely panting.

"Yes, a draw," Gralyre concurred, removing his sword from Boris' neck. He stepped back, and bowed to Boris respectfully, then turned and gave a nod to the wildly cheering crowd. At his show of gallantry, he won the people, and truly became the champion of the day.

Boris could not help the small kernel of relief at the outcome. His one miscalculation could have cost him everything. He turned upon his heal, and approached Matik.

Matik shook his head with a grin, and saluted his Commander smartly. "What a fight! Only ye could have fought Gralyre t' a standstill!" he praised.

"Tell me that looked authentic!" Boris snapped quietly.

Matik frowned in confusion. "It was no' real?" He handed Boris a tankard of ale, then pivoted to stand at his shoulder following his Commander's sightline. "By the gods! 'Tis almost a shame we have t' kill him. Laurazon has agreed t' assist ye?"

Boris took a deep draft of the amber liquid, pausing to wipe a sleeve across his mouth. "Aye."

"When?" Matik asked, turning to look up at the profile of his oldest friend.

"At the war council," Boris pronounced.

The crowd, unwilling to let go of their entertainment after the long dull winter, only grew larger as the archery bouts began. People jostled and joked, laying bets as to the outcomes, and evaluating the competitors.

Gralyre, Rewn and Dajin all joined in the archery contest, but at the end, it was a young man who had arrived as part of General Laurazon's contingent who won the shoot, beating Gralyre for the top spot.

The lad, Tryfin, was truly gifted, and Gralyre was glad to finally meet someone whose skills surpassed his own.

General Laurazon came forward to congratulate his man, lifting Tryfin's arm high in victory to the cheers of the crowd, causing the young man's face to flush red with pleasure.

Smiling, Laurazon drew a small wooden disk from within his shirt, of about two fingers in diameter, and winked at Tryfin. The crowd grew silent and expectant, as the bowmen pulled an arrow and knocked it. He nodded that he was ready.

General Laurazon flicked the small disk into the air with a quick snap of his thumb. Twisting and flipping, it rose high.

The bowman drew and shot, and the arrow struck a post further down the field. A man ran out from the crowd, and pulled it free. He began to yell, and jump in celebration. The wooden disk was pierced through the centre by the mettle barb of the arrow. The crowd cheered madly in celebration of the impossible shot, and General Laurazon thumped Tryfin on the back, well pleased.

As the afternoon progressed, test after test was thrown at the contestants. Though General Laurazon's man, Tryfin, had edged Gralyre out of a win in archery he remained unbeatable at all else. With a staff, he was formidable and unstoppable, putting up a whirling wall of defense that confounded all. He did things with a battle-axe that no one had ever seen before, and at the end of the melee stood shoulder to shoulder with his nemesis, Matik.

In hand-to-hand combat, he was the last man standing.

The more impressive the feats of his strength and skill, the larger the crowd of onlookers grew, as word spread throughout the fortress. The more difficult the task, the more cheers Gralyre received as, after each impressive feat, he bowed first to Boris and then to the crowd. His humble acceptance of victory made him even more popular with the Rebel spectators.

Though it was what he had conspired with Gralyre to achieve, Boris grew darker of temper with every win, to the point that even Kierdenan's needling faded into a background annoyance. He had never seen a warrior to match him; he was a breed unto himself, and with every win and every bow, Boris was reminded that he had almost lost everything, and that it was Gralyre who had saved him.

At the end of the tournament, Gralyre was declared the champion of the day. Boris presented the small purse of gold coins, his eyes hard and unfriendly, though his mouth smiled.

Gralyre wondered why Boris was not happier. The Commander had the win he had desired, and his Generals all seemed suitably impressed. The illusion was complete.

Gralyre waved at the crowd, smiling widely, as though elated at what he had achieved, while deep within he felt a large measure of shame for the victories. For though he had earned each win, he had so outclassed the other warriors that the tournament truly had been weighted in his favour.

But it was done now. Gralyre had repaid his debt, and he had regained a measure of his freedom as a Huntsman. He could leave the suspicious glares of Catrian, Boris and Matik in the overcrowded fortress, and walk free in the clear forest air. The win was at least worth that, and far more important to him than the heavy weight of gold in his pocket.

Gralyre returned Rewn's grin as he accepted the congratulations of the assembly. Unnoticed by all, Dajin shoved to the rear of the crowd, brimming with sulky envy over Gralyre's good fortune.

80C3

HEATHREN MOUNTAINS – LATE WINTER

It is the most vicious predator to ever walk upon the crust of this world, yet something as simple as snow makes It sluggish and weak, for It is a cold-blooded creature more suited to the warm southern climes than to icy mountain passes. 'Tis why the

Rebels build their fortresses so deep in the Heathrens.

Every dawn It makes Its den inside the ice of a glacier, or the deep pack of snow in a gully, and by nightfall the cold has so sapped Its strength that It is almost too weak to dig free without the assistance of Its minions.

The Demon Riders do what they can, building massive bonfires every morning to warm Its flesh throughout the day's hibernation, and to thaw the Deathren at night, who are usually frozen immobile by the setting of the sun. Sometimes, the 'Riders must be set to chipping bodies free from frozen graves.

Speckle Tail whines for its warm den in Brannock making It yearn to kill it, but It cannot spare the strength. It takes every resource to survive the winter-gripped mountains, and so murder must await a more opportune time.

Its one consolation is that Green Crest has lost much ground, for it travels without the assistance of the day walking Demon Riders. It is gaining on the denmate traitor, slowly but surely. Soon, It will bathe in its blood.

CHAPTER TEN

NORTHERN REBEL FORTRESS – LATE WINTER

The tournament's fair weather extended into the following day, and though the snow still lay thick upon the ground, the warm wind promised that winter was not to last forever, and made good upon its vow with every drip of melting ice. Rivulets of water flowed from the snowpack upon the high wall-walks, and flooded low-lying areas, freezing overnight to provide endless amusement for the fortress children who skidded with giggles of joy across the small patches of ice.

An uncommon somnolence had overtaken the fortress in the wake of the tournament, as though having had a day of enjoyment all were loathe to assume their burdens once more. The fortress was quiet, without the usual bustle that filled its walls to bursting.

The tournament had been a success despite the disaster that had been narrowly averted after General Kierdenan's manipulation of Commander Boris to challenge Gralyre, but now that the festivities were over it was time to plan for war. For the first time in generations the Rebels would take the attack to their ancient foe, but first, Boris had to convince his Generals of the course. Though they all owed allegiance to Commander Boris, the Generals were autonomous within their own territories, and obeisance was foreign to their natures. Without their consent, there would be no mobilization, and mankind would slip quietly into extinction.

The Rebel Generals and their Lieutenants entered her pavilion, and Catrian accepted their respectful bows in her direction with an acknowledging tilt of her head, taking advantage of their distraction, as they hailed each other and sought their seats around the table, to subtly invade their thoughts in search of the mental misbalances that heralded Doaphin's tampering.

Ewers of ale had already been placed down the centre of the board, with a mug and plate set in place for each man. Meats, cheeses, and breads rested in platters, a small feast, for the meeting was expected to run long, and they did not want the attendance of servers to distract them from their purpose.

Boris commanded the head of the large table, with Matik to his left, and General Chartrin of the west and his Lieutenant, Jon, to his right.

Chartrin's face was ruddy and handsome in the lantern light, and his golden earing peeked out from amidst his curling, windswept blond hair, as he leaned across Boris to congratulate Matik for his performance at the tournament. Catrian sighed and wondered why it could not have been he who had captured her notice instead of Gralyre.

When last Chartrin had travelled to meet with Boris, Catrian had been but a child, and her girlish fantasies had painted the pirate as handsome, and larger than life. She well remembered her fascination with the rings of shining stones that flashed upon his fingers as he gestured, and the heavy gold chains hanging around his neck that glinted richly whenever he threw back his head and laughed, which was often. Far from making him appear foppish, his adornments were displayed like trophies, yet now, after Gralyre, it was too much the peacock on display to tempt Catrian's adult tastes. Chartrin's forces held control over a large archipelago off the cost of Dreisenheld, from where his ships raided Doaphin's supply vessels for many cargos. It was not all for gain. Much of what Chartrin stole he filtered to the downtrodden people of the mainland, using the rare luxuries and goods to trade for food and supplies needed by the resistance.

In contrast, Chartrin's man, Jon, sat stern and rigid in simple black, unadorned by the jewels worn by his General. They had long been away from their pirate ships, travelling most of the dark winter months to reach this unprecedented war summit, but Jon's face, like his general's, was still deeply touched by the sun. His dark hair was clubbed neatly at the back of his neck, and he was fresh scrubbed from seeking out the comfort of water. Skimming his thoughts, Catrian could clearly see his love for his people, and his utter devotion to his General, though that trust did not extend towards this current company. Jon's brown eyes were narrowed, as he carefully conducted a suspicious evaluation of the assembly.

Seated beside Jon was General Kierdenan with his second at his side, Lieutenant Vetroy. Kierdenan's thin lips were twisted into his usual sneer beneath his flattened nose and puckered scars. His small, brown eyes glared at Catrian from beneath the thick, fury ridge of his brows, meeting her gaze directly, as she turned her attention his way.

She hated the way Kierdenan watched her, as though she were an object to covet, instead of a living, breathing person. There had long been contention between Kierdenan and Boris regarding Catrian's autonomy, for the General saw himself as the next Commander, and had made several proposals of marriage to Catrian to cement his claim. She did not delude herself into believing there was anything romantic about his courtship, for the only love in Kierdenan's life was the acquisition of power. A marriage to Catrian would gain him access to Boris' territories to join with his own, not to mention control of her sorcery for his own purposes. He was furious over this summons to the war council, but had come regardless, afraid that some important decision would be made without him.

Of all the Generals, Catrian liked this man least. He fought by their side, but his heart was twisted by hate for any creature but himself. And what he seemed to hate almost as much as Doaphin, was a woman with power. She was thankful that Boris had never seriously considered his proposals, as she could not imagine a worse fate than becoming wife to this man.

"Are ye in my head, Sorceress?" Kierdenan taunted softly. His remark went unheard by the others, lost in the noise of conversations between the Generals, as they settled themselves around the table.

Catrian stared at him levelly, not bothering with a reply.

"Read this thought then!" he smirked, as into his mind's eye came an image of Catrian, naked and helplessly tied to a post, while an equally naked Kierdenan assaulted her with grunting abandon.

Catrian's lips tightened with anger at the insult, but this was neither the time nor the place to seek redress. There were larger matters to be dealt with. Still, she could not prevent altering Kierdenan's image by shrinking his manhood in size and threat until it was undetectable in his fantasy, then releasing her likeness from its bonds, and fading it to nothing.

"Have your laugh, Sorceress. Ye will beg my forgiveness when ye are mine!"

"Hold your breath until it comes t' be," Catrian suggested haughtily.

In contrast to the waves of animosity rolling from Kierdenan, Lieutenant Vetroy was bored with the proceedings. His lank blond hair fell in clumps over his face, a secretive curtain through which his light blue eyes peered slyly out at the rest of the company. His wit seemed to extend only so far as to agree with his General in all things. The two men were a spectrum away from Chartrin and Jon, in both attitude and cleanliness.

Catrian's face betrayed none of her thoughts, as she took her place at the far end of the table. She did not trust the two men, but they had no love of Doaphin, which, like it or not, made them allies in the cruel and bereft world in which they lived.

General Ryes of the South, politely held Catrian's chair for her, before seating himself at her right hand. His oldest son,

Corr, who acted as his Lieutenant, sat by his father, and immediately edged his chair away from General Baldric, obviously intimidated by the spymaster's burning presence.

General Ryes' protectrate was located in the deserted southern territories, where the evil of Doaphin held full sway, and his Rebels were the last bastions of humanity. They spied upon the comings and goings from Fennick's Island, but did little else to support the resistance.

Seen together, the men of the south were disconcertingly pale of skin when compared to the other men in the room, for their territory was encapsulated in a thick blackness that they called The Bleak. Catrian wagered that this was one of the few times in their lives that either man had ever seen daylight. Many generations past, Doaphin had created The Bleak to ensure that his Stalkers and Deathren need not fear the sun's punishing rays during their occupation of the territories surrounding Fennick's Island.

In contrast to his drunkenness during the tournament, today General Ryes was sober and attentive to the occasion, though his mind was chaotic with impressions and colors, sights and sounds. Catrian pitied him his overwhelmed senses, for the bright sunlight, and all the colors of the world were a far cry from life within The Bleak.

Ryes' son, Corr, had acquired a burn on his face from standing in the hot sun during the tournament, which made him seem less wan than his father, though there their differences ended. He was as alike to his father as any kin that Catrian had ever encountered. He was as short of stature, as soft around the middle, and afflicted with the same receding hairline. His lips were a startlingly vermillion in his pale face, made less odd now by the sunburn that tinted his flesh. Neither father nor son wore a beard, which was as well, for the addition of facial hair would have made their faces even more moon-shaped than they already were.

Both men were in awe of the company they were keeping for though all the Generals had met each other upon occasion, this was the first time in memory that they had all held council together under the same roof.

Catrian's attention shifted to Corr's right, to General Baldric, the wolf to Corr's lamb. Baldric brushed back his long, straight black hair, sniffing so that his impressive black moustache flicked upon his chest. The General's flat black eyes, burning out from deep sockets in his swarthy face, had seen too much of the horrors of Doaphin's occupation, and only Catrian knew that his thoughts were oily with a blackness that bordered upon madness, for outwardly there was no sign of this inner tumult. It was said that he had collections of Demon Rider teeth that he had made into thrones, one located within each of his many spy headquarters, deep in the ancient sewers of every occupied city in the land. He was also rumoured to be starting on the decoration of his subterranean halls but Catrian forbore to delve deep enough to reveal that truth. His commitment to the cause was absolute, the devotion of a true fanatic.

General Baldric's second in command, Iptus, looked

nervously out of place. The thin, little man kept pulling at his collar, his twitchy eyes darting ceaselessly, and he seemed ready to bolt for the nearest hole in the ground at the least sign of danger; a rat in a room full of cats, a man more suited to skulking in corners than walking in the open.

When Matik cleared his throat, laughing at a quip from General Chartrin, Iptus jumped and overturned the tankard that had been set before him. With a dart of his hand, he righted the mug before more than a few drops spilled, and sopped the liquid with his sleeve, his eyes flicking side to side, his face flushing with nervousness, as he sought out any who had noticed his minor accident.

General Laurazon of the lowland north and his Lieutenant, Pedric, took their seats to Catrian's left, buffering her from the malodorous presence of Kierdenan and Vetroy. The territory under their sway was perhaps the most dangerous in the land, for their hidden base was situated within a seven-day journey of Doaphin's Towers. Though Laurazon sat calmly, lazily glancing around the table, Catrian knew him to be the most dangerous of the lot. Only such a lethal warrior could have survived in the very throat of evil for as long as he had. He was very smart, and very, very deadly, but a more loyal man in the fight, there was none.

Lieutenant Pedric was only slightly less dangerous than his General, yet he presented an affable demeanor, smiling at Lieutenant Vetroy disarmingly, as he poured them both a tankard. Vetroy did not bestir himself to smile back beyond a sullen twist of his upper lip, though he did accept the ale when Pedric handed it to him.

Catrian was privy to the inner landscape of Lieutenant Pedric's mind, and shivered at the cold calculations that were taking place, the numerous ways he could slaughter Vetroy should he need. She did not think Vetroy would have been so relaxed had he a notion of the brutal pragmatism hidden behind that charming smile.

All the men proved clean of the Usurper's taint, and she gave a subtle nod to Boris that all was well.

Boris nodded in return, and he and Matik both relaxed, moving their hands casually away from the haft of their weapons. It was not that they did not trust their own people, but only that any man was capable of falling to corruption and ruin, and this year's ally could be next year's enemy for the price of a sack of gold, or a threat to a loved one.

Commander Boris leaned forward, and rapped his knuckles upon the table. "Men, let us attend t' the matter at hand."

"We have come t' your summons, Boris," prompted General Chartrin, "despite it being dangerous for all o' us t' be gathered in the same place. If your fortress were attacked, the consequences for the resistance would be disastrous. In one fell strike, Doaphin could destroy all o' his enemies."

"Rest assured that I would no' have risked calling this summit if it was no' o' the utmost importance!" Boris settled back in his chair, and nodded to Catrian to begin. "My Generals, harken t' the words o' our Sorceress!"

Twelve pairs of expectant eyes swung in Catrian's direction, awaiting her words of wisdom, though she suddenly did not feel so very wise. Catrian and Boris had summoned the Generals in the fall, and it had taken these many months to assemble. She had intended not to be present for this summit, opting to overwinter in Verdalan but her uncle, angered with her defiance to his summons, had come to fetch her himself.

Now she had but one chance to convince them to go to war. Why did time and events always render down to naught but a moment?

"I have scried the future, and witnessed disturbing portents," she began carefully.

"Bah!" snarled General Kierdenan. "We have come all this way in the cold bowels o' winter for magic pig shit! Did ye read the entrails o' a chicken or throw bones?" He rudely pushed back his chair, and made as if to stand and walk out on the summit. His man, Vetroy, tossed his head to fling the overlong, lank hair back from his eyes, and made to follow.

Boris slammed his hands down on the tabletop, and the wood boomed loudly, rattling tankards and platters. "Sit down! Still your tongue, and hear her words! Do ye think I would have called ye here o'er naught?"

Catrian watched as Kierdenan realized that he did not have the support of any of the other Generals. He bared his teeth in a snarling threat, and motioned to his Lieutenant to rejoin him, as he settled back into his seat.

She tried not to take insult at his words, for she knew the

mistrust people had of magic. Their prejudice grouped all Sorcerers together in evil, refusing to see that it was not the ability that was corrupt, but the intent of the wielder.

Truthfully, she was more annoyed that he had compared her talents to a third rate hedge wizard, those whose noxious potions healed every once in a while, branding them as great sorcerers by the common folk, though more often than naught the people perished from their toxic brews. To be lumped in with these charlatans was a lowly insult indeed, and one that she was loath to let pass, but instead of knocking him through the wall of the tent, she calmly flicked her hand, and a wavering image appeared in the air above the table, having all the substance of a soap bubble held suspended upon the surface of water. From whatever angle, the scene appeared whole and flat to the viewer.

Iptus stumbled from his chair in a panic, before sheepishly sinking back down, as the rest of the group watched the phenomenon with growing wonder.

Miniature people walked in and around buildings, in a small market that was hawking summer fruit. It was the familiar scene of an enslaved lowlander village.

"What is this?" Ryes breathed in awe.

"This is the near future," Catrian stated tersely. "Watch, and see what I have seen."

The tranquil scene was marred by the arrival of Demon Riders, and the men watched as every human was slaughtered, and the streets ran red. The Demon Riders, inflamed by blood lust, literally ripped the villagers limb-to-limb, raping and killing until smoke from the fires finally occluded the gruesome images.

"So what," Kierdenan shrugged. "The lowlander sheep are slaughtered thus every day!"

"Aye," agreed General Baldric. "We have all seen such atrocities before, m'lady."

Catrian's gaze rested upon Baldric, though she did not reply, for they would soon divine the full truth for themselves. The scene changed and another village was devastated, then another. There were no survivors. The brutal images went on and on. No human settlement was spared. Finally, it was the city of Verdelan's turn. A small moan of rage escaped General Baldric, and he pounded his fist down on the table. Taking pity upon him, Catrian exerted her will upon her magic, the images shimmered and altered, and this time, they could all recognize this very stronghold, overrun by a frenzy of Deathren and Stalkers. The Generals watched in fear drawn silence, as fortress after fortress of the resistance was devastated in a similar manner.

"Enough, by the Gods o' Ill Fortune!' General Ryes gasped.

Corr patted his father on the shoulder, and Ryes gripped his son's hand to hold it there. His eyes were haunted with a father's fear while he searched Corr's face, as though memorizing his son's appearance.

Catrian viewed the Generals solemnly. "'Tis genocide. Doaphin means t' exterminate every human in the land." She waved her hand, and the disturbing images vanished. The room was tense and silent while she waited for the Generals to assimilate her horrific news. "Ye would no' have believed such without seeing it for yourselves," she explained, not unkindly, for each man's face betrayed its own measure of shock.

"For generations, we have considered ourselves out o' reach, and safe in our mountain fortresses, and General Chartrin on his isles," she censured, pinning each man with her hard gaze, "but that time has ended, and we must make a choice. Do we sit behind our fortifications, and await Doaphin's army and death," here she paused to gauge the responses of the men to her first option, "or do we ride forth, and fight for the lives o' the innocent, and make Doaphin pay a thousand times in blood for every human who dies?" As if her challenge were a signal, the men abandoned their silence and began to argue.

"T' ride against Doaphin is suicide! We must stay, and fortify our strongholds so that we can defend ourselves," General Kierdenan shouted.

"We are all dead!" General Ryes moaned in defeat. His knuckles were white from his grip on his son's hand.

"No! We must protect the people. 'Tis why we are here!" Baldric joined in. "We must fight! We must kill all o' them!" His flat eyes flamed with the dangerous light of obsession, and his long moustache seemed to stiffen with indignation, as he glared Kierdenan to silence. He had seen first-hand the foulness of Doaphin's occupation. He lived in the bowels of the lowland cities, and knew better then any the tortures the lowlanders endured.

"But why now? Why after all these years?" demanded

General Chartrin, sidestepping the argument brewing between Kierdenan and Baldric to demand an explanation.

A worry crease appeared between Catrian's eyes. "That, I do no' know. Something has Doaphin stirring in that evil pile, Dreisenheld! Something has happened t' precipitate this massacre." Catrian turned her haunted gaze into the far distance. "I only wish that I dared t' look closer, but if he knew where t' find me, this fortress, and these mountains, would be lousy with Stalkers and Deathren in a fortnight!" She could not control the shiver of revulsion that rippled through her.

"Ye are right t' hide yourself, m'lady," said Baldric, his chest still heaving with the force of his emotions. "Ye are o' no use t' us dead!"

"Thank-ye," Catrian smiled wanly, and inclined her head in his direction in response to his faint gallantry.

Commander Boris allowed the Generals their squabbles, waiting for their reactions to abate, as he shared a meaningful glance with Laurazon, and gave a slight incline of his head. It was time.

"This makes no sense," Laurazon stated and his lieutenant, Pedric, nodded in agreement. "Even a monster as insane as Doaphin, would no' be so stupid as t' kill all his slaves, for whom then would he subjugate? We must ask ourselves, what is the purpose o' these attacks? What end is Doaphin seeking t' bring about? What does he seek t' gain?"

"The end t' mankind, that is what!" General Ryes' voice quivered.

Kierdenan sneered at the man's weakness. "We canno' help the lowlander sheep! 'Tis too late! We must do what we can t' save ourselves!" Pandemonium erupted at his words.

"Think man! We live off the largess o' the lowlanders. Where will we find food after they are gone?"

"We have forewarning. If we fortify, we can survive…"

"…we are too few, and it is too late…"

"…Doaphin wants nothing. He is a madman! He needs no reason t' kill us all…"

General Chartrin leaned back in his chair with a cynical smile, a finger playing absently with an earing while his eyes shifted back and fourth around the table, gauging every man's thoughts. "Doaphin must hope t' lure us from our strongholds," he suggested to Boris. "He wants us in the open so he can destroy us. Perhaps he wants us gone from the passes so he can finally push through t' attack the Dream Weavers?"

Lieutenant Pedric made a rude noise. "It must be something more. We are no threat t' Doaphin. Never have been," he glared Kierdenan into silence when the man would have interrupted. "We are nothing but a mosquito buzzing about his ears. So what has happened t' change that? Why would he stir himself t' attack us after all this time?"

"That may be my fault," mused Catrian tightly, her face paling. "This summer we liberated a tithing wagon. There was a Demon Lord riding with the train, and I killed him. Doaphin's paranoia o' other sorcerers is legendary, and if he saw me as enough o' a threat, this could be incentive enough t' cause the jaws o' this trap t' be set." Catrian mouth turned down at the idea that she might be responsible for the coming purge.

Kierdenan lunged forward in his chair. "Then we will trade ye t' him for our survival!"

"Try it," Catrian challenged, as her face flushed with anger.

"Enough!" roared Boris. "Catrian is our only weapon. Ye do no' hand your only sword o'er t' the enemy on the cusp o' war!"

Laurazon inclined his head to Catrian. "No offence t' your powers, lady, but Doaphin has surely known o' your presence for years. Besides, ye are but one against dozens o' Doaphin's Demon Lords. He knows ye are no great threat t' his power."

"We should no' rule this out!" Matik defended Catrian's importance. "She could be in grave danger!"

"No, we should no' rule it out, but neither should we stick our heads up our arses!" Boris chided coldly. "If Doaphin wanted Lady Catrian, he would launch a magical attack directed at her alone, no' go t' the effort t' initiate a purge o' humanity."

"Men destroy what they hate and fear!" blurted Baldric's man Iptus, his hands working nervously against the wood of the table, his nails scrabbling against the grain over and over, as though he were trying to dig his way out of the summit. His face flushed at his temerity when all eyes turned his way, for he was a spy, a man of the shadows, and was ill suited to being the centre of attention. "Doaphin, for all his great powers and long life is no' immortal. He has hated us forever, that has no' changed, but he has ne'er feared us. So what do we have, what power do we hold now that Doaphin fears? What has changed between this spring and the last? 'Tis a riddle, ye see?" He squirmed in his seat. "What does Doaphin fear above all?" He looked at Catrian, and blushed to the roots of his hair, "E'en above other sorcerers?"

Laurazon answered him. "He fears the fulfillment o' Fennick's Curse. Above all else he fears this, so much so, that it has kept him locked behind the walls o' Dreisenheld for centuries! So much so, that he spends legions o' his troops every year in a bid for the Dragonsword!"

Iptus smiled nervously and nodded, as Commander Ryes added, "'Tis true enough. Every spring we watch, as thousands of troops are ferried t' Fennick's Island. None have ever returned."

Catrian paled when she saw Boris exchange a satisfied glance with Matik, and with sudden clarity she recognized a hidden agenda behind Gralyre's performance at the tournament. She had believed Boris, when he had insisted on Gralyre as champion to ensure a win, for there had been enough truth in the plan to allay any suspicions on her part, but Boris had outmaneuvered her!

Ever the clever tactician, he had ensured that Gralyre would stand apart from all others, deliberately and subtly bringing him to the attention of his Generals. Catrian's hope of keeping Gralyre off the agenda evaporated like water from a hot stone, and she spared a glare for her uncle. She did not yet know his purpose, but could clearly see the machinations of strategy that were turning like tumblers in a lock. What had he done?

"Why should this year be any different than the last three hundred? Surely ye are no' suggesting that the Lost Prince has returned?" scoffed Lieutenant Jon. "The Lost Prince is a hearth tale!"

"That means nothing." Iptus insisted. "Real or no' t' us, the prophesy is real t' Doaphin." Arguments flew back and forth across the table once more.

Catrian sensed the jaws of a trap being set to snare her, yet could not see a clear path to move the discussion away from Gralyre. She glared at Boris in silent accusation.

Boris returned a pointed look. He was not going to back down. "Tell them." He ordered quietly. All conversation suspended, as the tension between Boris and Catrian brought the men's full attention back to their hosts.

"Tell us what?" Chartrin demanded. "We did no' come all this way t' have secrets kept from us, Sorceress!"

Catrian drew a deep breath, and tried to smother her resentment at Boris' manipulation. Why had he not shared his plan, instead of ambushing her in this way? "'Tis likely nothing," she stated in an offhand manner. "An internal affair I had no' considered relevant enough t' mention." She paused to glare coldly at Matik's self-satisfied smirk. "But, as it now seems significant t' our discussion..." Her lips tightened as her hand was forced.

"This summer, during the same rescue o' the women ransom that I spoke o' earlier, wherein I killed a Demon Lord, we also liberated a warrior. This man has since made his way t' our fortress. He has no memory o' his life before last spring. All he has are recurring nightmares that possess an eerie resemblance t' the battle o' Centaur Pass, and the execution o' the Lost Prince. He even calls himself, Gralyre." For all her casual tone, Catrian tensed, awaiting the inevitable explosion of disbelief. "Ye all know him as the champion o' yesterday's tournament."

"Are ye telling us that ye believe the Lost Prince has returned?" Demanded Kierdenan with blatant scorn. "Ye think the man who overcame our best warriors is…?"

"O' course no'!" Catrian laughed disparagingly, trying to affect an air of unconcern. "The poor man suffers memory loss and madness."

"And…" prodded Baldric, his spy's senses intrigued by the hints of Catrian's uncertainty.

"And," she continued, her false humor collapsing into a glare Baldric's way to let him know of her displeasure at being pushed further, "he holds artifacts that could be construed as having belonged t' the Lost Prince." She held up her hands, forestalling their inevitable questions. "He possesses the royal ring and seal o' the House o' Lyre, or a very good copy o' it, a wealth o' coins minted during the era, and a letter that appears t' have been penned by King Lyre t' his son, Prince Gralyre, upon the eve o' the fall o' Dreisenheld."

"Impossible!" Baldric slapped the table with his hand.

"'Tis a trick! It must be!" Chartrin agreed.

"Who is he? Where did he come from?" Corr demanded. His eyes shone at the thought of a legend reborn.

"Who knows?" Catrian shrugged, choosing to address the last question. "He knows nothing o' himself, and I have been unable t' find his memories, nor discover his people. He believes his nightmares are his mind's concoctions t' fill in the gaps in his missing past by using the fable of the Lost Prince, and I am inclined t' agree with him."

Catrian had the sudden need to advocate Gralyre's usefulness, for a dark premonition had set her heart to thumping. What was Boris up to? By defending Gralyre was she aiding his plan, or sabotaging it?

"The only reason that this man, Gralyre, is still alive is because he has power. He is the first freeborn sorcerer, aside from myself, who has ever been found alive. With his powers joined with mine, we have a fighting chance against Doaphin in battle, to perhaps save more lowlanders from the coming purges!" Only if she could ready his skills in time, and if Gralyre was not a collaborator in disguise, she thought with distress.

After her passionate defense, there was stunned silence from around the table. Then Pedric, of the lowland north, spoke. "'Tis an obvious trap." He looked at his General, Laurazon, and they nodded to each other, as from around the table the others echoed their agreement.

"We considered that possibility t' be well worth the risk in order t' gain his magic," Catrian justified, a chill icing her spine, as her hands grew clammy with nerves, prompting her to press her palms flat to the wood of the tabletop to hide the light trembling that had begun in her fingertips.

"Where has the bastard gone? I will slit his throat myself, and present him t' Doaphin on a platter if it will save us all!"

Kierdenan stated hotly, drawing his dagger, and surging to his feet, his chair toppling over.

Surreptitiously, beneath the table, Matik drew his own dagger from his belt, and held it at the ready. If a fight broke out, his one intention was to protect Catrian.

It was just this reaction that Catrian had feared, and why she had sought to keep Gralyre's presence a secret. If the Generals overruled her at this meeting, she would be unable to protect him further.

"We canno' kill him," Catrian roared, the words immerging with far more vehemence than she had intended. When she beheld Boris' cynically raised brows, a blush worked its way up her throat, stemming from the shame burning in her heart. She had promised Boris that if the time ever came to kill Gralyre she would do so without question, but she was no longer certain she had the will to carry out such a sentence. By the Gods, just flogging him had almost destroyed her!

Kierdenan snarled, and slammed the point of his blade into the table. The hilt still quivered from the impact when he straitened away, and fisted his hands on his hips. "Why no'?"

Catrian's quick mind was ready for the question, using the same argument she had used to convince Boris those many months ago. "Need I remind ye gentlemen o' how very lacking we are in magic? We must have it if we are going t' survive!" Catrian skewered each General in turn with her savage glare. She could do nothing to control her ferocious reaction to their threat to Gralyre. "There is no army on earth that can defeat

Doaphin when he has a host o' Demon Lords at his back throwing magic at us from afar! We need Gralyre! We need his power! Else this endeavour is doomed t' failure, and we might just as well fall upon our swords, as bother t' go t' war!"

Kierdenan righted his chair, and threw himself back into it. He snatched up his tankard, and took a deep swig before wiping the spillage on his sleeve, and glaring sullenly around the table.

Pedric leaned over and whispered something to his General. Laurazon smiled in agreement before clearing his throat for attention. "There is one way t' prove if he is the true Prince or no', and gain more magic for our fight. We could try for the sword."

The blood drained from Catrian's head when Boris leaned back in his chair with the satisfied sigh of a man who had just been presented with a meal he found to his liking. Laurazon had seemingly arrived at the perfect solution to the problem, but it was one that could not help but end in Gralyre's death. Boris had played his hand perfectly, Catrian thought with bitter admiration, his strategy had been well planned, and executed with the finesse of the seasoned campaigner he was. She ought to have known that he would take action from the moment he had discerned that she had begun to develop a fondness for Gralyre.

"The sword! Of course," stated Corr to his father, smiling and nodding, as the subject under discussion entered territory familiar to him. "'Tis near t' the Spring Solstice. He would have t' leave immediately for Fennick's Island, or miss this year's opportunity."

"Ye are all mad!" Catrian censored, unable to keep her horror contained. To send Gralyre for the sword was naught but an elaborate execution! "He would die needlessly, when we could better use his magic in the coming war, no' t' mention his skills as a warrior. There was no' a man among ye that could match him in battle, just imagine what our armies could accomplish with his training!" She shook her head. "I fear we have become distracted from our purpose by fantasy, gentlemen. We need t' deal with what is going t' happen right now, no' go chasing after will-o'-wisps!"

"I must agree with Lady Catrian," pronounced General Ryes. The others might view him as a useless lowlander, without skills or backbone for the fight ahead, but he knew the dangers of Fennick's Island better than any man at the table for this was his domain. "At any one time, Doaphin occupies Fennick's Island with three legions o' Demon Riders, and at least five Demon Lords. That is no' counting how many Stalkers and Deathren roam the shores. Ye would have better odds breaking into Doaphin's Towers or Dreisenheld itself.

"During the Spring Solstice 'tis even worse, for that is when extra legions o' 'Riders arrive t' swell the garrison at Elevor. They are on high alert t' guard against anyone gaining access t' the ferry t' slip over onto the island, and the beaches are patrolled night and day. Over the years, we have managed t' smuggle a few men out t' the island, but no one has ever returned t' tell the tale. All that is known is that no 'Rider has ever returned either, and every year, more are sent."

"Trying for the sword is no' a bad idea," mused Chartrin as his fingers played with his bottom lip.

"Have ye no' heard a word?" General Ryes stiffened, offended that his knowledgeable opinion had been brushed aside. "'Tis madness! Death! It canno' be done, unless we mobilize an army, and even then we would likely no' succeed!"

Boris cleared his throat, and all attention returned to him.

"Give us your thoughts, Commander," Baldric invited. A glow of admiration lit his cold eyes, as he leaned back in his chair and smiled coldly. The spymaster appreciated the grand irony of sending a madman purporting to be the Lost Prince to his death on a quest for a mystical sword that had once belonged to the real Prince Gralyre.

"Catrian is right. The question o' Gralyre, is he a fraud or no'?" Boris shrugged, "Truthfully it does no' matter. But what Catrian has no' taken into consideration is how else he may be o' use t' us, over and beyond the magic he possesses!".

Catrian subtly shook her head at him, her face set and emotionless, though her gaze pleaded with him to stop. *'Do no' do this!'*

Boris looked away, and his words were measured, sure, and utterly committed. "Only imagine how we can rally the lowlanders if the people come t' hear that the Lost Prince has returned, and is questing for his sword! That would be real power! For years, we have been trying t' break through the apathy that grips them, t' awaken them t' their peril." Boris shook his head sadly. "I fear that even warning them o' the purge will no' impel them t' fight!"

Catrian started to relax. If Boris meant to use Gralyre as a banner, then he was safe for the moment, and she had to admit that it was a brilliant manipulation of the old prophesy.

"But give them a hero, someone they have been told o' since they were wee bairn? The Lost Prince Gralyre will return and kill Doaphin, and all will be made right in the kingdom!" Boris paraphrased, as he stared across the table at his counterparts, gesturing with his hands as he made his point. "The return o' the Lost Prince could be the incentive the lowlanders need t' throw down their shackles and fight!" His smile was cold and deadly. "The idea o' the return o' Prince Gralyre is a tool that we canno' afford t' toss aside! Catrian, despite her best efforts as a teacher, will admit that her pupil's magic will no' be ready for the fight." Commander Boris stared down the length of the table at his niece, compelling her to the truth.

"He is learning," Catrian vacillated, but at Boris' hard glare, she sighed with a heavy heart, as she admitted, "But Boris is correct. 'Tis unlikely that he will learn enough, fast enough t' be o' real use t' us in battle."

Boris nodded. "So he has magic, but we canno' make use o' it. If we take his power off the table, then how else may he serve us? As a figurehead t' the cause! We only need the lie t' stand until the end o' the summer. By then, the war will be decided, by one means or another, and what the people believe will be moot. So, I say send Gralyre after the sword. If he succeeds in recovering it, which is doubtful, it will only aid our cause. If he dies in the attempt," Boris smiled grimly, "well then, we have the perfect martyr t' impel the people onwards." He looked coldly across the table at Catrian. "Agreed?" he prompted the Generals, but his words were for her alone.

She measured the reactions of the assembled leaders, and reluctantly acknowledged that her uncle's plan was flawless. Before this winter, she would never have hesitated to sacrifice anyone or anything to keep her people safe. Gralyre was distracting her from her course, making her dream of impossible things. Boris was right to remove Gralyre's influence from her life. All that was important was that the fight against Doaphin continued! If her emotions had not undermined her so, she would have thought of this solution herself.

Deep resentment and hatred for herself, for her necessary, deliberate, calculated coldness drained the colour from her cheeks, where instead she wanted to scream a denial, and burn every man of them to ash for daring to suggest Gralyre's death. She had to concentrate on her breathing to keep her painful sorrow at bay. "Agreed."

One by one, the Generals responded with their own consent to the idea, all except General Ryes.

"Listen t' me. Unless ye are mustering an army for an all out attack, a larger force will no' make it past the sentries and the garrison. If ye are dead set upon this course ye are best served with a small group, seven…eight men…no more. If ye are serious about gaining Fennick's Island, o' giving this Gralyre a chance t' reach the sword, then ye must heed me in this!" His chest heaved as he sagged back in his chair, his face alarmingly red.

Ignoring the pang from her heart, Catrian pushed forward with the plan, eager now to get her mind focused back upon the coming war. "I will put together a small party, and send them south with ye, General Ryes. Ye know the way better than any o' us. Ye will know best how t' direct them once they reach the Island."

"Pick them carefully, m'lady," Ryes shook his head at the folly of the whole exercise, "for ye are surely sending these men t' their deaths. We must leave no later than five days from now, or we will miss the Solstice."

Kierdenan slammed his cup on the table for attention. "'Tis a weapon o' great power, that ye are putting in the hands o' a suspected spy, and a confirmed madman! I insist that I be allowed t' send my own men with him, t' ensure that he does no' turn upon us!"

Another argument erupted as the Generals each made a demand to add men to the quest for the sword.

Matik's gravelly voice rose over the din. "We have at our disposal our entire compliment, whereas the rest o' ye have only the men that ye travelled here with. There is no time for ye t' pledge men t' the endeavour unless they are here, now."

Iptus looked at Baldric. "General, what o' Jord?"

Baldric nodded, his fingers absently tweaking his moustache. "I have a man," he told Catrian, "good with knives, and good at getting in and out o' tight places. He would be a great asset t' the group."

Laurazon steepled his fingers in front of his mouth. "I think that ye could use Trifyn, our archery champion."

"Laurazon, he is but a boy," Pedric interjected.

Laurazon glanced at his second. "Do ye truly believe that he would be any safer with us on the battlefields this summer? Keeping him with us will no' grant him safety."

Pedric slumped, his face falling to the logic of Laurazon's words. Catrian discerned that there was a kinship there.

Ryes shook his head at their commitment to the plan. "Do no' look t' me t' add men t' this fool's quest. I would no' condemn them t' die in that cursed place."

Boris surveyed the table. "Does anyone else have men they would pledge?"

Chartrin shrugged. "If I were at home, there are dozens o' good fighters t' choose from amongst. But none o' them here that I would sacrifice t' this end."

"I have a man for ye." Kierdenan sat with his arms crossed over his chest, staring coldly into the emptiness above the table. He did not elaborate, and Catrian did not question him further.

Catrian's lips tightened. "'Tis decided. Have your men report t' me in two day's time," she advised the Generals, before she steered the council back to the original purpose of the meeting. How had it all spun so far from her control?

"Back t' the matter at hand." They still faced the hardest decision of all. "Doaphin will begin his purge in the spring, and humanity will fall. If we stay within the mountains, we will delay our own deaths, for a time, but die we will when Doaphin's hoards overrun our strongholds one by one. We face a choice o' mobilizing for war or staying within our fortresses t' await our doom."

She folded her hands carefully in front of her. "I urge ye t' ride in defense o' the lowlanders so at least some might escape through the passes into the lands o' the Dream Weavers, and perhaps find sanctuary. As ye know, the passes are well guarded by Doaphin's forces, and it will be heavy fighting t' win through, but it is our only chance. If we stay in the mountains, we will be overwhelmed, and die a pointless death. Or they will merely lay siege and starve us out, for we barely survive the winters as it is. Without access t' the food o' the lowlands, we are finished in any case." The men shuddered at the glowing power revealed in the grey-green depths of her eyes. "We need your council, Generals. Our fate has arrived, and a decision must be made."

"I ride with ye, Sorceress," General Baldric pledged fervently, zealous lanterns flaring to life in the depths of his black eyes.

"We ride," General Laurazon agreed quietly, his fist opening and closing upon the table.

"I can ferry lowlanders t' safety onto my islands," General Chartrin pledged. "Doaphin has no ships that can catch us, and we will be safe for a time, until he brings Demon Lords a'calling."

"We stand with ye, my lady," General Ryes stated with a

quiver in his voice. Catrian suspected he only agreed to save face, for he commanded few men, and did not have much to offer, but she would take all the help that she could get.

After a long pause that had the Generals and their men staring at him, Kierdenan gave his pledge, grudgingly. "I think ye are all fools, but I will stand with ye." It was plain to all that he was not happy with his decision.

When the men had given their support to the mission, Catrian heaved a sigh. So it was to be war. The tired part of her soul accepted the decision without triumph.

The rest of the day, and far into the night, was spent in creating workable strategies to save as many of the lowlanders as possible before Doaphin's creatures destroyed the world of man.

₧₨

"Do no' be wroth with me lass. I did what had t' be done."

Catrian stared at her uncle from out of eyes rimmed red with exhaustion. The meeting had only just concluded, and the weary Generals and their seconds had left to seek their beds. Catrian wanted nothing more than to seek her own, yet Boris lingered, determined to clear the air between them.

"'Tis done. I have no further say in the matter." She did not need to ask, to know that he referred to Gralyre.

Boris sighed and rubbed a tired hand over his pate, scrubbing at the short grey bristles, while he evaluated his niece's mood for a chink upon which he could re-attach a leash. Her life was not her own, she belonged to the resistance, yet she had grown unruly of late, distracted by Gralyre. He had to find a way to refocus her vast powers upon the cause, for the Sorceress could not have two masters.

"Gralyre is dangerous, he could be a spy…"

As he began to speak, she cut him short. "Enough, uncle! I know all o' the arguments. I know! But we had agreed that I would train him, that his magic could be o' use t' us. Why did ye change your mind and no' tell me? Why ambush me at the war council!"

"Ye have grown too attached t' him, and I sought only t' spare ye the heartache o' what canno' be. Ye admitted that he would no' have mastery o' his magic in time t' aid us in battle, so I have devised a new purpose for him, one that will negate the harm he could cause us, and aid the resistance at the same time."

Catrian shook her head, sickened with exhaustion and grief. For a blazing moment she hated the resistance with every fiber of her being. She turned her head away so that Boris would not see her expression. "I am tired. Please leave, uncle. Just leave."

Boris stood with a weary popping of joints, and stretched his arms above his head with a massive yawn. For a moment he stared down at Catrian's averted face, before his expression hardened. "Get ahold o' yourself, girl. Ye would do well t' remember what is at stake. Your bleeding heart has no place in war."

Catrian surged to her feet in a burst of rage, and pointed at the door to her tent. "I am tired, uncle," her voice trembled, as she held on to her control with everything she had, "and I no longer wish t' speak o' this."

The Commander's jaw hardened at Catrian's dismissal, but he gave a short nod before stomping out of the tent.

Catrian's pointing arm lowered slowly, numbly, to her side after he had left, leaving her staring sightlessly at the flap of her tent. A shudder racked her, then another, her shoulders heaved, and a heavy sob escaped.

She spun, pushed her filmy curtain out of the way, and threw herself down onto her bed, crying heavily, for in two days, she would send Gralyre to his death.

CHAPTER ELEVEN

Catrian's demeanor seemed calm, as she awaited the eight men and women assembled within her tent to settle into their chairs around her table, but inside she was angry and grieving. She had sent people to die for the cause before, a necessary evil, and this instance was no different... but she knew that for the lie it was.

It was different. He made it so. *Gralyre*. When this small group departed on their futile quest she would never see any of them alive again.

She had no say in the matter. The council had decided. Yet all night long she had found herself hoping against all reason that Gralyre *was* the Lost Prince, that he *would* return victorious with the sword, and thus prove himself worthy so that she would be free to pursue her foolish heart for the first time in her life...

Catrian gave herself a mental slap for her romantic foolishness. It was good that Gralyre went to his death, for if he stayed, her distraction would prove fatal to them all. Boris was right. The resistance needed her, and it was past time for her to remember to whom she owed her allegiance.

Her gaze passed slowly over the men and women patiently awaiting her council, fine warriors all, yet still Catrian fretted over the choices she had made, uncharacteristically unsure of herself. Like a death knell, she named them within her thoughts.

'*Gralyre, Rewn, Aneida, Mayvin, Jord, Dotch, Trifyn, Cian.*'

Rewn, Aneida and Mayvin, were obvious choices to send with Gralyre for they had hunted together and knew each other's ways, and as such, were not spooked by Gralyre's magic or mysterious past. Plus, Gralyre had been training them in combat, making their skills greater than most of the Rebel warriors from whom Catrian could have chosen.

And then there was Dotch, who just now sat back in his chair, eyeing first the company then Catrian, patiently awaiting his orders. As General Ryes had refused to sacrifice one of his men by supplying a guide for the fool's quest, Catrian had been obliged to spend the last day and a half seeking a warrior who could navigate The Bleak, an impossible task that had finally been blessed with success by the Gods of Fortune when she had discovered Dotch, a sentry who was about to be deployed for duty at the far outpost at the Eastern Pass.

Dotch had been born in The Bleak, and well knew its pitfalls, making him an invaluable asset to guide the company through to Fennick's Island. He was slightly older than the majority of the group, and would hopefully supply a steadying influence upon the younger men.

They had all been difficult choices but in the end Catrian realized that this second-guessing was purposeless, especially with time working against them. Once again she cursed how all choice narrowed down to one moment, and all the planning and forethought in the world could not predict the will of the Gods.

And then there were the three men that she had had no hand

in selecting at all.

Jord, who was of the spymaster General Baldric's company, flipped and played with two knives, his narrow face emotionless as he juggled. His thoughts were in a turmoil, yearning to be outside, and away from people. The desire was understandable from a lowland refugee from Dreisenheld itself, one of the last Humans to be birthed within that city.

He had only just reached his first score of years but already had the old soul of a seasoned warrior. The only thing youthful that he still retained was his thick brown hair, trimmed into a shaggy mess using the very knives he was playing with, and the lack of beard that revealed a prominent chin with a dimple offset of centre.

Jord had not participated in the tournament, not because he had not the skill to win, but because he bore a deep-seated need to remain unnoticed, making him a perfect spy for General Baldric. Catrian worried that, though he had deadly skills with knives and daggers, he was a survivalist to the core, and not a man to sacrifice himself for the greater good.

Seated beside Jord was Trifyn, the bowman who General Laurazon had pledged to the quest. Though he was of an age with Jord, Catrian's heart broke for the boy's youth, and for a life that was about to be cut short in vain pursuit of an unreachable talisman. Trifyn might match Jord in years lived, but not in life experienced.

The bowman fidgeted and peered at the others from the corners of his eyes, and by trying to ape their tough and ready poise, merely emphasized how very uncertain and overwhelmed he was. By all reports Trifyn could hit a fleeing rabbit in the arse in dense brush at midnight, from one hundred paces; a valuable asset who would hopefully gain his seasoning as he travelled.

And then there was Cian, who was Kierdenan's man to the core. Catrian was loath to include him in the venture, but was forced to do so because of the politics of the situation. She had quickly divined that Cian's sole purpose, should the sword be retrieved, was to ambush the group and bring the weapon to Kierdenan. The General was ever seeking more power and influence, and there was no way that he was going to allow Commander Boris and Catrian to take possession of such an important magical talisman. She would warn Gralyre of the snake in his midst, and leave him to decide how best to deal with Cian when, and if, the situation demanded.

Her attention rested briefly upon the subject of her thoughts, and became ensnared within his midnight gaze. She had a brief sensation of falling before she wrenched herself back to the business at hand. The decision was made; the course was set.

Seating herself at the head of the table, she opened a book she had previously set there, flipping through it to find the passage she wanted, which she marked with her finger, as she took in their expectant faces. "I ask ye t' keep all I am about t' tell ye confidential when ye leave." She awaited their nods of assent before continuing. "Doaphin has begun the final purge. This summer he will exterminate mankind." As succinctly as possible, she outlined the horrors about to be unleashed against humanity, watching their faces cycle through emotions, as they processed the eminent death of all that they held dear; fear, disbelief, shock, resolve. Gralyre, who had been told of the coming war by Matik merely kept his gaze steady upon Catrian's face, as she finished her report to the others.

She looked away, unable to watch the betrayal overtake his expression when she sentenced him to death. "If we are t' survive, we will need all the magic left in the land t' pit against Doaphin and his Demon Lords. We have chosen ye eight for a very important mission," she lied skillfully. "Ye will travel t' Fennick's Island, and recover the sword o' the Lost Prince!"

Rewn and Gralyre exchanged a look of deep cynicism, while the other members of the chosen group sputtered in surprise.

"Fennick's Island! By the Gods..."

"The Sword!"

"'Tis suicide!"

Tryfin looked around bodies towards Gralyre, his blue eyes guileless and young. "Your name! Is it because o' ye? I heard rumours, but could it be true? Are ye...?"

Gralyre made a chopping motion with his hand. "'Tis only a coincidence, bowman."

She awaited the comments to abate before she looked down at the book she held, and in a strong, clear voice began to read.

"*Be it known; this is a true history o' Doaphin's hoard o' evil that defeated the Black Prince Gralyre, and his men they called Vengeance.*"

She glanced up from the text to be certain she held their

undivided attention. "This is the only written account that we have ever found o' the passing o' the Lost Prince Gralyre. It was recorded by the great Dream Weaver Seer Chai'low who was trapped with the bulk o' the Dream Weaver armies on the far side o' the landslide at Centaur Pass. Unable t' reach the Prince, he did manage t' record a firsthand account o' that cursed day. It was entrusted t' the survivors o' the Prince's army, our ancestors, who founded the resistance. Ye are, o' course, all familiar with the story o' the Lost Prince, how he was defeated, and how the Sorcerer Fennick used the last o' his power t' change places with the Prince at the exact moment that Doaphin would have removed his head." It was a statement not a question for any bairn born of the last three hundred years had cut their teeth upon this legend.

Catrian glanced back to the book, scanning for the passage she wanted.

"Two o' Doaphin's own held the Prince captive for the executioner's blow. Doaphin swung the Dragonblade without care, beheading his own men along with the Prince. But low, when all three headless bodies had fallen, The Prince was no' amongst them. In his place lay the beheaded corpse o' the Sorcerer Fennick. Doaphin, in his madness and rage grasped Fennick's severed head, and lifted it before him, demanding t' know where The Prince had been spirited away.

"And the head spoke, leveling a doom upon the evil Doaphin, a curse as inexorable as time."

Catrian looked up at her audience, and quickly paraphrased

the rest of the text. "Then came the curse that ye all know;

Enigma rise from out o' mists,

Spirit waken with a roar,

Dragon perched on vengeful fists,

Fell Usurper rule no more!

"'Tis at this time that Fennick's head began t' laugh, and Doaphin threw it into the midst o' his own army where it exploded into an inferno, consuming about one third o' his hoard. Doaphin lifted the Dragon Sword o' Lyre aloft, and screamed for a hammer, determined t' destroy the blade then and there so that it could never fulfill its destiny. But even as he did so, the sword evaporated like mist from his grasp, withering his hand in the process, and far away, an island arose from the south-eastern seas."

"Fennick's Island," Trifyn whispered in awe, rocking his chair in his restless excitement, forgetting in the moment that he was seeking to portray the façade of a hardened warrior.

"One thing I never understood about this tale," Rewn spoke up, "was how the sword was able t' disappear with Fennick already dead?"

A smile feathered Catrian's lips. Trust Rewn to cut deeply to the heart of the matter. "Chai'low argued that the sword was actually Fennick's Wizard Stone."

She continued to speak over the collective murmurs from her audience. "'Tis a valid theory. Upon Fennick's death, all that he was, his essence, his soul, his powers, would have been absorbed by his Wizard Stone. If Chai'low is correct, the Dragon Sword o' Lyre now possesses not only all o' the magic and knowledge that Fennick possessed, but also his soul. Fennick is the sword!"

"And the sword is on Fennick's Island," murmured Gralyre, a scornful twist to his mouth.

"Yes." Catrian lifted her chin stubbornly. His expression was daunting, and she wondered what he was thinking. Excited crosstalk broke out once more but Catrian ignored it, her gaze arrested by the contemptuous expression on Gralyre's face. How could he suspect the real motives behind the mission?

She flipped the page of the book she held, trying to regain her composure by concentrating on the text. "We do no' know much about what ye will face when ye reach the island. Commander Ryes and his predecessors have ne'er been able t' successfully land men, and then bring them home. Most o' what we know comes from what Chai'low was able t' discern with his magic."

"*On the island is a labyrinth,*" she quoted from the text. "*In the centre o' the labyrinth rests the great sword, sealed all around by eight magic walls, each nested within the last, with but a single passage through each. Upon the cusp o' spring, the doorways in the rings align, and 'tis on this day, and no other, that one may enter the path and attempt t' recover the Prince's Sword. The way is open from sunrise 'til sunset. If one has no' exited the labyrinth by the setting o' the sun, they will be forever trapped within.*"

"Why can ye no' walk straight through t' the sword if the doorways are aligned?" demanded Aneida.

"Perhaps there are trials ye will face, perhaps 'tis a maze that ye have t' wind your way through. We do no' know for 'tis no' written here," Catrian slapped the text with the back of her hand. "Chai'low's magic was unequal t' the task o' divining the full nature o' the labyrinth. The only thing ye can be certain o' is if the test is failed, ye will be trapped, and ye will die."

"I suspect that conquering the labyrinth will be the least of our troubles," Gralyre prompted.

"I was coming t' that," Catrian replied testily, as she shut the book with a sharp snap, for Gralyre's perceptiveness was grating her nerves. "Ever since Doaphin realized where the Dragon Sword rests, he has had forces occupying the island whose only mission is t' guard against the return o' the Lost Prince, and t' stop him from reclaiming his sword. Doaphin is obsessed with the curse and feels that he can break it if he can but destroy the blade.

"General Ryes has reported that each year, on the solstice o' spring, when the doorways align, Doaphin floods the labyrinth with his creatures. Perhaps he hopes that the magic will be confounded by the onslaught, making the sword vulnerable t' thievery, perhaps he just hopes that out o' the thousands he sacrifices, mayhap one will conquer the labyrinth. In either case, 'tis at this time and no other, when their external defenses are depleted, that a small force such as this," she gestured to the group, "might be able t' slip through!"

Jord's daggers flashed, and he muttered, "Only t' face the legions who have entered ahead o' us? What good comes o' that?"

Catrian glared at him sternly until his ears burned red. "Maybe nothing, blademaster, or everything, for the magic o' the labyrinth is very powerful. Every year since the island first appeared, Doaphin has sent tens o' thousands o' his minions into the maze. None has ever returned." Grimly, Catrian searched the faces of the eight warriors, as they did the math in their head. Thousands of Demon Riders a year for the last three hundred years; Doaphin had sacrificed millions of his creatures to his obsession.

"The island is also guarded by Demon Lords. The number o' Stalkers and Deathren is unknown but expect many."

"We will no' need t' worry about them though, right? So long as we move only by daylight?" Tryfin fretted.

Dotch answered him with the fatigue of experience. "There is no daylight. Doaphin's Demon Lords created The Bleak, a black fog thick enough that the Stalkers and Deathren can survive by day, for the sun's glow is weakened nigh unto a midnight darkness." He snorted derisively, "Though they still smoke a bit, and ye can smell the burning from far enough away that ye can usually avoid them, if ye are canny and downwind."

"I will no' lie t' ye," Catrian said quietly. "'Tis likely that ye will no' survive this venture. If there are any amongst ye who wish t' stay, I will understand, but do so with the realization that we are mustering for war. Ye will be no safer here. 'Tis the end o' all things, for Doaphin's evil is upon us, and the fate o' mankind will be decided by the snows o' next winter. The Resistance is grasping for every advantage we can conceive o'.

Retrieve the sword, and ye may turn the tide o' the war."

Some of the faces before her were white, all were strained, and fear was a palpable presence, but her heart swelled with humble pride that not a one of them stood to leave. She gave them a moment to decide before breathing out a long sigh. "Thank ye for your commitment t' our cause. There is little time left before the Spring Solstice, and it will only be by the good fortune o' the Gods that ye reach the island by the aligning o' the gates. Tomorrow ye will depart with General Ryes' company. Ye will be moving fast, so pack lightly, and bring only what ye need t' survive. General Ryes will brief ye more adequately on the perils ye will face on Fennick's Island, as you travel south.

Her voice became husky with emotion. "Ye will meet at south gate at dawn tomorrow, so spend your night with care, and take the time t' bid your loved ones farewell, for ye will likely no' see them again." She nodded at them, clasping the book tightly to her chest. "May the good fortune o' the Gods be with ye all."

By this dismissal, their fates were sealed, and the meeting ended. Now was the time to build lasting memories to be taken with them like hoarded gold, to be brought out on a cold, distant, fearful night to shed warmth upon their doomed souls. One by one, they filed silently from the tent, these condemned men and women.

Rewn paused by Gralyre, who stood as a statue, staring at Catrian's averted face, as she placed her book back on the shelf. "Are ye coming?"

"Not yet."

Rewn glanced between Gralyre's stern features, and Catrian's indifferently turned back. Feeling the coming battle like the gathering of a storm, he made good his escape. "I will see ye at home."

When they were alone, Gralyre spoke. "Catrian."

She whirled as if startled, though she had been well aware that he had not left with the others. "Why are ye still here?"

"I have questions that still need answers." Like a stalking cat, he began to move towards her.

"What questions?" The palms of her hands grew slick with sweat, she, who could obliterate him with a thought, was nervous. Her heartbeat accelerated, and her stomach twisted from her guilt, as he came to a stop in front of her.

"What is the real reason we are being sent to Fennick's Island?" he asked mildly.

"I told ye," Catrian relaxed into her rehearsed answer. "We need the magic o' the Great Dragon Sword!"

"You have known about the purge for most of the winter, have you not?"

"Yes…" she began but he cut her words short, unwilling to listen to more of her lies.

"Yet 'tis only now that you have decide that you must have this cursed sword. After centuries, 'tis only now that the resistance cannot live without it?" His face and voice darkened with his disdain as he spoke.

"Our need has ne'er been so great!" she snapped defensively.

"You would have me believe that I," he thumped his chest with a fist, "the suspected spy, would be trusted with such a powerful magical talisman if it were recoverable?" He grasped her by the shoulders, holding her in place, as though he expected her to bolt from him.

Angrily, she tried to shrug free but when he would not release her, she used her magic.

"Ahg!" Gralyre snatched back his hands with a pained curse, as though he had gripped a live coal, a trick she had used upon him before.

"I do no' answer t' ye!" Catrian snarled, incensed by his challenge, as Gralyre shook his fingers urgently to cool them, and backed off several paces.

"Ye were given the option t' bow out, the same as everybody else!" She slashed her arm through the air, her hair flowing over her shoulder at the violent motion. "Ye are no' being forced t' go, 'twas your choice!"

The pain in his hands ebbed, but his temper spiked all the higher with a rushing pulse of blood in his ears. Only she could make him lose control like this! Only she had the power to anger him so! Gralyre clenched his fists, fighting to keep any composure he had left. It helped to see that she was struggling just as hard with her own emotions. "Enough lies, Sorceress! Tell me why I was chosen for this mission! If you want me dead, then kill me! Do not drag seven innocents into this mess between us!"

The knife thrust of his words stabbed into Catrian's soul, the guilt they caused dropping her heart to her feet like a rock in a stream. Her hurt forced her to attack. "Ye were given the reasons. Could it be ye are a coward?" she taunted. "Afraid t' go, yet afraid t' say nay in front o' the others?" She wished her words back even as they left her lips. The way she was talking and acting was not like her. Why could she not maintain her detachment with this man, as she had with all others? She had become a stranger to herself.

Gralyre's face went calm, utterly blank of all expression, and Catrian shivered, as the atmosphere of the tent seemed to charge itself.

"Do not play me for a fool, Sorceress," he stated in a deadly, mild, voice. "And do not ever try to throw lies up between us. Do not ever pretend that you and I do not know exactly what goes on here, or that I ever had a choice to go or to stay!" As he spoke, he slowly moved back towards her, though he did not make the mistake of laying hands upon her again, but instead used the force of his rage to pin her to his will.

"You want me dead, so you send me on a dead man's mission. I will die and be out of your way forever, or I will recover the sword and be killed for my troubles when I return," he growled into her white face. "But why the others? Why Rewn? Why Mayvin and Aneida? What have they done to earn their executions other than to be my friends?"

Catrian wanted to yell and scream and throw things, as he ripped apart her carefully crafted fabrication. She should have known better than to try to lie to him, but as usual, she had gravely underestimated him. A grimace at her own stupidity traced across her lips, as all of her desire to fight drained away. Why deny what he already knew? Gralyre only asked that he be told the truth of the matter, that she not glaze nobility over what was nothing more than a staged execution.

"Some o' what I told ye was the truth, if 'tis any consolation," she murmured tiredly. "Doaphin's purge will begin, and if ye stay ye will go with us t' war. Ye will die anyway." She shut her eyes against the pain of her foreknowledge. "We will all die." Watching the horror filled images, a tear slipped from Catrian's eye, and she shivered while her voice broke with emotion. "Doaphin will sweep across the land like a plague, killing every living being in his path. The Resistance is no' strong enough t' stop him, although we may slow him down. With luck we may even delay him enough t' save some." She sighed when she opened her eyes, her gaze steady, brave through her anguish. "But save them t' where?" she demanded of Gralyre. "The Dream Weaves, if they even exist anymore? There is no guarantee that Doaphin's shadow does no' already fall across their lands as well!"

"But you were to add my magic to yours! We were to fight side by side! Why have you bothered to train me if there is no hope?"

Catrian shook her head to still his words. "Gralyre, ye are learning quickly, but ye will no' be prepared in time. Ye can be o' no use t' us in battle. 'Twas naught but a dream o' hope. Ye are no match for a Demon Lord. Ye have the strength, but no' the skills!"

"And what of the others you have chosen to go to the slaughter with me?" Gralyre demanded righteously. "Rewn, Aneida, Mayvin, Tryfin…"

Gralyre would have continued to list them, had she not interrupted. "I thought that if I sent them with ye, ye might have a fighting chance at survival!" she cried out in pain, and immediately wished the words back, as a sob rose to choke her.

Just like that, Gralyre's anger evaporated. The moment held like a long drawn arrow in flight, silent, the deadly impact yet to be felt.

Catrian was appalled by what she had confessed to him, as she searched his face with painful intensity. She was a fool to have admitted to what could not be, but now, at the end of all things, perhaps it did not matter that she was unmasked nor that he might be a mortal enemy.

Gralyre's midnight-blue gaze burned like fire into hers, his face arrested by an emotion too great to name. With a sudden, wrenching growl, he dragged her into his arms, and his mouth took hers roughly with pure, raw need. He was no longer fearful of her burning magic, just fearful of losing her, as he ran a hand into her hair, anchoring her to his passion, and forcing her to accept his kiss.

Relief blasted through Catrian, and her heart bloomed open as all barriers and subterfuges, all the machinations and games, evaporated in the heat of their passion. His mouth was ravenous, commanding, and almost painful, the damn had burst and there was no containing the turbulent maelstrom. Overcome by the force of his desire, she pulled her lips to the side, her gasp a soft moan, her soul afire.

Gralyre lips slipped across her turned cheek, tonguing the tears from her cheek, as his mouth travelled to her ear. "Do not cry. Everything will work out. I will survive," he vowed. "I will return to you." His deep voice trembled, as he comforted her. He drew back slightly, and set his forehead to hers, keeping her safe in the circle of his arms, so near that the two shared a single breath.

Catrian's hands lifted to cup his lean cheeks. "Do no' try t' use your magic," she whispered brokenly between kisses she peppered against his lips. "The Demon Lords will sense ye, and your skills are no match for them. They will kill ye." Her voice caught on the knowledge that he was to die anyway. "I will maintain contact with ye during your journey, and teach ye as much as I am able afore ye reach the island." She knew even as she said it that it would not be enough to keep him alive, and more tears spilled down her cheeks.

Catrian's world narrowed to pure sensation. The beard on his face tickled the palms of her hands, hiding much of his expression. The hair was still patchy from being singed away by his nightmare's magical outburst of a fortnight past. She frowned in a moment of irritation, and Gralyre's thick black beard evaporated from his face, leaving him as exposed as she.

Her hands now burned hotly against his cheeks. Gralyre's nostrils flared, bringing the scent of her, the essence of her, inside of him, becoming a part of him for all time. Heather and sunlight. *Catrian*.

Helpless to deny himself, his lips took hers in another long kiss, a possessive moan rumbling out of his chest at the new sensation of her soft cheek nestled against the nakedness of his.

Catrian buried her hands in his hair, whimpering as she twisted her lips away from his, devastated by the intensity, and her confessions continued to pour from her. "Ye were right. I was slowing your lessons," she whispered harshly.

"I do not care. Not now." His teeth caught her bottom lip, in a gentle nip before his tongue soothed the sensual pain.

"Ah!" she gasped at the sensation, blinking rapidly to regain her train of thought. "I should have taught ye more. But I was frightened. Ye were learning so much, so quickly. Too quickly." Certain that he would now reject her, Catrian tried to pull away, dropping her hands to his chest, and pushing to try to create distance but with an effortless flex of his muscles Gralyre held her fast.

He gave her a tender smile. "It does not matter now. 'Tis alright." Gralyre's heart set up a howl of protest. Nothing was alright!

His hand travelled into her loosened hair, tangling in the length, trapping his fingers, taking a moment to appreciate its texture and silkiness, and trying to memorize it all. This was the end; he knew it, she knew it. He went to die on Fennick's Island, and Catrian went to her death in the war to end all wars. Now was the only time for them to put their battles and subterfuges aside, and brave that, which before today, would have been unthinkable to them both. In her face he could see all that he was feeling, and knew that his eyes echoed the torment in hers. There were no more words to be spoken.

Slowly, intently, holding her gaze, Gralyre lowered his head, bringing their lips into the softest contact, gifting her everything that she wrought in his lonely heart; his sorrow, his desire, his regrets.

Catrian's arms flew to his head, pulling his lips to hers in a tighter, more passionate play. *'Never again,'* her soul screamed in agony, *'never again!'* It was madness, it was dangerous but she could not stop the powerful emotions that were finally tearing free inside of her!

Gralyre's arms tightened, molding her body to his, letting her feel his rising passion. He knew that he must have lain with women before, somewhere in the murky fogs of his missing past, but was fervently glad that hers was the only face he now knew; her lips, the only ones he would ever taste.

She was nudging at his mind, asking him to open to her, and he let down all his barriers to let her in, realizing as he did so that she had already laid her mind open to his.

They basked in the fire that they found for each other. All lies and motives and schemes were stripped away, and this was the only truth. The heat of their bodies, hands grasping and tugging to find skin, to remove all barriers between them. His hand on her bared breast, her nipple tight against his palm. Her fingers digging hard into his shoulders, scraping roughly down the muscles of his back in her impatient hunger. The magic of their thoughts, in deepest, passionate harmony, arced like lightning between them, gaining strength with each strike.

Gralyre dragged his mouth free from hers, and pushed her back against the tabletop, roughly pulling her head back by her hair, leaving her throat arched and bare for his ravishment. She nipped his ear, circled it with her tongue. They were dissolving into each other, his soul melding forever with hers...

"By the Gods o' Ill Fortune! What goes here?" Matik's harsh, gravel voice shattered the spell that had ensorcelled them.

They fell apart guiltily, struggling to right their askew clothing.

Gralyre's soul still blazed for her, and Catrian's face was flushed passionately, her hazel eyes glowing. Both of them ignored Matik's sputtering accusations from the doorway. He did not matter; nothing existed outside of their stolen moment.

Gralyre drew a deep breath. Tasting her still upon his lips, breathing in the scent of her passion, he drew his dagger, and cut away a lock of her hair.

Catrian bit her lip, and her hand touched the place where he had made the ragged cut. Her eyes softened with understanding, as he lifted the tress to his lips in a soft kiss, his gaze steady upon hers when he sheathed the blade, and took a step back, the hardest thing he had ever done. "Good-bye," he whispered hoarsely.

'Good-by, not farewell,' Catrian thought in distress. The finality of their parting hit hard. "Good-bye," she whispered

back, utterly devastated by the knowledge that she would never feel his arms around her again, never touch his face, or hear him laugh, never feel rage at his challenges, nor be humbled by his honour. *'Gods! How am I t' bear it!'*

After one last heated glance roving over her passion softened features, the beauty of her form, Gralyre spun on his heel and stalked away from her. Grief for what could never be tore through his lonely soul. He did not see the hand she had lifted to stay him drop forlornly back to her side.

Instead, Gralyre's gaze focused on the sneering face of Matik, who blocked his path from Catrian's tent.

CHAPTER TWELVE

Matik sought to push past Gralyre into the tent to see to Catrian but Gralyre dropped a heavy hand onto the smaller man's shoulder, stopping him in his tracks, and dragging him along as he left. Catrian needed time to regain her composure. Besides, Gralyre thought raggedly, he would hate to go to his death without saying a proper good-bye to Matik. Gralyre's teeth bared in a silent, feral snarl, as his control slipped its ironclad fetters at last.

"What are ye doing?" Matik demanded as he was propelled off course. "What have ye done t' Catrian, ye poxy filth?" He struggled ineffectually against the iron hand that locked upon his shoulder with so much pressure it felt like Gralyre's fingers were meeting in the middle.

Gralyre growled, so consumed by the pain of his loss that he was incapable of speech, as he threw the smaller man away from him. His heart was lacerated, and Matik's denigration of the bittersweet goodbye he had just shared with Catrian only added to his torment.

With a surprised grunt of expelled breath, Matik landed face down in slush and mud, and slid a short distance. He spat out dirty snow that had sluiced into his mouth, and scrabbled to his feet, pulling his axe from its sheath and swinging it threateningly. The whistling sound of parting air sang counterpart to Matik's dirty chuckle. "So, 'tis t' be like that, is it? Ye are smart t' choose a fast death, instead o' perishing on Fennick's Island!"

Gralyre's dagger leapt into his hand. "Are you sure you want to travel this path again, Matik?" he hissed.

A crowd began to gather, attracted to the raised, angry voices. Entertainment was in short supply in the fortress, and a fight was a welcome distraction.

"Only a coward would assault a pure lass so! What is the matter spy? Do ye miss being buggered by your Demon friends?"

Gralyre realized that he could not kill Matik, for Catrian's need for her General would be great in the upcoming war. But there was no way he could walk away without retribution, not this time, though if he began he feared he would not stop until the snow turned a watery red melt from the hot spill of Matik's blood. A sound thrashing would have to suffice, he decided grimly as he sheathed his knife.

Matik witnessed Gralyre's action and howled, "No! No' this time spy! Ye will answer for what I just witnessed!" Matik cocked his axe for a devastating overhand blow and screamed a battle cry as he attacked.

Gralyre, so near to gaining control, tipped over into rage once more. He breathed harshly, deeply, as he focused upon a coil of rope lying to the side. The loose ends snaked from the ground, one end flying up to the saddle of a horse, and hitching to the pommel, while the other end whipped around Matik's ankles, tightening and pulling the man from his feet with a yelp of surprise, his axe bouncing from his grasp.

The crowd that had gathered for the entertainment of a fight screamed and fell back, quiet and tense as they realized more was afoot then two men fighting over a woman. Excited when they had been expecting blood sport, they now cowered at the unexpectedness of Gralyre's magic.

Into the heavy silence, Matik cursed and pushed himself up on his arms for the second time in as many minutes, his face, beard and chest filthy and dripping from the icy muck of the square, as he rolled himself over, and began to pull on the rope that bound his ankles. He howled in rage when he could not unbind his legs, and flung out an arm, searching for the fallen axe, but it was well out of reach.

"What trick is this?" Matik jeered, reaching instead for his belt knife to cut himself free. "Are ye afraid t' face me in a fair fight?"

Gralyre's brow knit in concentration, and Matik's clothing, his weapons, everything touching his body save for his beard, evaporated like smoke. Gralyre smiled triumphantly at working out the logistics of Catrian's spell to remove his beard, though he would not have much cared if Matik had simply vanished from the world in a spray of red mist. Gralyre was riding on a wave of exhilarated rage, unwilling to take up his restraints again until he had broken something, or in this case, someone.

The knife Matik had been reaching for was no longer there to grasp and he was left shivering in the weak winter sun, with nothing clothing his nakedness but his own hirsute skin.

A woman in the crowd giggled at the spectacle. Her friend made a loud comment that it could not be that cold out. The giggle caught momentum, until the watchers were laughing, with their sidesplitting guffaws drawing more people at a run to see what was so hilarious.

Matik's face grew red, as other parts of him shrank away from the cold of a suddenly brisk north wind. Unable to withstand the humiliating laughter, he hopped to his feet and lunged at Gralyre, his hands curled into lethal talons, wanting only to claw that cold smile from Gralyre's face.

Gralyre watched with unconcern, not even caring to step out of the way of Matik's advance. He waited until Matik's scrabbling hands had almost reached him...

'Now!' he ordered the horse.

With a charging whinny, the horse reared up and sprang into a full gallop. Matik's fingers had just brushed against Gralyre's chest when the rope pulled taunt, and he was jerked from his feet. He cleared the ground for quite a distance, scattering onlookers, as he landed on his face and was dragged away, backwards through the slush and mud. Under Gralyre's direction, the horse careened left, then right, and then left again, galloping madly around the square. Matik's yowls did naught but spur the horse to greater speed. The onlookers moaned in commiseration as Matik bowled through a woodpile, scattering firewood in every direction.

Gralyre crossed his arms and stared after the spray of snow

and mud that marked Matik's passage. Satisfaction warmed his eyes to a lighter blue, as he considered how many circuits he should allow the horse to make.

"Gralyre."

The soft, beloved voice made him whirl to see Catrian shivering in the cold, standing just outside her tent. Her face was strained and mottled with red. She had been weeping. He took a step towards her.

"That is enough. Please release him."

Gralyre immediately relaxed his will, releasing the snaking rope from around Matik's feet, and calming the horse to a trembling stop.

Matik's wild ride came to an end as he rolled up in a heap by Gralyre's feet, shivering and moaning, crusted in hair, blood and ice. Catrian lay a calming hand against Gralyre's arm for only a moment, their eyes locking with their shared regrets, before she brushed past, and wrapped a fur around the fallen man to cover his nakedness.

Frustration stampeded through Gralyre, as he watched her tenderly ministering his enemy. He stepped forward to help.

She thrust out a hand to forestall him. "I canno'… Gralyre please. Just go. Go now," Catrian's order was undermined by the strain in her voice.

He nodded tightly, unwilling to add to the distress he had already caused. Fingering the lock of her hair he still grasped, he forced himself to turn away, to leave her, hoarding his stolen treasure.

ഇൗൽ

Catrian glanced up with bloodshot eyes, as Boris entered her tent unannounced. She was wrapped in a blanket, curled up in one of her comfortable chairs set next to the lit brazier, as she sipped desolately at a cup of tea.

"Explain yourself!" the Commander barked. "Matik just awoke from his injuries, and told me he found you degrading yourself with that…that…lowlander spy! I should have him beheaded for his attack upon ye both!"

Catrian's face hardened, as she threw off her blanket, and surged to her feet. "That's enough! Ye have no right t' pass judgment upon me!" she yelled. Hot tea sprayed in an arc as she threw her mug at his head.

Boris ducked, and his face went slack with shock. In all her life Catrian had never raised her voice to him. "What has come over ye, girl? Ye are no' yourself! I warned ye against allowing him into your heart! I warned ye that naught could come o' it! What were ye thinking? Ye are putting everything at risk!"

"How dare ye! I do everything for the resistance. I am killing him for ye and for the resistance! Now ye would begrudge me one stolen moment for myself? And why did ye go behind my back and decide t' destroy him, uncle? He was learning! He could have helped us!"

"I made the decision for ye! Ye are distracted! Ye are putting him ahead o' your duties t' the resistance! By the Gods, I may be your uncle, but I am your Commander first, and ye will show me the proper respect!"

"Was it my uncle or the Commander who decided t' kill him?" Catrian spat back. "Ye made the decision for me, or for yourself?"

Boris slapped her, rocking her head, and Catrian staggered, catching herself on one of her chairs.

She looked up at him in shock, her hand to her cheek.

"Ye are no' like other women. Ye wield magic, and must always guard against corruption! There was a time I considered slitting your throat myself when ye were but a girl, rather than risk ye growing up evil!"

Catrian gasped, as her life and everything in it skewed sideways. "Uncle…" she whispered, horrified.

Boris froze at her expression, realizing he had admitted to a fear that she need never have known. "This man is dangerous t' ye, Cat. Look at ye! Defiant! Insolent! Ye would ne'er have behaved so afore he began t' woo ye! How soon would it be afore ye turned on your own?"

Catrian drew herself back to her feet, her face heavy with disdain that bordered upon hate, as she stood tall and unashamed.

"Ye are confined t' quarters until they leave. I suggest ye use the time t' find your way back t' the light, girl. If ye are no good t' the resistance, then ye are no good t' me!"

"Will ye then send *me* t' my death next, Commander? Do ye hold me in such little regard?" she demanded proudly.

With a ferocious glare, Boris turned on his heel and left.

ഇൻൽ

Daybreak was dark and sullen, an inauspicious beginning to
their quest for the Dragon Sword of Lyre. They began their
journey without fanfare, and with only a motley collection of
friends and family to send them off.

Gralyre kept searching for Catrian's arrival, using both his
sight and his magic, but was unable to find a trace of her. He
tried to shrug away the hurt he felt that she did not appear,
deciding that her absence was a kindness, that perhaps it would
make their parting easier, but a yawning emptiness had opened
within Gralyre's soul on the instant of quitting her side
yesterday, as though all hope had been scraped away to leave a
hollow shell. His spirits rose momentarily, as Commander Boris
arrived with the Generals in tow, but plummeted once more
when he saw that Catrian was not among them.

Generals Laurazon and Baldric stood at Commander Boris'
side as they oversaw the busy proceedings in front of the south
gate, watching as the horses were readied, and Generals Ryes
and Kierdenan's men assembled. General Kierdenan would
journey only as far south as his own fortress before peeling off
to return home to muster his own territories for war.

General Chartrin's pirates were also departing this morn, but
from the west gate, and so were absent from witnessing the
launch of the counterfeit quest. Chartrin had the furthest to
travel, all the way back to the west coast through enemy held
territory, and time was of the essence, for Doaphin would begin

the purge when the final snows had melted.

Gralyre wondered with a jealous pang if Catrian had decided to bid General Chartrin farewell instead of seeing him off. His mood sunk further.

He was distracted from his sadness when greeted by the young bowman, Tryfin, who passed by with his horse in tow. The lad was green, and Gralyre was not certain if he could be made battle ready by the time they reached the island. Skill with a bow against targets and animals was one thing; skill in the chaos of battle was something else entirely. 'Twas no kindness to send the boy to Fennick's Island. Far better to give the lad an opportunity to live for as long as he could for the short time remaining to humanity before Doaphin's purges destroyed it all.

Gralyre's gaze sought out the arrival of the other members of their doomed party, and immediately spotted Kierdenan's man, Cian, rudely turn his back on Rewn, and join his comrades-in-arms instead. Rewn's face knotted with ire before he brushed off the slight, and walked over to where his sister and brother waited. Gralyre would get the tale from Rewn later, but all of his instincts warned him that Cian was not to be trusted.

Distracted by a flash of reflected light, Gralyre's attention shifted towards Jord, who hovered on the periphery of the chaotic mustering of men and horses with his knives juggling and tumbling through the air. They caught little bits of the pre-dawn gloaming. The knife play had the effortless quality of long born habit, as Jord watched and evaluated all - alone within the company and obviously preferring that state.

Little Wolf whined and danced about, excited for the coming journey, eager to be away from the foul odours of the fortress, and back into the cleanliness of the wild. At just shy of a year old, he had almost reached his full growth, and his fur was thick with his luxurious black winter coat so that he appeared even larger than he was. In his eyes shone a keen intelligence that most people found disconcerting in what they thought of as a dumb animal.

In the interest of hurrying the group onwards, Little Wolf circled Rewn's legs where he stood embracing his sister, then bent and nipped him on the lower calf.

"Owe!" Rewn yelped, releasing Dara, hopping as he bent to rub his bruised calf. He glared at Little Wolf, who gambled away for a few steps before returning to circle him again. The wolfdog made a mock attack and Rewn jumped away - in the direction of the horses.

"Go away! I am no' ready t' leave yet," he yelled at the wolfdog, and shooed his arms in wide arcs, incensed that the beast sought to herd him.

Grinning widely in lupine delight, Little Wolf cavorted away in a mad circle, his tongue flapping comically, as he ran as though crazed.

Dara giggled, "Look," she chortled, pointing, as Little Wolf repeated the same trick on Trifyn.

Where Rewn was well used to the wolfdog's antics after travelling with him for months, Tryfin, the young bowman, took the attack to be real. With a yelp, he started for his horse at a run with Little Wolf in hot pursuit, tail wagging furiously, as he snapped theatrically at Trifyn's boot heels.

"Call off your wolf! Call off your wolf!" Trifyn yelled hysterically.

Gralyre turned and frowned at Little Wolf.

The wolfdog left off his mock attack, came to heal at Gralyre's side, and sat down, tongue lolling, ears perked in excitement and anticipation.

"Stop trying to hurry the people along," Gralyre chastised him. "We will be away soon enough."

With a small sigh, Little Wolf lay down, and placed his chin on his paws, though there was a twinkle in his eyes that bespoke an unrepentant soul.

"I wish they had chosen me t' go with ye!" Dajin's fervent yearning brought Rewn and Dara's attention back to their farewells.

"Be careful what it is that ye wish for brother, for soon enough ye will be going t' war with Doaphin, and will see more danger and excitement than I would wish on anyone in their lifetime!" Rewn replied, trying to dampen his brother's yearning for battle. Dajin knew not what he longed for.

"Yea, but I will be just one o' the thousands in the battle," a whine tainted his words, "Ye," Dajin gestured to his brother, "have been singled out. Your name will be remembered." Though he valiantly tried not to let it do so, the envy seeped through.

Rewn heard it and wondered irritably when Dajin would

grow up. Taking a deep breath, he placed one hand on his brother's shoulder and the other on Dara's. "Listen, the both o' ye. I will no' be coming back, do ye understand?" he shook them lightly for emphasis. "This is a death mission." He gazed into Dara's tear filled eyes, and saw that she realized the truth, but when he looked at Dajin, he saw that he might as well have been talking to a stone wall, for as usual Dajin thought only of the glory, never of the price that had to be paid.

"Ye might succeed," Dajin reasoned.

"Dajin," Rewn began, wondering what he could say to leave his brother with a sense of purpose, words that he would remember, words that would somehow encourage him to grow and mature. Then he had an idea. "Come with me," he said with a small smile.

Drawing his brother after him, Rewn walked to his horse and dug into the saddlebags. Finding the bundle he sought, he drew it forth and turned back to Dajin.

"I want ye t' have this. When I am gone, ye will be the head o' our house, and must carry on in the name o' our fathers past." Rewn held out the golden chain with the seal of their ancient house dangling off the end. The relic had been protected and hidden for generations, and had been the last thing their father, Wil, had rescued from their home in Raindell before they were forced to flee for the lives. With as much ceremony as the moment allowed, Rewn placed the chain over his brother's head, settling the seal around Dajin's neck, before embracing him.

"It falls t' ye now, Daj," he whispered hoarsely. "Ye must

protect our past and ensure our future. Live, and raise a family, and tell them..." Choking up, Rewn suddenly realized how much he was going to miss his brother. Looking after Dajin all this time had kept Rewn from feeling the terror of everything that had happened. With no one to be strong for now except himself, how would he keep his fears at bay? A shudder racked his frame, and he gripped Dajin harder.

"I know...I will. Be safe brother," Dajin whispered back, touched beyond expression by his brother's generous act of faith. Tears suddenly clogged his throat. "May the Gods o' Good Fortune smile upon ye!" As nothing else could have done, Rewn's premature bequeathing of the family heirloom finally hit home the truth that beyond this moment they would not meet again.

Rewn released him and stepped back. "Thank ye, Dajin." He nodded towards where Dara still stood. "Take care o' our sister, and Saliana..." Rewn frowned, as he realized that Saliana was not present for his and Gralyre's send-off. He had not missed her ephemeral presence until now.

Dajin's chest puffed out pompously. "O' course, Rewn. 'Tis my duty now!" he said importantly.

He all but strutted back to Dara, and Rewn chuckled through his tears at the spectacle, knowing in his heart that Dajin would never change. Rewn mounted his horse, determined to retain what composure was left to him.

Mayvin and Aneida kicked their horses to a walk and reined in beside Rewn. "Ye have said your goodbyes?"

Rewn shrugged, and brushed surreptitiously at the wetness on his cheeks. "'Tis as it is. I am ready. Have neither o' ye friends t' wish ye good journey?"

Aneida and Mayvin shared a glance. "No one." Aneida's smile faltered for a moment. "There is no one."

Mayvin reached over and tapped her hand to get her attention. *Together*, Mayvin signed. *We are together, and that is as it should be!*

"What did she say?" Rewn asked, then nodded as Aneida translated.

"Ye have us too," Rewn vowed. "Gralyre and me. We will all stand together!"

Mayvin nodded back, and patted Rewn's shoulder.

They would be underway soon. Tryfin and Jord, already mounted, were in conversation with their generals, nodding as they heeded their last orders. Spare horses were being added to the cue, and Rewn could see that Dotch was now taking his leave from his family. It would not be long now.

Dotch's wife leaned into her husband's strong chest, as he embraced her tightly. Though her chin quivered from suppressing her tears, she would not allow her two young sons to see her break so she tucked her face into Dotch's neck, as he held her for the last time.

"Do whatever ye need t' keep yourself and the boys safe. Anything, do ye here, Ella?" Dotch murmured fiercely into her ear. "War will be upon ye soon, and your only allegiance is t' yourself and our boys. Ye remember what I say! Ye stay alive.

Ye keep them alive! No matter what!"

Dotch kissed her brow, and wiped her cheek as he drew back. "Good-bye, lovey. Look after our sons. Raise them good and strong."

She nodded. "I will. I promise. And I will tell them all manner o' tales about their Da." She dug into the pocket of her thick cloak, and brought out a large, carved wooden flask. A small twinkle entered her smile. "I thought that ye could use a little taste o' home t' comfort ye, and remind ye o' why ye need t' live."

Dotch took it, pulled the stopper, and inhaled reverently. "Oh, lovey, where did ye find this?" He rolled his eyes appreciatively, and smiled, making the skin crinkle at the corners.

She reached out and brushed back a lock of salt and pepper hair from his brow, the hair she had trimmed for him just the night before, and smoothed down the fine shirt she had made, straitening the wrinkles. She patted him over his heart, feeling the warmth of the steady beat. "I was saving it for a special occasion." She smiled brokenly, and then cut her eyes downward with a little nod to encourage him to look to his sons now.

Dotch knelt and pulled both lads into his arms. "There ye are, pups. Ye are getting too big for your poor old man!" he whispered, as he squeezed them tightly, filling his arms with his entire life.

His youngest, eight-year old Demin, was crying with great racking sobs, while his brother, Kentle, at thirteen, was manfully stoic. Dotch leaned back, his gaze hungrily devouring their beloved faces to memorize each feature, trying to see them as they would be as grown men, a day he would not see.

Dotch cupped Demin's face, and smiled. "Wee Demin, do no' weep! I am going on a grand adventure."

Demin hiccupped. "But Kentle says ye will die!"

Dotch turned him by the shoulders, and pointed at Gralyre. "Do ye see that man, wee Demin?"

Demin nodded, snorting noisily.

"That is Gralyre."

Demin's eyes grew wide. "The Prince from the story?"

Why not? Dotch smiled, not at all reluctant to lie, cheat and steal for the sake of his child's piece of mind. "And he is taking your old man with him t' reclaim his magic sword!"

"Really?" Demin demanded with the excited belief that only an innocent trust could generate.

"Really," Dotch nodded, and watched his son believe his lie with every part of his being. Hopefully one day, when he was grown, he would forgive his father for it.

"Good luck, Da," Kentle thrust out his hand.

Dotch grinned through a sudden sheen in his vision, and his hand swallowed his firstborn's. "Thank-ye son. Kentle, ye are the man o' the family now, so I need ye to look after your Ma and brother for me. Promise?"

Kentle promised solemnly, though when Dotch stood and mounted his horse, Kentle hugged into his mother's side, as tightly as did his little brother, the two of them devastated, as they watched their father depart from their lives.

Gralyre saw that the others were finally ready, and sprung to his saddle. At his lithe motion, Little Wolf scrabbled to his feet, whining and dancing with excitement. All down the line, warriors were mounting, taking up their reins, and falling into line.

From where he had been in deep conversation with General Ryes, Boris walked back down the line of horses and supplies to where Gralyre waited in his saddle.

Gralyre watched him come, curious as to what the Commander had to say to him, now, at the end.

Boris halted and leaned in to keep from being overheard. "I saw what ye did t' Matik. Just be glad that ye are leaving today, for if ye were no' I would kill ye myself!" he blustered.

"Ye could try, old man" Gralyre gritted out insultingly. He was going to his death, and found that there was a freedom in no longer being obliged to convince anyone that he was not a spy. He was a dangerous man, and he need no longer hide the fact.

"The poor lad lost most o' the skin off his chest and received frost bite t' some very sensitive areas." Boris lifted an admonishing finger. "We need every able bodied man we have in the coming fight! For someone o' Matik's abilities t' be out o' commission is criminal!"

Matik? A poor lad? Gralyre's mouth twisted cynically, as he stared unflinchingly down into Boris' angry face. "Matik got what was coming to him, and you know it."

Commander Boris glowered at Gralyre's lack of respect while a dull flush began to creep into his cheeks.

"He is lucky that I have a sense of humour, and only incapacitated him," Gralyre continued in a soft, deadly voice.

Boris let the conversation slide in favour of more lethal weapons. "And what o' your attack upon my niece?" he demanded with all the outrage of a betrayed father.

One of Gralyre's eyebrows shot up incredulously, and he bared his teeth. "Attack?" Catrian's lock of hair seemed to burn where he had carefully braided the strands and tucked them next to his heart.

"Matik caught ye pawing at her, using your magic t' keep her from crying out for help!" Boris snarled righteously. The tendons and cords in his weathered neck stood out like vines surrounding the trunk of a weathered oak.

Gralyre's face froze of all expression, and his deep voice vibrated with threat, as Boris sought to taint the beautiful moment that Catrian had given him. "There was no coercion involved! You know better than anyone, Boris, that Catrian would have crushed me like a bug had my attentions been unwanted. She gave of herself of her own free will!" Outrage burned hotly through him. That they questioned his loyalties could be excused because they had no proof that he was not in league with Doaphin, but to question Catrian's honour was beyond insult! To debase the moment that had been shared between them, the only moment they would ever have, drew pure hatred from Gralyre's soul.

Boris reached out and grabbed Gralyre's forearm in a punishing grip, his fingers digging painfully into the hard muscles. "Catrian has no free will, she belongs only t' the resistance!" he snarled with frightening and unexpected fanaticism. "The fate o' us all rests with her powers! Ye confuse and distract her from the cause! She can never be yours! 'Tis good that ye go t' your death!" Boris finished cruelly.

Understanding roared through Gralyre, as this fool's quest suddenly came to make perfect sense. Boris was frightened of losing control of his greatest weapon; his niece's magic. He sought to keep her firmly in hand, isolated to all save his will alone, and to that end he would ruthlessly sabotage any relationships that Catrian sought to create. That Catrian had chosen Gralyre had just been an added evil in Boris' mind.

With casual strength, Gralyre reached over, and pried Boris' grasping fingers from his arm. Then he tightened his grip, grinding the bones of the Commander's hand. "You will find that I am not so easily murdered, old man!" He leaned down from his saddle, all pretense of civility fleeing from his posture and his words. "You send me after a sword of power, Boris! What makes you think that I will give it up to you when I return?"

Boris' smile split his face slowly, surely, though he had to work to keep the grimace of pain from bleeding through, as his hand popped and ground under the pressure of Gralyre's clasp. "No, I will no' see ye again. Your death is certain. Your influence over Catrian has ended."

Catrian. Gralyre's heart swelled with yearning, and he released Boris' hand with disdain. "I will retrieve my sword, old man, and return to claim all else that is mine!" he vowed coldly.

At that moment, the line began to move forward, and Boris was left to stare after Gralyre's retreating back. A chill worked its way beneath his warm cloak to his skin, and he shivered with foreboding, as he realized Gralyre had claimed both the sword and Catrian for his own. He had not factored the consequences should Gralyre actually retrieve the magical weapon.

Gralyre never looked back. The great wolf trotted beside his horse, its head reaching almost higher than the horse's belly, and as Gralyre cleared the gate, Boris shook himself free of his fears.

There was no fortune meted out by the Gods that would allow Gralyre to survive an assault on the most heavily guarded plot of land in the realm! It was a dead man that he watched ride away.

With a snort of derision for what had been nothing but a dead man's bravado, Boris turned away, his mood improving for the first time in months, as the problem of what to do about Gralyre was put to bed forever.

Dotch held his horse still as the line moved onward through the gate, memorizing the last glimpse he would ever have of his family. His wife and sons lifted their hands in farewell, and Dotch could no longer bear it. He spun his horse and cantered up the line to reclaim his spot.

"Goodbye! Goodbye Rewn! Goodbye! Mayvin! Aneida! Goodbye! Gralyre! Stay safe!" Dara waved frantically and called out as she chased the moving line of horses for a few paces. Dajin stood where he was and raised an arm in farewell.

Rewn, and the two sisters, Mayvin and Aneida turned in their saddles and waved back, with smiles on their faces but tears in their hearts, as they passed through the south gate, and their journey began.

EPILOGUE

DREISENHELD – EARLY SPRING

Within an opulent bedchamber, enmeshed in twisted silk sheets, a bejeweled hand claws out towards the ornately carved and gilded ceiling...

...Men ride south into a dawning sun that rises, hot and sure. Electricity hums through the air, and a portal to nowhere, guarded by the dead, gleams and shimmers like rising waves of heat from a pyre. A dragon writhes upon the hilt of a sword, its eyes glitter, rubies of glowing power. Lightning flashes to a cataclysmic crack of thunder. A man's hand holds the sword aloft in Victory.

Lightning cracks open the sky. Doom! Flash-Doom!

The dragon unwraps from the hilt and crawls down the arm, lashing itself around the wrist, tightening, claiming, and roars words, a curse that echoes from the past.

...Dragon clutched in vengeful fist,

Fell Usurper rule no more...

Flash-Doom! Doom! Flash-Doom!

Lightning and thunder strobe the air. Lighting stabs, Thunder crashes...

The Master awakens with a harsh scream. Through ornate, stained glass windows, lightning flashes, and endless rolls of thunder shake the chamber.

'The dream, the tempest - an omen. The sword reaches out to claim its own. Does He answer the summons?'

The storm is upon Dreisenheld. The end is nigh, yet all the players have yet to be revealed. Pulls the bell rope to rouse a servant. Paces. Schemes.

'The Rebels must not be allowed to reach Fennick's Island! Especially not if He travels with them. 'Tis not yet time for Him to claim the sword. Time. Three hundred years, and now there is no time!'

Pauses at the shimmer of movement in the dark depths of a large mirror. A strobe of lightning reveals haunted eyes and sweat-matted hair before shadows shroud the mirror once more.

'Soon the Stalkers will find Him. Soon all the years of planning, of waiting, will be over. There is nothing to fear here.' Thunder rolls over the castle, and gleaming teeth join the shadowy image in the silvered glass.

The servant silently arrives in a cloud of darkness, a shapeless thing of mist and madness.

'But just in case...'

"Send an extra legion to the garrison at Elevor. The Solstice is upon us, and the Rebels stir in their mountains!" Paces. Turns. An afterthought. "And bring us a slave!"

"At once, my Master." The dark servant seeps away under the closed door of the bedchamber.

"Draw him out! We must draw him out of hiding and end this. He must come to us!" Mumbling, musing, pacing. Distracted thoughts. Chaos, unfelt for hundreds of years! Exhillerating! Disturbing!

Halts and laughs deeply at the perfect symmetry of an idea.

'Yes! Let Him do all the work! He will obtain what was unobtainable. Then we will kill all of them! They will die, and He will come! He will bring the sword to us to save them!'

So be it!

The heavy, oaken bedchamber door squeals as it opens.

Anticipation!

The chains about his neck drag a screaming, struggling slave forward. His filthy, bare feet skid on the polished marble, and leave black marks.

Hunger.

Blood.

Death.

Pleasure.

Calm.

The End

of

The Rebel

Lies of Lesser Gods - Book Two

The Adventure continues in

The Sorcerer

Lies of Lesser Gods - Book Three

Visit our website for insider news and giveaways
www.lgamcintyre.com

Like us on Facebook
www.facebook.com/lgamcintyre

Follow us on Twitter
@LGAMcIntyre

Message from the Author

Do a good deed for a great read!

Post a Review

Please take a moment to post a review or click a star rating for **Lies of Lesser Gods** anywhere you purchase books or ebooks online, such as Amazon, Chapters/Indigo, Kobo, Kindle, or Apple Books.

Your opinion lets me compete on the same field with authors like Stephen King, George R.R. Martin (Game of Thrones), and J.K. Rowling (Harry Potter).

Independent authors don't have corporate backing. I owe all of my success to the support of my incredible fans who promote **The Lies of Lesser Gods** through posts and online reviews, and through sharing of my books with friends and family. Each fan's honest opinion helps my books rank higher in search engines, and in best seller lists, which in turn helps more people discover these great stories.

Thank-you for helping to make my dream of being a best selling author a reality. I'll make you a deal - If you keep loving my books, I'll keep writing them!

With deep gratitude,

                    ~ LGA McIntyre